Laszlo's Millions

Jon Elkon

First published in Great Britain by Andre Deutsch 1991
 British Library cataloguing in Publication Data.

Cover illustration: Willem Samuel. Design: Nicole Dreyer.

ISBN-13: 9781523706990
ISBN-10: 1523706996

Laszlo's Millions
remastered

Laszlo's Millions is a hilarious, mad picture of London in the 1970's as seen by Tom Bloch, a drug-fuelled spy who is also likely to inherit several millions from the lover of his dead grandmother Hazel. We learn how she met and fell in love with the priapic Count Laszlo Mindchyck, the Laszlo of the title, only to run away into the mists of war when bullied and tormented by his dreadful offspring. And how, many years later, she drops dead when informed that she is his heir...leaving Tom, her heir, likely to inherit everything. But there are conditions! The book is a weaving of stories, each bursting with life-loving characters, each determined to make Tom's life even more complicated than it is. We visit the parents of Tom's schizophrenic lover Mona, and discover what made her mad. The journey from Johannesburg and the Apartheid dystopia brings us the character of the Brigadier, who is now in charge of the BOSS spies in London. BOSS – the feared Bureau of State Security, the South African intelligence service, charged with identifying and terminating anti-Apartheid activists. Tom's employers. Whose headquarters is in the Gents' toilet at Sloane Square. The novel takes shape eventually with Tom's dreadful dilemma: should he abandon all his principles, assume a three-piece suit and thus win the inheritance from Laszlo? He has nine months to convince a panel of "Jurors" that he is a fit and responsible person to handle Laszlo's Millions. Which means selling out, abandoning his best friend Pieter, and heading into history...Zoom. In style, the writing is Tom Sharpe meets Monty Python via Kurt Vonnegut and a dash of Franz Kafka. Hilary Mantel described Elkon's first novel as 'fairly walzing the reader along...the prose is full of energy and humour and beneath the playfulness there is an undertow of pain...' (Daily Telegraph). This book takes off into territory as delightful, as charming, and far more challenging.

To you

(and for you I've added to, amended, fattened-up, slimmed down, substantially rewritten and vastly made more delicious this absurd story of mayhem and delight…)

Withers Stronglode Withers and Truelove
Solicitors and Commissioners for Oaths
5a London Wall London EC4

February 20 1971

Dear Sir

Re: Thomas Bloch

I have been fortunate in having obtained a small proportion of the immense folio of notes made by Mr Bloch before his disappearance. I append a copy herewith which I have attempted to arrange into some sort of order for your perusal.

As you will be aware there remains a great deal of controversy surrounding the circumstances of Mr Thomas' disappearance. The recent article by Fred Healey in the Guardian entitled 'The Vanishing Thin Heir' (appendix 17) proposes the theory that he was kidnapped by the South African Bureau of State Security ('BoSS') and reposes in some solitary cell deep in the bowels of John Vorster Square. There are many other theories, one of the most bizarre of which is that he and his vehicle were abducted by aliens, and quotes the notes found along the M4 as evidence that he no longer needed the essentials of earthly civilisation.

As for myself I prefer to think that the vanished Mr Bloch remains alive in a dive somewhere between here and there; that his disappearance is a result of the mental aberration so common in your family, sir.

I conclude by informing you that unless you want the enclosed published, you will see fit to reinstate me in my position and pay me shitloads of money.

Yours etc

James

J. T. Truelove BA LLB

1

One

One wet evening in March 1969 Robert Stone stopped snoring. His soul climbed out of his body and went for a walk in the sky. He died almost penniless, nearly brainless, in his smart flat in Killarney Heights, Johannesburg, which he had shared with his wife Hazel.

Three weeks later Hazel became a multimillionairess. Her good fortune lasted just sixty-two seconds.

Two

November 1938

A brother and sister hand in hand on the deck of the Union Castle liner the *Blenheim Castle* watched as the immense angular bulk of Table Mountain receded across a white-flecked brilliantly green sea. She had invisible tears. He frowned through a mist of pain. His name was Ian, hers was Hazel.

Their mission was to save Ian's life. He had a tumour the size of a peanut growing in his brain. Their destination was Edinburgh where Sir James McCullough lived and practised. He was the only man in the world who could possibly save Ian's life.

Hazel was tall with almost white hair above brown roots; a finely moulded face with high aristocratic cheekbones. She was dressed in a white pleated skirt and navy silk blouse. She was extraordinarily, excruciatingly beautiful. At eighteen, a virgin.

Ian was twenty two, thin and gangly, effete yet manly in a tweedy English Counties way. Had he not been addled with pain he would certainly have smoked a pipe. He was not a virgin.

Ian and Hazel loved each other jealously, passionately and exclusively. Ian's dalliances with other members of Hazel's sex had been resented and vigorously if subtly contested by her. None of his adventures had been turned into anything remotely resembling commitment.

They looked like a perfect couple there at the railing. 'What a perfect couple' Mannie Goldberg the industrialist said to his wife Myra.

'You know nothing', Myra replied testily. 'Firstly, they're brother and sister....'

'Really?'

'Really', she settled herself deeper into the deckchair and rearranged her shawl. 'and secondly, the boy has syphilis'

'Oh my goodness, don't tell me that'

'Or something....and what's even more sad – '

'There's more?'

'What's sadder is how they raised the money for this little journey...' she drew back, tapped the right side of her nose with her forefinger.

The Goldbergs shared a table with the Grants at dinner. Hazel was demure, withdrawn. She wasn't certain she wanted to sit at the same table with nouveau-riche Jews. Mannie was delighted – he had been fascinated by the scraps of information from his wife about the couple.

Mannie was a man with a dull corpulent grey exterior, a typical timber baron – smelling, of course, of whisky and cigars. Internally he was multicoloured and rich, a frustrated novelist, a people-watcher and tuppenny philosopher. He regarded himself as a Pragmatic Realist, who saw his wife as a compulsive scandal-monger and gossip who hid her love of interfering in people's lives under the cloak of Theosophy and her commitment to what she called 'Matters Spiritual'.

Ian frowned at the fish drowned in white sauce on a plate far too big for this poor dead thing, once so happy in the sea beneath their keel. Unfortunately for him, Ian was both intelligent and sensitive. He knew that he would soon be dead. Everything he saw or experienced had a flavour of the End Times. So he stared at the fish and thought his thoughts.

To be brought to attention by Myra attempting to initiate conversation with Hazel. 'I hope you don't mind me asking', she asked, knowing the answer, 'but are you related to Dora Grant?'

'She's our aunt, father's sister', she answered, observing that Ian preferred his own meditations to participating in social niceties.

'I thought so,' she said, 'I play bridge with her and she mentioned a nephew who could be travelling with us.'

'Oh yes', she said without interest.

'Yes, she suggested we might have something in common...do you play? – '

'No'

'Perhaps this voyage is the perfect opportunity for you to learn... you and your lovely brother! You two are *bound*, you know."

'Bound to what?'

'No no dear', she laughed, 'I am a psychic you see.' She grasped a hand too slow to slip away. 'Heavenly twins darling, bound together life after life...do you feel it dear?' she asked, turning to Ian and reaching for his hand.

'No', said Ian and collapsed into a foetal position on the floor, arms cradling his exploding head.

Hazel dropped to her knees, gripped by terror. (Mannie sotto voce to Myra 'I do hope he's not infectious!' Myra to Mannie 'Don't be silly you stupid man') A steward rushed over. The ship's doctor officiously demanded an explanation of symptoms and syndrome. 'No no please,' Hazel said, 'I know exactly what to do – just help him to our cabin ...'

Moaning Ian was laid into his bed. Hazel fetched a morphine ampoule, expertly popped the top off and filled a syringe. The Goldbergs watched in silent admiration as she rolled up her brother's sleeve and sank the numbing liquid into a vein. 'He'll sleep' she said and motioned them out of the cabin, following them out into the passageway.

Wordlessly they climbed the stair to the deck where Hazel began to weep. Myra's motherliness gushed up in her and she tried to put an arm around the girl's shoulders.

'Fuck off!' Hazel expostulated and the Goldbergs fled.

Ian and Hazel Grant sat on Sheraton chairs in a panelled room, at the receiving end of a vast carved oak desk. At the business end sat Sir James McCullough in a tweed jacket and plus-fours, which showed off what he considered to be his magnificent calves. He looked a bit like a music hall refugee with his bushy moustache and thinning hair.

'Well', said Sir James, 'the matter is not simple. It never is in these cases. The tumour is far advanced and the location makes it rather – uhm – inaccessible.'

'But can you operate?' Hazel asked. She glanced at her frowning brother who was pretending to be somewhere else.

'I won't mince words with you', the famous man replied, 'an operation would be extremely dangerous young lady. I am reluctant to undertake it.'

'I have a great deal of money here with me' Hazel said.

I'm as good as dead already, Ian thought.

Better alive and bankrupt than lose him, Hazel thought.

Oh goodie, the surgeon thought.

'Your brother is dead', said Sir James McCullough as he swept into the waiting room, brushing his hands together as if trying to remove dust.

Hazel in Victoria Station. Men in bowlers, men in khaki, women in soft flowing things and there were fox furs. The colours were: bright orange, pinks and pastel blues, red and dust. The sounds were echoey clanks grind puff and the subdued chitter of conversations. Sometimes someone shouted, or Cockney voices chopped the air. She felt as if she were fighting her way through soup, her straw hat cutting a path through it and insulating her from the confusion. Frightened alone girl with a mourning band on her sleeve.

How dare it be summer.

I loved him so much. I still love him. I love a bloated rotting body....no no, that's not Ian, what am I going to do where am I going, how could he desert me I can't go home

Not yet

Hello, Hazel

'What?'

'It's me, silly, where on earth do you think you're heading off to?'

'Ian? Ian! Where are you? You're – *dead*!'

'What was it that stupid woman said? Bound? We're *bound*, honey! Bound for where? You didn't think you could get rid of me so easily did you?'

A porter grins mischievously at the pretty girl talking to herself, who slips behind a news kiosk

'This is FABULOUS, ' Ian's voice chatters on in her head. 'There's no pain! The operation worked. I've found the best cure there is for pain. Death! I'm bounding with delight!'

'Very funny'

'So, where are we bounding off to?'

'I really couldn't face going home'

'Well, don't! Let's go on a Grand Tour. You know, like Byron or Queen Christina of Sweden or – '

'What about father and the family? They will be expecting me to come home....'

'Oh you don't want to sit around with all that misery and crying and carrying on. They'll only depress you. They won't ever be able to understand how happy I am!''

'Well...'

'Oh come on Hazel. We didn't come all this way not to see something of Europe!'

'...I hardly have any money left after your funeral and the medical expenses....'

'How much?'

She counted. £27 7s 6d. Then she went to the ticket office and bought a single one way on the Orient Express First Class to Paris. The she went to the telegraph office and sent a carefully worded telegram to her family in Johannesburg: HAVE ARRANGED BURIAL STOP WILL RETURN IN TWO MONTHS OR SO STOP NEED TIME TO RECUPERATE STOP

Three

Flat 52 Killarney Heights, Johannesburg. 1966 et seq

'I met the Count on the Orient Express', she said, pouring the coffee. 'I never want you to tell anyone my story, Tom. Promise?'

I nodded, knowing that shortly I would put the whole story into a novel in which Hazel would play the role of Wicked Stepmother. This was a cruel decision on my part especially when you consider how after her son Anthony's tragic death I became a second son to her. It wasn't easy for me; I had to take over Anthony's fawning relationship with her, the pretence of being her only confidant and true friend apart from her dead brother, despite the fact that we disagreed over so many things.

Don't misunderstand me - I genuinely liked her, probably perversely as no one else did. Plowsky and Michelle, my bitter brother and doll-pretty sister couldn't stand her. When we made the obligatory Sunday visits they would vanish into the garden to torment each other in the sado-masochistic ritual with which they expressed their mutual love. Mother Anne meanwhile managed to maintain a hypocritical step-daughterly appearance of polite affection beneath which lurked the purest hatred. Father Daniel would sit in the antique-ridden flock-papered lounge with a smug air of triumphant boredom, occasionally giving way to a flash of compassion for her poor brain-eroded husband Robert who sat day in day out in the same armchair in the same room and couldn't manage a sentence which necessitated linking more than five words together.

At some stage of those long afternoons Hazel and I would end up alone together discussing the antiques – which came to actually genuinely interest me – or some other such subject in which two totally dissimilar people could find a hillock of common ground. This usually happened while Mary the maid and Anne were together trying to push, harass and coax Robert to his bed, Daniel read the papers and picked his nose on the balcony and Plowsky and Michelle tried to murder each other five stories below.

Sometimes I went there alone, voluntarily. Our friendship developed to a point where we both began to believe in it.

And eventually Hazel told me the whole story of her brother Ian and her Grand Tour adventure and Count Laszlo and everything. I was sworn to secrecy. I'm sorry, Hazel, but subsequent events license me to break my vow.

Back to 1938. War clouds. Adolf on the strut annexing things and just beginning to gas and incinerate Jews, homosexuals, gypsies, the disabled and dissidents of any sort. A fine time for an eighteen-year-old girl alone in Europe – except, of course, for the chummy presence of her dead brother hovering over her left shoulder – to do the Grand Tour. And to meet a Count on the Orient Express.

Hazel never told me about the ghost of Ian, by the way. It just seems obvious to me.

The Count stared at the beautiful wistful so-vulnerable girl sitting opposite, all on her own, and his heart just jumped as if trying to escape and prostrate itself at her feet. Such well-formed slimness! So tight, held in that perfect shape by muscle and bone, so unlike the floppy sloppy women he knew, whose only hope of shape was defined by their clothes. So natural! So delightful! Those emerald eyes ...peroxide hair, true but the hint of auburn roots just made it more ingénue...and those cheekbones! Defining that aristocratic face....

Hazel looked up from her novel and saw brown ragged eyes with grey flecks pointing at her like a pair of flintlocks. She blushed angrily, returned to Louise de la Valliere, King Louis XIV, lace, roses, swords and secret kisses.

A tall dark stranger, she thought. Her heart went bloomp too, but she hid it. She couldn't hide the blush. 'Well well', said Ian. Probably.

The Count was forty two then, more than double her age, very slim and six foot three inches tall. His dark slicked back hair had just started a slow retreat from his brow. No moustache, Hazel was pleased to note.

He was, at that time, in recovery from the death of his wife Margita two years earlier. He was starting to enjoy the role of heartbroken widower despite the fact that even during their marriage he had been one of the most notorious womanisers in Paris, an habitué of the best and the worst brothels, with a list of conquests which included not just whores, but actresses, dancers, Americans...all of whom had fallen to the stunning power of his Organ.

This organ was known as the *Organo di Legno* amongst the girls at the Opera. This means, organ of wood. This was because it was huge and never went limp at all.

Every few months Laszlo would return to Hungary for a six week visit. There he would resume his domestic and manorial duties, make love to his wife, run the huge estate, kick peasants around and be the perfect father to his gorgeous twin daughters Lenke and Lilla, mischievous sprites who were a constant worry to their exasperated series of nannies.

Then Margita died. Laszlo was, to his surprise, devastated. She had fallen off her horse. A fence snapped her spinal column in two. The gamekeeper found her hanging backwards over it, her heels almost meeting the back of her head. Her horse grazed guiltily nearby.

For almost two years Laszlo had languished at home, half-heartedly attending to his duties and looking after the twins with the help of an increasingly rebellious army of domestics and his nearly mad mother. He moped. The legno remained sheathed except, occasionally for solo consolation.

Here is Laszlo's secret: I feel guilty telling you but it's relevant: Laszlo suffered from a very serious condition referred to by Freud (who had attempted to treat the Count) as Rampant Priapism.

The condition is caused by a constriction of the blood vessels at the base of the penis (not, as Freud had it, by the incident in Laszlo's childhood when his father had shown him his own erect dick after a drunken afternoon and said, 'See this? That's the family heritage. One day yours will look like this! Now you know why we are referred to as the Biggest Dicks in the Land!')

The result of his sad condition (happy?) was that Laszlo was clinically incapable of losing his erection no matter how many times he ejaculated.

Perhaps – I'm guessing again – Hazel's eyes had crept above and over her novel. Perhaps she noticed the beckoning bulge in Laszlo's trousers. Perhaps she was fascinated. She may have decided this would be a good opportunity to stop being a virgin. No doubt Ian egged her on.

Ian, being dead, would have been aware of Laszlo's previous lives I assume. He would have known therefore, that in his last life Laszlo had fitted comfortably into the huge corpulent frame of Chief Amaweza Umkulu in Zaire. This mound of flesh and laughter had slid his own wooden organ into the wet parts of thirty-two wives, sixty seven concubines and even, by mistake (it was a dark night) into the sticky part of his aged Councillor Mufima, who, it is said, thought all his birthdays had come at once and spent his remaining years praying to the gods for a repeat performance.

Enough of that, more of this: by the time the train reached Paris Laszlo and Hazel had engaged in conversation, exchanged ideas on the chances of war. Laszlo declared that Hitler was a dangerous maniac intent on conquering the world. Hazel wasn't too sure about this – she saw him as the strong man Germany needed, who had rescued his country from bankruptcy.

It was the first few seconds of their meeting which I am reflecting on at the moment – I am fascinated by those crucial seconds when two people destined to become lovers first notice each-other. Psychologists have worked it all out in modern times of course. First, the tentative eye contact. If the appearance appeals a smell is released which pheromone each unconsciously picks up. Next the poor slaves of passion suffer rushes of blood to various parts of their bodies. Lips inflate (adding to the attraction) nostrils dilate. The male may experience a rush of blood to the penis. Nipples of both sexes dilate too, which signal is rather wasted if the parties are clothed.

Hazel and the Count must have suffered all these rushes and inflations, increases in heart rate and breathing, even as they discussed the fate of Europe and the spectre brooding over their lives (sorry Ian I didn't mean you. I meant the Grim Reaper. Whoever that is.)

In Laszlo's case of course, his organ was already inflated. This left less for his heart to do in pumping blood about.

And Hazel had her virginity torn away by the ever rampant Laszlo in room XIV of the Georges V Hotel in Paris.

Ian no doubt gave her much encouragement and useful information in all this. He was delighted. He must have wanted to know what penetrating his sister's hymen would be like because he had always wanted to do it himself.

For Laszlo the experience was heart-shattering. Hazel was the first woman he had been with in the last two years, since his wife's death. And a virgin! The deflowering had been wild and more scintillatingly satisfying than anything the Count had ever experienced before. Even on his own. He ejaculated four times. Hazel had enjoyed five orgasms, the first of which happened even before penetration, with the assistance of the aristocrat's exploring lips and tongue.

They were in love. Or, to be more accurate, Laszlo *realised* that he was in love and Hazel *decided* to be in love.

He took her to the Opera. He took her to the Louvre. Together they went to the top of the Eiffel Tower. Mostly, he took her to bed. They were like infatuated newlyweds. And Laszlo didn't go to the Folies Bergere or the Crazy Horse or the Moulin Rouge or any of the other scenes of his previous debauches (although I wonder if when he walked the street with this fresh young beauty on his arm, was he parading her for any of the past conquests who may have been passing by?) The original purpose of this Paris trip had been to regenerate his interest in sex. He had imagined a whirl of girls impaled upon his wooden organ. Instead there was only one, and his heart was captive.

Four

Gyor (pronounced 'Dyur'), Hungary, 1938

The Mindchyck estate (pronounced mind chuck) was twenty nine miles from Gyor in the top left corner of Hungary, near the Austrian border. The scenery was (probably still is) spectacular. Greeny yellow pines and birches. Hills wearing forests like green hair shirts. Creatures in furs cavort about, fearing nothing. Birds feathered in ridiculous colours chitter away their tiny lives. Skies Wedgwood blue and fluffy white. It was early Autumn and the days were still long and sunny.

A winding dust road led up a breast-shaped hillock on top of which, like a nipple, perched the five-hundred year old pile, ancestral home of the Count. The house had been built on the foundations of a vast stone castle which had been destroyed by Vlad the Impaler centuries ago. Laszlo's ancestor who built the house had incorporated most of the stone and some of the architectural features of the previous edifice in the design of the new: it had towers and mock battlements which served no purpose other than to make a futile boast about past glories. There were rooms without doors. There were passages which led nowhere. But at the heart of the house the family occupied a charming, well-proportioned central section of the masonry pile surrounding a courtyard garden with flowers, stone paths and topiary mostly in the shape of dragons, because Demeny, the 90-year old gardener, handyman, chauffeur and butler was trying to make a point.

Laszlo and his new love were driven from the station by Demeny in a bad mood as usual in a creaky Daimler, dust-streaked and growling in protest at having to, yet again, get all the way from A to B and back. The first sight Hazel had of the house was magical. It was sunset and the red flaming orb sinking behind the nipple silhouetted a dream vision of unutterable mystery and romance, grand and awesome and so much out of her dream visions (she had, after all, read Drakula, the Castle of Otranto, Kafka's the Castle, every book ever written about Camelot etcetera ad nauseum....probably. Well I do know she had read Drakula at least. Gormenghast did not yet exist, Peake must have passed by after the war) that Hazel removed her hand from Laszlo's crotch and gasped.

The door was opened by a crone in a mouldy black dress and pearls. 'Who the hell is this slut?' she asked in Hungarian.

'This is Hazel, Momma', Laszlo said. 'I love her.'

'A ha-haaaa!' she shrieked, 'your lovely wife only just dead and you bring a whore home!'

'Shut up Momma.'

'Why doesn't she say anything? Is she dumb as well as stupid?'

'She only speaks English Momma.'

'English is it? English?' The old woman gathered her dignity up in handfuls, straightened her torn dress, twirled a pearl. 'Hello my dear', she said sweetly in perfect English. 'How lovely to meet you!'

'Oh,' said Hazel, extending a hand to be shaken.

'Come inside', she said grabbing Hazel's hand and pulling the girl toward her for a cheek kiss, 'come, get warm.' She added conversationally in Hungarian, 'the whore's an idiot.'

A long passageway led past dust-encrusted broken furniture to the occupied part of the house. The chauffeur followed, grumbling, with the luggage. A pink-faced maid greeted the master with a curtsy. 'Will you want dinner now sir?' she asked 'and who's she?'

'You will behave yourself Tanya,' the Count ordered. 'I am master of this house in case you've forgotten! This is your new mistress.'

'Really?' she replied, startled, 'should I get the girls?'

'Yes please. Fetch the girls.'

She rushed off, muttering murder to herself.

Hazel took a deep breath. There were mysteries here, she thought, dangerous mysteries.

The twins: Lenke and Lilla. Two simpering minxes ten years old, their lives circling around the adoration of their grandmother, the servants, the garden and a determination to get revenge on their father for having allowed their mother to die.

They had been experimenting with dyeing each other's hair. Lenke's was bright orange; Lilla's had a green stripe down the centre of her head like a tonsorial banner. Their faces were covered in smudged makeup. Lilla had determined to flout convention by using lipstick on her eyelids. Lenke wore two circles of blue on her cheekbones like a pantomime character from a horror movie.

'Darlings!' said Momma.

Hazel bore all this for a year. That year deserves a book of its own and I may write it. However, this book is not about Hazel, so she'll have to wait.

I'll sum it up: the year was like the desperate siege of a Crusader fortress. Hazel's troops attacked again and again, using first charm, then emotional blackmail (she was good at tears) then a dogged determination, then sullen resentment and finally despair. She learned Hungarian; she learned, or rather brushed up on German; she attempted to play with the twins but they seemed interested only in her lingerie; she fetched tea for Momma who threw it across the room and called for the maid...and the fortress stood. Eventually realising that the chance of victory had altered from unlikely to impossible, Hazel withdrew. Or to be more accurate she escaped. Laszlo had not been an ally in any of these battles. He had spent days away from the house, apparently trying to get the estate back into workable condition after the long period of neglect. With some success. But in doing so, he lost his wife-to be, who bribed the very willing Demeny to drive her to the station in the middle of the night.

It had been a ridiculous year, Hazel reflected as the Daimler made its bumpy, grumpy, annoyed way through the pitch-black countryside toward the town. (There were so many in retrospect unbelievable incidents, including the Attempted Poisoning, the Confrontation in the Orangery which involved some minor hair pulling; the Great Balcony Scene during which Laszlo swore that unless Hazel promised to be his forever, he would destroy his body by giving it to gravity over a great distance. To the rocks.....A novel in itself. Perhaps I will write it one day.)

Laszlo knew, with reflection, that there is nothing quite as silly as an old fox in love with a young chicken. But no one in the world could have prevented him from being exactly that silly.

While Hazel and Laszlo were acting out their absurd melodrama Adolf Hitler nee Schickelgruber, former painter, was making some progress in his world domination scheme, mouthing absurdities like 'we have no territorial demands. Germany will never break the peace.' Yes he did really say that.

It is likely he was Natya Vilkowsky in his previous life. Natya was the nagging Jewess who watched her husband die as he dangled by a rope from the tree in the village square, where the Cossacks had left him. 'I *told* you it would end like this. You never listen to me!' and 'It's all very well you going off and *dying* like that, what the hell do you think I'll eat now? *You*? And you so *thin*! It's not my fault you never eat! I make *food*, you only want to make *me*. Good for nothing! Good for nothing! Alive or dead!' And so on.

Hazel had another reason for leaving Laszlo. It was her fascination with Nazism and the Nazis. She was viscerally thrilled by the idea of an unstoppable master race strutting about Europe like an army of arrogant cocks. She spoke German fluently as well as Hungarian. So the news that 150,000 German troops had marched into Austria hastened her escape. She wanted to be there, to be part of it all. She imagined the proud, tall, young Aryans blond as gold, marching in time to the place where her legs met her torso. Compared to this dream the wooden organ had lost its attraction.

So she leapt onto the midnight train to Vienna clutching Momma's jewellery (enough to get by, not all of it.) and went choof choof off to Vienna. Wien.

When Laszlo discovered Hazel's disappearance (and the diminished box of jewellery) he went as mad as an ulcer sufferer who has inadvertently eaten a whole lemon. Or so Hazel surmised.

Five

'Vienna cured me of Nazism. I was so naive! I believed they were knights on a holy crusade...but then I was mercifully saved from that disease.' She handed me a plate on which the last fairy cake sat like the Mindchyck castle – like a breast with a cherry on top. I accepted.

'How?' I asked, nibbling at the nipple.

'Do you remember the couple I told you about? On the ship?'

'Oh yes, the Goldbergs. They were at my Barmitzvah you know.'

'That's right. Ghastly nouveau riche, very fat these days...it's disgusting. They should pay extra tax.'

Sensing a hobbyhorse about to canter into the conversation I said, 'Well go on Gran, tell the story.'

Vienna 1938

The Goldbergs were amongst the first people Hazel saw in Vienna. The first people she knew, anyway. The couple had gone to Vienna to see the famous Lippizaners at the Spanish Riding School, eat apfelstrudel and drink coffee at the Kohlmarkt, go to the Opera. Well, tourism was the ostensible reason for their visit. Having spent most of the year on the Cote d'Azur, in Paris and in London, they apparently wanted to broaden their horizons...

The real reason was far more sinister. In London Mannie had met a gentleman with the unlikely name of Franz Muller at a reception given by the Chief Rabbi. Herr Muller brought stories of a programme of extermination of German Jews which, while not yet in full operation, he believed to be a growing emergency of terrible proportions. While Dachau had opened in 1933, few people knew what went on there. Herr Muller had an inkling – his brother was a guard at that camp, had seen its potential for murder, had boasted about it. Kristallnacht on 9th November 1938 had only just happened. Being a liberal-minded Christian intellectual, he had been horrified by the mobs of hate-maddened people burning and looting Jewish shops, attacking people in the street, destroying lives and businesses.

Franz came to London with a determination to warn the British press and people. Both of which seemed uninterested. The British public was afraid of the German military, preferred to believe Adolf's protestations of nonaggression and didn't want to offend him.

Mannie was riveted by Herr Muller's speech and engaged the man in conversation afterwards. The result of that discussion and subsequent meetings was that Mannie resolved to go to Austria and thence to Germany to meet with Jewish leaders and others and find out the truth. If things were as bad as Herr Muller suggested, Mannie promised to mobilise South African Jewry behind a grand scheme to rescue as many German and Austrian Jews as possible, and bring them to South Africa.

Besides, thought Mannie, what a great idea for a novel!

So Mannie and Myra in all their innocence travelled blithely to Austria, assuming their status as South African citizens would protect them from harassment. Just in time for the Anschluss. Just in time to see the red and black flags popping onto the flagpoles. Streets turning grey and brown with uniforms. The population standing on sidewalks watching their conquerors invading their country and cheering like crazy. They chucked their Emperor out and threw their lot in with a foreign power. They gave away their country, abandoned all semblance of Democracy. And cheered and cheered and heiled and heiled.

The Goldbergs couldn't believe their eyes when they saw Hazel climbing out of the train. 'Hey! Hello!' they shouted.

'Oh. Yes. Hello indeed,'

'What on earth are you doing here?'

'Just travelling. The Grand Tour.'

Mannie smiled. Myra cringed. She didn't need her psychic powers to work out the question Mannie was about to ask.

'Where's your brother – Ian wasn't it? – how is he?' Mannie asked.

'He's dead', Hazel said cheerfully.

'Oh.' Mannie wasn't sure quite how to react. 'Uh – let me get you a porter - '

'I'm so sorry dear,' Myra said, patting the girl's arm sympathetically. 'Dreadful for you'

'Not at all,' Hazel said, 'He's quite happy about it.'

They pushed their way through the crowded station with its Nazis, panicked porters, Jews, homosexuals and Gypsies.

They shared a taxi to the Furstenberg Hotel which was swarming with Nazis who appeared to have annexed the Hotel as well as the country. At the desk they were involved in a passionate argument with a tall blond uniformed German called Manfred Leitz. Who, no doubt as a reaction to Mannie and Myra's surname, insisted there was no room at the inn.

'But we've booked a room!' Mannie, exasperated. 'Thomas Cook in London booked us a room. I presume you've *heard* of Thomas Cook?'

The name had no magic for Manfred. 'Show me your papers,' he said.

They parted reluctantly with passports and travel documents. Hazel felt like an observer, watching Manfred's manly attempts to converse in a semblance of English. She was sorry for him. She hoped at some stage to ascertain whether *all* his hair was as blond as the hair on his head. She hoped he would realise that she was actually on his side.

A thought occurs to me as I type this. Hazel doesn't seem at this time to have noticed that she was Jewish, or if so, that this had any relevance whatsoever. She had never actually bothered to be Jewish, I presume. I never saw any evidence of any particular identification with this particular brand.

She did not see fit to reveal at this time that she could speak German. She had learned the language at school. She had read Schiller. And Goethe. She had read 'Brush up your German' alone in bed on long, lonely nights when Laszlo was away. It was the only (at least part) English book in the Castle. This was probably on the advice of Ian, probably suggesting she keep her aces up her sleeve.

Manfred studied the passports intently. An officer strutted up to the little party. Manfred showed him the documents. They went into a huddle at the back of the reception. Words like 'Achso!' and 'Turisten' and 'idioten' and 'Juden' floated about in the air. Hazel grinned to herself. Her companions frowned anxiously.

The Officer's head popped up from the huddle. 'You vill come vit me' he ordered.

The Officer, Oberleutnant Franz von Buhling, came from an aristocratic Bavarian family. His grandfather had been one of the chief architects involved in creating mad King Ludwig's fairytale castles, including Linderhof and the incomplete Neuschwanstein. Von Buhling's family lived in a miniature version of Ludwig's planned Falkenstein, a monster of Gothic proportions, the only similar monster in Europe being owned by Count Laszlo Mindchyck in Hungary. Like the king, von Buhling's family had always been tinged with insanity – and a long tradition of eccentric liberalism. The Oberleutnant was secretly deeply distrustful of Hitler, and despite the holy oath of fealty sworn by every German soldier, he dreamed of unseating the dictator and restoring democracy. Preferably with him as constitutional monarch.

For this reason he apparently became one of the most conscientious of the younger Nazi officers. His Party membership gained him many privileges. People snapped to obedience when he gave orders. He liked that. They did what he wanted them to do. So he told them to arrest liberals, shoot Jews, crush all opposition to the Master Race. His rise in the army was rapid. Before the end of the war he was a full Colonel, still dreaming of destroying Hitler. No-one believed this story at the Nuremberg trials.

This nutcase decided that the foreign Jewish couple were undoubtedly spies, tools of the International Jewish Conspiracy. And Hazel was certainly their dupe.

His interrogation of the trio was not pleasant, not polite, hardly diplomatic, despite the Oberleutnant's moral anguish. Hazel, Mannie and Myra were, to put it more clearly, treated like shit. Exacerbated by Hazel's ruinous attempt to take Franz aside and say to him, in perfect German, 'I'm not really *with* these people, you know. I am on *your* side!'...the effect of which was to infuriate von Buhling beyond bearing. The traitress! No loyalty even to her own people!

...and had the British Embassy not come to hear of their detention (actually secretly from von Buhling, according to him at his trial) and intervened, the trio would certainly have been imprisoned as spies and probably shot.

Six

Killarney Heights, Johannesburg

'Well, that's the story Tom. How I could have been a Countess...We left on the next train and before I knew it I was back in South Africa...'

'Amazing,' I said, taking in the latest instalment and another bite of fairy cake.

'And that's why you find me here, a lonely woman with a half mad husband, despised by her stepchildren and deserted by her only son...'

'He *died* Granny, that's not the same thing.'

She flinched as if I'd slapped her, then came rare tears. I cringed as if it were I who had been hit. I managed to put an arm around her bony shoulders. 'Oh Tom,' she said, 'I miss him so much!'

Yes I knew that. Anthony's death had been sad and bizarre and it had resulted in even we, her family, gathering round to cluck-cluck and tush tush with the best of them.

It was only once we got home when, in the apparent solitude of the grape arbour I heard Father, unaware of my presence (I was burying the family cat at the time. I forget if it was dead or not), let out a series of giggles and guffaws which threatened to overwhelm him and cause strangulation by previously repressed delight – that I suspected there may have been more to Anthony's death than had been told. That sentence is a crime against grammar but it does what it has to do.

I did find out later. I will try to remember to tell you.

I watched Hazel's face as those dreadful memories replayed themselves in her mind, and interrupted 'I wish I could go to Europe. I want to do a Grand Tour too.'

'I don't see why you shouldn't, dear,' she said, angrily dabbing at a tear. 'As long as it's with your parents' blessing.'

'After my recent adventures I don't see Father letting me loose again.'

'Well, I feel a little as if his attitude has changed toward you somewhat you know.'

'Really?' I asked, 'Why do you think that?'

'If I didn't know better dear I could swear that when he tells people the story about you running away from home and going to Durban that time, there's just a trace of – *pride* – '

'I don't believe you,' I grinned.

'Frankly I don't understand why. I think your behaviour was disgraceful, fighting with your father, going off without any money. I worry about your sanity sometimes you know.'

I laughed. It's a pity I laughed. I would never have laughed had I realised how serious she was. 'So do you think I should?'

'Would you?'

'Yes! Sweep through Europe like a cold wind. Get some rocks off. Sow some wild oats. Like you did. I may just not come back.'

She tried to hide a mischievous grin. 'Wait until you've finished university my boy, they'll never agree otherwise.' she said, and leaned back on the rose-printed chair. 'I will tell you one thing I learned from my trip – '

'Go on, what?'

'Waste of breath of course. You won't listen.'

'Come on Gran. What wisdom do you impart.'

'Something I read, I think Goethe. Or somebody. Wherever you go, there you are.'

'Oh, ' I said musing. 'How trite.'

2

One

The Liar's Club, St James', London, England

'So that is your idea is it?'

'Yes,' the young man said, simpering, 'she must be in South Africa. It's logical.'

'She said she would never go back there. She said she was finished with all that.' The old man lit a cigar and leaned back, blowing a cloud of smoke at the innocent ceiling.

'That was a very long time ago.' The young man felt his collar nervously as if checking whether his companion had sneaked a piano wire into it. 'Besides, she may have been – how can I say this – misleading you?'

'No no no! If you mean lying, she would never do that. She was a model of probity.'

'Of course, of course...'

We'll cease our eavesdropping for a moment so that I can describe the participants in this conversation.

The older man is stoutish, but his face is leonine and he wears a shock of white hair dragged from its natural place at the back of the head to the front, in a combover of brash determination to hide the obvious. His face is that of someone who has suffered much and schemed much. His suit is perfectly cut in Saville Row for a man of his size, but the white shirt is fighting a losing battle with the lower part of his gut. Below the belt the bulge in the crotch area would only be missed by a blind virginal eighty year old nun.

He is Count Leo Mindchyck.

His companion here in the lounge of the exclusive Liars Club (an establishment for gentlemen and those claiming to be gentlemen in London's Pall Mall) is tall thin and gangly, about thirty four years old. His name is James Truelove, the youngest and avowedly most brilliant partner in the firm of Withers, Stronglode, Withers and Truelove. He has been Laszlo's solicitor for three years.

The Liars Club, incidentally, was founded in 1768 as a place where gentlemen (and those aspiring to be gentlemen, as the brochure shamelessly avers) could practise the skills essential for success in business, commerce and society. Membership is exclusive, by invitation only, and hellishly expensive. Laszlo bought the place in 1966.

'Hm,' Laszlo said. He dipped his spoon into a bowl of Swiss Muesli, 'so she is living in her home country again. I can't completely blame her.'

'What would you like me to do sir?'

'You're my lawyer. What would you advise me to do?' Laszlo asked, mouth full of mush. 'Should I go out there?'

James shook his head. 'In my opinion that would be quite wrong. I will appoint an agent out there to research more deeply. We need to find out if she's married – '

'Married! That could not be? I hope you're not reverting ...' Laszlo is referring to Truelove's horribly embarrassing gaffe on first coming to the club. The unfortunate young man had thought that the name of the club meant that everything said on its hallowed premises should be untrue – as a result of which he was almost strangled by his client when he haplessly remarked that Laszlo's chauffeur had attempted to rape him.

' She's not young any more, anything could have happened...'

The old man blinked myopically at his solicitor. Memories of the gorgeous springlike gay young girl paraded through his mind.

'I'm sorry.' Truelove genuinely was. He had a great deal of affection and admiration for his client. He especially loved (and hoped to emulate) the way the Count gave such a gentle and urbane impression to all the people whose heads he planned to have removed. He dealt with business the way a trout-tickler deals with his meals-to be. Truelove wanted to learn everything from this man. And then beat him.

'Does she have children even?'

'I don't know yet. I've only just started to do the research...'

'They should have been ours, hers and mine, those children. Well you had better get me the full picture. Let's see what kind of life she has. Get your people to make me a full report. All right?'

'Of course.' Truelove grinned.

Two

BOSS, the Bureau of State Security, was founded in June 1963 as 'Republican Intelligence' by an ex Nazi (ex?) called H. J. Van der Bergh. He had certainly supported the Nazis during the war, as had so many other members of the ruling South African Nationalist Party. The existence of BOSS was a closely held secret – one of those 'secrets' generally known by most of thos actively opposing Apartheid, but never officially admitted to until at least 1969.

It operated under the beady eye of Justice Minister B. J. Vorster, who became Prime Minister when arch Apartheid architect Verwoerd was assassinated in the House in 1966. Vorster's elevation also meant the promotion of BOSS to a position of immense power, with a huge budget and no restrictions on its activities either inside or outside South Africa.

BOSS' objectives can be summed up as follows: infiltrate, undermine, destroy, kill, slander, control, betray, bribe, propagandise all those it considered 'enemies' of the State – that is, anyone who didn't support Apartheid. All of whom were presumed to be card-carrying members of the Communist Party, or fellow-travellers, or dupes who were, in the opinion of Vorster and his minions, were determined to infiltrate, undermine, destroy, kill, slander, control, bribe, and so on the God-loving Afrikaner volk....and therefore likely to commit terrorist acts at any time.

One of the priorities of the paranoiacs who ran BOSS was the penetration of NUSAS. The National Union of South African Students was considered a highly dangerous organisation: because NUSAS was always organising protests against Apartheid. Inevitably B. J et al assumed the students were Commies and therefore potential terrorists, saboteurs and therefore to be infiltrated, undermined, etc etc etc.....

That Pieter Mostert, son of the Afrikaans mayor of Ventersdaal, was set on going to the University of the Witwatersrand, that nest of pinkoes and radicals, had come as something of a surprise – as well as an unpleasant shock to his parents.

'What do you want to go to that Commie place for?' his father asked.

'It's a good university.'

'No son of mine is going to a comminis' school!' his mother Hester sputtered.

'But I have to go to Wits!' Pieter protested, running his thin fingers angrily through his straw-coloured hair.

The natural place for Pieter to pursue his higher education would have been RAU – the Randse Afrikaans Universiteit, which had just opened across the road from Wits. The South African Government had decided on this location because it seemed like a good way to annoy the pinkos at that austere bastion of liberalism and 'progressive' ideas. The students at the RAU were mostly from small towns, or from farms. They were Nationalist supporters, every one a passionate advocate of Apartheid, regarding their near neighbour as a promoter of the *swart gevaar,* the 'black danger'. (The RAU has since moved to a smart new campus miles away. Who won?)

'Why can't you go to the RAU?' Hester asked, 'Like any good Afrikaner? That Hennie van Rensburg, he's going there, so is Fanie DuPlessis. All your friends from school will be there.'

'Mother!', Pieter sighed. Now he knew he would have to tell them the truth.

It made them very proud.

University of the Witwatersrand, Johannesburg. August institution, founded on gold and diamonds. In 1896 as the South African School of Mines, because the diamond miners of Kimberley decided it may be a good idea to educate their children to handle the vast wealth daddy hoped to prise out of the carbon heart of the earth. Then, when gold was discovered in the Transvaal, in and around Johannesburg, the School upped sticks and transformed itself into the Transvaal University College and thereafter the South African School of Mines and Technology by 1908. Which suggests that it was originally set up to make (white) miners even better at ripping the heart of gold and jewels from the screaming protesting body of the African earth. Having said that, the University had admitted 'non white' students all the way up to 1959 when the Government passed an act designed to enforce Apartheid even in hallowed academe. This is a novel not a history. Head for Google and dig out the story –it's fascinating.

By the late sixties, when Pieter and I invaded the place, the University had been established in its present location since 1922. Its grand porticoed classical architecture spreading over hills and vales. Its growing portfolio of property including not just the campus, but caves, archaeology, a farm, showgrounds... money no object, then. Which could explain why the place was so hated and feared by the Afrikaans establishment and especially, the Nationalist Party. Or maybe it was more the fact that it was a nest of liberals, anti-apartheid activists, or, as the Nats would have it, pinko Commie terrorists who were, in their eyes, a danger to the state.

Which was why my parents approved my choice of University – it was assumed, anyway, that I would go there. If there was any choice, it would have been between Cape Town and Wits – Cape Town was pretty much the same sort of place, just with sea and mountain as a background. And without free food free laundry and free bed.

I was doing all 'nice' Humanities – Philosophy, Political Science (very dodgy in a semi-fascist state) and Law (toxic combination – equipment for revolution.)

My parents particularly wanted me to be a lawyer. They were good white liberals. They were also nouveau-riche Jews.

First generation Jewish immigrants usually scrape a living. Often, their children decide not to be poor and scratch and bite their way to the top of the pile, like my father. And they push their children into the professions, because Daddy doesn't want his children to have to do the same immoral, dangerous, sometimes illegal things they had to do to reach the top.

This is not, of course, an immutable rule. Many first generation Jewish immigrants made a pile, of course. In these cases, their sons usually went into IDB (South African joke. It could mean either Illegal Diamond Buying or, in this case, Into Daddy's Business) and frittered away their newly won fortune. Their sons would become doctors or lawyers in order to save father from the bankruptcy court. Hence the Jewish Mother's anthem, 'My son the doctor...' or lawyer, or accountant. As far as daughters were concerned, their job was to marry a doctor, lawyer or accountant. And go shopping.

My Jewish Momma wasn't originally Jewish. Her conversion had seemed a good idea at the time of the marriage. Which made momma, always a great actress, determined to outjewishmomma the Jewish mommas. She wanted to be seen as Jewish (emphasis on the ish) in every way.

The role did not suit her physically. She was in those days slim, blonde (chemically assisted) attractive (plastic-surgery assisted) intelligent (evening class assisted) if neurotic (psychiatrist assisted) woman who spoke Standard BBC English. My most useful inheritance from her. Rescuing me from the vowel-squeezing of my contemporaries, but obviously greatly assisting the bullies in High School.

Back, or rather forward to the University of the Witwatersrand. It was a time of ferment. Spring 1968. To celebrate the advent of hippiness I grew a beard, smoked pot, joined NUSAS the Students' Union in thumbing noses and general mayhem of protest against the Armoured Beast of the State. (More Googling suggested – look up the SRC and NUSAS at WITS and CTC in the sixties and seventies. Wow. I sure missed some exciting times!)

1968 at Wits was the year of the Spies. Mired in their conviction that this university represented a threat to the Apartheid state, BOSS was rumoured to have riddled the student body with secret agents spying, undermining, meddling, infiltrating. Paranoia ruled.

The President of NUSAS that year was Rob Bailey. This angular, dark haunted young man seemed to have assumed the burden of the liberation of South Africa's oppressed peoples singlehanded. Others could be used to help, but could never be entirely trusted. Especially if their own safety were to be threatened. This was rather clever of him, especially as there were definite cases of NUSAS documents going missing or being mysteriously altered. Of the NUSAS office having been searched and not very cleverly tidied up afterwards. When demonstrations were planned, there could be no doubt that the police had foreknowledge – on several occasions permits were refused even before application had been made.

So Rob made a decision: the only way to prevent the office invasions and searches would be to mount nightly vigils on campus, around the Hofmeyr Building, which housed the Union. Bleary-eyed undergrads were rotaed to sit in trees, crouch on balconies, hide in cupboards – in the hope that some of the culprits would be caught. No-one considered what we would do to the spies if they were caught!

Naturally Pieter and I volunteered. Unfortunately, due to a mixup (which I now know Pieter engineered) we were allocated different nights: his was Thursday, mine was Tuesday.

....there was this guy with this particularly good DP, the best grass produced on the entire East Coast of Africa (you can keep your Zanzibar Cob, buddy) I can't blame him, I suppose. I could try blaming my natural generosity or something but that would make me sound as if I'm trying to make out I'm a good guy or something. Anyway, I wish that good DP hadn't inserted itself into our lives, I wish I hadn't decided to take Pieter some that Thursday to make his vigil a bit more pleasant.

I drove Mother's Jag up to the gates of the University around 10 p.m, showed the half asleep gatekeeper my student ID, parked in the space marked 'Professors Only' and went off to the Hofmeyr building, torch in hand, to look for Pieter.

I expected to be challenged, leaped put upon, attacked – nothing. Everything terribly quiet.

Unmolested I strolled across the quadrangle, Still no sign of Pieter.

Halfway across there was a bench. I stopped to listen to the night. And realised that a jacaranda tree near the entrance was emitting strange jerky movements from its branches, rustling sounds suggesting a lurking jaguar. Or two. I tiptoed nervously up to the tree. 'Pieter,' I whispered.

There was a frantic rustling from the branches. I tensed to flee. A pair of pink panties fluttered down at me and the pink face of Martin Bernstein emerged, just visible, through the leaves. I shone the torch upward. 'Whatsat? Whosat?'

'It's me, Tom' I said, relieved.

'Oh shit!' Another pink face glimmered into view. I recognised the petite Karen Williams.

'Hello Tom,' she said, with obviously a major attempt at inappropriate nonchalance. 'We're –uh - on watch.'

'So I see,' I said. 'Have you seen Pieter?'

'In the office, I expect' Martin said. 'I think that's where he keeps watch.'

'Thanks Martin. I'll go check up on him.' I turned to go.

'Tom, don't say – well, you know, anything. I mean we are on watch here you know'

'Of course', I said, thinking I have always wondered how arboreal marsupials procreate...Karen Williams!! With that pink-faced lug!!

'Uh Tom, won't you – uh ' he pointed at the panties lying on the ground.

'Sure', I said, picking them up and putting them in my pocket. Pieter would love this....! Rapidly I strolled to the unlocked door of the Students' Union office and slipped quietly inside....Karen Williams! With Pinky Bernstein!

I tiptoed up the stairs and went down a corridor, listening briefly at each door. Finally I came to a door marked 'President'. There were sounds, unidentifiable sounds within. It stood very slightly ajar. A pale secretive beam of light escaped.

I pushed the door gently open.

And there, in the light of a torch propped against a filing cabinet was my best friend photographing documents so intently, he hadn't heard me entering...

My heart was going bang bang so loud it must have been audible to him. But it wasn't.

'Pieter', I whispered.

'Shit!' he said. The camera flew out of his hands and a revolver pointed at me.

'Pieter! It's me! For fucksake! Don't shoot me!'

'Tom! Oh, Jesus!' he said. The revolver continued to point in my direction. It was shaking now.

'This is ridiculous' I said after a few terrifying seconds in which anything could have happened.

He stared from me to the gun. From the gun to me. He put the gun down on the desk. Then he sat on Rob's chair, deflated, head in hands. 'I suppose this is what's called red handed', he said glumly.

I stared silently at the tousled yellow hair and the bitten fingernails that clutched at it in hanks. 'No pun intended I hope', I said drily.

'Don't joke Tom', Pieter said, looking up, still shaking.

That made two of us.

'I don't believe it. I seriously don't believe it. You of all people...'

'There's a time for clichés Tom...and I suppose this is it.'

'I suppose...' I said. Then, 'I don't know what to do next!'

The possibilities. Both of us trying not to look at the gun on the desk. Both trying to look at the gun on the desk. Both considering fight vs flight. Both remembering how together we had faced death before, as brothers-in arms.

'Maybe I have to try to explain...' Pieter said at last.

'Ok,' I said hopefully, 'Explain.' I sat at the desk from him, the raped documents between us, the gun just out of reach of both.

'It happened like this, Tom,' Pieter said. 'You remember when we were in the hospital? You were in ward 2C and I was next door.'

I remembered all right. Lying there waiting for my body to mend so that the Army could hang me.

'Yes'

'Well, I had a visit from the Brigadier, Tom, Brigadier Maartens, you know, the one from BOSS.'

'Yes, he visited me too. Didn't say much, he was the one informed me we were heroes, that Absolom told him we had engineered his capture so we weren't going to hang after all.'

'Well he said much more than that to me...'

'Go on'

Pieter fought reluctance, won. 'He told me – sorry Tom – he told me you were delirious, you know, and there was somebody there to write down every word you said – '

'And what – ' Fear made me gasp

'And they're not so stupid as you thought. I mean, they knew everything, Tom, everything that really happened...'

'Jeez! So why the hell did they let us off – '

'They reckoned we – or rather, I – would be far more useful spying for them. Especially here, at Wits.'

'And you agreed? You agreed! After all our discussions!' I had always assumed Pieter and I shared the same views – about BOSS, about the police state, about Apartheid...was this how he had managed to persuade his parents to let him study at Wits - ?

'We'd both be dead if I didn't. Don't think it was easy, Tom. Lying to you was the worst!'

'You did a good job of that...'

'I haven't slept since. My stomach just churns up. I think I'm getting an ulcer. The only thing that has kept me going is how I keep them happy...'

'Keep them *happy*???'

'Yes. Look!' he pointed to the sheet of paper he had been photographing. It was headed 'Canteen receipts March – May' It was a list of items sold, prices and totals. Like 'Orange Juice 5 cents, Bacon rolls (buttered) 15 cents', stuff like that.

'And this, ' he said. A fat sheaf of papers headed '100 yard sprint. Best times.'

'And this – 'Acceptable Music for Public Dancing at SU Fresher's Ball'

I looked up at him. He was grinning sideways. Come to think of it, so was I. Next thing, we were laughing. 'Oh my God,' I roared, 'how the hell are you getting away with it?'

'So far so good,' he said. 'But I won't manage for ever. BOSS won't stand for being made a fool of. Even if they *are* fools.' A shadow of gloom flitted across his face. 'And then fuck knows what will happen.'

I nodded. 'Fuck knows.' I said. 'You should have told me.'

'How could I? They reckon you're a hopeless case, a pinko commie druggie terrorist. It's you they want me to watch, along with the others.'

'Hm'. Thinking, Pieter will always have BOSS on his back now like a hump. Or a bomb.

Each of us leaned a chin on a hand and studied the other. 'Oh well, when in doubt as they say...' I said and rolled a huge fat DP joint to Pieter's relieved delight.

We did a lot more giggling after that, especially when Pieter told me some of the other documents he had presented for the scrutiny of the Security Police. Like lists of stationery ordered, a First Aid leaflet and then finally, to placate them, a copy of dear Pinko Bernstein's screamingly boring thesis on 'The Theatre of the Absurd – Pataphysics, Surrealism, Dadism and Existentialism', which no doubt caused several agents hours of frustrated reaching for dictionaries and attempts to draw a call to arms out of Bernstein's ridiculous plagiarised thesis.

And after we were giggled out I said, 'So what are we going to do now?'

'What do you mean "we"?' Pieter asked.

'Hey, I'm part of this now. You can't carry on alone. I wish you told me before.'

'I know,' he said, ashamed, grateful.

'Look – I can come on Thursdays can't I? You can join me on Tuesdays.'

'And - ?'

'And we'll keep BOSS running around in circles chasing its own tail for so long they'll get giddy and collapse in a heap.'

'It's playing with fire Tom,' he said gloomily. 'When they finally realise there's no secret codes or Communist plots in the laundry lists, they'll have my guts. '

'You haven't got any.'

'Stop being silly. Just think what you're getting involved with.'

'All right, all right. Look, we're in this together. If it hadn't been for me blabbing in that hospital you wouldn't be in this fix. So we'll collect stuff for them. Together. We'll keep to the useless stuff you're collecting, but we can add other things that will make them think you're doing your job.'

'Huh?' Pieter flicked hair out of his eyes. 'Like what?'

'Well, there's the official NUSAS typewriter, right?' I pointed at the machine. 'We can fake documents can't we?'

'Huh?'

'What they want is names, right? Minutes of meetings. Names of members of the political clubs and societies. So that's what we give them. *Our* versions.'

'Boy oh boy,' Pieter said, 'You know what?'

'What?'

'You caught me just in time. That Maartens has been pretty heavy on me recently. To be honest, I don't think I could have gotten away with it for much longer – '

'So aren't you lucky to have a friend like me? I smiled. Then, conspiratorially – 'by the way, you'll never guess who Pinko has got with him doing whoopsie in a jacaranda tree...' I whipped the panties out of my pocket and waved them toward his nose....'come on! Let's sneak up on them.....!'

From then on, on Tuesdays and Thursdays, in the dead of night, the Bullshit Production Society churned out volumes of documents, forged papers, plans for protests that never took place, lists headed 'Committee for the Liberation of the Oppressed' or 'Marxism Discussion Group'.

Like all double agents, we were always on a tightrope. When we produced route plans of marches, we had to persuade Rob for some spurious reason to change the route at the last minute. And when we gave lists of suspect people, we always included campus jocks, members of the Traditional Dance troupe, every *kuggel* on campus and of course anybody we didn't like.

We knew how dangerous the game we were playing was. If BOSS realised that they were being played with we would have as much chance of living out a happy life as a dead chicken has of crossing the road.

Three

A clique formed around Pieter and I. We were the guys who knew everything, like where to get Dexedrine – essential for exams. We always had the best grass. We knew who was doing what to whom and why. In class we constantly made asses of ourselves by arguing with lecturers (because, after all, we knew *everything*). Some of our peers loved us for that. To others we were assholes, and they were, of course, right. These poor souls had their names given to Maartens for special attention.

We wore our hair long, of course. In my case I wore my hair frizz. We dressed in jeans. Sometimes we murdered flowers and wore their dying corpses. Few of our fellows hadn't read the *Time* article about the Hippie phenomenon, and many wanted to jump onto this flower-bedecked bandwagon.

The only missing piece of the multicoloured pied-piper procession was the drug at the centre of it all in the USA – LSD. The mind-altering consciousness opener, lauded so convincingly by Leary, Wolfe, all those beautiful people in the vanguard of this social and political revolution, visionaries of the new spiritual age.

Then one day acid arrived. In a letter to one of our circle, 'Baby' Frewin, was a sheet of blotting paper. The sheet was divided up into one-inch squares. It had been sent by a friend of his from Hippie Heaven, holy San Francisco. There was no explanation with the gift. But we knew it could be only one thing.

There were twelve little squares. The battle to be amongst the apostles was intense. People grovelled shamelessly to Baby. I didn't have to grovel because Baby was my friend and I was, after all, the only guru around. Pieter didn't have to grovel, as he was my friend.

Baby (sweetness and innocence itself, he was called Baby because his cute fat little face hadn't changed substantially since infancy) was inundated with offers of drugs, sex, money. To my knowledge – being a man of integrity – he only yielded to the drugs and the sex.

Eventually the apostles had been chosen and a meeting was set up in the flat of Piers Mallory. A tatty basement in Hillbrow surrounded by boxes of people and streets of dogs, dust and grime. Apartmentland.

We thirteen sat on the floor around a low table upon which were displayed the ritual objects. The blotting-paper and scissors, the pipe, the grass, the cigarette papers, the matches. A vase with a sickly rose. A wooden incense holder, in which two sticks of Jasmine incense glowed and puffed.

'What shall we listen to? ' Piers directed his question to me, as the Master of Ceremonies.

'Let's start with Beefheart.' I said, glancing at Pieter and Baby for confirmation.

I made the ritual cuts, handed a square out per person. We chewed, drank tea.

Beefheart finished, turned over, finished.

We sat. Made joints.

Incredible Stringband finished, turned over, finished.

We waited. Chatted. Giggled.

Bob Dylan finished, turned over.

Suddenly Henry was tripping. Henry was a scrawny farm boy type whose stubble, made of steel, was impervious to razors. We knew he was tripping because he started saying things like 'O wowwwww...!' and 'Whoooooooooah....' and 'AmAAAAYzing.....'

Piers, Baby, Pieter and I went into the kitchen to discuss all this. 'It is obvious to me,' I said, 'that this acid is not.'

'What about Henry? He's on something more than grass!'

'Hmmm yes. There must have been some acid on the sheet. Maybe most of it evaporated. Maybe he got a corner where it was all concentrated.'

'I'm sorry guys,' Baby said, 'This is really embarrassing...'

'What are we going to do with Henry?' Piers asked.

'I suppose I'd better take him away somewhere. He could get paranoid amongst all these non trippers staring at him.' I enjoyed taking control of the situation. Good thing I had absolutely no real idea as to the right thing to do in a case like this. Perhaps I just wanted to escape from the embarrassment. 'You guys play them music, give them a good time, send them home'.

I went in to Henry. 'Let's walk'.

Hillbrow night streets, flashing neon madness of people in pairs and singles looking to be pairs, towering blocks of crumbling concrete and wan lights behind torn net curtains. The Kingdom of Hopelessness. Shambling figures addled by alcohol, steamed by smoke, driven by need.

I began to realise that this walk was a mistake. Leaving safety with this mad-mouthed babbling idiot with the grin splashed across his face like a wet rag.

'Wowww thisisamazing...look him, whoa! This is so good Tom, you're SO good! Hey whatsat.... o wow o wow o wow....'

Sooner or later even in these streets someone is going to notice... me thinking cops round here are all in cars for their safety so they'd just think another drunk, I hope...

I guide him toward an alley, a space between buildings where I hope we'll be less conspicuous. He stops, leaning. 'Oh Tom, thisss isss...oh God you are beautiful...look a' you...beautiful...' staring at me. Scary. '...you can fuck me. Tom, I want you to fuck me...!'

'Jeez Henry...' he makes a grab at me, holds my arm really hard, tries to pull me toward him 'Now, now Tom, thisss isss...fuck me...' the other hand is unzipping his jeans...'fuck me...fuck me....'

'Henry, put your trousers on!' I pull away but he chases, grabs at me, 'No Henry! Forget fucking! Look there – look at the lights...'

He tries to reassure 'No Tom, safe here isssalllright...you can fuck me, it's fine, really....beautiful....beautiful...'

'Leave me alone Henry I don't want to fuck you....' I break away again, Henry, trouserless,, his erection visible between the tails of his shirt, chases me down the alley.

Flying tackle - oh no I forgot he was in the rugby team. Splam! Onto the filthy ground surrounded by trashcans. A dog whose territory we have invaded goes crazy. So does Henry, who rips at my clothes – *pop*pop go those carefully sewn buttons on my plaid shirt *rip!* The zip comes away from the jeans. *HELLLP....*

This was the first and only time in my life I was glad to see the cops. Konstabels Myburgh and DuPlessis of the South African police arrived just in time to save my virginity. Mouths agape, jaws at floor level. 'Stop it!,' Myburgh yelled, 'Stop it you bleddy *moffies!* Get off! Polisie! DuPlessis, get water...'

DuPlessis emptied the contents of a bucket of filthy drainwater over us. Henry jumped up, yelled 'They're after me!' and vanished into the night. I was dragged off to the Hillbrow police station.

So my parents had to come out in the middle of the night to face the awkwardness of their eldest son having been arrested for public indecency. Despite my protests Father paid an Admission of Guilt fine, that is, *he* admitted *my* guilt...'but I wasn't...I was the victim...! I didn't...'

'Shut up moffie' Myburgh said.

'Do you want to go to court?' Father asked murderously. 'Do you want this to get into the papers? Do you want your mother and me to have to hide our heads wherever we go?'

'But you don't understand! I didn't – '

'If you want to be a homo that's your affair. But if you get arrested in the process, it becomes ours!' Father snapped.

Mother just wept. Smudged her mascara.

The rest of the family avoided me for the next few weeks. Both brother and sister seemed not to want to be in the same room as me. Which was almost as galling as Henry's apparent amnesia about the whole evening. Apparently he had made his way back to Piers' flat where he was cleaned up, sobered, put into trousers and despatched home. For a while the twelve probably believed that I had taken advantage of poor drugged Henry in an alleyway, who had only just escaped with virginity intact. Which only went to strengthen my reputation as an advocate of Free Love so I didn't suffer *too* badly...

Hazel didn't avoid me and on the next Sunday came over for a Birthday Braai. It was *her* birthday. Mother, riddled with guilt, knowing that otherwise the old lady would spend the entire day alone in her room weeping over a picture of Anthony, had persuaded Father that a small family celebration would be a good idea.

Hazel, knowing that her 'godawful' new maid Minnie (all her maids were 'godawful' – Hazel and Robert expected the same service from the one maid they could afford as they used to get from three) would look after her sick husband, albeit godawfully, had not needed to be asked twice. She had heard the story of my arrest from one of her grapevine buddies. By the time the story got to her it had become somewhat exaggerated, as I learned after lunch when Mother and Father were having their afternoon nap (or 'screwing' as Plowsky and I called it) and my brother and sister were avoiding Hazel and me by tormenting and being tormented somewhere in the depths of the house.

'I hate to say this Tom,' she said, trying to melt herself into the shade of the mulberry tree despite the unwillingness of the cast-iron Victorian garden bench to be moved into the shade, 'but it does seem as if you are going down the drain.'

'What the hell do you mean?' I asked. I was lolling on the lawn at her feet, trying to keep out of the shade she was trying to get into.

'This orgy business – '

'Huh?'

'Marion Bloom told me all about your little experience with the police. The fact that your mother didn't see fit to share it with me is no surprise.'

'What do you mean orgy?'

'Don't be coy with me. I know all about it. Marion had it from Linda Ginsberg and she heard it from someone who works at the Hillbrow police station. Homosexual orgies on campus! It's just not very tasteful. And so indiscreet....'

'Homo – '

'Oh don't play the innocent. I'm completely *au fait* with all that and I assure you it really doesn't bother me if you are – what's the word – gay – What really annoys me is – '

'I'm not! Honestly!'

'And all those drugs and so on. Don't think I don't know! I've read the articles in Time and Life. All people with long hair smoke LSD, especially the men. I think you'll agree I'm a woman of the world Tom, but I just don't agree with it. Are you an addict?'

'Really gran – '

'Be honest with me Tom. You and I have always been friends. Do you think you are addicted?'

'Of course not!'

'Goodness it's hot...always brings on my headaches...' she dabbed at her face with a huge man's handkerchief. 'I don't know what to make of you. They say drug addicts lie to everyone, even their nearest and dearest. I wonder if you should see a psychiatrist. I don't dare mention that to your mother, she'll think I'm interfering. That's what she thinks of me anyway. A nag. An interference. A nuisance. An attention taker. I love your mother in my way you know....'

Yak yak yak moan groan complain I thought, and turned my ears off.

Four

I met Mona like this: Philosophy tutorial. Arguing with the lecturer about Determinism. Pity I hadn't then read Mensonge.

Poor Professor Kramer lurking behind his glasses and beard and pipe smoke, terrified of us all and happy with his stereotype. 'No, but – ' I said, and the Professor's heart sank because he knew that my 'no, buts' would make it impossible to get to the end of the tutorial without a headache, 'surely we are the end result of everything that has ever happened?'

'That is the Determinist argument, yes. But if you consider Oedipus – '

'That's not the thing. You know what I mean. What about our previous lives, for example?'

'What?'

'Our previous lives. And our parents' previous lives – '

'Of course, childhood influences are taken into account – the so-called "Soft Determinists" –'

'Not that. I mean the lives we had before we were born – '

'Ah, reincarnation!' He blew a cloud of pipe smoke at the innocent ceiling 'in this context, this is nonsense.'

'No it's not. Some of the greatest thinkers in history believed in reincarnation. You can't ignore the effects of billions of years of life after life – '

'Look, Bloch –'

'No but. What we are and what we do is the result of the subtle intertwining of billions of factors. One.' I counted off the factors on my fingers. Other students settled themselves into their hard chairs for a good nap. Only one was paying attention.

Her eyes kept grabbing mine. I sought other eyes but my gaze kept being pulled back to those big blue pools deep in a smiling, rapt face.

After a few sentences I stopped trying to avoid them. And allowed myself to enjoy this beautiful thing which God, in one of those moments when he believed in himself, had made.

Her face had a dangerous roundness, like a mortar shell. High forehead, wide cheekbones. A smile prickled the edges of her cheeks. Big turquoise plastic earrings framed the smile, masses of flimsy purple material framed a body that seemed to have enveloped the tiny chair.

So I played to my audience of one. Kramer had ceased to be of any interest to me. 'One: the evolution, history and geography of the planets and the solar system. Two: the evolution of man and the beasts through life after life. Three: thus and therefrom, History. Four: our childhood experiences, development of character dependant on all these factors, as well as those determining the characters and attitudes of our parents.'

'Groan,' said a classmate, just audibly, but I wasn't bothered about him. The girl was slaughtering me with her smile.

'Five: Everybody else's previous lives and childhoods. Six: natural events, evolution, disasters...'

I sat, smiling smugly. So there, radiated from me like a miasma.

Oh God, the Professor thought, why do I have to teach pricks the wisdom of the ages when they think they know everything?

'Determinists, you said, are "hard" or "soft" depending on whether they believe that all our actions are determined by the past, or only some of them – that is, the amount of free will – '

'So, Bloch,' the Professor enquired with a sigh, 'does that make you a hard prick or a soft prick?'

The Freudian slip had escaped way before he could check it. The classroom erupted in uncontrollable mirth, and the next thing I knew I too had escaped, slipped out of the door with hooted laughter and 'you soft dick' clattering after me down the corridor.

...pursued, it would seem, by a girl buoyed up in bubbles of delight. 'Say, wait up!' she called.

'Hey,' I stopped. 'You're American!'

'True, but it's not my fault,' she said, grabbing my hand. 'Hi! – I'm Mona.' Her touch was alarmingly intimate. Patchouli wafted over us.

'Yes,' I said, feeling warmth from her fingers spreading through my body.

Gently, she let me go. 'And you're Tom.'

'Yes. Kramer is not going to be happy with you – '

'Or you, walking out of his tutorial. Hey, I don't think you're a prick – let's go outside!'

She grabbed my arm with ring-clacking fingers. Again that warmth. And led me to a flowery bank beside the swimming-pool. 'Whew!' she said, letting the innocent earth know she had arrived by yielding to gravity in no uncertain terms. All those ants and insects dying so that she could wallow on the lawn. All those tiny spring flowers crushed into the purple of her dress.

I sat down next to her, adding to the insect death toll. For them too History had just ended.

She removed an elegant porcelain pipe from an invisible pocket and filled it with pure grass. 'Want some?'

'Yes.'

We smoked. The sky had pale white high clouds. Summer would happen soon. I suppose there were birds.

'Some of what you said back there was great,' she said.

'Some?' I smirked like Columbus, waiting to see Queen Isabella to report on his new territories.

'You know, a lot of what you said, I've been thinking for a long time. I mean, even the reincarnation thing. You spoke about that as if it's just plain *obvious*, it doesn't bear questioning – '

'Well it doesn't.' I leaned back, took a noisy toke from the pipe. 'You may think it's weird,' I said, smiling at a cloud, 'but I've felt as if when I meet some people I just know who or what they were in their previous lives. Just some people. Clear as anything!'

'Me too, meeee too!' she said excitedly. 'Say – ' she raised herself up on an elbow, turned an elfin look full on me. 'what about me? Can you tell anything about *my* previous lives?'

I sat up and looked into her. And she looked into me, and there was a dropping away of everything between us: two people unclothing their minds for each other....then, suddenly she pulled away and I felt as if something I had almost grasped had been torn out of reach. I had to find out more! 'Not yet,' I said. 'But I will, I will...'

She looked away, refilled the pipe. 'Maybe...' she said. Then, 'some of the other stuff you said was true, too.'

I laughed. 'Whatever "true" means.'

'No, what I mean is. If it wasn't for that great list you gave, you wouldn't be lying here in exactly that pose. Exactly there. With those pants on. With me. Smoking this pipe. You wouldn't have that mole!'

'I forgot to mention genetics.'

'What the hell. It was great. It was all great.'

'Thank you.' My smugness radiated like nuclear waste.

'I mean, everybody the centre of their own little world thinking they're a person. But all they are is part of this – this – whole thing – this wonderful pattern – '

'Yes and – ' I accepted the pipe

'Centres – each one. Of a circle. Like an eggshell. Limited by their ignorance.' She was getting very excited. Purple radiance. ' but infinite. Like little circles in infinity...'

'That's right – '

'Points in space! Just points!'

'Hey, what are the dimensions of a point in space?'

'There aren't any!'

'Do you realise,' she said, waving her arms about so wildly that the pipe left her hand and did an aerial ballet, 'that's what we are. Points in space! And points in space have no dimensions!'

'They are infinitely small!'

'Which is the same as saying infinitely big!'

'Which is the same as saying they don't exist!'

'So if we're circles, we're points in space, we're infinitely – uh – infinite – so – '

'So there are no limits!' I screamed.

'Yes and – ' she cried

'This means – ' I howled

'WOW!' we chorused.

We decided that this was Enlightenment or something much like it. I laugh now, but for three days our feet did not touch ground. We were wild with the wonder of it all. We felt we had transcended karma, had a vision of the real. We thought we had found the Secret of the Universe.

Leaping about the place in mists of delight, we glided through people and places. There were no obstacles.

Except of course for other people. Explaining to them, or trying to, was impossible. We could not explain it. We couldn't convey the excitement.

Least of all Hazel. She just frowned and said 'Perhaps the first veil has dropped from your eyes. Or it could be that you've gone mad. Frankly I don't know which one it is.'

It took me years to discover how right she was. Now I know that:

a) I know nothing, but not very well, and
b) Enlightenment is No Big Deal.

A plush office. London.

'Well?' Laszlo wheezed impatiently. 'What have you found out?'

Truelove sipped at his gin and orange in what he hoped was an elegant and casual manner. 'The children are quite grown up. Well, one is, anyway.'

'The other is young? Isn't she too old to have children?'

'No, her child is dead. A boy. Apparently something to do with a dicky heart and enforced *coitus interruptus* – '

'Look young man. I am aware that you are a lawyer. There is no need to spout Latin at me to prove it. I had a good education too!'

'Sorry,' Truelove said, taking three deep breaths and repeating to himself 'Calming the breath-body I breathe in, calming the breath-body I breathe out' as recommended by Swami Jenkins, his personal guru.

'Well what about the other one – the daughter?'

'She's married, has teenage children,' Truelove said.

'Owww' Laszlo groaned in pain 'I could have been a grandfather...' then 'What are their names? Are they good people? Do they get a good education?'

The lawyer told Laszlo about my brother Barry (known as Plowsky to those in the know) my sister Michelle and myself. When I say all, I mean he told the old man how tall each of us was, what we had for breakfast last Friday, what we had said when presented with that breakfast by the bored and menopausal cook Bella, who couldn't have given a toss about whether we liked the dried-out fried eggs and the burnt toast. The sort of information available to a man standing in the kitchen of the Bloch home for at least ten minutes that Friday morning.

The man was Armand Bennett, a Private Detective hired by Truelove in Johannesburg to report on our domestic arrangements. Dressed up as a black delivery man from the chemist's, he had stood about jawing with the servants on Friday morning on the pretence that he was awaiting his 'Christmas Box' (the annual tip) which my mother refused to give him as she had never seen him before. *Joshua* always delivered from the chemist's and she had already given him his Christmas box.

Luckily for Truelove, the information seemed to satisfy his employer. (Who wasn't actually listening very much. Perhaps he was thinking about his two daughters, the twins, killed by the Nazis while they were in occupation of the Castle – apparently their constant bickering and trickery had finally driven the Kolonel to call for a firing squad. They were lauded as heroes of the Resistance ever after.)

'Tell me lawyer, is my Hazel happy? Does her husband give her what she needs?'

'From what I can discover the husband is doolally. Spends all day in a wheelchair laughing at everything.'

'Good God,' Laszlo said with a smile. 'How dreadful!'

'Yes it is,' Truelove said, agreeing with the sentiment in spirit. 'Well, I can have him put out of his misery - ?'

Laszlo looked thoughtful. Then he grinned like a hyena watching a kill from afar. 'I don't do things that way', Laszlo said. 'Any more. Now you just listen what you have to do...'

Discovering that I was in love with Mona and that she was in love with me wasn't a surprise. Nor was it particularly special, compared to what we had already shared. It was the inevitable result of all that. We were each half of a perfect being, we thought, a creature which could see without opening its eyes. Neither of us had any doubt, intellectually at least, that this conclusion was perfect for us, would last our whole lives, would take us further than anything that had ever happened to us before.

The emotions came later. All very well to have this mutual understanding thing. But the warmth and need and delight and longing grew. Very quickly. Well, her face was so very beautiful...her body was big, true. In an enveloping way. Flabby, yes, in a friendly way. Flouncy, draped in purple silk and chiffon, likely to take furry stuffed toys to bed, stick paper flowers onto cutesy handmade 'I love you because' cards...in an adorable way, at least to a teenage virgin in love. Who, lost in her perfect blue eyes, could so easily forgive all that in the conviction that her fart smelled of roses.

We paired like Siamese twins. We defied parents together. We cheated in exams together. We gave unofficial seminars on Truth and Enlightenment in the canteen together. We even decided to go to London together, when the year was over....London! Mecca of the sixties for South African Hippies. San Francisco was much too far away and foreign. London seemed to be the place to go to be really free, man. Where you could dress free, speak free, be totally, like, free. And, of course, free to take drugs lots of them. Especially LSD. When Mona and I discussed acid and we shared what we had read about Leary et al, we agreed that acid would be the door that would open to perfect spiritual understanding, liberation....

Most of our friends regarded all this intensity as rather funny. Pieter certainly did.

'Has she plucked your cherry yet?' he asked, laughing one day as we sat waiting for her in the canteen.

'uhhh...'

'She hasn't! Bleddy hell man! What are you waiting for? Old age?' he leaned across the table to slap me on the back.

She hadn't and neither had I. I won't deny I thought about it. Often. It just didn't quite feel right, not yet...

'It's not actually funny Pieter. She and I are...'

'Ag no man, don't say it! Just too high and mighty to get down and dirty! Is that it?'

'Pieter...what the hell is it to you? - don't say you're jealous?...' Mona and Pieter were so similar. They held the same political beliefs – hated Apartheid, longed for justice. They were as counter-cultural as each other. They loved drugs. They loved me.

'Don't be stupid! I just want you to be happy.'

I leaned forward, I had to tell him. 'We're going to London together' I announced.

'No...really?' He seemed to be trying to hide a flash of annoyance. 'When?'

'End of the year. If the parents will wear it.'

'Jislaik. I was thinking of going some time also....'

'Great.' I said, and the conversation shattered at the entrance of Mona, in a cloud of angels, like a Baroque heroine...

The dreaded Sunday braai, ritual occasion of insincerity, eating dead things and drinking smelly fermented things in order to share the experience and the indigestion afterwards in the hope that somehow all this unpleasantness would result in a cementing of family relationships. Every Sunday in summer the parents hosted this lunchtime ritual for a variety of guests which always included Hazel and Robert, as well as a small selection of close friends or family – those privileged enough to be invited knew what they had to do: eat, drink and buzz off by 3.30 at the latest so that my parents could go for their 'nap' – meaning their weekly sex game while we children played, fought, masturbated or generally amused ourselves.

This Sunday only Hazel and Robert had turned up; the weather in the December of 1969 was so terribly hot, most of their friends invited had invented an excuse to stay home.

There was a great clanking and rattling as Silva, the manservant, weaved his drunken way onto the patio above which the grapevine struggled for existence on its posts and wires. The trolley he was pushing was laden with raw steaks, lamb chops, T-bone steaks. It looked like the bloody aftermath of a battle.

I shifted on my sun lounger, grasped at a slippery bottle of sun lotion, sat up as mother emerged from the house in dressing gown and bikini. 'Hello darling' she said, greeting her stepmother and father with a polite peck on a cheek. 'Just put them on the fire will you Silva'

She collapsed on the plastic-plaited garden chair next to me. 'God it's hot,' she said, sweating almost as much as I was. 'How are you feeling?'

'Your son wants to go to Europe,' Hazel announced. I sent her a frown. I wanted to say that.

'Me too,' Robert offered. He had a habit, these days, of trying to pretend to be involved in conversations. He was, of course, ignored.

'Good heavens dear,' Mother said. 'What a silly idea. You've only just started university. You have to *finish* your studies first. That's not too much to ask!'

'I'm doing really well in Uni mom. I'm fit and healthy! I'll carry on with Uni when I get back! 'That new girlfriend of yours is behind this I'll bet.' Mother was no fan of Mona. To her the girl represented all that was fake and plastic about Americans – while a fan of Kennedy and American Liberalism, she saw Americans in general as the most hypocritical of foreigners. 'You ask your father. He'll only say the same.'

Father came dripping from the pool. 'What on earth – Silva what do you think you're doing?'

He thrust the man rudely away from the braai which was sending volumes of smoke and flames into the upper atmosphere. 'You have to wait until the flames and smoke have gone down. How often do I have to tell you? Go inside and get the salads.' He shook his head bitterly as he plucked crisped blackened anonymous flesh from the griddle with a fork and tongs. 'That boy is so stupid!'

'He's been at your whisky again dear...'

'I'd like a whisky...' Robert said.

'Drunk as well as stupid...' Father muttered.

'Such a shame you can't get decent servants' Hazel said, the subtle stress on the 'you'. She was smugly thinking of the new maid she had recently taken on – the twelfth since the sainted Mary had died, admittedly, but this time Hazel was convinced she had found a paragon.

Mother ignored the barb. 'Darling, Tom wants to go to Europe before he's finished university,' she said.

My heart sank. Father in this bitter muttering mood would not agree to anything.

'That's a stupid idea. He must finish first.' He snatched a towel and dried himself off.

'I can go for the summer break, dad. Be back for the next year,' I said. ' I need to see something of the world, don't I gran?'

'So do I,' Robert said with a smile.

'You must do whatever your parents think is best dear,' that traitor said blandly.

'Frankly my boy,' Father added, 'after the last little expedition of yours I'd rather you stay nearby where we can keep an eye on you. I mean, we never know what you are going to do next, do we? No no. First University. Then we'll see'

'Nonsense!' I sputtered, 'I'm almost eighteen!'

'Don't shout at your father,' Mother said wearily.

'We did our best to bring him up, what does he do? Gets feted by the bloody Nats! "Hero of the Republic"! It's shameful! What are we to make of that?'

Last strawsville Arizona, I thought. How much more explaining do I have to do?'

'I'd like a whisky and soda,' Robert said.

'I'm over all that,' I said, 'you heard the Brigadier. I've got my discharge from the Army. Then I'm free!'

' We'll see. In the meantime I want a continued guarantee of good behaviour.'

'You mean I can go?'

'If you're completely fit, we'll think about it then.' Mother chipped in.

'Whoopee!' I yelled, leaping up and knocking the trolley with its load of death over onto the slasto. 'I'm going to Europe!' and I dashed for the swimming pool, Father racing after, where I most satisfactorily dive-bombed Plowsky and Michelle in the middle of another of their attempts to drown each other.

'I'd like some whisky. With soda. And a slice of lemon,' Robert said.

'I have a headache,' Hazel said, 'I'm naming it Robert.' Perhaps she should have called it Ian.

Which all meant months during which my legendary trip to Europe became a blackmail guarantee of good behaviour – and any slightest infraction, or suggestion of infraction, or even the very ghost of the slightest possibility of infraction, would result in the threat to ban the whole expedition. Do you know what convinced them in the end? I told them that Mona and I were now so deeply involved in politics at Wits that we could be arrested any day. There was nothing they could say about that!

Three

Mona's parents' reaction to her news that she would shortly leap from the family nest, fly (metaphorically) six thousand miles with a stranger who looked like a freak was, to say the least, fatalistic.

MONA'S STORY

Cyrus, her dad. Cerise, her stepmother. Mona's real mother had vanished years ago when Mona was eleven after a messy divorce. Her first eleven years was as the centre of a civil war, a battle-to the death between two fanatical sects like Shiites and Sunni, Cavaliers and Roundheads, Catholics and Protestants – only worse. Family pressures from both sides (including, she says, huge financial pressures relating to a legacy or a trust fund, something like that -) insisted they stay together. In the same house. Have sex. Have a child.

Mona's real mother was called Corinne Cohen, scion of a huge Brooklyn Jewish family. Her father was a tailor. Mother was a professional mother, who managed to breed twelve children before finally her body wore out and she lay down to die.

Corinne ran away to Hollywood after her mother died. She changed her name to Corinne McCarthy and failed to become an actress, despite several screen tests and several more appearances on casting couches. She was extremely beautiful but as good at acting as a dead fish is at billiards. Nevertheless with a face like hers she was bound to land on her feet.

Her feet eventually landed in the bed of Joey Carroni, gangster to the stars, supplier of their cocaine, women, boys and murder, when needed.

It was one of the latter contracts that necessitated what Joey called 'a decamp' to Dallas Texas. Within months he had snared most of the important folks in the city in his rackets: gambling, porn and drugs mostly. Corinne got to meet the Best People – her cutesyness, charm, intelligence (an autodidact of distinction, Corinne boasted that she could have a conversation with anyone from a professor to a pervert, and her best were when the two combined -) and above all, her great tits – made her hugely popular.

Dallas was boomtown – as anyone who has seen the TV soap knows, God in his wisdom had gifted a bunch of ignorant pork-scratchers and cow lovers with a bonanza of liquid gold. Strange how He always gives millions and millions of money to those with the least taste, the least morality and the most guns on this planet. I suspect his sanity. So Dallas stank of money, and Joey was determined to get his hands on as much of the filthy stuff as he could in a city where the biggest money outside the oil industry was in gaming, prostitution and religion. Without actually selling his own butt. Or starting a new church. As soon as he arrived, therefore, he bought a grubby nightclub called Cats, changed the name to the Cat's Pause ('Pause! Paws! Gettit? Place where cool cats can pause! No? You stupid bitch. Claws? See? Like dat? Ha ha haaaaaa....') right in the centre of town on Gaston Avenue, and began to ply two of his favourite trades.

One of the first customers Corinne met was Cyrus Porter. He was a big (six-four) craggy, grizzled old young man of twenty-eight. She was (only!) twenty. He had a face full of hollows and pockmarks – the legacy of years of scraping pimples with tobacco-stained fingers. The face was well carved, possibly by the same guy who sculpted Mt Rushmore. But in colour - blue eyes, light brown hair which could have been blond had his genes shifted a tiny bit to the right. He was very nearly handsome. Corinne was in love. He was so different! Joey Carroni was dark, suave, pot-bellied, unhealthy, moustached, continually loud and jokey – funny-irritating. Continuously making sickly puns. Ok for an hour or so. Unbearable for more. Cyrus was so – *American.* Grubbily clean-cut. Enthusiastically ardent. So apparently naive, sweet...sexy. Corinne's image of a WASP. American aristocrat.

Cyrus was in deep trouble. He owed Carroni a great deal of money, gambling debts. Carroni had subsidised the young man because he knew that Cyrus' father was filthy with rich.

Unfortunately Cyrus was not beloved of his father. The only child of Jed's only marriage, Cyrus had been brought up by an aunt while his Father made his megamillions. His mother had died giving birth. Jed never forgave him. They hardly knew each-other by the time Cyrus reached eighteen, when Aunt Delice met the love of her life and ran away to New York with her, leaving the boy with his bemused and confused father.

The old man was megarich with oil and as far as he was concerned, the words 'black sheep' were far too mild to describe his oldest son. Despite his hopes that Cyrus would go to Harvard (daddy had the inflated respect the undereducated have for a University education) and become a magnate of some sort – probably own Texas, or the world, or something like that. Instead Cyrus, fresh out of High School, met a croupier in Vegas. The affair had lasted two years, involved midnight suicide threats, and a huge amount of gambling by the young man who would do anything to be as near as possible to his love, even if it involved great portions of his allowance. And, of course, more.

They swore to love each-other until death. So, after the thirteenth suicide threat, they decided to marry. Cyrus went home to Dallas and Daddy. Daddy said Never!, raged, assured his eldest that the affair was over. Then he sent someone to Vegas with fifty thousand dollars.

Cyrus never saw his croupier again.

When the boy realised that she was entirely accurately and for ever gone, he started gambling again. This is how he came across the oleaginous accommodating Mr Carroni who, realising that this man's papa was certainly a legion of cows worth milking, ensured it wasn't long before the boy owed him Huge Sums.

So he met Corinne. So she fell exactly in love with him.

It was in a smoky corner of the Cat's Pause, about 1am. There had been a great deal of mooning from a distance before the couple finally spoke to each other. She had watched often as the boy continued to fritter away not just his allowance but vast borrowings from the club's owner, but it was several nights before Corinne finally got her chance to corner the innocent lad alone, while Joey was 'dealing with business'.

For his part, he was certainly flattered. She made no secret of the fact that she had tired of her pet gangster. She moaned about his going to whores. About his not giving her big enough presents. About him simply not giving her enough attention. Cyrus lent her his ear, largely because he did have a big heart and knew it would do no harm to have his dangerous creditor's gal on his side.

Then, poor boy, she finally told him she loved him. His big heart took a great jump. Mostly fear. Carroni was showing off to some out-of-towners, possibly French. She took both his hands in hers. He sweated. She said 'Cyrus, you are a real man. You are the real man for me!'

'Oh shit,' he muttered.

'I hope you understand,' she whispered. I love you. I just – '

'Gee,' he muttered.

'Take me away from all this!' she said, having forgotten that the standard of her acting was Dead Fish. Remembering, it must be said, what Joey Carroni had told her about the megawealth of the boy's parentage, as well as what her friend Cassie had said about tall men with small feet. She looked up, right into Joey's eyes, leaning over the back of the plush red velvet of the semicircle of sofa. Stab of fear and guilt. 'Hey baby baby' he said, 'having a cosy little chat with the Persian Emperor here?'(she had, in a drunken moment, mentioned that Cyrus was named after an ancient Persian king and since then Joey had referred to Cyrus teasingly as 'your highness' or 'majesty')

'Sure I am,' Corinne pouted, 'no-one else wants to get cosy with me...'

'Hey kiddooo' he slapped her playfully across the face 'well you just keep him happy, I got French to fry...hey, didja get that? I said French fries! Ha haa! Got Frogs legs to eat. You like that yer majesty?' and roaring to himself (inviting others to join in admiration of his incomparable sense of humour) he went back to the French couple he had been annoying with his unwillingness to set up a table for *chemin de fer*. Because he didn't know what it is. And didn't want to admit it. Neither do I. I admit it.

'Come for a walk' she instructed her unwilling beau, and led him down Gaston Avenue to where White Rock Lake gleamed in reflected moonlight. In those long ago days, Mona assured me (I received this tale in her voice – I have only added the odd detail, tiny embellishments and three outright lies) there was a tangle of bushes around this lake which was less a lake, more a mere bog upon which almost floated a collection of ill-thought out yachts, rowboats, as well as a selection of unidentifiable dead things in states of decomposition. Surrounding the lake was the scrag-end of a forest or wood. Inhabiting this wild woodland in those heady summer nights was a writhing mass of couplings, suitable, unsuitable, legal, illegal and downright disgusting. In those days, 'he took her down to the woods' (or him, or them, or it,) meant only one place, and one thing. Or two. Or three.

Corinne did not know all this. To her (she had only seen the place in daytime) it was unutterably romantic, a perfectly suitable place to embark on romance. It is, after all, purely a matter of taste. So arm-in arm they strolled by the lake, she at least perfectly unaware of the writhing bushes between them and the soporific city.

Whereas Cyrus, as a native of Dallas, knew exactly what this place was renowned for. Further, he had heard dreadful tales about the place: of lurking villains, armed and dangerous, who leapt on all sorts of lovers and robbed them of all their jewellery, and sometimes of much more too. Unwilling to show any fear – suspecting she was testing his courage – he clutched the gun he kept in his waistband and bravely circled her waist with his other arm.

Inevitable, I suppose, that this innocent lovers' stroll should end in tragedy. 'This will end badly won't it?' I asked, handing Mona her little pipe.

'Well no, Tom, it ends up with me here with you, here at the end of strands and strands of Karma....it's ended great!' we surveyed the inside of her perfumed bower. A suitable place for Karma to have brought us to.

'...and strands and strands....' I giggled...'so link it up. Describe the strands some more.'

I bet you guessed. That spooked by rustling bushes, alert for robbers and rapists, poor Cyrus would shoot poor Joey dead when he came looking for them, mad that Corinne should have gone off with some punter, bang bang...

'Not quite,' Mona said, 'Good guess. No, poor Cyrus got such a fright when the fellow came running after them that he did let out a shot. Which injured her pet gangster, who said, 'He shot me honey! Get the cops! I swear he tried to kill me...!'

Well-brought up as he was, Cyrus launched into a hectic apology. 'I'm so sorry! I didn't know it was you!'

'You yellow dog,' Corinne said, grabbing the gun off Cyrus.

'Good work honey', Joey croaked and she shot him dead, right between the eyes.

....so Cyrus and Corinne resolved on getting married. It was a necessary solution to the possibility of a murder conviction, and was, I suppose, tangled up with things like alibis and mutual lies. With a fair amount of blackmail thrown in.

Daddy was pleased, initially, because he was allowed to think that Corinne was the daughter of a rag trade magnate in New York who had died leaving everything to her brother, the Senator.

Aha, you'll say. How did Corinne get away with the wedding, having to admit she wasn't the Senator's sister? She didn't.

The wedding was scheduled for November. The couple had met in July. Corinne had no intention of waiting long. She was terrified of being found out...

Old Jed Porter did have a twinge of suspicion. His twinges had served him well all his life. Twinges had given him his wealth – starting, it was rumoured, with the twinge of a dowsing rod above a lake of oil.

Strange how, he thought, I get a twinge every time I see this girl? Not a penile twinge either. Something much more..., yet she was so well educated, Wellesley and all...(remember Corinne, the autodidact? Well, she could chat about anything, young Corinne. Proust – the topic of her thesis was, she said, 'Proust and the Age of Enlightenment', American History – she could go on for hours about how Ben Franklin had warned the Americans when the British were coming ; Paris, and how lovely the Rhine was flowing through the city, past the church of Notre Name and the Grand Tour of Eiffel; above all, she could bore for hours about Italian Opera and almost delighted the old man by trilling 'Your Tiny Hand is Frozen' on any inappropriate occasion)...It seemed so wonderful and right that the boy had at last found a college girl, a real intellectual who seemed fine for settling down and becoming a good Texas wife.

But he was certainly not at ease. Twinge, twinge. And why the hurry? And why couldn't he meet her family? Especially the senator? (Republican, Maine). He decided to look into the matter and within weeks his people had discovered that not only did the Senator not have a sister called Corinne, but the girl seemed to have no living relatives whatsoever, had been associated with some rather questionable people in the underworld of the town and...

...and she was pregnant.

...with his grandson.

...by his gawky goddarned black sheep of a drinkin' gamblin' whorin' shithead of a son!!!!

Twinge!

The old man hit the roof. Again.

(Incidentally and by the way. Jed's famous twinges were actually caused by cancer of the bowel. This wasn't discovered until the autopsy. He must have had a great deal of pain in his life. He was one of those people who never visited a doctor. Jed boasted 'the last time I was seen buck-naked by a quack I was one minute old! Haw haw.' His poor dead wife was a constant doctor-botherer. He should have learned the lesson. Perhaps he blamed the medical profession for her death. Perhaps and maybe. It wasn't the cancer that got him in the end. But that's another story.)

Back to hitting the roof. Which resulted in Corinne rushing Cyrus off to Mexico where they were bound together in Spanish-accented English by a drunkard. She knew what she was doing, that girl. And when, months later, they crept into Dallas with her great big bump, Jed had calmed down. A little. It was what she called a Fate Accomplished, the sort of move Jed had made many a time in business. He had to admire it, despite all the money that would have been wasted on wedding preparations had they not eloped.

Instead of getting a contract out on his son and daughter-in law he gave the boy a job. President of Porter Oil's subsidiary in South Africa. That would keep him out of trouble and, more important, out of Dallas. He didn't want the whole of Texas giggling behind his back.

By the time the couple arrived in South Africa they hated each other. This is not surprising. Cyrus had a brain that didn't work too quickly. He took things as he saw them. Did not digest. Once somebody at school called him a pustule. It was three days before the offending kid was found unconscious behind the school with the Concise Oxford Dictionary open at the letter P stuffed in his mouth.

So it took a little time before he realised that he had married a fortune-hunter with a huge appetite for expensive things, who was quite unprepared to give him anything in return, even sex. For her part she had lost respect for him as soon as she heard him apologising to Joey for what she considered his botched attempt to free her from the gangster's stifling clutches. She had stopped seeing him as a sex god and he had become a mere meal ticket – which suited her well, as all she wanted was to start a new life.

She continued to remind him that she could easily disabuse the dumb cops in Dallas of their false notion that Joey's death was just another gangland killing. And, after all, what would Daddy think?

Besides, she was pregnant which disgusted her heartily.

Her hatred grew as she counted the reasons she hated him. He would not stand up to his father; he was slow as a tortoise in a hair race; he farted in bed; he couldn't be relied on to commit murder effectively; and, finally and unforgivably, he had spots which sometimes – horror! – leaked blood or pus. She also suspected that the old man, to get his revenge for the runaway marriage and etc and etc, might have cut Cyrus out of his will.

War was declared. Having said that, it was a while before Cyrus realised it. The birth of their daughter didn't even rate a ceasefire. Yet they could not divorce – Cyrus could never admit to his father that he had made a mistake. She couldn't leave him because she could not find anyone rich enough to give her all the precious things she 'needed'. They were bound together like Siamese twins locked in mutual hatred, sharing a pustular body...and fur feathers and crockery flew throughout Mona's young life. As soon as she could understand, she realised that her mother's whispered words were full of hate ('See how he is to me? Your father is a *Spineless Runt*! He's suffocating my cultural *life!*'), and her father's, when alone with her, begged for pity ('see how she is to me, cruel critter! She's chewin' my balls!')

Corinne took to playing opera at full volume whenever he was in the house, knowing how it drove him to fury. So Mona's early memories of her mother were peppered with the coloratura trills of fat ladies dying.

Then when Mona was eleven the old man died. Joseph was killed by a man with a Magnum. A hole four inches across went right through his heart. Somebody had hired a killer. Another story.

The family went to Dallas for the will. They said they were going for the funeral.

The will was read. The entire Porter fortune went to the Republican Party. There was a proviso: that Cyrus was to be President-for life of Porter Oil South Africa. That was the old man's final revenge – exiling Cyrus to South Africa for ever.

So the trio trooped back, and, as they waved New York goodbye from the deck of the Queen Mary (I would guess that maybe the trip to NY included popping into Brooklyn so Corinne could show off her new family to what was left of her old family. Just guessing. Mona wouldn't say. Intriguing.), Corinne said 'I want a divorce.'

'Fine, bitch.' Cyrus answered.

'I'll screw you for every cent'

'Do that. I ain't got a cent.'

'Mummy I want to swim' said little Mona.

'Go swim in the goddam ocean,' her mother said.

Then came the scene which has haunted me since Mona told me about it, there in the perfumed stuffiness of her boudoir....

The Divorce Court. Cyrus stands one end with his lawyer, Corinne at the other with hers. Mona in the middle. A court official has an arm around her. The Judge asks Cyrus, 'Do you wish to apply for custody of this child, Mr Porter?'

'No your honour'

'Well then, Mrs Porter, I assume you will apply for custody?'

'I certainly have no intention of doing that your worship.' Corinne says, seeing her freedom in jeopardy.

'Oh dear,' says the Judge. This is the first time in his twenty years as a magistrate that this has happened to him and he is getting emotional. 'Come now Mrs Porter, I realise you are upset. She *is* your daughter you know. I would regard your application sympathetically.'

'Don't be ridiculous. She is a nuisance, that girl. Hanging on to me. Rude, argumentative – '

'Mommy,' Mona says.

'Please Mrs Porter, this is a *child*!'

'Well I have my own life to live. Why do you think I'm divorcing that idiot over there?'

The Judge feels despair. 'Mr Porter I appeal to you. Unless you assume responsibility for the child the state will have to do it. Is that what you want? Your own child?'

Cyrus thought for two long minutes. 'Hell,' he said, 'I don't even know she's mine! Besides, I pay my taxes.'

We should try not to hate Cyrus too much. His own emotional life was, after all, a tangled mess. He had been ignored by his own father all his life, regarded as a nuisance when he had to come home after Aunt Delice found herself and came out after which, of course, she went out. All the way to New York. Everybody he had ever relied on or loved had deserted him or let him down. That was just the way things were.

The Judge, not knowing all this, was distinctly annoyed. 'Come with me my dear' he said to Mona. 'Let's have a little talk in my chambers. Court will be adjourned until 2pm.'

The girl was crying already and did much more of that in the Judge's room. Luckily the Judge was a nice man. Patient. Had a normal family. All he wanted for everyone else was to have the same. Nice man.

Eventually Mona calmed down and they had a little chat.

At two the court reassembled. The Judge glowered down with distaste at the jumble of messed-up humans he had to sort out. 'Now,' he said when everyone was seated and awaiting his Judgement, 'It is my decision in this case to grant a divorce on the grounds of irretrievable breakdown of this marriage under Section 4 on condition that – can you understand me? – one of you takes custody of this lovely little girl. OTHERWISE I will grant divorce under the reason of mental illness, or continuous unconsciousness of BOTH parties as per *Section 5* of the Divorce Act. I can only conclude that anyone refusing custody is actually crazy and the girl will be taken into the care of the state.'

There was a stunned silence and a gasp from almost everyone in the room. 'Outrageous!' his lawyer said.

'I protest!' her lawyer spouted.

'No surprise!' Mona said.

'Well? Which is it to be?' the Judge turned to each party. 'Section 4 or Section 5?' Hasty whisperings between lawyers and their clients resulted in growled 'Section 4 your honour' from each in turn. At last! Agreement between both sides – not to be forever labelled as insane! Or even 'continually unconscious' whatever that meant. Dead, presumably. The shame the shame...

'Very well then. And since,' the Judge continued, with a blatant wink at the girl, 'neither of you will assume the responsibility, I will ask Mona herself to choose. Mona dear, will you tell us what you think? Do you want to live with your mommy or your daddy?'

Mona was very clever. Years later an IQ test gave her a score of 150. She stood there and puffed out her chest just like a real lawyer and addressed the court.

'Thank you your honour. I have been giving this matter some thought for quite a few years. I thought, if mother and father split up who would I most like to spend my teenage years with? Oh yes of course I knew you would split up! But, silly me, I thought you would both want me...'

A moment to wipe away a tear, not just for Mona but everybody in the room, except of course for her parents.

'...and I thought a court would send me to Mother. That's not quite how it's turned out – ' she looked straight into her mother's eyes. Dramatic pause. 'Mommy, why do you hate me?' she asked suddenly.

The room trembled for an answer. Corinne just shivered. 'You see?' she looked around for affirmation. 'You see how she embarrasses me? You see?' addressed to the Judge as if this explained everything.

'Daddy, you don't hate me as well do you?'

Cyrus looked up from his contemplation of the Imbuia table he and his solicitor occupied. 'Of course not' he mumbled.

'Then *why* don't you want me?' Mona dropped the question into the silent courtroom like a corpse into a pond.

By this time the Judge himself was awash with emotion. 'Answer the question Mr Porter,' he said hoarsely.

'I – I don't know what to say,' Cyrus said helplessly.

'I know what's going to happen to you two,' Mona said sadly. 'Mommy will eventually find some nice rich boyfriend who will believe her lies and marry her. And Daddy? You will just go on, not knowing what you want, never being very good at anything, never making decisions...so I guess I'll stick with you, Dad.' She turned to the Judge. 'At least he's got a steady job.'

The whole room turned its attention to the Judge, whose raised eyebrows were threatening to take flight. 'Do you agree Mr Porter?' he asked.

Cyrus stared into the distance, the stodgy cogs of his brain churning away.

'Section 4 or section 5, Mr Porter?'

'Uh – yes I will', he said, as if in a marriage ceremony. Then, with a snort, he began to weep...

Mona became the ruler of the household, wore the trousers. And she loved her father very much, though she never forgave him for the 'I pay my taxes'. Yet she understood him and when he wept in the courtroom she decided he must feel something for her, or contrition at least. In gratitude she resolved to take control of his life.

He responded to the change in her and made changes of his own. To the surprise of his staff he began to take an interest in the business. He made decisions. Some of them were rather good. The business expanded.

Mona meanwhile began discovering sex. Her first inkling came from a magazine called *Mammoth Knockers* which she discovered hidden in the secret drawer of her father's Sheraton Bureau. After studying it carefully she came to these conclusions: One: big bazooms were important to men. TWO: Daddy liked to be very secret with this magazine. She had to find out why.

So, one night hiding in the cupboard in her father's bedroom, she watched astonished as he laid the book on his bed and lay down and paged through. Then, with muttered words of love and passion, he kissed the centrespread several times and removed his pyjama bottoms.

Gosh. She watched in amused amazement as he squeezed out from his deepest self the milky liquid of life and, after much fuss and bother, wiped it away with a man-sized tissue.

This was certainly a clue. And the next day Mona extended her researches to the copious bookshelves which had been filled wholesale by her departed autodidact mother, to 'make the Study look right'. There, by careful analysis and extrapolation from books like *Tarzan and the Hidden Gold, Primitives and Baboons, The Origin of Species* and, finally, to bring all the clues together, *Lady Chatterley's Lover* she reckoned she had worked it all out. Intellectually at least.

Which was all very well, but by the time she was fifteen she knew she had to find out how it worked in practice.

She enlisted the help of the sixteen-year old garden boy Johannes in this scientific quest. The boy was himself discovering sex, though he was not a virgin. His first experience two years before had scared him out of his wits. He had almost concluded that he was homosexual when the young mistress invited him to her room one sunny afternoon when the crickets were dying in the swimming pool and dragonflies were screwing in mid air.

Well, Johannes knew at least the *mechanical* side of the process and wasn't shy in explaining it. Mona was more a friend than a boss to him, after all. But when the young missy wanted a practical demonstration the boy came over all blushful.

She was insistent. Explained that her interest was purely scientific. That it wouldn't hurt at all. That secrecy was part of the deal, there would be no repercussions. That it would earn him fifteen rand.

Convinced at last by the latter argument, the boy made his attempt, the young missy was pleased, paid her debt and he ran off never to be seen again except hanging around gay bars in San Francisco years later. (Lucky boy missed out on the Aids epidemic...fell in love with a politician who kept him in purdah – another story.)

Good, she thought. Next thing I have to do then is to get Father to replace his magazines and other paraphernalia with the real thing. So she set out to find him a wife.

In the afternoons after school she haunted the shopping malls – Rosebank, Hyde Park, Birnam – where the nice middle-class ladies went to shop and sip, shop and lunch, shop and stare.

Finally in Rosebank she struck gold. Sitting at an outdoor table of a cafe was a petite well-dressed woman of around forty. An absence of rings suggested an absence of attachments. Just enough sadness in her eyes to hint that she could be a widow or a divorcee. And, most satisfactorily of all, quite disproportionately big bosoms that obviously resisted any attempts at imprisonment in anything but the most copious of brassieres.

Just Daddy's type. Someone he could loom over. She'd fit well under his armpit. Some character in that jaw suggested she had inner toughness – which Daddy needed. Mona watched carefully for a while, until the woman noticed, shifted, looked annoyed, uncomfortable.

So she went up to the woman, apologised, and asked her name. 'Cerise', she said and Mona knew this was Right. Cyrus and Cerise, perfect. Like a Country and Western duo.

Cerise was a little taken aback, but intrigued by the American accent this tubby freckled charming young girl sported. (Footnote: skip this if you want to get on with the story: Mona's American accent was an essential part of the Monaness of her. Yet she hadn't been in America since she was twelve years old, so had plenty of time to acquire the squeezed vowels of the South African English speakers. Why hadn't she? When asked, she said 'I decided not to', and that seemed the end of that. Still unexplained, however, is the fact that her accent was no way Texas, like her father's. When asked she said, 'I decided not to.' That's so Mona. My accent at this time, by the way, was pure English RP. But that was the product of years of elocution lessons paid for by Hazel who wanted me to be 'classy'. I'm really not.) In those days foreigners were rare in South Africa and were courted and shown off to friends. Foreigners were Interesting, and what's more, they had seen TV! There was then no TV in South Africa; the Government was afraid that if people got to see what was actually happening in the world they would turn instantly into Communists.

Mona introduced herself and suggested that Cerise buy her a cup of tea. Cerise was taken aback, but she was lonely and bored, so she agreed. Mona asked Cerise to tell her about herself. Bemused, she told her story. She was a divorcee. No surprise. The split had happened three years ago when she found out that her husband was a serial adulterer and a compulsive liar. She owned a very exclusive men's boutique. She enjoyed her freedom but occasionally thought it would be 'nice' to marry again.

Perfect, thought Mona.

'And what about you?' Cerise asked. 'What do you do?'

'I'm at school of course,' Mona replied offhandedly. 'I do lots of things. Say – ' she said, as if she'd just thought of it, 'you'd like my dad. He's also divorced. I have a picture – ' she hauled the best photograph she had ever seen of her father out of her capacious purple flowered bag. He looked craggy but handsome. No trace of blood or pus.

'Now wait a minute,' Cerise giggled, intrigued by the picture. '-are you trying to matchmake or something?'

'Sure', Mona said.

Six months later Cerise and Cyrus were married. Mona made a pretty purple plumpy bridesmaid. Her father had fallen for the plan without a trace of resistance. Love at first sight. Of Cerise's tits.

This last episode was unravelled for me on the grassy bank by the campus swimming-pool, where we had first bonded. 'Gosh,' I said, 'I think it's absolutely horrific.'

'Horrific? Why?' she asked blandly.

'I mean, what a hell of an experience for a young girl.'

'Which? Adopting a new mother or losing the old one?'

'Phew! Both!'

'Listen Tom,' she said, 'It was good for me. It made me strong, self-reliant. And my relationship with the C's couldn't be better.'

'Really?' I said, brushing a hungry red ant off my calf. 'Have you told them about our plan to go to Europe?'

She shrugged offhandedly. 'Sure.'

'How did they react?'

'Well, Cyrus said "Of course dear if that's what you think is best"'

'Gosh.' I said.

'And Cerise said "I hope you'll be happy dear"'. She giggled.

I stared in a mix of compassion and admiration. 'I love you.' I said.

'And I love you too baby' she said and we kissed.

'When will you let me make love to you?' I asked.

'Hmm...that's not so easy...'

'My parents are out tonight.'

She held my hands and smiled with, I thought, deep relief. 'Then tonight....we fuck.'

'I don't want to fuck with you, I want to make love with you.'

'You don't think that the mere entry of your prick into my body will make a difference between us do you? I mean, will it spoil things?'

'It has to happen. We're committed.'

'So be it.'

So that night at last I finally and deliriously abandoned my virginity. All those people who had tried to tease it away, to rip it away, to beg, coddle or stroke it away had failed up to now. And all those people I had begged to take it away had refused up to now. I don't know why it took me so long: maybe I was dithering between boys and girls as sex objects. I had certainly fantasized about both – male strength, muscle, purpose. Female soft parts, cuddly parts, depths and supple mounds. And, after all, that deep secret cavern within which a man was consumed.

It was a hard decision...and a soft one.

So it was that Mona made the decision for me because she had said yes and she was chockfull of soft parts.

I didn't tell her I was a virgin. I didn't have to because she took charge straight away, as we got to my room. I had been thinking all afternoon, what if I muff it? Pun intentional. What if my Gentleman refuses to be upstanding? What if I don't fancy her once I see her nude? Whatif whatif whatif...

But as we closed my bedroom door (Michelle and Plowsky were out too, by the way. Convenient!) Mona made me forget every whatif ever invented. Because immediately I turned from the door her hands were on me, sliding up into my shirt, terribly clever cool fingers unbuttoning me without a hitch and my chest was stroked so gently I shivered, as if my lover was a ghost who with her long-nailed fingers tweaked my nipples in passing, and boyoboy I can tell you my Gentleman stood, screaming, let me *out*! Let me *in*!

She wasn't ready for that quite yet. She was in complete control of me, making me, moulding me to her body. I felt as if my muscles were melting as she pulled me over onto the bed on my back and ran lips and tongue over my straining chest and I didn't realise she had unzipped me, even feel the top button of my trousers yielding to her busy fingers, but I knew that her lips were around my cock all right, and my trousers somehow vanished from my legs.

And when she straddled me, her warm wetness sucking me right into her, direct passage to her heart, I knew that this dream, this glory, this joy had to be mine as often! As much! As wide and as long and as deep and as far...

'Ah ah ahhhh,' she said, 'JEEEZUS fuck me! Fuck! Oh Tommmmmm...' and she collapsed on top of me and I realised that we had both, at almost and exactly the same time.

Later as we lay side-by side on the bed, each in sweat and sweetness, I said again, 'I love you,' and I did.

'Obvious. And. I. Love. You.'

'Hey,' I said, turning on to my side, 'I've got a good idea – '

'I know, something to eat?'

'In a bit. Look, how much money can you get together for our London trip?'

'I don't know. Dad will give me a couple hundred I guess.'

'Mine won't give me much. His theory is if he keeps me short I'll come running home in no time. What would you say if I told you I know how to raise a helluva lot more?'

'I'd say great!'

'Well...all we have to do is...' I circled her nipple with a finger.

'What, Tom?'

'Get married.' I said.

'Huh? Did you say Get...Married...???'

I had been thinking about that almost since we met, though the apparent ban on sex during our first few months had made me confused about what precisely our relationship meant. But now we had done it, broken the barrier, crossed the Rubicon...'Why not?' I asked joshing, afraid that if I was too serious I would be risking rejection.

'Hey, I believe that constitutes a proposal...'

'I suppose it does...'

'O.k. It's a good idea. A great idea!' she said, her face split by a smile.

'That counts as an acceptance.'

'Guess so.'

'Golly,' I said, overawed by the sheer Bigness of it all.

And to my amazement my parents, having eventually yielded in the Europe row, seemed inured to saying 'yes'. And they did. Numbly. Eventually.

'Well at least you'll be a respectable couple', Father said, no doubt with a secret sigh of relief that his son may, after all, be heterosexual.

Mother had other worries. 'Tell me something, Tom, is Mona Jewish?' Mother asked innocently, believing she knew the answer.

'Ha! That's what it's about!' Plowsky sniggered, mouth full of peas. 'She's a shiksa! That's why he's been – '

'Because if she isn't, dear, she would have to convert.'

I was so stunned by this I dropped the oversized bit of lamb chop I was about to try to stuff down my throat. I couldn't believe that Mother, who had been a Shiksa herself, could possibly object to my marriage. 'Now wait a minute,' I sputtered.

'What's the difference?' Michelle asked sweetly, 'they're in *luhvre*',

'Good heavens' I said, amazed. 'It's the voice of reason – '

'-and he'll go away with her. And never come back!' Michelle continued with relish.

I manoeuvred some peas onto my fork and flicked them at her. 'Mommy! Look what Tom's done!' Michelle screamed, standing and dabbing frantically with a napkin at the green on her white blouse.

'Now now' Mother said.

'Stop it both of you. Your mother is right,' Father contributed.

'Wait a minute. Hang on...' I said, the story Mona told me yesterday reviewed itself in my mind. 'Isn't there a Jewish law that says if a mother is Jewish the child is too?'

Mother nodded. Her studies during her conversion had confirmed this. 'Yes that's true', she told the family.

'Well,' I said, sitting back in smug triumph. 'her mother's name was Cohen...!'

'Ah,' the family chorused.

A JEWISH VEDDING

Our wedding day was brash with tasteless sunshine. The garden of the Sydenham Synagogue, which had been chosen by Mother as the 'least bad option', bloomed and basked. A wirework arch festooned with climbing roses was the centrepiece. The smells of a thousand flowers twined about the dapper guests who stood around in various states from awkwardness to becalmed boredom. Her parents and my parents regarded each other across a chasm of embarrassment. Mine knew that hers didn't like me; hers knew that mine didn't trust her. Yummy. Hers hated the fact their daughter was marrying a Jew (Mona had failed to notice that Cerise was a dyed-in the hair anti-Semite when she paired the woman with her slow-witted father, who had always been anti anyone he was told to be anti). Besides they believed me to be a notorious hippie corrupter of youth who had seduced their innocent daughter under the influence of who knows what drugs.

Mona's father was tall, lean, moustached, grey and craggy-faced. He smoked cheroots, wore tweeds and a ten-gallon hat. Her stepmother Cerise was in cashmere and pearls, fitted well under Cyrus' armpits despite her impressive mammary display. Legs thin as twigs. Face pale as paper. Terrified. She had never been near a synagogue before and was certain someone would lend her money or eat her children. They prayed no-one would try to have a conversation with them. They wanted the ceremony over as soon as possible in the hope that the waves it made would be tiny and none of their friends would notice it had happened.

Amongst the guests were fellow students, including Pieter who looked as happy in his ill-fitting suit as a medieval knight would be in a tutu. Baby Frewin in black and white. Piers Mallory in purple (in honour of Mona?) – even Henry had made it, on release from Sterkfontein, the mental asylum. And Patrick Lebokeng, newly enrolled at Fort Hare, smart and crisp in his Brooks Brothers. Patrick, who everybody predicted would one day be a lawyer. And a leader of his people. Hazel made a grand entrance at noon, dressed in flouncy silks and lace, trailed by her driver who wheeled a semi-conscious Robert along in a wheelchair. The others were friends and sundry business acquaintances of my parents, doing their duty, and all the uncles and aunts were there too.

The few blacks there, aside from Patrick, were friends from the townships and the whole household of the Bloch servants. These latter, while feeling quite uncomfortable, were 'very heppy for baas Tom!' and Salva in particular was delighted to be in the presence of a potential source of alcohol.

Needless to say, Mona and me, and all of our friends, were very very stoned. That morning Pieter had arrived at the house early with a large chocolate cake. 'Is that it?' I asked.

'What it?' he grinned.

'Our wedding present? From you?'

'Look closer ou maat! O *doubting* Thomas....!'

'Huh?'

'Approach nose first....'

'Do I smell what I think I'm smelling?' I asked.

He nodded. 'I used half an arm', he said.

An arm is a measure of grass. Half an arm would be about an ounce and a half of quality marijuana. Pieter was certainly exaggerating, but even so...

'Oh my gosh,' I said and ran delightedly to the kitchen, fetched plates and a knife and cut us each a generous portion. We ate. Then I cut another slice and put it in a paper bag so that I could give it to Mona before the ceremony.

Which I did! I sneaked into the room in the synagogue in which she was sitting in state on a bridal throne. She was wearing a white and purple wedding dress, each fold carefully arranged, so that she looked like a Doulton figurine.

'Tom! What are you doing here? It's bad luck!'

'No it's not,' I said, handing her the piece of cake. 'Eat this!'

'Don't mind if I do,' she said with a grin, and I slipped out.

Father grabbed me by the arm in the garden. 'I don't know what you're so happy about,' he said, seeing my inane already-stoned grin. 'Her parents hate you already. Great start!'

'I know' I giggled.

'It's not funny. I'm trying to have a man-to man with you. Apparently that's what fathers have to do on a wedding day.'

'Haha' I said.

'I don't understand you. I mean- she's not exactly a Playboy centrefold is she?' He interpreted my smirk as a knowing grin. 'oh well, ' he sighed, 'I presume she has – other talents.' He winked. It didn't suit him, this attempt at man-to man.

He sighed, gave up. 'Well come on then, let's get this thing over with. Your future starts here.'

He propelled me towards the arch, up the long path along which the guests had gathered like an opera chorus. Faces. Friends, relatives, acquaintances, strangers. Hazel's face, winking. Pieter caught my eye – a wave of relief. Smiles meet. A few more friendly faces. Relief. It's going to be fine, I thought.

Father and I stood side-by side under the flowering roses. A Rabbi approached. Good God, I thought – a dwarf! He was four foot high. He wore a top hat out of which two plaited side whiskers tumbled. His beard was pure white, one foot six inches long.

I bit my tongue hard to stop myself from giggling. Tore my eyes away from this apparition and surveyed the crowd. Oh dear how embarrassing. Hee hee. I wish I wasn't so. Oh goodness that table heaped with food over there. Hungry! I could just do with. That cake! Nice, right by Robert. Hang on.. that cake...isn't that the? Oh no, it bloody is. That grinning hole in it three slices big. Oh no, MUST –

The Rabbi is rattling on at me, trying to tell me what to do. He's saying how happy he is I'm so happy.

I've GOT to get that cake away from there.

'Hello, Mr ? Are you listening to me?' the Rabbi says.

'Oh yes of course, there's something urgent – '

'It's too late for that!' Father snaps. 'Just hold it in. You can go after.'

The Mendelssohn Bridal March squeezes its way out of the speakers and flows all over the lawn. Cloying, rich as toffee and cloves. The lyrics I always associated with the music – well, since I first either heard or invented it as a child, I forget which – Here comes the bride/ All fat and wide/ She's got your baby/ Stuck up inside....and it was just Too. Fucking. Much. Especially when Mona came flouncing down the path. So silly! Flouncing in purple and white, above which floated this mad black lipstick grin, easily visible behind her thin veil, as was the trowelled-on makeup, kohled eyes...

My hand too late to my mouth to stifle the escape of fugitive laughter. And when Mona saw me properly from the diminishing distance in my suit and silliness, haircutted scrubbed pink and glowing it was too. Fucking. Much. For her as well.

'A Veddingk!' the Rabbi hisses 'is a very serious time!'

Mona, alerted by the hiss to the venerable absurd figure in all the ridiculous pomposity of his greatcoat, top hat, whiskers and small stature, could do nothing but pray 'Oh no please God, pleeeeeees...' to no avail. God turned his back, so that she could erupt into gulps of inchoate laughter.

Equally, God ignored my desperate attempt at self-control. I bit my tongue until blood came. When I tasted the blood I managed a pause. 'Bite your tongue!' I whispered hoarsely, spraying her bridal gown with droplets of blood which...made things MUCH worse

It took a while. Surrounded by bemusement, embarrassment, unease, annoyance, we corpsed, as they say in the theatre. And on and on. Until, finally quite exhausted, we managed a semblance of control.

There was a moment of suspension. Time just stopped, while Father wished for a sjambok. Mother wished she was in a bridge tournament. Cerise wondered how many pearls there were in her necklace. Cyrus imagined himself in Dallas. With a gun in his pocket. Our friends, I imagine, simply held their breaths, longing for the next chapter...

We stood before the Rabbi hand in hand, trying not to look at him. Or down at him. Our mouths full of blood. Our clothes spattered with it. He took a deep breath and intoned sacred words in a foreign language.

Many many words.

Too many words.

My attention wandered. What was I thinking about before? Oh yes, the cake. The what! And my eyes travelled to the buffet table where the cake sat smugly awaiting more victims. If only I could signal Pieter in some way. Heyyyy, there seems to be a somewhat larger amount missing and nobody else near – apart from – apart from Robert in his wheelchair and his driver. And what's that on Robert's lap? A plate? Sprinkled with dark brown crumbs?

Ohhhh noooo! I jerked my attention back to the Rabbi. I've GOT to do something about that cake. I hold up my hand, open my mouth. This ceremony had to pause –

He's saying something in English. Oh shit! Control. Control. I glance back toward Robert who, catching my eye, waves happily. Grinning his head off. I gape. He imitates my gape, points at me, starts giggling.

'Mr Bloch. Mr Bloch!' the Rabbi is trying to get my attention again. 'Would you break the glass now please?'

Aha, he wants me to put my foot on a glass goblet lying on the rug at our feet. And to smash it. It's traditional.

Which is a very expensive act of vandalism. Even I can see it's very fine crystal which has travelled a long way from Waterford in Ireland, travelled safely too, only to be smashed to smithereens by a Jewish bridegroom in South Africa to symbolise. Something. Probably how rich we are.

The glass sensibly decided it wasn't going without a struggle. So, when the slippery sole of my new leather shoe came down on it the forces of nature and Fate shot it up in the air – *wheee*- and with all the elegance of a guided missile it arced up into the air, reached the limit of its momentum until gravity took charge of its accelerating descent directly onto the Rabbi, knocking him and top hat backwards into the lap of Robert who, laughing hysterically, propelled himself away, scattering guests like ninepins.

Our beautiful wedding was chaos. Bodies flying, people screaming, Father shouting for order, Cyrus trying to help, mother emoting, Mona and me giggling in heaps with our friends now standing, lying, laughing, all over the place, Rabbi on the grass hatless and swearing in Yiddish, various aunts calling for ambulances and/or police, until, eventually, Father's effort began to gradually take some element of control. The Queen Mary finally turned around by the tugboat. Rowing boat....people picking themselves up. Robert's driver disappearing into the distance trying to catch his Boss.

The Rabbi, mollified at last by Father's hasty promise of a considerable contribution toward the new roof for the synagogue, picked himself up, dusted himself off and started all over again (yes he was a fan of musicals. This doesn't mean he was gay, necessarily, though who knows?)

Mona and I composed ourselves. Pieter composed himself. Most of the people present composed themselves. The glass was smashed and made an Irish noise. The Rabbi pronounced us man and wife. Not me and the glass. Me and Mona. It was like a sentence, I thought.

Which was when another sentence was pronounced. It was this: 'Hands up! Everybody stay calm now. Hands up!'

The garden was swarming with SAP – South African Police, all pointing guns at the stunned wedding guests, all of whom froze in terror – except for Patrick Lebokeng, dear friend, who made a run for it. Not for long. A shot and he fell, not dead, just winged. Surrounded, picked up, removed.

'Sorry to bother you all on such an occasion', said the Brigadier apologetically. 'You can put your hands down now. We've got our man' and the cops disappeared as quickly as they had arrived...with a brief nod from Maartens toward Pieter, and a 'Dankie ne'.....

The reception had been cancelled. All the guests had gone home or to their doctors for more Valium. Except for poor Patrick, who lay on a cot in a cell in John Vorster Square, waiting for his torturers to come back for more.

'They arrested my friend! How could they arrest Patrick?' I said, and found myself almost hysterical again. 'I can't calm down. I can never calm down again. They made a mistake? What do you mean a mistake???'

'That's what they're like,' Mother said. 'Patrick has connections with the ANC. They assume he's a terrorist. Took the opportunity to arrest him. They'll realise they made a mistake.'

'It just makes me sick. I met him through the Liberal Party. He hates violence. He wants to be a lawyer. Why?'

'Don't get hysterical again dear,' Mother said and gave me another little yellow pill. 'We know how you feel darling. Your father and I feel the same.';

'They're bastards,' Plowsky said. 'But anybody can make a mistake.'

'Shut him up Mother, just shut him up.'

'Wal, I know what he means', Cyrus drawled. 'Someone reports screaming and mayhem and murder and stuff and you see all these blacks standing round, what do you expect?'

I don't throttle him because he's my father-in law, and I know Mona likes him. Instead I go to my bedroom and lying next to my sleeping wife I try to understand.

Two days after that Robert died. Hazel seemed remarkably unperturbed. 'Really darling,' she whispered to me at the funeral, 'It's a relief. Anyway – he died happy...' I'll bet! Especially if there was any of that cake left wandering about in the remains of his brain...

Three days after *that,* the Daily Mail tells me my friend Patrick Lebokeng is dead. 'Fell out of the ninth floor window' at John Vorster Square, the police headquarters 'while trying to escape.'

That night I nudge Mona in a vain attempt to wake her. 'We've got to get out of this country, Mona - do you hear me? It's time to gooooooooooo!'

3

One

Parents, step-parents, parents-in law, friends wept or pretended to weep as Mona and I climbed aboard the Blue Train bound for Cape Town and the ship that was to glide our bodies over the choppy Atlantic to Barcelona. The families were a hub-bubbling crowd of advice, anxiety, sadness and (guess whose siblings) pleasure. 'You'll be back realising this is the only place where you can live a life of riley' - Father. 'It's cold in Europe dear. Make sure you've packed the TCP Coricidin D and vitamin C!' Mother's sure-fire recipe against colds. 'They're all messed up in Yurp, hadta save them from Germoney twice! Cowards all!' Cyrus. 'You're doing the right thing dear, it's what I did at your age. Or a little older. Have fun!' Hazel. 'Goodbye, good riddance' Plowsky, Michelle. 'Here. A present.' – Pieter.

The ship was the MV *Europa*, an Italia Line vessel, sleek and stylish even in Second Class. In those days travelling by sea was much cheaper than travelling by air, but that didn't mean our fellow passengers were scum. Well not all of them.

We had a cabin with twin bunks which didn't impede our sex life, not even slightly. Though I will admit to a good selection of bumps and bruises by the end of the voyage. Mona, being rather better upholstered, had fewer.

Our first day was ecstatically gorgeously romantic, filled with delightful discoveries. First, the ship: attired in white like an expensive gigolo, smelling of Brylcreem and cigars, throbbing with that deep and sensual power of engines strong enough to move twelve thousand tons through thousands of miles of ocean. Gorgeously appointed (even in second class) the ship shimmered with white paint and brass, twinkled and sparkled with polish, bustled with white-coated stewards whose twinkling eyes and beaming faces promised any. Goddam. Thing. You could ever. Want.

I still dream of that throb. That promise. That tremendously masculine promise of a ship's engines.

(Ending in a screw. Sorry. Couldn't resist. Ghastly pun. Sorry.)

And the receding breathtaking scenery of Table Mountain and the soporific city of Cape Town as we churn away, past Robben Island where Nelson Mandela has already served four years of his life sentence, out into the choppy vastness of the Atlantic, under which lie many ships as proud as this....

Leaning over the railing of the upper deck we had our first smoke of the voyage while the stewards like seagulls chattered and fluttered on the deck below, determined to raise the revenue of the line and increase their own earnings. And the funnel, way above, got high on its own smoke.

And we saw our first flying fish soaring alongside the ship a few feet above the water and laughed. For that was what we were doing, soaring feet above the water.

We were very high that day and I don't think the grass we'd smoked had much to do with it.

That evening, (the dining saloon panelled, white tablecloths looking as if carved from snow, silver cutlery, three varieties of glass at each setting. Yes, even in second class.) after a meal that still tasted good hours after eating it, we sat on the lower bunk in our cabin and went through the cards and little gifts our families and friends had left us.

'Fifty rand, can you believe it?' I held out a card and some grubby paper money from Hazel. The note said 'I can't decide whether you are being utterly crazy as usual or are making the right choice. Still, I did the same thing myself and am a better person for it.'

'I know she can't afford much but *fifty* rand...!' I said.

'Hey, look at this!' she stared at the contents of a dismembered envelope. 'From my dad. Two hundred shares in his company. What are we supposed to do with that?'

'Shit!' I laughed. 'Look!' I held up a wallet. 'Real ostrich! From Plowsky. Hang on – ' I extracted a note my dear brother had slipped inside the wallet. '"This reminds me of your mind. Empty. I hope you find something to fill it with."' We laughed. 'He has a sense of humour, my brother' and filled the wallet with the anon money, my money (around R500 which had been lying in a post office account since my Barmitzvah) and Mona's money (R400 from Cyrus).

'Fat enough now?' I waved the engorged wallet in the air.

'We're rich,' Mona laughed. 'Hey, who's this from?' she held an envelope out at me.

'Ah,' I said, taking it, 'It's from Pieter.'

I opened it. A sheet of blue airmail paper was folded carefully around two tiny pills the size of saccharine, coloured purple. I stared.

'What is it?' my wife asked.

'Listen baby, ' I answered softly, almost breathless, 'there's only one thing these can be. This is acid.'

'Let me see!' she snatched it from me. 'Wow! So small...hey, what a beautiful colour...'

'Mmm.' I said. 'Your colour.'

'Where did he get them? I thought it was impossible to get acid in South Africa –'

'No idea. I mean, why didn't he tell me?' I took the paper again, read Pieter's brief message: "Well, now you've GOT it, what you going to DO with it?" 'Yeh', I sighed, 'that's the story of my life...'

'Well,' Mona asked, 'Now we've got it what *are* we going to do with it?'

I smiled, took her hand. 'Well I'm certainly not going to smuggle it into Europe, that's for sure. So I suppose....'

'So do I.' She nodded excitedly.

'But we'll wait till we're a few days out. Everything must be perfect.'

'Perfect.' She said.

'Like you,' I said, hiking up her dress.

Two days later we had our first storm. The sea darkened early in the afternoon, as if furrowing its brow over a deep problem. Yellow whitecaps lay on top of the waves like pus. The wind grew steep and angry. The ship yawed, rose, fell. Deep up, breathe in!, deep down, splash, a moment of fear that it would never rise but then, shaking the water from the decks, up again like a phoenix. Our afternoon sexgame abandoned, I grabbed Mona's hand and inadequately dressed we raced along the decks, grabbing at each other to deprive the sea of its human titbits as it voraciously attempted to ingest the ship. Howling 'Yesssssssss!' and 'Wowwwwwwwwwww' and 'Hurrah!!!!!' each time the howling yawing elements failed to sink our beautiful gigolo.

The other passengers with a few exceptions had disappeared into their cabins. Exeunt lunches. (We slipped over a number of exeunted lunches on the promenade deck.) But still we raced, up and down the up-and down decks, laughing, wet and wild, certain of our invincibility because we were in love, weren't we, two halves of a whole that could never be sundered, right! Who together shared the Inside, the Outside, the Around, and the True.!

Couldn't we?

The storm was two days long. By the time it abated we were sick of it. Not seasick as such – unlike most of the passengers and quite a few of the crew – we seemed to be unaffected by the great liftings and fallings. But when we awoke that morning and saw a gentle, relaxed ocean out of our porthole we were heartily relieved.

'Perfect day,' I said.

'Mmmm.' Her head went down under the covers.

'And I'll tell you what we'll do, if you're good – '

'What?' Her muffled question filtered through the blanket.

'We'll open our heads to the sky.'

She emerged from the bedclothes like Venus from the sea. 'I don't do riddles...'

'...with the aid of two purple friends...'

PIETER'S LITTLE PRESENTS

In the event it wasn't until that night that we unwrapped the two purple pills Pieter had given us and stared at them together in the white throbbing womb of our cabin.

We had decided to eat our pills after dinner when passengers would be drunk in the bar, or safely stowed in their bunks or each-other's bunks out of our way, and the crew would be busy sleeping or driving the ship or standing about waiting for tips or sex. Besides, we needed the day to share everything we knew about LSD.

I so wanted everything to be *right*. From what I had read, set and setting were critical. Set being the mental attitude, preparedness and confidence; setting being a safe place, preferably beautiful.

All very well for *you* to say, Mr Leary, Mr Alpert *et al...*

But why didn't you warn me about the 1,000 microgram tablets made by Mr Owsley specifically to blast the minds of seasoned trippers into the cosmos? Enough to give *four* novices like Mona and me eight hours at least of mental dissolution? Had I known, I would have broken those purple poisons into two, or even four...or thrown them to the Flying Fish, to add some hallucinogenic variations to their aerial cavortings.

But you see, I wasn't worried. I had as much faith in Mona's ability to ride the cosmos as I had in my own.

Which is why, after a day in which we had chatted easily about how much fun we were going to have (an eavesdropper would have heard references to Huxley's Doors of Perception, Blake and his visions, Coleridge's Xanadu, Leary's Psychedelic Experience (throwing in the Tibetan Book of the Dead as well as the Egyptian one for good measure), and called the police. Or an ambulance. Or Pseud's Corner. Admittedly, most of this was guessed. Or invented. Or only partly known. Or heard about from others...looking back I despair of me then. How true it is that when we're young we know everything and as we get older we only know one thing: that we know nothing. Cod profundity signifies how reluctant I am to write my account of that night. It still hurts.)

(Here goes anyway.)

'Hello little purple pills,' I said. 'Say hello to Mona.'

'Hello little pills' said Mona, laughing.

The pills did not reply.

'Say "AH"'

'Ah.'

And we, believing ourselves nascent gods, each ate 1,000 micrograms of that which separates that which is between the self and everything else.

Within three quarters of an hour I knew everything had changed and was changing for ever. I breathed and the ship breathed with me, its throbbing engines warming and deeply thrilling...it felt red and good. I glanced at Mona. Yes, she was feeling it too. 'Let's go outside. Quick!'

The moon was bigger than the ship that night. It sat on the sea like God's misplaced beach ball and tinged the tips of the waves with silver. The stars, awed, gave up their pale attempts to prick holes in the night and sat, smudged, on their thrones.

We side-by-side on the upper deck facing the bow of the ship which, cleaving its way through the silver-tinged blackness of the night, began to fly. 'All right?' I asked. She muttered something. And vanished

I was riding this surfboard through skies spattered with diamonds and rubies which breathed and laughed. I inhaled them through my pores and dissolved. For an eternity, I became a little then nothing and there was no me...

For hours

And hours

No beach no sky no ship just an ecstasy for hours

And hours

Every now and then a sparklet of me would emerge, take breath and glimpse Mona and the sea and the ship and everything then back to the space to where I belonged

For hours

For no time at all

Emerging again and the remaining sparklet of me saw the space where Mona had been and for an instant wondered where and why

I knew that Something had happened in the Here, something important. I tried to take hold of it in my mind but I couldn't, because the sky beckoned and there was more surfing to be done. I breathed in, my eyes closed

Soaring, riding up there, glorious Silver Surfer on waves of joy, plunging into the moon and out the other side! Catching planets in a net, inhaling them, mists of jewels and colours sinking into me, no hope of control, no chance of return, no hope of a return to earth, not even for a second...

Stupid shit.

So when eventually I emerged from the night, from my elevation, and was able to contemplate the empty space beside me where there had been Mona.

'Mona? Mona?' I floated down to the cabin, where there was no Mona.

'Mona?' I scanned the corridors right and left of the door. I began to shout running along companionways, up stairways, across slippery heaving decks. Pushing past lurching drunks and a couple of puzzled passengers making for the safety of their own cabins. The sea had turned rough again, and the sun tried to raise itself above it all like an unshelled egg.

'Mona! Monaaaa!' I ran on out into the heaving dawn, shouting.

Until I found her, trapped like a wild creature against the railings, her arms battened down like broken wings, held fast by three sailors while she raged and swore and spat and fought to escape from her mad ghosts.

Now I know how far she fell. In her account: she said it started with a mocking voice, which taunted her. About her mind, her body, her wishes, her likes, her whole purple persona. Then the door opened and in came an army – a voracious horde of angry and vengeful spectres or ghosts or spirits, raging at her, hacking, plunging swords into her body, killing and killing. Blaming her. Raging at her for all the evil in the world. Telling her that it was she who had Broken It. She who had ravaged cities and killed the good and cut off their breasts and split their children's heads like coconuts against marble columns. Fifteen thousand people dying as she sacked the city...lying on the deck of the MV Europa, her head full of screams. There had been only one way to stop the screams, but three sailors didn't agree....

The ghosts were to be with her for the rest of her life. Their lying taunting voices unleashed within what had become what they refer to as paranoid schizophrenia. How little they understand it.

Psychiatrists and other armchair students of the mind would probably say she was genetically inclined toward this 'illness', and it would have manifested itself eventually. That LSD was just the catalyst. Or perhaps not. Sometimes I think there are millions of cruel nasty vicious disappointed ghosts who, denied admission to whatever heaven they may have believed in seek out open doors which admit them into the mind of a victim they can bully into madness, murder or suicide so they can swell their ranks.

Or maybe that's not it. Maybe what tore the hole that shipwrecked her mind was that scene in a courtroom, when a father said 'No I don't want her' and a mother said, 'Neither do I'.

I carried her back to the cabin, my broken bird, and she slept in my arms for twelve hours like the dead don't.

Later we discovered that during the night of madness she had emptied my shoulder bag into the sea. A gift to her ghosts, an attempted bribe perhaps. I still had our passports (locked in a drawer in the cabin) and the money I had in my pocket. But my wallet had gone, my notebook, some grass I had brought for the voyage, my diary, my traveller's cheques, the loot from the wedding and my Barmitzvah long ago. We were broke.

She refused to leave the cabin. She refused to eat or walk. Or even talk at first. When she went to the toilet I had to beg her to come out again. God I was frightened. I kept saying to myself, this is temporary, she'll soon be over it. But day after day was the same. She just lay there. Refused the food I brought back from the dining room. Ignored kind Giovanni, the steward who begged and begged her to eat. Eventually she told him to 'Fuck off you fucking blimp" and he did.

The new Mona. Shipwreck.

The bubbly grinning wide-eyed girl I had known had left. The creature by my side was a sullen thing often lost inside herself. Who would burst into tears for no reason. Who dialogued audibly with invisibles. Her tormentors. Her accusers. Sometimes she resisted them, sometimes she agreed with them, nodding and accepting her culpability for everything.

Harbour of Santa Cruz de Tenerife, Canary Islands, Saturday

Dear Pieter,

...so that's what happened dear friend and brother. I can't blame you, you couldn't have known what the effect would be on her. I am frightened about what may happen next. I can't seem to be able to bring her back. God I love her so much, this is ripping me apart. I feel so – well, guilty, as if I could have done something...should have done something, but honestly I was so taken up up and away I could do absolutely nothing. I just want to take her into my arms and hug all this crap out of her. But I can't. She lies there like dead. I talk to her but she cries about things, hardly ever looks at me, relates to me. You won't believe this but she's losing weight like mad. I don't see that as the bright side. There is no bright side.

Whatever happens I have to stick by her now. I have to protect her. I managed to get her to have some salad yesterday, just a mouthful, it was such a relief. She seems to believe she's responsible for all the evil in the world, so maybe she's trying to die?

I know I sound self-pitying and I am. I feel helpless. I wish you were here. I wish she were here. I don't suppose you could spare us a little money could you? She threw it all overboard. I can't possibly let the parents know anything about this. Anything will help! Send c/o American Express in London.....

Barcelona finally arrived on the port side of our ship and there we disembarked, and with luck, our thumbs and the many kindnesses of strangers we pointed ourselves toward London. On that journey every now and then Mona would appear out of the muttering scary gloom of her new self. For periods of time it was as if she had never left...but then, something would trigger a retreat and a look would come over her face as she fought off or didn't fight off her demons. Or somebody (say, for example, the gentle laughing truck driver with his broken English who happily drove us to all the way to Toulouse) would say something she would misinterpret as a stinging secret attack which showed without doubt that he was in league with her demons...and she would quietly, then loudly, then hysterically demand to be let out... even in the middle of a strange town with pools of darkness in its midnight streets.

People fed us, let us spend nights in their houses, they knew something was wrong and in their foreign hearts wanted to help to put it right – what did they think of the stern man and the muttering girl who would take no food who looked more like a familiar than a wife? They gave us food, shelter. In Amsterdam, a man got me a job working at the docks where I was ribbed for being small and only half as capable of lifting massive things as they were. While Mona stayed at his home in the day with his lovely family and to my surprise seemed a little at peace as she played with their clever little daughter. Thank you Henk and Marie. And especially Annie.

It took us a month, but eventually we had enough money to cross the channel and pay a token amount for our board and lodging. We arrived in the Kingdom of Great Britain (Harwich) a week before my twentieth birthday. February 1969.

Two

He had decided to take the bull by the horns. After, it must be said, two stiff brandies he had quaffed in rapid succession before the meeting. 'She's dead,' he said and sat back waiting to be gored.

In the dining room of the Liar's Club, noon. Waiters bustle. Grown men do fart jokes. The faux-wood panelling peels. Outside, winter grinds London to a stop.

'My boy you had better not say that again. Because if you say it again I may kill you.' The old man glared at the younger one, daring him to strike.

Truelove attempted to unpick the green carpet with his eyes.

Then, like a penny arcade mechanical swami into which a coin has been dropped, the old man started to move. Laszlo's gnarled hand tightened on the brandy glass. His sanity seemed on the wobble again. As did the world. He leaned forward. He had to know. 'Alright Truelove. I'll grant you amnesty. You can forget we're in the Liar's Club. You look at my eyes. You say the truth. Is my Hazel ...' the word stuck in the throat, amidst the dried-up tobacco and dregs of years. Eventually: '...dead?'

Truelove nodded. Only his knees were shaking.

The world hung, suspended. Then at last, 'Tell me exactly what happened' he said at last. His voice sounded as if it had been recorded on a wax cylinder a hundred years ago.

'We carried out your orders exactly. At a quarter to six in the evening our man Bennett knocked on her door.'

'Yes yes' the old man said waving away a waiter who, fearful of violence, hovered, ears akimbo. 'I chose the time carefully. I wanted her to be relaxed, ready for dinner, having her evening cocktail.'

'Go on.'

'She came to the door in curlers. She was getting ready to go out.'

'So soon after her husband's death?' Laszlo said like a stage villain. 'Well she couldn't really have cared for him. And then?'

'As agreed he told her you had died and that she had inherited everything. The film camera recorded it all. The film should be on its way – you'll see for yourself.'

'I want to hear it from you. What were the words? Tell me the *words*.'

'Something like this.' The Lawyer consulted a sheaf of notes. 'He: "Good afternoon Mrs Stone". She: "Good afternoon." He: "I have some important information for you." She: "Well you had better come inside. But you can't stay long. I'm going out. And I have a headache." He: "I have to tell you the news here on the doorstep." She: "Why?" He: (pointing to cameraman) "The moment is to be filmed. Those are my instructions." She (hiding face) "You're the Security Police aren't you? BOSS? It's Tom isn't it? He's not in the country! I don't know where he is. Now go away." He: "No, I assure you – "'

'That wasn't in the script!' Laszlo interrupted.

'I can't help that – '

'When her husband died we agreed the script. Your man was to be tactful, solemn – ' he was wagging a finger now, like a parent admonishing a child for bedwetting.

'I know – '

'Your job was to find out if she still had feelings for me. Not to scare her to death!'

'I know but – '

'Oh carry on, read me the rest of this!' he tapped Truelove's notes with his forefinger.

Truelove, recalling the advice of Swami Jenkins, breathed deeply six times and continued. 'She: "Whatever he's been doing I had no part in it." – He: "I assure you I am not with the Police. My card. I am the South African representative for Messrs Truelove Stronglode and Withers, the solicitors and executors of the estate of the late Count Laszlo Mindchyck formerly of London...' here Truelove dared a glance above the notes and saw Laszlo tracing patterns in the spilt wine on the tablecloth. "Who?" He: "Count Laszlo Mindchyck."

'You're lying. She must have known the name!'

'She remembered. She remembered,' Truelove said hastily. 'Look. It says so here.'

Laszlo snatched the sheaf of paper from him and read aloud tonelessly. '"She: Wait a moment. Laszlo? *That* Laszlo? Old wooden prick?" He: "I have come here to tell you that the Count is dead." She: "They must have had to make a special coffin, with a bulge in the middle." He: "His last thoughts were of you." She: "Old wooden prick! Ha ha ha." He: "He has left you all his fortune, which is considerable." She: "Ah...!" Mrs Stone drops to floor. Ambulance called. Dead on arrival. Brain Tumour.'

'Hm.' Truelove said.

'So she's dead.' Laszlo said woodenly. 'The only woman I ever loved is dead!'

Truelove sipped tea. Waited.

Eventually the old man went on. 'She loved me so much she decided to join me.'

The lawyer tried to conceal a sigh of relief. 'I'm sure' he said.

'Tell me about this Tom. Her grandson?'

'Her grandson. Apparently she loved the boy obsessively. Left him all her worldly goods. He doesn't know she's gone yet. Apparently he's here, somewhere in London. Her solicitors are searching for him –'

'Strange she left nothing to her children –'

'She doesn't like Tom's mother much – she's a stepdaughter. Her only son is dead. She thought of Tom as her son.'

'Right,' Laszlo said, 'you go to her lawyer, see you're appointed their representative in Britain. Get a copy of that will. I want to study it. Then find the boy. If she loved him he must be something really special.'

'Um he isn't *actually* – '

'Don't give me any of your ums! Just do it!'

Loud haw haw from across the room. Lord Harmsworth just got the fart joke.

Dear Tom

Well I hope you're really liking London and Mona is feeling better. I am going to have to tell you it's all my fault. You are my brother-at arms and I am going to be completely honest. It's easier by letter because I'm too far away for you to punch me.

Well not really ALL. Those little presents came to you courtesy of the Brigadier. God knows where he got them. Maartens said – as he handed the pills to me – 'here, give them to that Tom, these hippies like these druggies, tell him this is a first payment from his country for the work he's going to do for us in London. Understand? This is the Proper Stuff they tell me. Made by a bloke called Owsley especially for the CIA. 1,000 micrograms each. Enough for eight people. Tell him. It'll make him very happy'. I was going to tell you in a letter to you in London. I never thought you'd take them on the boat! I thought they'd be easy for you to smuggle in and didn't want to put the details in a letter for Mr Customs to read. And you took a whole one each! I feel so bad about that. Just lucky you're both still alive is all.

Here are a few rands to keep you going for a little at least, you know I haven't got much but a few of the people put some together.

As for me, I am deep up to my neck in things you know about and things you don't want to know about. Who knows? Maybe you'll see me sooner than I think...or just maybe, never

Bests

P

There was a knock on the door. I looked up and around at the bare dirty room. Mattress on the floor on which my wife lay curled, hardly breathing. Cigarettes and joints stubbed out on the torn rug. A day old plate of Chinese takeaway replicating bacteria. Tin box of tobacco, lump of hash, cigarette papers. A turntable amplifier and speakers, a pile of records. Faint smell of jasmine incense lingers around the corpse of the burnt worm that released it.

Fucking police. Not going. 'Tom for fucksake'. Mona rolled onto her back. Mind you police wouldn't knock.

I went down the uncarpeted stairs, opened the front door and took a telegram from a sneering postman. For me? I signed, tore it open.

WILL BE IN LONDON TOMORROW ON BUSINESS STOP MEET ME AT COFFEE MACHINE LEICESTER SQUARE 2.30 STOP FATHER

I ran back up the stairs. Look at this!' I yelled, waving the telegram at Mona. 'We're saved!'

She read it as if it was a message from another dimension. 'He'll only want something from you. He'll want us to go back.'

'We're not doing that. Ever.' I said without conviction.

'When you reach twenty one – if you reach twenty one – you're likely to be extremely rich,' Father went on. 'Are you listening to me?'

'Rich', I said, listlessly stirring the cup of cappuccino which, with its lukewarm chocolatey messiness, represented the state of my mind pretty nearly exactly. In preparation for meeting dear Father I had smoked a great deal of Nepalese hash.

'I don't think you understand me boy.'

'Yes Father.' I lie. 'Can you advance us a hundred for now then?'

'What did you do with all the money you took with you? There must have been more than a thousand rand – '

'We lost it. Kind of overboard.'

'What!!!???' For a moment I fear this could end in violence. Actually, as we're in public, I don't care. As long as he initiates it.

'It was an accident. I got the traveller's cheques back from American Express. Pieter lent us some. It was the cash that went....'

He takes a deep breath. Realises he's in public. Focuses on his tea.

He'd do anything to get me back to South Africa, I think to myself.

A formica-topped table separates us, barrier of plastic and steel. On the table is a sugar container with a long chrome tube which is supposed to dispense a teaspoonful of sugar every time it is turned upside-down. It hadn't worked for me. Much sugar sprinkles the gap between us. A plastic cruet sits next to the useless sugar bottle. The salt and pepper containers are marked with thousands of tiny scratches. I am trying to work out if they make any sort of logical pattern.

Police sirens scream. Somebody has stabbed somebody in the alleyway next to the Prince Charles Cinema.

'Tom! Are you with me?' Father waves a hand in front of my face. I pretend to listen. 'Now your gran is dead – '

'Huh?' I reviewed what the word 'gran' meant to me. Surely not Hazel?

'Didn't you get my letter? The one with the money order? I explained everything.'

Two difficult concepts. Dead gran. Money order. Money order? I hadn't had a letter with a money order. This was not a huge surprise: most mail at the squat where we live in Notting Hill Gate was removed by bailiffs or stolen or chewed up by an Alsatian belonging to Mr Ratty. 'I thought you hadn't sent any money.'

'I sent you a hundred pounds. So you didn't get it.' He sighed, reached into his wallet and pressed a wad of fivers into my hand.

I drank more slushy coffee. Then conversationally, 'Did you actually say Hazel is dead?'

'She passed away almost three weeks ago. It was in my letter. I was surprised you didn't reply.'

'Oh,' I said. 'So what happened to Hazel?'

'Seems she had a brain tumour, which maybe explains all those headaches she had. I always said there was something amiss with her brain...which may explain why she left her money to *you* I suppose. Maybe she thought we are well off enough. But when she died she had no idea how rich she was...so you don't know the story then?'

'No I don't. Tell me.' What he had said began to drip in to my stoned brain. A sadness rose like gas. Hazel was dead. She was a kind of...friend I suppose, never really a gran. I kind of liked her. She certainly liked me. Ok, I never actually loved her as a granny but I always liked her. I enjoyed her company. But my liking was always somewhat tempered by Mother's Wicked Stepmother stories. (see Umfaan's Heroes or just take my word for it.)

'Your grandmother, or rather, your step-grandmother had a great love affair apparently before she met your grandfather Robert. I don't know the details. It was a while ago when she was in Europe. He was a Count from Poland or Hungary or Transylvania or some such. Do you want a donut? No? Well, they had rather a fling.' (at this point I play back the stories Hazel had told me...oh, *that* Count!)'Then when she left him he fled from his castle or whatever to get away from the Nazis. His whole family was killed. He went to England, made a fortune – and when he died, he left everything to her!'

'Gosh,' I said.

'Gosh indeed,' he said.' Well, after many years of searching his lawyers tracked her down, found her in Johannesburg. They told her of her good fortune and she died.'

'Huh?'

'The tumour that had been growing in her brain just burst or something. It was a Thursday, I was playing golf, got a phone call. Apparently the whole thing was filmed by the lawyer – her being told, her dropping dead, – they gave us a copy. From inheritance to death in 62 seconds. Sad really. Your mother says we should sell it – call it the Shortest Multimillionnairess. The only way we will get anything from her...'

Silence opened between us. Hazel's face hovered in front of me, obscuring my view of Father. It was her face as an old lady, but I could see there the high-cheekboned impenetrable beauty she had once been. The woman Laszlo spent his life dreaming about, longing for, regretting, seeking. I stirred the futile coffee again which was now mere sugar and froth. 'She'd decided to join Ian, her brother...her brother died of a brain tumour too you know. He was the only man she ever loved...or maybe he came for her...'

'Nonsense. She just died that's all. Probably had the tumour for a long time. If she said something maybe we could have had her treated.'

I sighed. I even felt a tear in my eye. So romantic! Father would never understand. 'It's sad,' I said.

'Never liked the woman myself. Neither did your mother. The point is, you are her heir.'

It hit me then. The miasma of hash in my brain finally dispersed. 'Me? Me? I get Laszlo's money?' I let the spoon drop.

'It's not as easy as that. There are conditions.'

'What?'

'She didn't know she would die so rich when she made her will, obviously. Any rate, you and Mona need to come back to SA straight away.'

'Was that the condition?' I asked.

He hesitated. 'Not exactly. I don't know how to put this. Her words were, "provided he is a fit and responsible person". Hah! That will be the day! Failing that, various charitable organisations get the lot.'

'Like...?'

'Oh, feral cats, donkeys, that kind of thing...'

'What does "fit and responsible" mean?'

'Well – ' Father was nonplussed. 'Probably anything her lawyers decide it means. She also used the word "sane". She had doubts about your sanity.' He grinned. 'I know just how she felt.'

'Thank you for your confidence', I muttered. Then, 'Who are her lawyers? Who decides? How? When?'

'They've appointed this fellow Truelove here in London apparently. He's acting for her estate and I believe for the Laszlo estate as well. He explained the whole thing to me on the telephone, so I came here on the first available flight. I wanted to tell you before he gets to you. He's got some mad plan or other –which is why it would be so much better for you to catch a plane straight back...'

'What mad plan?'

'Listen to this: they are going to appoint twelve people, like a jury, to observe you for the next nine months, until you're twenty one. Then they'll report back.'

'Of course I'm sane,' I erupted.

'The way you live? I'm told you and Mona are in a squat.'

'Yes....'

'And do you still take drugs?'

'Not much.'

'And why didn't you bring Mona? Can I see her? I don't have much time, I have to get back. Surely you can arrange your busy programme –' his sarcasm had an edge of desperation – 'so that I can see my daughter-in law?'

'Uh no, she's ill. It's infectious.'

'Really.' Not believing. 'I suggest you come back to Jo'burg. We'll bribe some psychiatrist or other to swear you're as sane as a judge. Then I'll invest the money for you. Find you a nice cushy job. What do you say?'

'One word,' I said, 'No.' And I stepped out into the street.

I arrived back at the house as Ratty was leaving. 'Hey man,' he said, brushing past me, 'Gotta go. People to do. Things to see. She's in the kitchen.'

'Thanks,' I said.

It was Nick the Rat who had helped us to find somewhere to live shortly after our arrival in London. We met him in Regent's Park. He was a ragged wizened old young man (he said he was twenty one, looked fifty) with dead blond hair, a scrag of beard and the manic manner of someone who was just too busy to stop. He seemed to think faster, move faster, talk quicker than anybody I had ever met. He stared into one's eyes as if he were devouring one's brain.

He had taken pity on our moneyless state. Or more likely he guessed that we, being nicely middle class and foreign, were likely to have access to pots of the stuff. As a poor boy from a poor family determined to Make Good he latched on to the Flower Children of the bourgeoisie and filled his house with them. Favourite drug: Methedrine which he drank from ampoules. No-one else in the world could stand the taste.

Nick loved it. Mona and Nick (she refused to call him Ratty as everybody else did) got on famously. Why? They were both cracked, fed on each-other's madness. The Cockney Dickensian villain and the spoilt kid with the genius IQ sat head-to head for hours. Crazed chortles rising now and then from the huddle of heads.

The others in the house kept their distance from the pair. So did I at first, relieved that at last Mona seemed to trust somebody other than me. Though prone to jealousy I realised that there was no sexual element in their relationship. They simply shared a chip on the shoulder, the belief that they were the hard-done bys of the world, allies against the Dark Forces that ruled the world.

I eavesdropped once or twice. They always spoke in terms of Us and Them. I realised that Mona was sharing her conviction that she had been invaded by the forces of pure evil – and I did have a tiny hope that maybe the Rat was humouring her, trying to put the voices in their place...but who the hell knows.

'Mona, they want to give me money.'

'Do They?' She was standing at the kitchen window. Water was gushing into the unplugged sink, splashing over and about a pile of plates and mugs. Mona ignoring it, just staring out of the window.

My heart gave a lurch. I had heard the capitalisation of that T. For a moment I saw her as Father would have seen her, had he been standing at my side. Her eyes glaring from deep-set darkness like rubies. Her floor length crumpled purple dress. Her very pale face, very red lips as if lipsticked.

'Have you eaten today?' I asked.

'Of course I have! I've eaten what I can. What money?'

'I don't believe you. If you don't eat you'll die! Mona I'm so sick of this –'

'What money? From your father?'

I held my breath. Getting angry with her only made her withdraw. Then, forcing myself to speak in a calm, conversational tone, I told her about the Inheritance and the conditions.

'Oh,' she said, seeming to be thinking deeply about all this. Then, 'I know what's happening. They're trying to get to *you*, now, to buy you onto their side - !'

'Who? Who are we talking about Mona?'

'They! Call them what you want – the Dominant five percent –the Moneylords, the Slimpkings. The people who make all the cars and televisions and the arms and the wars. The people who want to get us all sewn up. Or think they have –'

'For fucksake Mona – '

'No, listen. They all conspire *together* to fool us, ask Nick, he knows what I mean, they want to get into your head too, only certain people understand – '

'Mona that's bullshit. That's the paranoid scenario the Nazis used as an excuse to kill anyone who wasn't Aryan. They called it the International Jewish Conspiracy –'

'They were at least partly right. Of course some of Them are Jews. But some aren't.'

I could hold my temper no longer. 'For chrissake Mona, that's all dangerous rubbish and you know it!'

'You won't listen to me! You won't believe me and they'll have you. They've been watching all the time, planning. Trying to get you away from me. If it wasn't for me and Nick –

'Oh Christ', I groaned.

'Yes Jesus is part of it all. He made it possible for Them in the first place, getting the ordinary people to open to him – '

'I'm going for a walk.'

I slammed the door on my way out but it didn't help. I was angry and frightened. How to separate Nick and Mona? Before this International Conspiracy madness became an International Conspiracy. Under the direction of Mona and her pet Rat.

...and now this Inheritance business. Honestly. I strode out into Notting Hill Gate thinking of all this. And all that, as well. Sane...? Me? No idea. Money...how much? Why?

The evening was surprisingly warm, fresh. I counted the money left in my pocket. £85. Father's gift. I'd have to make sure Mona and the Rat didn't get their hands on it. Come to think of it, it was probably he who had found Father's money letter on the doormat. And taken it, the swine.

I turned right at Ladbroke Grove. Everybody, it seemed, was on the streets. Suspicious characters hussling bags of parsley at tourists 'Best ganga?'. Gays careened by in feathers. Long-haired bearded men sat in doorways with long-haired bead-bedecked girls deep in discussion about Transcendental Meditation. A frowning priest in grubby surplice looked for somebody to save. Pieter came out of a doorway.

Huh?

'Pieter. *Pieter!!!*'

'I don't believe it! *Tom!!!*' We collapsed laughing into each-other's arms. I felt so relieved. Light had appeared in my darkness. I wanted to kiss him! But would have hated to have offended the staring priest who was doubtless forgiving us as we are God's children too.

'I sent you money – did you get it? – then I just sent myself when I didn't hear –'

'Yes yes, at American Express - You're the best thing I've seen for ages! How amazing...'

'How long have you been here?' I asked, an arm around his shoulders as we sat on a once fine Georgian porch.

'Only a week – I *knew* I'd find you!'

'Tell me everything – what's been happening – you had me so worried in your last letter – what the hell???'

`So much! I couldn't write what was really happening! For a start...'

Yes yes and yes. Two men arm in arm sitting on a grubby step on a lovely Spring evening exchanging lives, heads no more than a foot apart, babbles and roars of delight! An old lady, her life in carrier bags, passes in a dust cloud of memories, streams with tears.

PIETER'S STORY

This story is told in Pieter's voice:

When you left I found myself in a difficult position. I was about to start my second year BA and people were becoming really suspicious of me. Not just NUSAS – obviously, me being one of the few Afrikaners in the place – but BOSS as well. The info you and I fed them was, as we knew, useless and they didn't manage to make any arrests that ended in convictions.

Well they wanted to catch commies and, let's face it, there weren't any.

And as for NUSAS, they began to add one and one. The two being me and you. We being the only ones around when documents went missing and even though they were mostly lists of rugby teams and other *twak,* they weren't happy.

So one day during the holidays Brigadier Maartens came to visit me. I was sitting on a koppie overlooking Trichardsdal, near where the Pandokkies used to be – you remember? Where we spent the night waiting for Umfaan.

A light rain was falling but it was quite warm and I sat there in a T-shirt and jeans smoking a joint. I was amazed to see this wet fellow in full uniform struggling up the hill. You can imagine! I threw the smoke away. Then I recognised the Brigadier.

'Mostert! He shouted.

I leapt to my feet and saluted. This was involuntary. 'Morning Brigadier.'

'What are you doing out here in the rain?' he asked, seating himself puffily on a dead tree. 'Sit for Christ's sake. You should know better than to salute without a hat on.' He removed his own and wiped swear away with a handkerchief. 'We're not happy with you Mostert', he said.

'Why not?'

'Results, boy, results! I'm not in a good mood. I've driven two hundred miles to see you to tell you that. I'm hot and I'm wet./ All because you don't give me results.'

'But I've given you piles of papers and things - !'

'Useless the lot of it and I think maybe you know it...yes you gave me lists of names. We tapped some phones. I allocated twenty two men to watch the people you told me were plotting revolution. What do we get?'

'I don't know, Brigadier', I said, even though I did know.

'Nothing! That's what we got! Then: you gave me lists of demos the Commies planned. They're going to march down Eloff Street on Tuesday for example. So I goes to the Minister and tell him to ban all marches on Tuesday. And what happens?'

'I don't know, Brigadier.'

'Yes you do. The bastards march down Rissik Street on Monday.'

'Maybe they found out – '

'From who? You? Three: you gave us minutes of meetings. And what do they contain? For example, dissatisfaction with the state of the squash courts. So my people spend months trying to work out what the code words "squash courts" stand for. And what do they stand for? – '

'Are you asking me?'

'Squash Courts! That's what they stand for. Tell me Mostert, how did an idiot like you get accepted for university?'

'You told them to accept me Brigadier.'

'Don't play the fool. Look me in the eye now, boy. Tell me you're not playing games with me.'

'I'm not playing games with me.'

'I can't work you out,' he sighed. 'What was that you threw away when you saw me coming?'

'What thing?'

'This.' He bent over to retrieve the half-smoked spliff which had somehow stayed dry. He looked at it for a couple of long minutes. Then he removed a lighter from his pocket, lit up and inhaled gratefully. 'I just don't understand you' he sighed and passed the joint.

The rain stopped and a beautiful sunset started. 'I've come to give you a last chance,' he said, grinning involuntarily. When the Brigadier grins, he grins! You remember how like a toad he looks.

Well, when he smiles, the top half of his face tries to leave the bottom half. It's quite something.

'Do you know Karen Williams?' he asked, accepting the joint back again.

'Of course,' I said. 'She's screwing Bernstein.'

'We want her. Understand what I am saying? We want that pinko. I don't care what you have to do. Get the goods on her, see? And here's the Official Warning: if she's not in John Vorster Square with enough evidence to convict a saint by May, I'll have your cock stuffed and mounted on my wall!'

I gulped. I'm rather attached to that part of my anatomy – and at the moment, it's attached to me. 'What has she done Brigadier?' I asked.

'That's for you to find out. And even if she hasn't done anything at all, you make sure she does! This is your Assignment. You will not fail me.'

'I will not fail you,' I said. I am rather good at looking into peoples' eyes when I'm lying.

'You had better not. Or you will force me to use a rather tired old cliché. It goes like this: "Or Else"'

'Yes Brigadier.'

'Or else means a whole lot of things. We could, say, hang you for murder...maybe even arrest you for this – ' he waved the joint at me. 'Whatever, if you fail me you've had it.'

'Jislaaik.'

'Exactly.'

You may pop out for some ice cream and sweets now, while Pieter and I go to Charing Cross station. Yes this is me, Tom, again.

Why are we going to Charing Cross station? Because Pieter is living in Bromley, Kent, and has invited me to go back with him to meet the people he's staying with. There's a chance they'll offer Mona and me a room.

I telephoned Mona from the station., (Yes the squat did have a phone, thanks to some Ratty business)

'I'll be home rather late. You don't mind do you?'

She did. 'No,' she said, 'why should I?' Indifferent, subdued.

'You'll never guess who I met in Ladbroke Grove. Pieter!'

'Really. That was nice for you.'

'He's taking me to meet the people he's staying with. They might have a room for us.'

'I don't want to live somewhere else.'

'Well we'll argue about that later.'

'When will you be back?'

'I don't know. Later this evening. I'll see – ' The phone goes click. Well, fuck you.

Sometime, somehow I've got to get her out of there I thought.

Right, Interval over. Pieter resumed the story on the train:

Well, term started and I had to get to know Karen Williams. I couldn't understand why BOSS wanted her so badly. She is a tiny sparrow-like being, you remember, with sunken eyes, black hair, always looked a little – greasy. She seemed so inoffensive to me. Admittedly she seems a little – um – secretive, but I always thought that was to do with her disliking everyone. Except, of course, for Martin Bernstein.

Karen and Martin were obsessed with each-other. They were so in tune, people concluded that the two of them had the whole telepathy thing worked out. You know, finishing each-other's sentences and such. As you can imagine getting to know her was a hard egg to crack.

So fairly early in the game I came to the conclusion that the couple definitely had *some* sort of secret. The way they always kept themselves apart from everybody, never joined in any group or clique. Maybe, most people thought, they were so involved in screwing there wasn't time for anything else. I didn't think it was that simple.

I managed to arrange to be in the same Political Science tutorial group as Martin. It was bloody clever Tom, actually. What I did was, I sat next to the creep. And while he was disputing with the lecturer about Malthus and the influence of the Industrial Revolution on the development of Marxism – Christ, was he boring! – I stole his notebook.

Later in the Canteen I sidled up to him - he was sitting next to Karen naturally – and said, 'Martin, I'm so very sorry.'

'What?' he said, 'What about?'

'I seem to have taken your notebook by mistake. In the Tutorial. It's so similar to mine you see.'

'Oh it was you' he said without interest, extending his hand for the book.

'Brilliant!', I said, seating myself uninvited at the table. 'I didn't know you wrote *poetry*'

He snatched at the notebook. 'Give me that!' he sputtered, going a bit pink.

I avoided his grabbing hand. 'No, I think they're great, really! This image – a beam of light to represent the whole of human experience. It's brilliant!'

'Is it?' I had found his weakness. Stroking made him purr.

'Yes! Amazing. And your use of assonance – '

'Yes?'

'So original! So – vibrant!'

'Well,' he said, 'I didn't realise you could be so discerning'

'I may be an Afrikaner', I said, 'but I recognise brilliant use of English!' I handed the book back as if it was a precious and fragile thing. 'I've got a great idea,' I had his attention now. 'Listen to this'.

'Why don't we go home?' Karen asked.

'Just a minute honey bear,' Martin said impatiently. 'What idea?'

And I outlined my plan. We would get the Poetry Society to run an open competition. They could publish a Slim Vol of the entries, and I was certain he would win.

'So who's going to put up the money for all this?' he asked. 'It costs money to print books. And give prizes. Who gives a fuck about poetry anyway?'

'Leave that to me,' I said and zipped off to a phone box.

'WHAT!' said the Brigadier. 'You want us to finance a *what*?'

'A poetry competition Brigadier. It's absolutely essential. You want Karen Williams. Well, if you finance a poetry competition I'll have her boyfriend. I'll be in with her, you see.'

'How?'

'If we get him I get her. This is the very best way for me to worm my way into and between that little couple. Believe me.'

'You had better not be taking the piss, Mostert. That's all I can say. Just remember this is your last chance. How much do you want?'

Well, I won and the Great Poetry Competition was announced.

Entries trickled in. There were three. Keith Franks, the Organiser (his official title. He eschewed Chairman, the traditional honorarium, as it was too macho. And Keith was NOT macho.), a lanky fellow with eyelashes an inch long, pouted despairingly at me. 'What are we going to do, darling?' he asked, 'What on *earth* are we going to do?'

Well, I took a leaf out of your book, Tom. 'Simple,' I said. 'We'll cheat!'

Incidentally I explained the arrival of three hundred rands in a brown paper envelope marked 'Poetry' in the NUSAS post as a gift from a culture loving farmer called Basie DuPlessis. 'This had better work,' the Brigadier's voice crackled through the tapped telephone in the Canteen. 'I had to raid a whole week's petty cash for this blerry rubbish.'

'It'll be worth it,' I said. 'Don't worry about a thing!'

All very well my saying that. I was worried sick. Though the Competition gave me a great many excuses to talk to Martin (I even managed to force an invitation to dinner from him when I implied I would be 'heavily involved in the judging') I hadn't managed to turn up a single tittle of evidence against Karen.

As I got to know them better, I began to hope fervently that I could be instrumental in putting Karen away. With Martin preferably in the next cell, separated from her by barbed wire. God they were irritating!

That dinner gave me three days of gutclenching agony – not just the tofu and brown rice, but all the bloody *poetry* I had to listen to!

Having a sensible conversation with them was impossible. Whenever I got Martin talking about politics or poetry or the theory of internal resistance Karen would interrupt with 'Isn't it late? I hope this isn't going to take too long.' Or 'Haven't you got a home to go to?' I couldn't get any useful opinions as far as the Brigadier was concerned anyway, from either of them. Which was in a way a relief of course. What I could never understand was why he didn't just arrest them – since when did lack of evidence deter BOSS from arresting and interrogating people? I would guess they had powerful parents...

Anyhow, I became quite a poetry expert. I could recite the whole of Ginsberg's 'Howl' by heart...*Big Deal saith Tom, who couldn't?*...We had given ourselves six weeks to get the entries in and print the booklet before the prizes would be announced. Franks and I began to write poems frantically, inventing wilder and wilder names for the fictitious entrants.

Then as Judgement Day approached, I decided to have another go at Fortress Karen.

The only card left up my sleeve was the Ace of Hearts.

Having ascertained that Martin was out, I loped off to their flat in Hillbrow. She was alone, yes. 'Oh dear,' I said, 'isn't he in?'

'No,' she said. 'Go away.'

I waited on the doorstep. 'Can I come in for a bit? I'd like to talk to you.'

She thought for a full minute, then she let me in. I found out why as soon as I sat down. 'Listen,' she said, 'is he going to win?'

I removed a grubby little teddy bear from a painful place beneath my bum. 'I can't actually *guarantee* that,' I said. 'The judges are entirely independent.'

'Rubbish,' she said, shifting the third volume of the Encyclopaedia Brittanica off the settee onto the floor. She sat next to me. 'You said you organised the whole thing so's Martin would get his chance. What are you going to do about it?'

'Well – ' just what I was hoping for...

'Never mind Well,' she said. 'Listen to me, you little shit. If you let him win, I'll have your guts for garters.'

'What???' I was totally mystified. 'I thought you – '

'I can't have him winning! He's so obsessed with this shit now he's no fucking good to me. Now he wants to be a romantic bloody *poet*....! What a waste of space!'

'I told you, there's nothing I can do...' heart sinking.

'Very well,' she said. 'I've tried friendly persuasion. Now I have to revert to blackmail.

'Huh?'

'I know all about you Mostert. I know who you're working for.'

Can you imagine? I was absolutely. Well, wouldn't you be? 'What - ? How?' I blurted.

'I know what your game is,' she said and smiled a very thin smile. 'You're CP, right?'

CP....CP......Communist Party...?

'...and therefore you know Martin and I are part of Red July. You know about us. The last thing we need is publicity!'

'Of course...' I said, not understanding.

'Martin doesn't agree with me, see. He's got an ego the size of this building. It's disgusting how you grovel to him. It makes him unbearable. You will make sure won't you?'

'I'll do what I can' I said between bafflement and relief.

'Good. That was the Blackmail. Now I add bribery. Do you want to fuck me?'

Though it had about as much appeal as necrophilia, I did my duty. I was confused, sure, but to my horror I knew that now I had her (both ways), I had what the Brigadier wanted – I just needed details, evidence and these two would be finished. When I was dressing, she gave me a salute, clenched fist to chest. 'Long live the Party,' she said. 'Long live the Seventh International!'

Now I understood. Red July was a group of violence- orientated white intellectuals, more radical even than Umkonto WeSizwe. So she was the real thing. An actual fanatical. The Brigadier had been right all along! I had always thought that the 'Communist Threat' was a state-sponsored fallacy, the Common Enemy syndrome necessary to retain the support of the poor whites.

And she thought I was one of them.

Gee.

Now what? I don't believe in Communism – as it's practised anyway. But I don't agree with Apartheid as you know. And I certainly don't agree with bombing innocent people. So Tom you can see I was in a serious dilemma. I never thought this game was serious, just a way to keep going the way I was keeping going...

I know you'll find what I did next hard to understand, Tom. I just felt myself carried away on some kind of wave out of my control...maybe I just didn't agree with what they were doing anyway....anyway, I'll go on:

I had no hard evidence against Karen. To get some, I would have to win her over completely. And the first thing to do was to make sure Martin didn't win the competition.

This was difficult, as the other poems were all considerably worse than his terrible efforts. I approached the three judges, a brace of ancient literary queens Keith had found somewhere in the dusty depths of the university. But no negotiation was possible. The poor things were overwhelmed with Martin's 'brilliance'. There was only one entry of any merit and that was Martin's and if I didn't agree I 'shouldn't be at University'. They were determined to give that slimy shit the prize. Karen would disembowel me.

Deadlines approached. On the night before the announcement I was lying sleepless when somebody knocked. 'You bastard! You shit!!' said a demented Karen, standing dishevelled in the corridor.

Numbly I let her in. 'Calm down,' I said, 'tell me what's happened.'

'It's Martin! He's useless! He's so wound up about the competition, he's been drinking all day. He's no good at all!'

'Oh well,' I said beginning to unzip.

'Not now you idiot! Get your coat. We've got to go.' She clapped her hands imperiously and we left.

'Where are we going?' I asked as we clambered into her battered Renault.

'It's a Mission,' she said. 'Bugger it. It was supposed to be me and Martin. You've fucked it all up with your stupid Competition. So *you* have to do it.'

'What? Do what?'

'Shut your mouth. I am an Adjutant so I'm your superior. You do as I say. See that package on the back seat?'

'Yes...'

'It's set, ready to go, understand?'

I understood....'Where?' I gulped.

The horrible truth. 'The railway station', she said grimly. 'Where else? This is the plan. Are you paying attention?'

'O.k. So I suppose it's a bomb, right?' I asked rhetorically.

'No,' she said sarcastically. 'It's sweeties for the cops!'

'What do you want me to do?' My mind seeking an escape. I didn't want to be responsible for blowing people up, for fucksake.

'Now listen,' she said, 'I drop you at the back entrance by the taxis. You go into the concourse. Find a rubbish bin. Put the packet – carefully – into the bin. Then amble slowly to the front entrance where I pick you up. That's all. Do you understand?'

'Front entrance. Back entrance. I understand.'

'Good,' she said, accelerating past a troupe of schoolchildren attempting to cross the road.

Almost literally shitting myself, I hopped out of the car at the back entrance of the station, package clasped. We pantomimed a soppy goodbye. 'Have a good trip darling' she said as she drove off.

Diddly dum. Just me and my bomb. Tiddly om-pom-pom. Where to dump it? How long the fuse? Damn thing, I swear it was making a ticking sound.

I have to admit to you Tom I began to panic. The Railway Police, I thought, I have to find the Railway Police. At this stage of this game all I could think of was how much I wanted to stay alive.

Secondary considerations – like this is my chance to prove myself to the Brigadier...and/or to Karen...this is my chance to save lives... hardly played a part. All I could do was rush about the concourse with my ticking burden in a flurry of indecision and blind panic.

I saw a sign. Police. It was the RP office. I burst in. A half-asleep Sergeant sat at a desk. A couple of plainclothesmen lounged about. A weeping homosexual arrested in the toilet sat at a bench.

'A bomb!' I shouted. 'This is a bomb! What do I do with it?'

The Sergeant looked at me cynically. 'Try the Left Luggage office *meneer*.'

'What??' I burbled.

'Only joking,' he grinned. Then he took the package and held it to his ear. '*My Fok*! A bomb!' he yelled. 'Evacate! I mean, evacuate!' and within a few seconds the office was empty, leaving only me, the wide-eyed homosexual, and the bomb.

'I think we should get out of here', I said.

'I can't,' said the man. 'I'm arrested.'

'But this is a bomb!' I said, putting it down on the desk and dragging him protesting toward the door.

'Please,' he wept, 'they've sent for my *parents*! I'd much rather die!...'

WHOOOOOOMP! Went the bomb and I was flying.

I woke up in the hospital (This is something you and I seem to do a lot, Tom) and guess who was sitting next to me on the bed...

'Did you get her?' I asked, as soon as I realised where I was and who it was.

'You idiot!' said the Brigadier. 'So you've decided to live!'

'Am I alright?' I asked. 'Will I walk again?'

'You're so bleddy stupid! How do you manage to dress yourself on your own in the mornings?'

'Am I all right? Please tell me.'

'Of course you're all right!' the Brigadier said. 'Physically anyway. As far as your brain is concerned, I suppose it's as useless as ever.' He grabbed me by the shoulders and shook me furiously.

'WHY didn't you warn us? WHY didn't you stop her? WHY did you let her get away? Tell me!'

'I couldn't...I didn't have time...there wasn't anything I could do!'

'So you blew up the copshop instead. Do you know what the pinko press are saying?' Letting go of me, he sank back despairingly on the chair. 'They're having a big laugh at us! They're saying the Terrorists can get their explosives right into the very heart of our police stations! Even the Afrikaans papers are saying the police are incompetent. Nobody is safe.'

'Well at least you got Karen didn't you?'

'How could we got Karen! Where's the evidence, hey? Only *your* word for it. And as far as everybody is concerned, you're the terrorist who planted the bomb. Bernstein's dad would make mincemeat of you in the dock.'

'In the *dock*?' I said, aghast.

'Well we got to hang *someone.* Since you're all we got we got to hang *you.*'

'But I – '

'Don't panic. There is an alternative.'

Groan. Haven't I heard this somewhere before...'What alternative'

'We're going to spring you. Tonight you will be spirited away by three black men dressed as guerrillas. You will be smuggled across the border and you will end up in London. This is going to make us look stupid all over again but it will be worth it.'

'Why - ?'

'I don't want you in court! Who knows what an idiot like you could say! Besides, you'll be invaluable in London. That Karen will send you all her bloody contacts when she hears. This could be a big break for us.'

'But – '

`Your credentials as far as the Commies in London are concerned will be impeccable. You blew up the Station. You escaped. You didn't squeal, despite the torture – '

'*Torture???*'

'A few little electric shocks, nothing serious. We'll get that done this afternoon. We have to make it look good, for the press you see.'

'No!'

'Don't worry, you'll manage.' He handed me a Mogadon. 'Just eat this before they come. You won't feel a thing. But make sure you scream like hell. There's Commie agents everywhere.'

Groan.

'By tonight you'll be on your way to London. When you arrive you will establish yourself. You will meet all the lefties and Commies and hippies, all the people who are trying to undermine this great country of ours. We will send you a salary of course. You will be contacted by our network over there. Everything clear?'

'It's that or be hanged, right?'

'Correct. You see I have no choice.' The Brigadier stood.

'Just one question Brigadier,' I said. 'What happened to the *moffie*?'

'The what?'

'The homosexual. The one I was trying to drag out.'

'You mean Willie Nel? That was no homosexual. That was a hero of the Republic. Blown to smithereens trying to detain a terrorist. If he hadn't been behind you to take the full force of the blast you would have been very dead. He's having a military funeral this afternoon. Full honours. So there's no chance he could have been a homosexual hey?'

I nodded. 'Well, his parents will be pleased.'

'Damn right,' the Brigadier said. 'Especially his father. He's a minister in the Government you know. Well, *totsiens* for now...' and he left.

(Insertion from Tom: Martin and Karen were in fact the only real Commies on campus. Martin's father being a barrister of international renown meant the Brigadier wasn't going to make a move without concrete evidence. I think Martin became a Minister in the Mandela Government after 1990. Karen died of cancer in 1989, sadly. They were never lovers. Martin was homosexual.)

Four

Well hello. This is Tom again. Pieter's story, which could have taken us three times around the Circle Line, in fact occupied half an hour while we waited for a cow to be removed from the track at Hither Green.

Peter and I are now walking through the tree-lined streets of Bromley Kent. The dusty ghosts of Victorian pomposity ooze out of every house. Here, they seem to say, no gentleman *ever* raises a fist except to a bounder, every woman is perfect of nail and niceties, no person of any remotely criminal bent ever walks these streets. Voices are never raised above a well-modulated drawl. Everything is as solid as the Empire never was. The houses are rotting just a bit now, stonework fraying at the edges. But the happy ghosts who prowl about the place in broughams, hansoms and on foot cheerfully reassure each-other that everything is as it always was.

'What do you think of the place?' Pieter asked, waving a hand about.

'Very nice. No, very *naice*. By the way,' I said, 'did you ever hear who won the Poetry Competition?'

'Why,' Pieter said laughing, 'Me, of course! I heard it from Franks who was in London last week. Very embarrassing for him. Very surprising for me! I was convinced Martin would win.'

'What was the poem?'

'It was called The Reckoning. I wrote it in the name of Stephen Wilkes. It went – I remember,

When I wrung the neck of the cock
I thought, "What have I brought you?"
The delight of night,
Sudden, true.
And what in turn will you give me?
An hour's gnashing
Of your flesh, a sucking of your bones
An indigestion of juices.
I think you
Win.'

'Uh uh' I said.

'I tell you Tom, if it's that easy to write poems, I could really make my fortune. I won't have to be a professional spy any more. I've got millions like that,' He got out his notebook.

'No more Pieter,' I begged. This could get out of hand.

'You're in luck,' he said. 'We've arrived.'

And so we had. At a tall terraced house in a quiet street. Victorian red brick with stucco curlicues.

The door was opened by a thin man in grubby cords, early forties, harassed to raggedness. His hand whipped through what was left of his hair. He was in the midst of a discussion with someone invisible. 'Yes yes' he said, 'I'll *do* it darling when I get a moment just be just a little *patient* I have to answer the door now I can't do *everything* at once you know, it's Pieter darling and – uh – come in, come in.'

We came in. 'This is Tom,' said Pieter. 'This is Grant' I shook a gaunt abstractedly proffered hand.

'Yes yes' said Grant. 'I'm just – nice to meet you, uh. Come through won't you?'

He led us into the half-decorated hall. Wallpaper couldn't decide whether it was going up or coming down. The floor was bare-boarded. Decorating implements were scattered about like props.

'Who is it? Who IS it?' a female voice megaphoned down the stairs, echoed off the walls.

'Yes yes' Grant answered. Frustration, petulance, exasperation brimmed over. 'I *told* you dear it's Pieter and – uh – dear.' He added the last word dutifully.

We followed the muttering Grant through into a half-decorated lounge. There had obviously been a dispute about whether the walls should be grey or magnolia. Grant retrieved a paintbrush from a paint pot and splashed a line of magnolia onto the wall. 'What do you think, uh? Whatsname. Is this not better than that?'

'Don't bother with that *now* Grant', a voice reverberated through the room.

The source of the booming sound was not, as I had supposed, upstairs. It was a large woman on a sofa in a long Laura Ashley dress of pink and purple flowers. She was huge, and the poor sofa (Biedermeyer. Restored, worth plenty. If it survived the next few days.) sagged beneath her. Her hair was done in a plait which reached her waist. Her pasty face was bubbling with chins and cheeks. Somewhere in there was a gorgeous smile. 'Welcome the guest! Hello darling,' she said, extending a hand as if to be kissed. 'Lovely to meet you John.'

'Tom,' I said. 'Hello' and I awkwardly shook the beringed extremity.

'Have you two eaten?' she asked.

'Why don't you ever *listen* to me, Nora. This is a *neutral* colour. It goes with *anything*!'

'Not now darling' she said in a voice so sweet, I looked around for the ventriloquist. 'Take John to the kitchen darling,' she said to Pieter. 'I can see he needs feeding up.' I couldn't help wondering at her use of the phrase – would I be the next meal?

'Well actually,' said Pieter, we were wondering...'

'Come on Pieter, you say,' Grant said, waving the paintbrush threateningly. Gobs of colour met the floor. 'Grey would be so dull, so dark! Don't you think grey is dull?'

'- whether you had found somebody for the front room yet?' Pieter continued, ignoring him.

'Why does everybody ignore me?' Grant muttered.

'Ignore him darling,' Nora said. 'Of course John can stay, can't he?' She asked rhetorical confirmation from Grant, who gave an exasperated gasp which could have meant anything.

'Tom,' I said.

'And his wife of course,' Pieter added.

'Ten pounds a week. And help with decorating,' Nora said. Then, to Grant, 'Why did you say his name was John?'

'Come and see the room,' Pieter invited, and led me up to a large front room made small by a vast quantity of cardboard boxes and tea chests full of books, filing cabinets, broken Victorian chairs and other bric-a-brac. 'It'll be fine,' Pieter was reassuring. 'They need the money and they sort of collect hippies.'

'Well,' I said, with a grin meant entirely for myself, 'here are two more for their collection.'

I glanced around the room, taking it all in. Hopefully there would be somewhere to put all the trash and treasures. It seemed fine to me, although it was rather upmarket and would be very smart if the decorating ever got finished. A tiny bit intimidating for scruffy hippies. The Notting Hill squat was no way secure and besides it would be excellent to put a few miles between Mona and the Rat. Bromley couldn't be far enough.

And being with Pieter again was great. Even though, despite his excitement and enthusiasm, he was looking haggard and strained.

'It's great,' I said. 'So who and what are Nora and Grant?'

'Nora's sort of an artist, and Grant's a producer at the BBC, medical programmes I think. They're very – accommodating.'

'A bit on the arty side,' I said.

'A bit.' He smiled. 'Let's go to my room.'

And there, beneath a red lampshade which gave us both a rubicund glow, and between inhalations of delicious hash, we continued our story exchange until finally I ended with the Tale of the Golden Carrot.

'So you see,' I said, 'if they decide I'm whatever they would regard as sane, next year, when I'm twenty one, I'll be ridiculously rich!'

Pieter laughed.

'Why do you laugh?'

'At you! The great anti materialist! Always going on about despising money and all that. Hating the rich.'

'I know,' I sighed. 'But I didn't plan it. Besides, I've been thinking about how much good I could do with a lot of money.'

'Aha,' he said, 'that's the trap you see. You think you'll feed the sick and give succour to the poor, right?'

'Well – '

'Oh you won't. You'll suddenly discover that you control a dream machine, with which you can convert any wish into reality. Money corrupts, *pallie*, and absolute megabucks corrupts absolutely.'

'Not always.'

'Oh come on. All those rich philanthropists, it's just a tax dodge to them. A way to keep more of the money for themselves.'

'Sometimes,' I said thoughtfully, 'when I tell people, even friends about it, I get a feeling like – like they're *jealous*.'

'I hope you don't mean me. I don't have to be jealous. My pa owns thousands of acres of prime farmland. One day I could be, if not mega-rich, at least a Rand millionaire. If my dad didn't disown me, that is...'

'Hmm.'

'If they ever let me back in South Africa....'

'Hah!'

'Anyway,' he said, taking a delicate drag on the roach-end of the soppy joint, 'I think I'd prefer fame to money.'

'They often come together,' I said. 'Besides you're already famous enough – at least in S.A.' He laughed. 'Anyway, why fame?'

'Because then people would listen to what I have to say. I've learned a lot. About life, people, motivations and so on. And anyway, why not? Listen to this.' He scrabbled through a pile of papers on the small Victorian kitchen table which served him as a desk. I groaned inside as he started to read.

> Sometimes I see so *wide*, so *far*
> I see just why people are!
> So how come when I come to explain,
> My words are always drowned by rain?

'I know what you mean...' and I did. 'You're taking this poetry business seriously, aren't you?' I asked.

'Sometimes.' And he slipped the sheet of paper back into the pile.

'Well then, if I get rich I'll buy a publishing house, make you famous.'

'Ag no *man*!' he laughed. But I could feel the longing in him, the ragged yearning of a person living in the conviction that whatever he did, his motives would be misunderstood.

The door opened and a boyish man came in wearing underpants and nothing else. The underpants clung to a half erection. The face was sweet, hair coiffed. 'Hi Pieter,' he said, 'Lissen man bit of a hassle, she's being a bit whatsname again, you couldn't spare me a doobie could you?'

'Sure,' Pieter said, handed him a shred of hash. 'Brian, this is Tom.'

'Hi,' Brian said, without interest.

'He's moving into the front room.'

'Oh great man' Brian said and shuffled out.

'Who's he?' I asked.

'That's Brian. Sort of hairdresser to the stars. Pretty boy. Nora's in love with him.'

'In love for real?'

'Probably would never admit it. She says he's the son she never wanted.'

'He's not that pretty...'

'Oh, he looks much better when he's done his hair and had a shave. He's about the campest straight I've ever met. Takes hours in the bathroom.'

'It's hard to believe he's straight...'

'Well he certainly is hetero by preference. Lives on the floor above with his latest girlfriend. The longest lasting for ages, called Kath or Katke or something....his pattern is protestations of love forever, cheats, they fight, goes on to the next one. When I first met him he had two black eyes. Well deserved probably.'

'Who else is in the house?'

Another couple, a bit bland. Don't see much of them. They are really anonymous together, you'd think they were two halves of a single wit. Then when they're alone together it's as if Siamese twins were fighting each other for independence...'

'Really,' I yawned involuntarily.

'You'd better sleep here tonight,' he said. 'There's a sleeping bag over there.'

I crawled into it, my eyes closed.

'Good night,' he said.

'Goodnight' I mumbled. But my thought machine gently ticked away, going over the events of the day. Nice place...pray Mona likes it...great to see Pieter again...pity those bastards won't let go...funny thing, Fate...somehow so often things kind of come right in their way...

'Tom, are you all right? Need the loo?'

'I'm fine...no'

'You're making funny noises.'

'Really no, I'm fine...o.k....'

I couldn't have been more wrong.

Five

Room 121, Withers Stronglode Withers and Truelove London EC4

Armand Bennett shifted uneasily in Truelove's famous Visitor's chair. Or rather *on* Truelove's famous Visitor's Chair. The 'chair' was actually a large beanbag on the floor of the lawyer's office, upholstered in jolly pink and blue fabric. This was a concession to the hippie lifestyles of many of Truelove's clients.

Truelove himself sat in an Executive Lounger Mk IV behind a desk which looked as if it had been hacked out of a lump of plastic.

'You fucked up in South Africa....' Truelove said, leaning forward menacingly 'now I tell you, if you fuck up here you're back on the cheapest tramp steamer you can find all the way home, and I hope the rats get you!'

'I'm telling you Mr Sir,' Mr Bennett said, 'I know exactly what is what. The boy has moved!'

'All right, so he spent a night away from home, this is your evidence he has moved?'

'Well yes boss sir. See, this is his friend the bloke Pieter I told you about. He's asking the Tom to move out of town, to the suburbs...'

'And the wife is still going nuts with this maniac in Notting Hill! This does not make sense! Bennett you have cost my client a great deal so far and all you've done is fuck up. '

'But sir boss this is not my fault – I only report what I see – '

'Stop bloody arguing with me you idiot. Hie thee to Notting Hill! Sort it out!

Knock knock knock. 'Mona...! Nick...! Paul....! Anyone...! Let me in! I've forgotten my fucking key! MONA!'

I picked my way through the rubbish-strewn alley at the side of the house, entered through the back door. Deserted kitchen, unwashed dishes, grub and grime. A thick red wire carrying stolen electricity nearly tripped me up. A tap dripped stolen water; loudly.

Up the stairs to our room. 'Mona?'

Opened the door. A corpse grinned at me from the bed.

NO!

Blood everywhere.

MONAAAAAAAA!

No, it's not her. Shaking, get closer. Too ratlike, rat drowned in blood, gawping open throat, on our bed, neck ripped open,

A fly hovers

I ran

Blue uniforms everywhere. I can't stop shaking. A policewoman holds one of my hands. She is shaking too. A moustachioed face barks at me, 'When did you kill him, hippie? Why did you kill him? *Jealousy*, was it?' He sprays the word.

I wasn't here last night I want to explain. He won't listen. Flashbulbs bang, red and white. I cry into the policewoman.

The doctor straightens up from his examination. 'You can leave him alone,' he says to the policewoman. 'He didn't kill this hippie. It was suicide.'

WHAT???

He waves a six inch nail in the air. 'This is what killed him,' he says. 'He drove a nail into his chest. This hippie,' he points contemptuously at me 'probably slit his throat later. Jealousy I should think.'

'Well well,' Moustache says, re-entering the room, 'you are a *stupid* hippie aren't you? Such a lucky little stupid little hippie you are, aren't you...I'd just love to get you into the cells I would – '

'But how – '

The Moustache ignores me, goes to the doctor and they mutter together.

'How - ?' I turn to the policewoman.

'Hush now,' she croons, stroking my head as if soothing a child.

'How can someone hammer a nail into his own chest?'

'Ssh,' she says, 'don't you worry your little...'

'If he did it, where's the hammer? No, please answer me. And' I gulp, 'where's Mona?'

'Never mind dear,' she says. 'Your wifie will be here soon. She'll look after you. She's probably popped out to do the shopping.'

'This is a nightmare,'

'Have you got somewhere else to stay?' concerned. 'I nod. 'Well, off you go then. Leave your address with me. We'll send your wifie to you when she arrives.'

'But – ' unable to stop myself, 'don't you see? She did it! She must have! She has delusions you see. She thinks she's Boadicea and – '

'Run along, Mr Block. Leave the detective work to us.'

I pull away. 'It's *BLOCH*'. And I leave.

On the way out I caught sight of a letter lying on the mat. Thomas Bloch Esq. I read it on the train to Bromley.

Withers Stronglode Withers and Truelove
Solicitors and Commissioners for Oaths
5a London Wall London EC4

June 20 1969

Dear Sir

Re: Estate late Hazel Stone

As you will know, we are acting as the solicitors in this matter and I am acquainting you herewith the wishes of your deceased grandmother Mrs Hazel Stone regarding the conditions upon which you may inherit the Estate, including all monies, properties and appurtenances.

These are to include the Estate of the late Count Laszlo Mindchyck, of whom she was the sole beneficiary before her death. I believe something of the vast extent of this Estate has been explained to you. While she drew up her will before knowing of her inheritance from the late Count, legally the conditions still apply.

Her instructions to her lawyers in South Africa, of whom we are the sole UK representatives, are as follows:

'Should Thomas Bloch, my silly bugger of a step-grandson, prove himself to be a sane and responsible person a year after my death he is to inherit everything I have. It's not much but he likes old things. Which is why he liked me. If not, my property and possessions are to be sold and the proceeds donated to the Hendrik Verwoerd Memorial Fund.'

The responsibility of the decision as to whether you qualify has devolved upon us and in the absence of clear and distinct guidelines as to the meaning of 'sane and responsible' from the Testator, we have decided as follows:

1) You will be assessed by a panel of twelve carefully chosen people over the next nine months, hereafter to be referred to as 'Jurors'.
2) These persons shall observe you without making themselves known to you.
3) After the expiration of this term, a meeting shall be called at which each Juror shall submit his or her report, in the presence of yourself and under the chairmanship of this Firm.
4) You will be given the opportunity to defend yourself if necessary and to make representations on your own behalf.
5) The decision will then be taken by a democratic vote. The expenses incurred will be deducted ultimately from the Estate as we are acting as Executors in this instance.

With best wishes for a happy outcome

James

James Truelove BA LLB
UK Executor for the Estate of the late Hazel Stone

'Well?' Laszlo lit a cigar, drew deeply, coughed. 'Everything according to plan?'

'Indeed. The boy is nailed, the girl disposed of.'

'Good good,' Laszlo smiled like a sheikh in a harem.

'I must say sir it did seem a little drastic...'

'Drastic? Look young man. If you want to work for me you must realise that I know what I'm doing. She's no good to us as she is, agreed?'

'Yes.' Truelove mused. He was feeling smug indeed. Bennett had been worth the airfare. He liked this picture of himself as totally ruthless, able to casually carry out whatever actions were necessary to fulfil a client's needs. And getting Laszlo whatever he wanted would get him, Truelove, whatever *he* wanted. And the Aston Martin was now what he wanted...soon! It was as easy as that.

'I trust you have made arrangements for Phase Three?'

Truelove purred. 'All set up.' He settled his angular body a little more easily. He imagined the leather seat of the Aston massaging his butt.

'The boy has a lot to learn,' Laszlo said, absently stubbing the cigar out on the white tablecloth. 'And not much time to learn it. I have great hopes for him.'

'I'm not so sure –'

'Not sure?' The Count's eyes narrowed. 'Well I am. My darling wanted him tested so we'll test him. Then you'll see!'

A waiter dashed over with a jug of water, tipped it over the smouldering tablecloth and retired, cursing in Italian.

Six

Two days later and still no sign of Mona. Down at Bromley Pieter and I are going over everything for the thousand and fourth time. I'm sick of it all. And Pieter isn't helping.

'Just tell me how a six-inch nail in someone's chest could be suicide,' I said. 'It must have been her, Pieter, I'm telling you. Shit it's a nightmare...'

'I can't believe it of Mona,' he said. 'She's a little crazy, sure, but not *that* crazy.'

'Not that crazy? I wonder. You have no *idea* what happened to her on that ship. With that acid you gave us. She went completely schizo. Certifiable. You don't believe me? She thinks she's Boadicea or someone. She's got to be found! What if she does it again?'

We were sitting in the garden. It was late in the afternoon, still very hot. Pieter sat in a pair of boxer shorts. The fly gaped open just enough to be annoying. I sweated in a T-shirt and jeans. My arms were going pink. Glasses of half-drunk shandy posed precipitately on the uncut lawn. A tube of paper containing dried leaves and the resin of an exotic plant linked us.

'You blame me in a way don't you', Pieter said sadly.

'What, for giving us the acid? No, hell. Maybe it would have helped if I'd known how strong it was...but I survived fine! Her mind was wobbly. You weren't to know. Neither was I. Thing is, I still love her. I'm worried sick for her. I miss her!'

He took a sip of shandy. 'Did I tell you how I got those tabs?'

I sighed. 'I can guess. The Brigadier, right?'

'Right.'

'Your fucking boss. Knows how to bribe hippies. He's such a bastard.'

I loosened my shirt from my trousers, wondered whether it would be worth taking off for the last gasp of the sun.

'I hope when you're a millionaire you'll take out a contract on him,' Pieter said wistfully.

'You might as well forget that. There's no chance I'll get my hands on that money. Not after all the crazy things that have happened to me lately.'

'Hm.'

'What do you mean Hm?'

'It's just all a bribe, Tom. A way to destroy you. Put you in their camp. Make you just another moneygrubbing – '

'They'll never do that!' There was a kernel of annoyance at Pieter in me. I didn't really know why. Perhaps in a way I *did* blame him for the acid. *And* for supplying the cake at the wedding. *And* for not trusting me to resist the allure of the money with my principles intact. Besides! He had sold himself out to the Brigadier – in a way – hadn't he? 'You sound just like Mona when you say things like that. Plots. Us and Them. Urgh! I hate it!'

'Well perhaps there's some truth in it.'

'Jesus Pieter shut up. Who the hell can I talk to if I can't talk to you? Why do you say such bloody stupid things?'

'I'm sorry Tom,' he said handing me the joint. 'I just want you to be objective about things, that's all. You're going through a horrible time.'

'I'm *trying* to think objectively. But one can't reach the right conclusions without knowing all the facts. And we don't have them.'

'Umfaan used to say – '

'Stuff it Pieter, I'm not in the mood for any of that bullshit.'

'Umfaan used to say...'

I sighed, pulled my shirt off and lay back, trying not to listen as Pieter conjured up the ancient face of the black Sangoma, Umfaan, who both of us revered in our teenage years. Who claimed to have lived in the bodies of thousands,,,,

The Director

'There was a time,' Peter began, 'when Umfaan was a Boer farmer on the border between the Boers and the Fingo, you know, by the Great Fish River.'

'For fucksake Pieter – '

'For fucksake, you'll say, because the Border Wars were fought long before Umfaan was born. And how could Umfaan conceivably have inhabited the life of a white farmer? Well, Umfaan would say, that's a stupid question. Because Umfaan has always been alive – it's only the body that has changed.

'Anyway, when he was a Boer farmer back in the days of the Border Wars, he farmed three thousand acres of the very wildest part next to the River, and every few days he lost cattle to the Fingo from across the river. To them, cattle were wealth and they didn't see why the Whites should have so many cows.

'Well, one day they took forty head of the very best of the herd and you know there was nothing Umfaan could do but cross the River to punish them *severely*. So he went to his neighbours and borrowed men and arms and set off to his fate.

'There were thirty-seven of them, each armed with the most modern percussion rifles, and each mounted on a fearsome great horse. You may think this was a small force indeed to confront tens of thousands of Fingo and their friends the Xhosa but you must remember that all those poor Blacks were equipped with was prickly spears and shields of cowhide; they dressed in loincloths made of dead animals and covered themselves ritually in blood and dung when they went into battle. So the Boers were convinced that God was on their side, because obviously he wouldn't be seen *dead* in the company of a bunch of Blacks with no clothes sense.'

'You invented that part yourself,' I complained, wondering if Pieter hadn't invented all the other Umfaan stories he'd told me.

'Ok, I invented that part myself,' Pieter admitted with his Little Boy grin. 'Anyway, the Fingo were too smart to get into battle so they ambushed the dumb whites instead.'

'How'd that happen?' I asked, wanting a little detail.

'Whoosh woosh bang bang zip scream,' Pieter said.

I giggled. My doomful gloom had evaporated for a while. 'Go on,' I said.

'Well, when Umfaan woke up he was tied like a chicken in the hut of the Big Chief of the Fingo and through the doorway he can see the dead and riddled bodies of his former troop, doing their duty for Nature by feeding their bodies to the flies.

'"Shit!" Umfaan thought to himself, "Now I'm in for some serious torture and mishandling", but he was entirely wrong. Because the next person to enter the hut was a smooth, suave Black Man dressed in the height of London Fashion, which consisted of a swallow-tail coat in crushed maroon and top hat. He was smoking a large cigar. The sight of a Black Man in this getup threw Umfaan into fits of terror.

'"How do you do?" the man said, shaking hands with the outraged Boer. "Mr van der Merwe I believe?" I should have told you, van der Merwe was the name Umfaan was wearing in that particular life.

'"Who the hell are you - ? - and *what* the hell are you??" Umfaan asked, all in one breath.

'"I'm the Director," the Black Man said. "I'm the one who has to make sure everyone stays in his or her role. I mean, it would be all wrong if the Xhosas and the Fingos and the Zulus and so on would start to speak in Oxford accents and called each other 'old boy' now wouldn't it old boy?"

'"What the hell are you talking about?" asked Umfaan who was now beginning to believe he was, after all, dead and in hell.

'"And it would be equally wrong if you stupid Boers were to suddenly realise that it is *our* land you've stolen, and our occasional thefts of your cattle are merely an attempt to gain some sort of recompense? Wouldn't it? The world would turn upside-down, no?"

'"It's not *your* land! It's *our* land!"

'"See what I mean old boy?" the Director drawled. "You're saying all the right things, the things expected of you. And if I were to say that what we have here at the Great Fish River is the meeting point of two warring expanding people, you would possibly agree?"

"Possibly."

"Or try this one: there were Blacks on all the land you call yours centuries before you came over the seas with your guns. And if we had discovered gunpowder first, it would have been *us* invading *you*. You would be very confused if you believed that, wouldn't you? Especially if you were to go about saying it to all your friends!"

'"I would never say anything like that," Umfaan said.

'"Of course not. And you would never tell anyone that a black man could get as educated as any white, wear the same clothes as they wear in the most fashionable parts of London, or that – as is plainly the case here – he could be more intelligent than you?"

'"Aaaargh!" Umfaan screamed, because his van der Merwe brain had just given out, cracked open like the egg of an ostrich hit by a bullet.

'The end of the story is obvious. The Director took out his Colt 45 and shot van der Merwe dead, to put him out of his misery. See?'

'See what?' I asked in some frustration.

'Well, it's obvious. When Umfaan found himself disembodied, floating up there, he was presented with a choice of new bodies to inhabit. He *had* to choose that of the Black traveller through time and space we know so well – '

'I repeat. See what?'

Pieter sighed like a schoolmaster who has been trying his best to teach somebody with no brain. Then he stood up. 'I think I'll go and see if anybody is boiling the kettle,' he said.

I stared at the letter lying on the Notting Hill mat. I was there to pick up my things for my move to Bromley. The handwriting on the envelope was unmistakeable. It lay there like an amputated limb of my body. My own and yet not my own. My stomach gave a heave. I picked it up, refusing to open it. Shoved it into my bag. Sulked all the way in the train. Resisting the impulse.

Finally, when I was alone in my new room I wrenched it open, started to read, threw it aside. Then, breathing deeply, read again:

Dear Tom,

How exciting! Here I am on my own at last, and this is the first chance I've had to write to you. The first few days were rough, but I'm getting more together all the time. At last I have found my Mission, a point to my life, and I have found some people who go along with me.

I am SO sorry you are not here with me. I need your clear bright view of things (even though you are usually wrong!)

and your arm to lean on when the going is tough. But deep down I feel you are not one of Us. You still have doubts, even though we saw the Light together.

I will love you forever darling. I will love your misguided head and your well-guided prick.

But then you were always a prick, weren't you. That's my new name for you.

Kisses, Mona

Damn it! I thought. What the hell does she think she is doing? I stuffed the letter into a drawer and pulled some papers over it. I could smell her on it, not a perfume, rather the scent of her desperation, her fear and above all her mania. It was as if, even through the dull blue marks on the paper, her hand was reaching out and clawing at my throat.

I tore myself away and went for a walk. Let her go her own way, if that was what had to happen. I stamped my anger into the pavement as I walked. Nora was the only person I told about it eventually. I couldn't bear any more of Pieter's 'objectivity'.

Nora, in her role of Earth Mother, was everybody's confidante. A lapsed Catholic, she liked receiving confessions. For this reason we all trusted her. Telling her our secrets was like putting them into a sealed box.

In return she confessed we were her surrogate children because she couldn't have any. Grant's fault, she said. Low sperm count. Working for the BBC probably caused that. Ok, maybe not, but it certainly used and sapped him. His eyes always ringed with black from late hours and multiple arguments. His stoop, that of a much older man. His testiness. Not an easy man to have sex with, I would have thought.

In the days that followed I got to know my new adopted siblings rather well. I even got to like Brian. An only child orphaned at the age of fifteen (both of his parents were killed in a car crash) he had inherited twenty thousand pounds, a fortune in the sixties, which was to be held in trust for him until he was twenty-one. This nest egg didn't have a hope in hell of lying in a bank gathering interest, for Brian had discovered that on the strength of this inheritance he could borrow.

What fun.

He went on world-spanning holidays, consumed vast amounts of drugs and women, bought funny little businesses that failed almost as soon as money changed hands.

By the time he was twenty-one (which was when he met Nora and Grant) there was a hundred and twelve pounds left unpledged. So, realising that the money had run out, once his creditors were paid he got himself a job as a hairdresser's apprentice and learned the art of making ladies' hair do incredible things.

By the time I met him he was coming to terms with the fact that he was no longer a gentleman of independent means. Though extraordinarily generous, he was the sort who saw no reason not to have anything – or, to complete the cliché –anyone he wanted. He always got anything he wanted, even when his parents were alive. If not with money, with his incredibly long eyelashes and his facial beauty, which was astonishing, feminine, vulpine.

A more sober and critical analysis of his facial features would lead one to conclude that the ears were certainly too large, the lips too thin on a wide mouth, the eyes too far apart. Praxiteles would have made edits. Looked at as a whole person, he radiated confidence and sensuality. Blond, slim, boyish, pretty. (I think the main reason he seemed to like me so much was my refusal to be drawn into those big eyes...like so many pretty people burdened with too much intelligence, he respected most those unaffected by his physical charms)

His latest girlfriend Kathe was a tiny Luxemburger with great big brown eyes, intelligent, sensitive and much in love. We theorised that Brian had chosen her because however mad he was likely to make her, she was just too small to beat him up. She was the child of a diplomat, terribly well brought up, finishing school and all that. We were a little in awe of her, never could figure out why she had fallen for Brian.

The other couple were a symbiotic pair of lookalikes. He (Dick) was a thin hectic short being with scraggly hair already thinning at the age of twenty. She (Moira) was Welsh, bony and long, prone to interminable monologues the message of which was always defeatist. The couple used 'we' as practically their only personal pronoun when referring to themselves. The First Person Singular seemed to be in a language foreign to them.

They had loud prolonged fights most nights. After the ritual dinner *en famille,* Battle hour would commence. Dick and Moira would vanish upstairs and the confused sounds of ultimate warfare would rock the house. Everyone else pretended to ignore it, Grant occasionally giving a frustrated sigh between brush strokes; Nora slapping down the dishcloth and saying 'a family that *sups* together should wash *up*! Together'

Nobody ever mentioned Mona, asked about her, brought up the subject in any conversation – unless I did so in conclave with Nora. She would have been as out of place in their happy little commune as a Salvation Army trombonist would have been.

'You know what I think, love' Nora said one night when she and I were doing the dishes. It wasn't our turn. Just saying. 'I think you need to get a job.'

The idea startled me. I didn't need money much as Father had started sending me a small allowance. True, I was bored. I had even tried being depressed and didn't like it. I often missed Mona terribly and thought about her a great deal. In some kind of strange way, though, I suppose I was relieved she had disappeared. It took responsibility off my shoulders.

Or did it?

Pieter and I had made expeditions to the West End a few times to look for her amongst the derelicts at Charing Cross, as well as some of the hostels which looked after hippies and homeless. Once I thought I had glimpsed her. A dirty ragged thing with two carrier bags scurrying off into the shadows beneath a railway arch like a rodent. We pursued, she vanished.

What was I going to do with her if I found her? Tell the Police? I wasn't going to do that. They were the Enemy, the Fuzz. One didn't. Whatever she may have done. *Whatever*???? Murder??? A relief not to have to make that decision!

So when Nora said, that night, 'I think you need to get a job' it sounded like a pretty good idea. And I really don't know, so don't ask. In case you didn't, I'll do your voice: 'To what extent oh Thomas you semi-fictional hippie freak with your rat-taily hair and bit of facial, your red eyes and manic manner, consider that having a job would make you more likely to inherit the millions of the Laszlo creature?' If I try terribly hard to remember, I believe that in the depths of my ragged mind, that messy mess, I have to answer 'probably.'

I decided to consult Noel. Noel was an Englishman in his forties. Or fifties. Or thirties. Balding, slightly plump, who I had met in a club in Durban when he was in S.A on business. I tried to sell him a girl but soon realised he was far more interested in me. So instead I sold him some dexies and we became good friends for the brief period. After that we exchanged the odd letters (his were *very* odd) and when I had found myself in the UK I had telephoned him once or twice when I needed advice about basic English things. Like why the English weather was so shitty and more important, where to get decent dope. We always ended the conversations with 'we should get together some time.' 'Of course, give me a call when you're free' 'will do'.

So finally, unable to think of an excuse for not doing so, I went to see him in the terraced house in Battersea on a far-too cold day for the time of year.

'Tell me about your job,' I said, settling myself on a collapsed sofa in his *pot-pourried* lounge. His mother, a deaf old dear of eighty-five, half-snoozed in an armchair. A fire crackled in the hearth.

'Very boring darling. It pays the mortgage, that's all that matters.'

'That's not all that matters Noel,' I said. 'I have to have a job myself, now, you see. I need to – '

'Why do you need a job darling? Why don't you just sell your body? That's what I did when I was your age.'

I snuck a glance at Mother, who was snoring. 'I do not intend to sell my body,' I said.

'Why on earth not?' he asked, passing me a joint. 'You're fairly luscious you know.' He reached playfully for my crotch. '*I* wouldn't say no...'

'This is serious', I said, seriously moving his hand away. 'I need a job, let's say, for family reasons.'

'A hand job? No? So your father is nagging you is he? Still on an allowance?'

'No. Just tell me about your job.'

Noel sighed and stretched out on his side of the couch. Suddenly, Mother shrieked 'Cuppa tea!' and fell asleep again. Noel ignored her. 'Goodness, you are an impetuous youth. I am a little embarrassed about it you see. So no Shock Horror Revelations in those novels you're always writing please.'

'Promise,' I lied.

'Well I work for a company called, rather appropriately, Grabkin, as you know. The Company was founded around the end of the last war I suppose. It began as a supplier of furniture parts like knobs and locks and things. Hinges. Those ghastly bits of brass they put on cheap repro furniture. Well, exports went terribly well especially to

Africa and the Middle East and the customers there kept asking if we could source other things like metals and construction materials, that sort of thing. Eventually the directors decided in their holy wisdom that it should no longer refuse these requests and they set up a subsidiary to buy and sell stuff like that. We became an international Trading Company.

'Customers were delighted and in a few short years we were trading almost exclusively. Buying things we never got to see and selling them to customers we seldom met. All one needs for this kind of business is telephone, telex and typewriter. Then people spend lots of money and reap the rewards. Like that.'

'Sounds easy.'

'Not always. Nowadays we deal in absolutely everything. Sugar, tractors, frozen chickens, condoms. We're huge. Last year we were taken over by an international conglomerate, who just want us to go on doing what we're doing.'

'So how do you fit in?'

A loud snore from Mother.

'I'm a negotiator. I sit on the telephone, run up horrendous bills talking to people from Albania to Zanzibar. It's great fun. A fellow says get me steel wire. I phone a fellow and say can I have some steel wire please. Then we argue about the price. Then I make the sale. International Letters of Credit later, the company is richer than ever.'

'Interesting,' I said.

'Actually it is. But also boring darling.'

'So! How do I get in on this one?'

Noel smirked in mock amusement. '*You* darling? Good Lord, who would ever have thought the King of the Colonial Hippies would be having this conversation with me! Grabkin is at the vanguard of capitalism in the Third World. We're corrupting and screwing millions of innocent foreigners. How can you, with your immaculate social conscience, become involved in all that?'

'Well,' I said, 'it's just temporary. A year maybe. No more. Won't you see if you can do something for me?'

'We'll see,' Noel said and leaned across the room to gently nudge the old lady. 'Cuppa tea love?' he asked.

Brian's navy blue suit bit into my armpits. The trouser bottoms had been shortened by two inches and were secured by safety pins. The shirt – Grant's – shone whitely and gave off puffs of sweat-smell, mixed with cloying deodorant. Only the tie was mine. An orange and blue thing, four inches wide, which I had bought months ago as a joke.

Miss Parkinson the Personnel Officer stared at me through glasses designed to hide her squint. Her print dress had wide white lapels which framed a bony neck. She looked very like Katherine Hepburn playing a nineteenth-century schoolmistress.

'You're Bloch,' she stated.

'Yes marm' I said. I had decided to treat her like a schoolmistress.

'From your cv,' she said, reading from a piece of paper typed by Grant at my dictation, 'you seem particularly inappropriate to work here.'

'Don't be fooled by that, marm,' I said. 'I'm keen as a mouse turd, sharp as rat's teeth, bright as a bosom!'

She *had* to smile at that.

She didn't.

'You're a South African,' she said, as if that concluded the discussion. 'Have you considered the small matter of the Work Permit? I presume you have a Right to Remain? Or are you here on a 3 month permit? What is your status?'

I had no idea. They stamped my passport when I entered the country three months ago. That was all I knew. I hadn't looked at it since then. 'I don't know,' I said.

She gave a delightful exasperated sigh. It could have been a 'tut'. I was warming to her little mouth. The sensible glasses. The 'I live at home with mother and a cat' smell about her. 'Work Permits are difficult to get these days. Unless you're a nurse, a chambermaid...or an au pair.'

'Um, obviously not,' I said. 'Wrong sex.'

'Don't be sexist please Mr Bloch' she said, swallowing with distaste. Which made a lovely little movement in her throat. Which made the adam's apple wobble. Which made me think, haven't I read somewhere girls don't have adam's apples? Or is that a sexist thought? 'If we were to decide you were worth applying for a Work Permit for, we would have to prove that you, an Alien' she said the word the way some Afrikaners say the word 'native', 'can do a job no British person can do.'

'Oh dear,' I said.

'Can you do something no British person can do?' she asked.

'Anything,' I said.

'Thank you Mr Bloch,' she said. 'We'll let you know.' She stood, a certain sign the interview was over. Extended a hand for a wet fish shake. I stared at it. Yes, I thought, a man's hand.

On the way to the tube there was a *pop!* from beneath each armpit as the stitching in my borrowed jacket gave way.

'No good,' I said to Pieter when I got home. 'It's all something to do with Work Permits. I can't prove that no British person could do the job.'

'What are you going to do?'

'I could become a nurse or a chambermaid apparently. So if I change sex I'll be fine. And that woman who interviewed me, she'd changed sex I reckon!....'

'How do you know that?'

'Hairy hands... Adam's apple.'

'Sexy!'

'And if I have no job I get no millions.'

'Tut tut frankly. You'll just be one of us humans. Having to struggle through life. So sad...'

'Did you realise that you and I are officially Aliens?'

'What?'

'Aliens, apparently if we're not British we're assumed to be from another planet.'

'You mean they've found out our secret?'

Haha.

We went out into the night. I had to shake off the cloying feeling that destiny was enfolding me in its suffocating embrace. The sense that whatever I actually wanted to do with my life (getting stoned listening to music laughing with friends having sex) (and nothing much else)Some Thing or Some One was doing their best to make that impossible. Was I looking for a job because I wanted Laszlo's millions? So that I could spend the rest of my life doing the brackets above? Did I want the hassle?...the way things were looking, the only way I would ever get the millions would be to go back to South Africa...never! Never!

Right now all I wanted was a really good FUCK.

And I met this girl at this club, see.

We were in the Underground, smoking a joint in a corner. Watching psychedelic green blue and purple bubbles blooping and popping and growing and flipping about. Discussing the morality of riches. Then she came over, hand out to share the joint.

She was everything Mona wasn't. Blonde, slim, birdlike. Her eyes were a frightening green. Her tits were high and tight. I looked into those eyes and knew that the itch between my thighs was about to be scratched.

So we did the statutory giggling, chatting, cuddling, dancing routine and she invited me back to her flat. Fine, I said, and waved Pieter a fond good bye.

Her bedsit was on the top floor of a house in Clapham. The room was a cavern of silky hangings in rich reds and greens, tassels, beads.

Incense. Candles, with their legacy of stalagmites and stalactites of melted wax. The bed on the floor. A dressmaker's dummy stood in a corner wearing a tie-dyed T-shirt and a broad-brimmed hat. When I entered the room and glimpsed her lusciously female figure I started in fright.

Maria laughed. 'Meet Emma,' she said, then, to the dummy, 'Emma, meet Tom. Emma's my friend! I have to dress her up!'

'Why?' I asked.

'Studying Fashion at St Martin's' she said. 'She tries all my creations on. Tells me if they are any good.'

'Nothing you design would not be beautiful,' I said. 'As for you, you would look even better in nothing. Come here.'

I reached under the stretchy velour of her blouse and my hand met a firm breast. I cupped it and stroked it round and around till I reached the nipple. I pinched it gently, then sent my other hand into the blouse so that her other breast would not feel left out.

Her hand cupped my crotch. I exploded out of my trousers. Clothes littered the air. We rolled in the glorious softness of the bed reaching for all parts of each other.

Our hands get to know every part of each other.

Every part gets to know every part.

This is not just because I haven't had sex for so long.

This is something else...

Seven

Morning. I staggered back to Bromley via tube from Clapham South and train from Charing Cross. The journey passed in a stupor of muggy happiness. I stared at the going-to-work fools in their pinstripes or dowdy dresses and pitied them. Inferior mortals! Who have not tasted the joys of freedom and the bliss of last night...

Still euphoric, I let myself in.

On the floor a blue airletter. *Tom Bloch. Airmail/Lugpos.* Bugger. Parents.

Dear Tom,

I am sorry you saw fit to run out on me in London. I hope that you have had time to reflect and that you and Mona will shortly be on a plane. I assure you there is very little chance of your being declared sane and responsible while you and your wife continue in your present lifestyle. If you return we can sort everything out together. I can probably offer you a job with my firm, in a junior capacity at first, but it would give you at least the appearance of respectability.

The Laszlo millions, I am sure you realise, are not to be sneered at. Mannie Goldberg, my solicitor (you know him, his daughter was the one I wanted you to marry) tells me the Estate is worth around fifty million pounds in property, stocks, bonds and Impressionist paintings and all that. I therefore beg you to take all this very seriously indeed. I hate to think what you are likely to do with such wealth and I am always ready to help with my experience and expertise. I would remind you that I have twenty years experience in business and Mannie also will be there to give you sound advice. Your mother and I are ready willing and able to devote ourselves to the equitable handling of all this wealth should you be lucky enough or clever enough to merit the inheritance.

I am happy to send you air tickets straight away, you just have to call.

Your Father

Darling,

I hope you are well and happy. We are missing you so much, especially at Yomtov. Please come home.

Love, Mom.

Never! Never! Never! I tore the letter in half.

Then I tore it into quarters. Then eighths. Then it wouldn't tear any more.

I went into the kitchen. Nora was eating a bowl of muesli at the table. I ignored her, dropped the letter down the sink and turned on the grinder. On less for the Things Pending drawer.

Mash, mash.

'What on earth's the matter?' she asked.

'My father thinks I'm an idiot. He's sent me a job application! For him!'

'What on earth are you talking about?'

'I'll bloody show him who's the idiot...'

She smiled indulgently, humouring me. 'So what happened about the job you applied for?'

'Nothing doing,' I said, plonking myself on a chair and pouring muesli into a bowl. 'Work permits and things.'

'Listen dear,' she said, leaning over to me and putting an unwelcome arm around my shoulders. 'If you set your heart on something you'll do it. I'm sure you will.'

I wasn't so sure. I spent three days trying to be depressed. Ignoring everyone. Snapping at people if they tried to be nice. Living on brown rice, chickpeas and a quarter of an ounce of Moroccan. Which made depression rather hard to maintain.

On Friday I phoned Maria.

'Hello.'

'Hello.'

'Who is it?'

'Tom.'

'Tom. Tom! Why didn't you phone before? I thought our night together was...special! You know?'

I tried arch. 'You could have phoned me...?'

Offended. 'I'm not sure I want to talk to you.'

Oops. 'Yes you do. Meet me at the Disaster in Earl's Court. Two hours.'

I rang off quickly, so she couldn't say no. Risky. Shut myself in my room. Rolled a joint. Read a chapter of Charles Fort about rains of frogs, blood, lightning, stones. Felt like I'd been under them all. Fort knew there was something hysterically weird about the world but never quite got it. Nowadays of course, this matter has been cleared up.

Two hours later I was sitting in front of what looked like a picture of my mind: a slice of meat on a bed of limp lettuce in a sea of bloody ketchup. Maria came in, looked around, didn't see me. As she turned to leave I shouted her name.

'Don't shout,' she said, coming over and sitting red-cheeked opposite. She's one of those people who get embarrassed. I almost never feel this particular emotion.

'It's good to see you,' I said, clasping a hand with both mine. She was pleased to see me too. 'What will you eat?'

'Nothing thanks,' she pulled her hand away. 'Well? How are you? Why didn't you call before?'

'I did,' I lied. 'No reply.'

'Well,' she said, 'I'm honoured.' She smiled reluctantly. This wasn't going well. I had to change the script.

'I need to talk to you. It's really confidential. It's really special. It's really awful.'

'Really?' I had her now...so I told her all about the Inheritance. Everything. The only thing I didn't say a word about was Mona. She wasn't ready for that yet and neither was I.

'Gosh' she said when I had finished. I felt a wave of frustration. Was that all? Here I was baring my soul, or at least some of it and all I got was 'Gosh'. Maybe she's not as smart as I thought. Or foreign....I just so wanted her to like me. Well, to fuck me anyway.

'Do you think I'm sane and responsible?'

'Hm...' she said. 'I hardly know you. I do know you have a lovely bum.'

Aha. We're on a wavelength. Or something. 'Please Maria,' I said, 'this is important to me. I think.'

'Do you want to be?'

'What?'

'Responsible. Sane. Rich.'

'I don't know. I mean, I hate the idea of strangers judging me. Who has the right? At the same time...I doubt if I have a hope in hell to be honest.'

'You do want it, don't you.' She smiled blandly, reached across the table. A perfect tit just missed the ketchup. Pity.

'I do and I don't. Hell I'm sorry. I'm getting obsessive.'

'There's a cure for that,' she said.

At last, synchronicity.

That was a lovely weekend, it really was. The whole time with Maria, mostly in her bedsit apart from a few food buying expeditions. And then came Monday, and she had to go to work. And I had to go back to the cursed real world...

At least the looming shadow of Mona seemed to be receding. At the very thought I felt guilty. It was so easy pretending there was no Mona. But just not for long. Suddenly I felt a rush of pity of sadness of love. Mona where are you? Do the police know? Care? Who knows? If only I could get to her, get her treated, cared for, fixed...but...

And as if she had heard me calling to her, Mona telephoned. The phone was ringing as I let myself into the house.

'Hello lover.'

'What? Shit! Mona! I was just – where are you?'

'Safe dearest, very safe. But I can't use this phone for long. Hey, what do you think about Nick?'' Her voice was squeezed, thin.

'What do you mean what do I think?'

Horrible.

My heart bumped with fear.

'Nailed, eh? Nailed at last! Nailed to the mast! Crucified! It's what he wanted you know. Shut up you. And you! They'll get another one soon!'

'What? Who?'

'The ones that killed him! They're after us all! They won't get me, though. They knew we were on to them you see. Oh Tom, I hope you're safe! Hide out my love, hide out!'

'Listen Mona, please listen! You've flipped. You need help. Tell me where you are I'll come and fetch you. Tell me. Where are you?'

'Don't tell me. Please don't tell me. They've got to you haven't they? You're bought, aren't you. They've bought you with their yellow money. Oh, I was so wrong about you! You're a drip!'

'Mona please...'

'I've got to go now. They're stalking me. They don't like it if I use the phone. I just sneaked out, you see. Bye ex lover! I still love you!'

Click! Went the phone.

I ran out of the house, up London Road. I didn't stop until I got to the Police Station. 'You've got to help me,' I said to the policeman at the desk.

'Oh yes?' he said, omitting the word Sir. Evidently in my creased clothes my unwashed, beardy state I didn't merit politeness.

'It's my wife. She's missing, had a breakdown you see. She's already attacked somebody. She'll attack again, I know!'

'Women...' he said shaking his head theatrically. 'Tell me about it. My wife's the same...'

'No, you don't understand for fucksake, it's much more serious than that! She's really mad, seriously cracked! Hears voices! Don't you get it! Is nailing people!'

'I think you had better come with me,' he said and led me to a room inside the station. 'Now strip!' he said.

'What?'

'Whatever you're on, if you have any on your person we'll find it and I'll be happy to arrest you for it. And for wasting our time. So strip!'

Thank goodness I had nothing on me. And when finally I staggered out of there as full of righteous anger as a raped nun, I knew one thing for certain. From now on, I was alone. I could expect help from no-one. No-one could understand. .....

And what's more, *I* couldn't understand...how did she get my number....?

Eight

In multi-occupancy dwellings (or what were, in those days, referred to as 'hippy communes', to which stereotypical neo-socialist collective our household had a resemblance. In that we were mostly stoned all the time anyway) there are usually two people who have taken on themselves the huge burden of always answering the phone. In the case of the Bromley house the official martyr was Grant, and his acolyte was me. The unspoken rule was that of Grant hadn't grabbed it within twelve tring trings (and he was, after all, out all day – but that didn't alter the rule) it was down to me. Nora was always 'too tired' and her job was to sigh to anyone within hearing, 'darling who can that be? Get it for me?' As for the others, they were simply too stoned. Or screwing. Or arguing.

But when the next morning after my unfortunate experience with the local fuzz the tring trings began, I ignored it. Twelve trings. Thirteen. It's her again I know it is. Fourteen. Fifteen. Teeth set I snarled into the mouthpiece. 'Hello!'

'Mr Bloch?' a female voice asked.

'Grr.'

'Is that Mr Bloch?' Mona putting on a different voice?

'Wuff woff' I said.

'Pardon? This line's not very good. I can't hear you.'

Not Mona. Deep relief. 'Wuff,' I said. 'Also, growl.'

'Good heavens,' she said. I could hear the grin. 'Can I speak to your Master?'

Shit! I knew who it was! I made some clicking noises with the dial and started again. 'Hello?'

'Hello,' Miss Parkinson replied. 'Who on earth was that?'

'Probably a crossed line. Or a dog. Something like that.'

'Quite amazing,' she said. 'I wish my little Axel would answer my phone. He's a Schnauzer.'

'Oh.' I said, wondering what kind of weapon that is. 'This is Mr Bloch. How can I help you?' I asked in business-like tones.

'This is Miss Parkinson Mr Bloch. We met last week. We would like you to come and see us. Mr Boles the Chairman would like to meet you.'

'Does he? Heavens. I mean, of course! When?'

'Tomorrow at noon. Looking forward to seeing you then. Goodbye.' She didn't wait for my goodbye. Just click and there I was in mid air. Trying not to shout with joy.

Well, how ABOUT that! What to do now? In twenty-four hours absolutely everything could change for me. Forever. Ha! Cream always rises to the top! I must prepare. How? I know, phone Noel. He'll know.

'She phoned!' I announced.

'Oh noooo darling!'

'Not *her*, though she did. No, I mean Miss Parkinson-'

'Who?'

'Your personnel woman. I'm to see your chairman tomorrow.'

'Boles?' he whispered. 'Tomorrow?' as if terrified of being overheard.

'Noel, you sound like a parrot. Yes tomorrow. What shall I do?'

'Look, where are you? At home? Stay put and I'll phone you in a couple of minutes'. Ding plunk.

What why? I put the phone down and tangled up the chord.

One minute. Two minutes. Tringtring. Bleebleebleeblee. Ching.

'Ha Tom. Now listen, don't speak. I haven't much change. About Boles. I can't talk in the office, you understand. I swear the place is bugged. I'm in the cafe across the road. Tom? Are you listening?'

'You said not to speak.'

'Don't speak. Listen! Subject: Igor Boles. Self made. Jewish or something. No-one knows for sure. Bombastic nouveau-riche type. Pretty screwy.'

'Screwy?'

'You'll see what I mean. There are rules with Boles. Here they are. One: Never look him in the eye. He'll think you're challenging him. Two: never contradict him. Under any circumstances. He can fly right off the handle. Three: Agree with all his opinions, whatever they may be. Then expand them. Run with them, if you see what I mean.'

'What if – '

'Darling, you're interrupting...' blee blee blee ching. 'Shit! – One more thing – '

'Yes.'

'Get a new suit would you? Oh, and a haircut for heaven's sake.'

'But – '

'Not but, there's a love. Just do it. Clear? And – '

'And???'

'Just box clever. Toodleoo.' And he cleared, with pennies to spare.

That night Brian cut my hair and it was terrible. I mean the experience, not the haircut. In those days cutting your hair, if you were a bloke, was like being castrated. Surrender. Sellout. To top it off, I let him shave off my beard. The pain!

The family babbled around sympathetically – they felt my pain.

'You'll need a briefcase,' Grant said, and shot up to the attic where he remained for the next hour, sounding as if he was being attacked by an army of dwarves.

Nora pressed twenty pounds into my hand. 'Tomorrow,' she said, 'you go and buy yourself a nice new suit. You can pay me back when you get paid.'

'Heck. Thanks!'

'You can use my blue shirt', Dick said brightly, flourishing a colourful blue rag printed with yellow flowers. The collar had spaniel ears.

'I can't wear that!' I protested, laughing.

'Of course he can't wear that', Nora grinned. 'I'm sure Grant has something plain. White maybe.'

'I've got a lovely white silk blouse,' Kathe chirped primly. 'Mutti gave it me.' And she went to get it.

Brian patted my new hair proprietorially. 'You do have a little problem you know,' he said.

'What?'

'Look.' He said. Holding a hand mirror behind my head so I could see the back of my neck in the glass in front of me.

'What the hell have you done?' I asked.

'Not me, you!' he said. 'You fell asleep in the sun yesterday. See that ring around your neck and face?'

He moved the hand mirror about.

'Jeez!' I panicked. 'Why didn't I leave it long!? She saw me with long hair – '

Moira pounced to the rescue. 'Makeup!' she said. 'Stage makeup. I have some!' and she dashed off to get her Leichner five and nine.

'You'll have to take your earring out you know.' Nora said sternly.

'Nora,' I moaned, 'I've just had a *haircut.* Isn't that enough?'

'Don't argue with me darling. You MUST make sure to take it out before you leave the house tomorrow.'

Pieter strode into the room and came to a dead halt. '*Here Jesus!*' he said. 'Who the blerry hell is *that*? Have we opened a moffie beauty parlour or what?'

'It's not funny Pieter,'I said, 'That woman from Noel's place phoned. I have to meet the boss. They could offer me a job.'

'Bleddy hell, they got you now *pellie*.' Pieter said and he wasn't joking. 'By the bollocks.' And he strode out.

'Don't worry about him,' Nora said, holding me down in the chair to prevent my following him.

Kathe returned with her white blouse. 'I forgot about this.' She said, pointing to a flourish of ruffles cascading down the front. 'I can cut it off ' and the brave girl proceeded to attack her mother's heartfelt gift with scissors.

Dick sprawled on the couch, meanwhile, manufacturing joints with conveyor-belt efficiency. 'You're going to look *so* sweet,' he giggled.

'What the hell is this?' Grant said, returning covered in dust from his expedition to the attic. In one hand he carries a briefcase which looked as if it was made of ancient papyrus. In the other he held a sheaf of letters. He waved them at Nora. He was furious.

'Oh my goodness!' Nora moaned. 'Those are private!'

Grant threw the briefcase at me and he and Nora stomped off to their bedroom to have a battle which continued most of the night.

'Oh dear,' Brian said.

'Oh dear dear dear dear dear dear dear' Dick giggled and threw a burning joint across the room. Several of us made a dive for it to save the carpet. Heads banged. Dick roared with laughter.

'Look!' Kathe said, waving the remains of the silk blouse, 'I did it!'

Moira bustled in with her makeup box. 'Now,' she said, 'I am going to make you *really* pretty!'

'Nooooooo' I protested but they jumped on me and held me down. My shirt was ripped off and the silk rag forced on. Streaks of blue and black were smeared all over my face. My earring was painfully removed. And when they had finished I was made to stand in front of the mirror by my raucous stoned family and confront the bizarre parody of the businessman I was to become.

The next day, replete in navy blue suit and white shirt fresh from Burton's Oxford Street (£29) and a pair of Grant's Hush Puppies, I stood before a plate-glass mirror and inventoried my appearance. At the sight of the whole Bloch, the Bloch face fell and the Bloch heart sank.

The day was already hot. The process of wiping sweat from my face had smeared Mona's careful makeup about my face, and the collar of my new shirt was stained with Leichner. Hell.

Half an hour to go! I decide to fix what I can, item by item. Hair: It'll do. Face: streaked but judicious application of handkerchief sorts that out. Shirt: collar stained as explained. But ok if I hold my face *so.* Tie: ok once straightened and the frayed narrow end tucked in the shirt. Trousers: fine at the waist but the bottoms folded up (they're an inch too long). They may stay up. Keep checking. Shoes....shit. I can't wear *brown* shoes with *blue* suit!

I slip into the next door shoe shop, realise I have no money left, wait until the staff are otherwise engaged, pop some black shoe dye into a pocket and find a bench in Golden Square where I apply the black over the tan.

Ok, chaps. That's me ready!

I was half an hour late. Well, I got confused, having taken an insurance piss in the gents at Piccadilly Circus, I exited from the wrong exit and went down the wrong road. Then the next wrong road. Then the next, and ended up right near Trafalgar Square which is blocks away. I was still a little stoned, sorry.

I was shown into a vast office on the top floor of the mock Georgian building. The carpet was deep. I felt as if my feet were sinking into a swamp as I as I trudged to the little group of four low armchairs which clustered around a rosewood coffee-table. 'Wait there', Miss Parkinson whispered, and closed the door behind her with a genteel click.

I sat as softly as I could, so as not to disturb the intimacy of the atmosphere, and looked about me. Everything was in shades of the subtlest variants of beige. Evil-looking African tribal masks glowering from hessianed walls threatened disturbers of the beigeness with a voodoo death. A cavalcade of elephants carved from a single massive tusk leapt up politely from the beige carpet. A trail of black outlines of the soles of my shoes recorded my journey from the door. Intimately.

'Hrrum.'

?

'Stay there,' a splintered voice crackled from the other end of the room. Behind a massive rosewood desk a tiny figure crouched over a desk pad writing furiously. 'I won't be long.'

I stayed. The only sound was the scratching of his pen. Time was squeezing through a bottleneck.

Finally he stood, and was not much taller than he had been sitting. He tottered towards me. 'Well well,' he cackled. 'Well well.'

I stood, extended a sweating hand. He shook it. His hand was all flaky skin. Bits stuck to my palm.

'So you're Tom Bloch.' He said, looking me up and down and nodding very, very slowly. 'Well well,' he cackled again.

He was about five foot two. Older than very old. His head was inadequately covered with a black wig which was worn rakishly, like a skewed beret. From a wrinkled face tiny brown eyes sparkled at me. I held his gaze for a second, then remembered Noel's instructions. I looked away. 'Sit boy,' he commanded.

I sat.

His eyes swung down to the footprints on his carpet. Then back to me. Then down to the carpet. Then to my shoes, the trouser-bottoms now dangling down, smeared with black. Then back to the carpet.

Then he said 'It's about time for a new carpet!!!!' and he let out a great shriek of laughter. The bizarre sound was too much for me, and the last traces of the last joint had their say and I joined him, both lost in laughter.

Eventually he sat at the coffee-table opposite me. 'Shut up.' He said.

I shut up.

'So you want to work for me do you? Hm! Well well.'

'Yes sir,' I said, trying not to look at the carpet.

'Shut up. So why do you want to work for me?'

'Answer!'

'You said shut up.'

I had gone too far – a stab of annoyance across his face. 'You will learn this boy, a time to stay silent. And a time to speak. Why do you want to work for me? Drink!'

'What?'

'Yes, what. Do you want to drink. Speak.' As if I was an idiot. Or a foreigner.

'Um...coffee?' I answered, hoping I had it right.

His hand crept to a button on the table. A bell rang raucously outside the door and his secretary sprang instantly into the room. 'Monica!' he shouted, as if she was deaf, 'Two teas!' and she left, backwards. 'An idiot my boy,' he said smiling. 'I bought her from the Sheikh of Bahrain. Cheap.'

I nodded.

'Joke!!!' he shouted. 'Laugh!!!'

I laughed.

'Why?' He snapped.

'What?'

'Don't waste my time boy. I'm a busy man. Everybody wants to work for me. I'm a wonderful employer. Do you know why?' He sat back in his chair and twiddled his thumbs. I waited, breath held. He stared into the distance. I waited some more.

'Why?' I ventured to ask.

'I knew you could talk!' He beamed triumphantly. 'Because,' he leaned forward confidentially, whispering nose-to nose, 'because they're all *skivers* boy. That's why.'

'Uh – skivers?'

'I'm a soft touch you see. That's what they think. As soon as I am out of the office they all down pens and chat away. Always chatting. And going to the toilet. Where they chat more. Mostly about me, of course. Complaining. Always whining mining and complining. They have cups of tea. Hundreds of cups of tea. Over a thousand pounds a year of cups of bloody tea!'

'Tea?' The door swept open and a shaking Monica entered with a tray upon which a cup of tea had spilt about a third of its contents. 'My God girl,' Boles said, despairing, 'I said *two* teas!'

'Oh,' she said, 'oh dear!' and shot out with her tray leaving a fine liquid tea spray in her wake.

'You see?' he said in answer to the unspoken question, as if everything had now been demonstrated and proven beyond question. 'How they take advantage of me. All the time.' He stared at his entwining thumbs and at the flakes of skin fluttering to the floor. 'Look at my hands my boy,' he said, holding them out for my inspection. 'See how they're flaking, falling apart?'

I nodded.

'That's *their* fault! Every weekend I have to come into the warehouse and pack the dangerous chemicals for the customers in Iran so they'll be ready for the Monday. Do any of them offer to come in? No! And it gives me dermatitis. Everything gives me dermatitis.'

'That's terrible,' I sympathised.

'Yes it is. It's terrible.' He pointed accusingly at me. 'So why? Why do YOU want to work for me?'

By now I had come up with a possible answer and I decided to try it out. 'Well sir,' I said, 'I really want to make my contribution to the export drive. I feel that with my experience...'

'Bullshit bullshit and bullshit!' he sputtered. A piece of sputter landed on my chin. I didn't dare wipe it off. This chap was madder than a Hindu in an abbatoir.

He stared at his hands which had resumed their twiddling. 'My woman, whatsname,' he said quietly, 'tells me you don't have a Work Permit. Is this true?'

'Yes sir,' I said.

'And your friend Noel tells me you would consider me daft enough to pull precious strings at the Home Office for you.'

'Uh – uh – no, I mean – '

'Quiet, boy,' he said, thinking. Flakes of skin dandruffed gently to the carpet where they beigely blended in tastefully to the decor. 'I suppose you speak Afrikaans?' he asked finally.

'Um. Yes.'

'I may be able to claim that you are indispensible to our South African trade. With sanctions always an issue the government needs the business...did you think of that when you decided to work for me?'

'Um – '

'No, I supposed not. Unless you're clever. Are you clever?'

'Um – '

'Hmm,' he said. 'Well, answer the question!'

I took a risk. 'Yes,' I said.

'We'll see.'

'Thank you.' I said.

'Thank you. Get out. Scuttle away,' he said and I scuttled away.

Outside his door his secretary skulked, still sniffling. As I closed the door she looked up. 'Tea?' she asked, forcing a smile.

'Oh – '

'You mustn't let him get to you,' she said reassuringly.

'He didn't.' I lifted a dripping cup from the tea-swimming tray and downed the lukewarm sticky reassuring liquid. Duty.

'Quite right,' she said, her face regaining its fading prettiness.

Her telephone tinkled and she snatched it to her ear, nodding at it several times before replacing it gently, as if it was a baby chick.

'I'm to offer you two thousand five hundred pounds a year and a car, starting Monday.'

'Gosh!' I sputtered, shakily replacing the empty cup.

'I'll see you Monday', she said. Then, as an afterthought, with what can only be described as a seductive wink, 'If I'm still here'

'Gosh,' I said again.

Noel sashayed into the room. 'Congratulations,' he beamed, extending a hand. 'Well you are a clever little sod aren't you? Welcome to my mad world!'

4

One

BOSS's operations in London at this time were run by Piet Schoemann, First Secretary at the South African Embassy. His secretary Charlotte Hamilton was responsible for the agents themselves. The network was split into cells. Each cell was led by a Controller who was responsible for his or her own cohort of spies. Amongst these were journalists, politicians, writers, professional people, street sweepers, postal workers, toilet attendants, tramps. I think that's everybody...oh yes, and a Nursery School teacher in Shipston on Stour. Their job was to infiltrate and disrupt Anti-Apartheid organisations and individuals. And sometimes, recommend 'Communists' for termination.

Amongst the scams BOSS was involved in at this time were: A plan to free Nelson Mandela from Robben Island so that he could be shot trying to escape; a four million pound forgery plot; the infiltration of the Stop the Tour organisation led by Peter Hain so that Hain could later be framed, discredited and destroyed as an 'enemy of the state'. All this in addition to their standard run of burglaries, phone tappings, buggings of the offices of the Anti-Apartheid Movement, the ANC, SACP, Amnesty International and anyone else who displayed the slightest abhorrence of racism or refused to buy Outspan oranges.

Armand Bennett stared suspiciously at the filthy tramp lounging casually outside the marble and chrome entrance of Grabkin Inc. It's strange, he thought, whenever I'm on Obbo there's millions of tramps about. Is this what they man by the Elephant Syndrome - ? when someone mentions elephants and that's all you see all day? What are they all doing here anyway? They look as bored as me. Jeez, Bloch's been in there for a while. I must have been mad to volunteer for this. I reckon I'll pick up my pay at the end of the month and buzz off to Joeys. Blow it all on *skokiaan* and *dagga*. And women.

And here's a funny thing: the tramp Bennett was staring at so suspiciously was thinking exactly the same thoughts. Word-for word.

'So you've sold out', she said.

'I have NOT sold out Maria.' I faked a laugh to show I hadn't been hurt.

Her voice squeezed playfully through the receiver. 'I knew you would!'

'Look *darling*,' I italicised the word, 'it's all part of the Plan, right? The Grand Design. In a few years' time the whole of big business, even government, will be in the hands of ex hippies?'

'Don't be silly,' she said. 'You're just rationalising. Finding excuses. Most of the hippies will be dead from overdoses before they're old enough to get their hands on anything.'

'Rubbish,' I aid. No-one was going to spoil the glow of triumph I was nurturing. I fought to hold my rising irritation down. The telephone was slippy in my sweaty hand. 'You sound just like Pieter,' I said.

'Who's Pieter?'

'My oldest friend. He won't speak to me.'

'Don't worry darling. I'll speak to you! Though speaking isn't what I want you for tonight…'

'Mmmmmmmmm….'

I got home by five and had to fight off an army of excited family. 'I knew you'd do it,' said Nora, forcing an embrace on me.

'We did it,' Brian said, ruffling my hair proprietorially.

'We're gonna be rich!' Dick chanted, and the others joined in, dancing around me. Pieter was, unsurprisingly, nowhere to be seen.

'Hold on hold on', I said, extracting myself from the suffocation of Nora's embrace, 'I've got to do something!' Something even more important than washing the black dye off my feet.

...so I went into the lounge and made a collect call to Johannesburg. 'Mother?'

'Tom! Where are you! How are you! How's Mona? What's *happening* with you darling? Why haven't you called for ages?'

'Fine thank you. Listen, Mother. I've got a job.'

'Oh. A job. Oh. That's.......good...does this mean you're not coming back? Hold on, I'll get your father!'

'No, please don't get him. Just tell him my news. Tell him I'm paddling my own canoe from now on. All right?'

'So when are you coming home...?'.

'I'm not coming home Mother. Give everyone my love.'

'But dear – '

'Goodbye Mother.'

Then I went upstairs to bath and change. I dugout an ancient pair of sports trousers, found a smart short-sleeved shirt. I ironed everything like a young executive about to go on a date. Yes, that's what I was! The commune may well laugh! I didn't care. I had already resolved that Priority One would be to find my own flat.

During all this there was no sign of Pieter. I was glad about that. He would have lurked like an Ogre of Conscience.

Maria! More important! A celebration screw.

I hotfooted it out of the house. Leapt onto the train. Leapt off again at Charing Cross. My boots flew. I leapt onto the tube. Off again. Upgoing escalators couldn't keep up with me.

Never touching the ground, my fleet flew me up her road, past all those lovely Georgian mansions with their crumbling gentriness. They need me...they need me to paint! Their Doric and Corinthian and Ionian columns purple, yellow stripes and spots to shout hello! With Chagall frescoes on their white white outside walls. I will save them, I will throw out the blue-rinsed faded ones who live in them, put the colonels and generals with their racist memories of fuzzy wuzzies out to pasture where the cattle can eat them as a superb source of fibre, install raving visionaries with real dreams between the curlicues and extravagances of the faded baroque…

Ring ring ring!

Patter of slippered feet tripping down the stairs, opening the door. There she is! In a silky night thing. 'Darling!' Bunch of blooms purchased at the station between our breasts.

'Darling!' she said, extracting herself from flower-crushing embrace. 'What happened to your beard? Your hair – '

'Shut up,' I said, dragging her into the little flat and shutting the door.

She sucked at me with kisses. 'You look *so* much better!'

'Candlelight dinner?' I gabbled between her lips

'Not yet lover,' she said, pulling away. 'Tell me first how things went! Coffee?'

'Not now,' I said. 'Later.' Growff.

'Yes now,' she giggled. 'I insist!'

I gave in, despite my ponderous erection and followed her into the kitchen.

'Can't it wait?' I asked again, making a grab for her waist.

'Hold on,' she said, shaking herself free.' Mind the kettle' and slipped out. 'Bathroom.'

She was gone a fair while. I counted all the spices, rejected most as a means of getting high. Stared about the room.

Everything has a place. The kitchen is fairly bare, extremely clean. Compared to Bromley anyway! Pots and pans, I thought, opening a cupboard, all look brand new.

The fridge contained a pint of milk, a croissant, a couple of frozen dinners.

I yawned. Come on, woman!

Eyes strayed over the tiles. Followed plugholes by wire to their tame gadgets. All these labour savers looked brand new too.

One double-adaptor had an inexplicable plug the cord to which vanished into the lounge.

I decided to play bloodhound. I put my nose to the wire and sniffing loudly, with the odd doggy whine interspersed, followed.

'Sniff sniff!'

Maria's voice came from the bowels of the flat. 'Tom, what are you doing?'

'Me bloodhound. Woof woof. Sniff sniff.' I said.

'Don't be silly,' she said, a little alarmed. 'Go and see to the coffee!'

'Sh!' I emerged into the living-room. Followed the bulge the wire made in the carpet. Sniff. Sniff.

She came out of the bathroom. 'Tom? What on earth are you doing?'

The wire emerged from the carpet. Slid behind the floor-length velour curtains in the bay window. The relentless bloodhound pursued.

'Tom! Stop that!'

The Hunt was becoming serious now. Why did she want me to stop?

'Tom, come on, stop this!' Her hand on my shoulder.

'Sniff! Sniff sniff sniff sniff sniff!'

Her hand tightened on my shoulder. She scurried to keep up with me. She didn't want me to solve the mystery. That made me want to solve it more. Towards the bedroom…

'Tom! Let's go to bed!'

'Wuff. Wuff.'

I got to the bedroom. Both her hands were on my shoulders. Almost riding me. Her soft rump on my back.

I tumbled over and we thrashed about like fish in a net. Rolled into the curtain.

A savage Crash! Sparks exploded with variety of hissings, buzzings and crackings. I jumped up in a panic, pulled the smoking curtain aside and there! Hundreds of pounds of camera and recording equipment going *sput sput* on the floor.

'Oh no! No!' Maria screamed, leaped up, held her hands in front of her face as if trying to blot out the sight, or trying to avert a blow…

Oh well, I thought, if that's what I'm supposed to do – and I slapped her hard on a briefly exposed cheek.

She reeled back screaming.

As I left, the smouldering curtain burst into flame.

Laszlo laughed. 'So much for your covert observation techniques! I *like* this boy!'

'Oh yes oh yes very likeable,' Truelove muttered.

'Come come Truelove. You can't tell me that you aren't – how shall we say? – rooting for the boy?'

'Perhaps,' the lawyer smiled reluctantly. 'But it's what he does next that's important, now I've lost one of our best people…'. His fingers went automatically to the silver ankh at his chest.

Two

It has started then! Bastards! Dogging me! Shits! And Maria is one of them! Thank God I didn't fall in love with her! I think. Did I?

I stared both ways down the street. No-one but an old tramp. I shouldn't have hit her!! But she was actually about to film us making love….what the hell is my lovemaking to do with them? Did they expect to see me demonstrating insanity – in BED? How? By assuming unconventional positions? Anal sex? Urgh!

'Hey man, you got a light?'

'Fuck off.'

I should have let them have their dirty movie. To think I was actually getting serious about that bitch! Dammit, got to get SO stoned I forget who I am and why….!

'Watch where you're going young man!'

'Fuck off.'

Where AM I going? Noel. Yup. Noel. I snatched a cab. I can trust Noel.

'Darling!' he mock shrieked. 'What a surprise! What brings you to my spider's lair?' He had been preparing himself for a night out. A towel was wrapped around wet hair. He wore a short towelling dressing gown with a monogrammed N in Script Italic.

'I need to talk. And get stoned.'

'Come in darling. My, my! Don't tell me you're yielding to my charms at last.'

'Shut up you twit,' I said, following him in. 'I just need to talk to someone sane.'

'Well you're in the wrong place for *that!* Say hello to Mother.'

'Hello,' I said. Mother lay in a heap on the sofa. The television winked at her from the corner.

'Hello pretty boy,' she said, smiling. She looked almost aware tonight. 'Who are you?'

'This is little Tom,' Noel said. 'You've met him at least twelve times dear. Honestly!'

'Well mind you don't make too much banging upstairs,' she said.

'Don't be disgusting Mother!' Noel was genuinely embarrassed.

'He thinks I'm disgusting,' she winked. 'What's there left for an old woman except taking joy in the sex of others? All I got left is me porn…'

Noel pulled me upstairs to his bedroom. 'Talk to me while I get ready,' he said as he dried his hair.

'Where are you going tonight?' I asked.

'Well, it IS Friday night dear.'

'And?'

'You can come with me if you like.' He reached for a hairdryer.

'A club, of course!'

'One of your gay clubs.'

'We'll pick somewhere a little mixed, just for you. Where's your whatshername?'

'Maria? Fuck her!'

'No thanks. I thought she was he love of your life?'

'She was,' I said, and told him the story of the evening.

Noel clucked. 'Well you just can't trust anyone these days, can you' He reached for much-bedecked jeans and a blue-red-purple-yellow t-shirt and put them on slowly and ostentatiously, hoping I was looking his way. I looked at his bookshelf. Burroughs. Ginsberg. Kafka. Kerouac. Shakespeare (Collected and Illustrated). An incense burner. Records.

'That's true. Can I trust you?'

He giggled. Dabbed himself from a bottle of Patchouli oil. 'That's your affair. Make a joint.' He pointed to a green onyx box.

'I mean it. Can I?'

He smiled. 'With your life,' he said. 'Well? Are you coming?'

'OK.'

Walking through Earl's Court in groovy gear borrowed from Noel's extensive collection of groovy gear.

Swinging through this ghetto of cool. Gays labelled St Laurent or Levi. Australians hunting sheilas to dip their Antipodean wicks into or, failing that, and they usually did, booze to dive into. Starving students hollow-eyed seeking drugs, or, failing that, food. A gaggle of wide-eyed South African Afrikaner chicks hunting the legendary Black Cock.

Memories of when Mona and I first came to London. Staying in an hotel called the Strathridge, till the Landlord threw us out. We hadn't had the courage to do much exploration then. Too dangerous. And Mona shrank in crowds, Boy, it felt so good to be free of any tie to anyone, worry-free, conscience free…

To the Masquerade, deep in its cellar. Filled with teeth n' eyes, teeth n' eyes, lit by sharp flickers of disco ball light in every colour of the spectrum, gyrating, shouting at each-other, crowds of gawpers, brawlers, drunks, lunatics, stoned visionaries of all the sexes, each there to find something. Anything. Preferably something NEW.

Yes there were women, I was pleased to note. Some would be dikes of course, but there was also a sprinkling of happy fag hags, hanging on to their Gay Best Friends for life.

The sweet waft of freedom! No-one, no one knows me here. No jurors or spies or lovers or people I have to make happy.

Noel vanished quickly into the gloom. He may have asked me if I wanted a drink. What I wanted, however, was to disappear. I felt so light, mischievous, happy! Decided to explore. Made my way around the whole complex of rooms, feeling very detached from everything. I bought a pint and perched myself on the edge of a beer-strewn table. I was waiting for somebody to try to chat me up.

'Hello,' my first customer was a thin creature with thinning hair and a thin-lipped smile. 'Do I know you? Have I seen you here before?'

I adopted a Spanish accent. 'I am, how you say, touristical.'

'Well, how nice,' he said. 'Can I buy you a drink?'

'I have dreenk' I said.

'So you have. So tell me, how do you find our country?'

'Turn left at Calais?'

'No, I mean,' he is taking me very seriously – 'are you a student?'

'A Stupid? Why you call me a stupid?'

'No, I mean, are you here to study?'

'Stoddy?'

He's losing patience. 'Look. What do you do?'

'Ees my business!' I hiss, threateningly.

'I don't mean in bed. I mean – '

'You say you don't like me gringo?'

At this point he slowly, carefully, deliberately emptied his pint over my head. Then he shrugged and disappeared into the crowd.

Behind me, a gale of laughter. I turned wetly. 'Oh God you deserved that! That was SO beautiful!'

....not as beautiful as the girl sitting at the table. Black haired, blue eyed, high cheekbones, the lot. She wore huge gold earrings and a light blue lace blouse with tight pink satin slacks. 'Here,' she said, and handing me a flowery cotton scarf helped me wipe away beer from face and front.

That was how I met Julia. We just – hard to describe – you know the way magnets call to each other across a room? And the nearer they get to each other, how the attraction becomes more and more.... and there we were. Only a foot apart.

Her beauty was radiant and feminine – yet boyish. Her laughter so quick and liquid. Her intelligence, sharp! Her body...slim, shaped...I was in love from the moment her scarf touched my face and her breath, like a puff of air from a passing swallow's wing, touched my cheek.

'That was a lousy accent,' she said, laughing as she mopped my face.

'I know,' I said. 'I guess you're right. I deserved that....better go and rinse some of this off', I said, and pushed my way to the loo where all the cocaine was happening, as well as a bit of casual sex in a closed cubicle.

I was quick!

And she was still there when I got back!

'Do you want to dance?'

We danced plenty. 'Are you *sure* you're gay?' she asked as I clasped a great wadge of bum during a slow number.

'Of course I am,' I said, 'and only you can save me!'

'Well that's good,' she said, 'Well I'm gay too! And only *you* can save *me*!'

Ok, so there was something masculine about her. Her body was strong, muscular, lithe. She smoked small cigars But I didn't believe her that night.

We spent hours wrapped around each other, and not only physically.

We plumbed each other's lives (not easy when disco music throbs and bumps and grinds all over the place. The trick is to cup a hand over an ear and point it at the speakers. Who has to put a hand over the appropriate ear. You'll get the hang of it. Sorry, forgot you have.) Another damn American – for some reason they head at me – and did something very clever in the financial world. A proper business-woman. She was on secondment to the British branch of an American banking house for a year. She had been in London two weeks. This was the first time she had been in a British Nightclub.

I claimed to be a 'Negotiator' for Grabkin Industries. 'What section?', she asked. I had to admit that I hadn't started working there yet.

'Well,' she said, 'you'll have to let me help you'

'How?'

'I have plenty of very useful contacts,' she winked. Meanwhile as we leaned close to each other across the table, her feet played with my feet. 'I've got a bottle in my car,' she said.

Outside, momentum flagged. Both unsure. Did we both want to do this? If so, what did we want to do?

Hell yes. Second thoughts: I damn sure knew JUST what I wanted to do...!

Her car was a lambent blue Triumph GT6, gleaming with care, proud with pedigree. Inside was full of maps and dogends and trash, most of it friendly. We sat in the car and talked and talked and drank half a bottle of Blue Nun. Waiting for a clue as to what to do next.

Finally I asked the question. 'Where do you live?'

She sighed. 'Chelsea,' she answered.

'I live in Bromley. It's miles away.'

'Oh,' she giggled. 'I guess the onus is on me then. I invite you home!'

'Onus?' I laughed. 'Well, if that's what you want to do that's what I want too!'

'Ok,' she said. 'I've got something there you'll like...'

The car gave a growl and a roar.

She lived in a gaunt Victorian house in quaint Cheyne Row, a few yards from the Embankment and the Albert Bridge. The flat was on the top floor, a typical Company let. Sparse furniture but all of it good quality. Some antiques. Deep cream carpets. The smell of polish.

We were still playing out the fantasy that both of us were gay. So when we entered the flat neither wanted to make a move. Awkward. The flat felt so empty, so much like a model or photograph, hard to disturb. Company sofa. Company curtains. Company nest of tables.

She went over to the company record player and suddenly Led Zeppelin shattered the corporate air.

'Right!' She said decisively, 'first I'm going to make some coffee. Ten you can have one of these.' She held out a handful of big white pills. 'Then,' she smiled, 'I'm going to convert you...'

While she made the coffee I did a quick recce. No cameras behind drapes. No microphones. I sat back on the couch and checked the spines of the books. *Dhammapadda.* Tolkien. Moorcock. Perfect Cooking. She came in with a tray. 'Brought those from home to impress the guests.'

'I'm impressed,' I said.

She sat next to me, placed the tray on the coffee table. The pills reappeared. 'These are well impregnated,' she said, breaking one in half.

'Not wanting to seem ungrateful,' I said, 'but with what?'

'Acid, good stuff. This was the best way to get them through customs. Drops on antacids.'

'Oh,' I said.

Gulp.

She rolled a thin American style joint with pure grass. Music filled the room, crept into all the corners. Pink Floyd. A relief after Zeppelin. Smoke trickled heavily down the walls, steamed in ripples along the floor.

(If you know what an acid trip is like skip the next part. Also if you don't want to know. You've read he last description for Chrissake. If you'd like to join in, read on.)

Julia kissing me, this tastes so good

A night full of jewels, we hand in hand through the heart of an emerald

Which solidifies into a stone within which we merge and find ourselves integrated into the Machine itself which

ROARS

Then….

Silence.

(I find it so hard to write that trip. It was so fucking amazing…hey I bet you guessed *which* Floyd! I think she just kept putting the same record back on about twelve times. I'm not even sure exactly what happened. Hell, I have no idea what happened. It was….so…fucking….amazing….)

I woke to a light in the room amidst a rubble of cushions and clothes, an upset ashtray. Julia naked beside me, her sweet face so strong in sleep.

Sensing my gaze, she gradually awoke. 'Jesus,' she said, looking around the room, 'What a mess!'

'You think that's a mess!' I said, pointing to my head, 'you should see what it's like in *here*!'

She laughed. 'That's Vonnegut you thief!'

'Sorry.' I grabbed at her.

Suddenly serious, she drew away. 'Don't fall in love with me Tom,' she said very softly.

'Why not?'

'I wasn't kidding when I told you I was gay.'

'Rubbish,' I said. 'You're as gay as I am.'

'I gathered *you* were straight!' She stood, pulled on a dressing gown and began to make a token attempt at clearing up.

'I don't believe you,' I said. 'I mean we did have sex last night didn't we?'

'Sure.'

'It was good, right?'

'It was drugged. You're nearly cute. It was…good, ok?'

'But didn't we – I mean – '

'Get dressed Tom. Go.'

I dressed slowly and a little sadly. 'Will I see you again?' I asked as she washed cups.

'I don't know.'

When she wasn't looking I wrote down the number from the dial of the telephone.

'I've done all I can boss,' Armand Bennett said from his seat on the cushion of Truelove's office floor. 'Now you know what? I want to go home.'

'Back to South Africa? How nice.' Truelove sneered.

He stared down at the pudgy little man in the tramp outfit with derision. 'The trouble with you lot is you don't appreciate a good client.'

'Oh it's nothing to do with you, boss. It's just – this job never really suited me. I mean everything I do seems to go wrong. And anyway, yu don't need me now. The rest is up to you. Just pay me and I'll bugger off.'

Truelove sighed. He remembered one of Swami Jenkins' favourite sayings, 'Nirvana is only for those without time on their hands' and wondered what it meant, though he was quite sure in some way it was appropriate to this case.

'Besides,' Bennett interrupted his musings, 'whenever I'm on obbo I could swear there's some filthy tramp obboing *me*! It's bloody unsettling, I can tell you. So boss, I've had enough.'

'Obboing you? Is that so? Do I detect a trace of paranoia?'

'No honest! I've been n this business a long time. I know when I'm being followed.'

'I see,' Truelove said, his mind wandering back to the weekend retreat…'first you must go blind,' the Swami had said, 'then you will truly see!' He wandered whether any of the more fervent acolytes would plunge red hot pokers into their eyes and shuddered.

Three

I used to think that for me having a job would be like an elephant having a go at a high wire act. But I was wrong. I discovered to my surprise that many of the people who have jobs are people. Some, anyway. You know, creatures with thoughts and dreams and emotions and aspirations beyond the damn place they work. Some are quite spiritual. Few are actually corporate capitalist greedy robots. Those are just the bosses.

Marge, switchboard and reception: a fifty year old who looked forty, only because her face never stopped moving so no-one ever had a chance to count the wrinkles. A powerful barge of a woman, always laughing, madly curious about everybody she came across. I never learned anything about her life: cold flat with a cat or grannie of a big brood? No idea!

Monica, Boles' secretary became a friend too. Naturally a timid creature, she had worked for the man for twelve years. Her timid image belied her steel spine. She made a confidant of me and told me at length about her Derek, who took up all her free time with mountain climbing, water-skiing and nightlong parties. 'We never seem to have the time or energy for sex,' she moaned, and used that as her excuse for the subject of sex being an apparent obsession.

June was my assistant. She can't be called a secretary because she did so much more for and with me than a secretary could have done. In fact she could easily have done my job, and she resented me at first.

So I seduced her mentally, using my little boy persona until, unwillingly at first, she began to be protective and she came to me. She clucked and fussed and sorted out all my terrible mistakes, even taking responsibility for one or two.

By the end of the first month I actually started to enjoy the game. And the games within the Game. The hierarchy of arse-lickin' and arse kickin' forms the basic rules; then comes the fun of the Appearing to look Busy while actually phoning all my buddies in South Africa game; the Having an Important Meeting in the West End while actually sunbathing in Finsbury Park game; the Taking a Dump in the Executive loo in order to stink out the place while actually getting the Guardian crossword done game ; the dining in the Executive Dining Room with Brian who was pretending to be a client from Martinique game; all of which was made even more fun by discussing all the wheezes with the lovely Heather tea-lady in the kitchen whose delight was always worth mining.

Did I do any 'useful' work? Well I did, or rather, June did. At 9 every morning she would come purposefully into my cupboard of an office – just big enough for the rather smart desk which had been Boles' first (I found it in a store-room and immediately glommed it for myself). I realised that initially the main part of my job was to gather lists of potential clients and write to them, or telephone them, offering our services. As traders we would find out what commodities international customers wanted, source the stuff, and sell it at a profit. So once I found a client I would find a supplier. Bingo. We seldom handled the goods at all.

I soon discovered that the DTI (Department of Trade and Industry at the Government) sent out regular bulletins of international tenders, of companies or countries seeking stuff to buy, and companies or countries with stuff to sell. They didn't seem to have any reservations about who we dealt with – neither sanctions nor any remotely ethical considerations had any relevance to them. If I had doubts, I'd telephone the person at, say, the Uganda desk and after a brief conversation, would have not only the help of the British Consul in that country, but every necessary instruction as to how to trade with them. The interesting one was Rhodesia – trading with Ian Smith's self-declared racist 'Republic' was undertaken by the simple process of 'triangulation' – which involved selling to a third country, say Iraq, or more often South Africa, who would then sell on to the beleaguered regime.

I did try to expand trade in many countries apart from South Africa, in my defence. Trade directories were terrific places to advertise and to trawl through for customers and suppliers all over the world. As was Crones Directory, which would barrage us with Update Cards which had to be inserted into the ring binder that bulged with uninserted updates. Bloke in Malta looking for tarmac. Syrian Harbours Authority wanting cranes. Cheap copper scrap available in Portugal. Saudi Prince seeks timber. Nigerian Timber Industries offering Sapele Mahogany. Bingo, marriage proposed, money made!

So June and I would set her work for the day, which would include mailing hundreds of letters to lists we had unearthed; sending offers by letter or telex; phoning the world to chase up supplies or orders.

By say 10, or 11, she'd be gone. Busy busy.

And I'd be alone. In my tiny cupboard of an office. With a telephone. Hence the phoning of all my buddies in South Africa. The 'meetings' or 'visiting the DTI Library' (which I did a couple of times. A vast basement at 1 Victoria Street FULL of paper documenting the world.), the sunbathing, the hours spent in the kitchen or on the loo, the fun….

Strangely enough, all my – uh - hard work, as well as June's – resulted in thousands of pounds of business.

Hence, as well, this book. I was bored. And decided to document it all.

The atmosphere in Bromley was soured by Pieter's attitude to me. I couldn't work it out. At first I thought he avoided me, or snapped at me when he couldn't avoid me, because he thought that I had sold out. But it was deeper than that.

Finally late one night I heard him going down to the kitchen and after a moment's thought, followed him there.

'Pieter,' I said, trying to control my anxiety and irritation, 'you and I had better talk'

'I don't want to talk,' Pieter said, pouring boiled water onto camomile tea.

'If we don't talk I will go crazy. I'm really sick of all the snide remarks, those little asides you make to other people. We used to be friends. Tell me what is upsetting you!'

He sighed, turned around to face me. 'I just can't stand your hypocrisy, that's all. All right? Now let me go to bed'

Anger grabbed me. 'But I tried to explain to you. I'm the same person I always was! It's just – I'm getting an opportunity offered to me on a plate, see – '

'Don't bother. I know exactly what you're going to say – '

'Please don't interrupt. I've got a chance to get right in where the action is, where the crowd who run the money machine hide out. They're letting me in the gate – '

'Oh yes, and you think of yourself as a Fifth Columnist, do you, working to destroy them from the inside?' he said, with a huh! 'You'll never do it! You're becoming just like them. Look at you! Company car, three piece suit. I can't believe this is the same Tom who stood arm in arm with me, facing the pigs!'

'And what about you? I snapped, 'you joined the secret police! BOSS, for fucksake! So you could be a Fifth Columnist?'

'That was survival! You can survive without being a total hypocrite – all you want is money!'

'I think you're jealous. You're riddled with fury because you think 'll be – '

He retreated up the stairs. 'You're an arsehole Tom. When will you find out which hole is for speaking and which hole is for shit!'

I followed, too angry for any sense. I had to make him *see.* I really believed I had some sort of Gran Design. That if I had lots of money I could buy and undermine the establishment I professed to hate. 'Pieter, listen to me - !'

'Go away! Go and make a contract! Go sell arms to Rhodesia!'

'I need you to understand – '

He straddled the stairs like the Rhodian Colossus. 'You have no idea what you're doing!' he howled and doors opened all over the house. Then his anger went out of control and his booted foot flew out. At least I swear that's what happened because all I knew was big pain in the face and me, spurting blood, falling back down the stairs. Pieter disappeared into his room and locked the door.

I staggered into the kitchen where I bathed my face in cold water. There were tears with the blood in the sink.

Nora came in, nightogowned, put her arm around me. 'Here let me – ' I shook her off.

'Sit down Tom,' she said. 'Come on. Let me mop you up. Let's talk.'

'I don't want to talk,' I said, and meant it.

'No Tom, you have to talk.' She steered me to the table, sat me down and patiently dabbed my face with a tea-towel. I wished she'd go away.

'I've exhausted all the words Nora. I don't know what you want me to say.'

She put the tea towel down and reached for my hand. The anger welled up again, but mixed with guilt.

'You know why you are so frightened Tom? You're scared he may just be right?'

I pulled my hand away. 'Rubbish!' I said, resenting the intrusion. She didn't understand either.

'No, think about it! I understand you, really I do. You're split in two at the moment. The old Tom and the new. Admit I'm right.'

Was she right? There was only one Tom. Is there still only one Tom? Perhaps. 'Yes.' I sat again. She clasped both my hands. Four sweaty hands.

'Pieter is the best friend of the old Tom. You resent him because he won't accept the new. You want and need his approval. But he won't give it. And the reason?'

'What?'

'You haven't got your *own* approval yet.'

I nodded dumbly. Not sure whether I was humouring her or she was right. 'But Nora, I feel the same as I ever did. I'm just me. I'm the same person I was a year ago – '

'You're both going to have to understand that. He's your greatest friend. The friend of the real Tom, the person underneath, behind, above all the rest. To him this aspect of you represents the part of himself that he fears. The need for – I don't know, certainty, security, what he can't have.'

I sort of grasped that. Also, thinking to myself – does Nora know about Pieter and BOSS? How he has to be two people?

I understand it so much better now.

'You two will have to be separated for a while, and soon, or you'll murder each other.'

'Do you think so?'

'Absolutely Tom.' She stared into my eyes and again I resented her naivety. And her insight. Sometimes I hate the truth.

So I realised that it would be me who would be cast out. Baby birdie thrown from the nest. This household was too small for me now. 'We love you Tom,' she assured me. I wanted not to believe her. I wanted to think that she didn't understand, she didn't really like me, was throwing me out onto the street...not fair! *He* hit *me*.

But I knew she was telling the truth. She did love me. I had to go.

Luckily, when all that happened, all this had already happened:

Julia.

I was determined to make her love me. Like most stupid male chauvinists, I considered her declared lesbiansm to be a reflection of a rebellious nature, or the result of an early bad experience with a man. AAAaaargh. I know now how wrong I was. But a lot of semen flowed over the sheets before I realised how wrong I was.

Well, she had after all admitted that she had enjoyed sex with me. After all, *she* seduced *me*, believing I was gay. Maybe it was the idea of two gays of opposite genders doing sex under the influence of hallucinogenics was ok, I don't know.

I had telephoned her the Wednesday evening of my first week of work. 'Tom! – ' she said, 'I knew I wouldn't get rid of you so easily.' Despite the words, she seemed pleased to hear my voice. 'How's your first week as a cog in the machine?'

'It's o.k. Hell, I'm a bit nervous some of the time but it's also fun….' I drew some witty sketches of my colleagues. She laughed, so I knew I could ask her 'When can I see you?'

'Tom – I uh – I mean I wasn't joking when I said – '

'Yes I know.'

'I was just lonely. You seemed fun. I – '

'I know.'

'Stop saying I know.'

'Sorry. Look, I'm not looking for sex – if you don't want to. I really like you as a person.' That was true. Well, the second part was.

'All right. What are you doing Friday?'

'Nothing yet.'

'Let's go to movies. Is that all right?'

We went to movies. I decided on a comedy, to defuse any tension. M*A*S*H. American, peripherally political, cynically revolutionary. What I wanted her to think of me. Without the asterisks.

While people laughed I got hotter and hotter, started to sweat. Not just because of the heat on screen either. My wet hands wanted so much to stray over her legs. When she leaned against me in a pally way, which said share this hilarious moment with me, and I wanted her body to say, share this body with me.

I accompanied her home on the tube. We had two joints. Tension was rising. Every now and then I felt an electric shock in my loins. My penis wanted to play. I tried really hard to tell it not to try really hard.

'Well,' I said suddenly, I'll be going then,' hoping she would protest. But she just gave me an expressionless look and painful though it was, I left.

On Sunday, I 'happened to be passing' and range her bell. She was alone, sorting out clothes. I was bright, witty, and we were like two close friends who had shared the same woman and were avoiding the subject of which she really fancied.

I stayed two hours and went home.

I had to make her trust me.

The next couple of weeks were sprinkled with telephone calls between us. We went to the cinema twice and a restaurant once. I had borrowed some money from the bank on the strength of my job. I used the loan for new suits, shirts and shoes. I even bought a sock or two. Oh, and underwear. But when Julia and I went out together, I let her pay half.

We grew very close. Closer. Not quite close enough for me of course. She haunted my solo erotic world. I drew pictures of her clothed, nude. When we walked arm-in arm down the Mall I pitied passers-by who, seeing us so close, would imagine us to be a perfect couple – and I enjoyed their envy.

The day after my terrible row with Pieter I telephoned her. 'Julia, I'm in trouble. You've got to help me'

'Of course! What's happened?'

I told her. She clucked. But she didn't extend the invitation I wanted. So I hadto suggest it. 'Julia, how's your spare bedroom? Just for a short while…'

'Tom, I really don't think it's a terribly good idea.'

'Why? I'll be a perfect tenant, I promise.'

'It's not just that – '

'Julia, I'm in trouble. Please. I can't bear the thought of going back there. I just can't face him. I promise it won't be for long. I'll leave as soon as I can afford my own place. Honest.'

'Ok.' She melted with a sigh. Then she said the phrase that sums up the bourgeois American attitude to life. It ignored the fact that I had a Company Car, that Bromley is miles away from Chelsea, that money is of any importance. 'Grab a cab,' she said.

I laughed.

Four

So I began my new life.

We lived together first like strangers, fearful of walking on eggshells, then, after a couple of weeks, like brother and sister. Knowing each other very deeply, tolerant of each-other's habits, impatient of foibles but ultimately forgiving. The transition was so swift it was almost seamless. Something to do with trust, I suppose. First she had to realise I wasn't going to tiptoe into her bedroom at night. Then I had to realise that it was her right to use the bathroom first in the morning, and when I used it, to drop the toilet cover and wipe up even the teensiest drips on the floor. I knew she really appreciated my cleaning efforts – I very quickly learned how to use Jif, the 'Hoover', a duster… so she just took a deep breath one day, I guess, and began to quite like my presence.

The difference was that I was soppy with love and had to hide it. It hurt! Her smells drove me mad. Pieter had said to me once, you can tell you're in love when her shit smells like roses. Everything she did smelled like roses. Yet – for a reason I can't quite work out – now I was living with her, sex and seduction seemed even less likely than before.

I kept my secrets from her. I didn't tell her about Laszlo's millions. I knew the story wouldn't impress her or make me seem more of a worthy person. Probably the opposite. I wanted her to think I had got myself a job because I was reforming my own character, not because I was being bought. And I told her very little about Mona. I didn't want her pity – or contempt.

It had to happen. One night she announced her intention of going 'out'.

'OK, where are we going?'

'Not *we*. I said *I* am going out.'

'Uh huh. Where are you going?'

'Tom, I can't live celibate for ever.'

'I have the solution to that - !' I pretended to joke.

'No you don't.'

'Oh. So you're going to one of *those* clubs – '

'Apparently, there's only one. Called Gateways. I'm going to take my bath now.'

While she splashed and thrashed about I brooded.

The process of her getting herself ready for the girls upset me more than I could hide. Yet when she emerged all scrubbed and shiny I forced myself to chat and joke, but obviously a bit too much because eventually she said, 'Tom, just stop being jealous. You're the lodger, right? You're also my friend!' She grinned and pinched my cheek so playfully it hurt.

'Right!' I laughed.

'So behave. Why don't you go out somewhere?'

'Uh I don't think so. I think I'll just watch some TV'.

'Well,' she said, pulling on a bunny jacket, have a good time!' She gave me a sisterly peck on the cheek and was gone.

The door clicked closed. 'You too,' I said to the empty hall.

I watched TV until the little dot was absorbed by infinity. Must not! Wait up for her! Must NOT be awake when she comes in! ooooh shit, what if she doesn't come back alone - ?

Haveanotherjoint. I was befuddled with dope. Saturation point beyond which no more stonedness was possible. Bored and wide awake, I went to her room and searched it until I found the great white bottle of pills. I ate one. A whole one.

Then I locked myself into the bedroom with the record player, the dope box, and a book of Impressionist paintings.

I've had *pints* of acid in my life. On pills, in liquid, powder, blotting paper. And that night was the first time I ever had a Bad Trip. None of my coping strategies worked – Water splashes, jumping up and down, even the *breathing* trick was futile.

It was BAD. It was so bad. Because of Mona probably. Well yes, because of Mona. She was there with me in the room as real as she could be. Firstly, just as a whisper, a suggestion, a scent of her, something that fed off me, grew bigger and bigger, inhabited me, shared my body so much, I became convinced she had died and had waited until I was open, and then, came in.

And was right there talking to me, her sweet voice chiding me for my neglect, nagging me for my forgiveness, accusing me of having *betrayed* her...*Tom Tom* she said *thirst of my life my brother my lover come to me Tom I love you so much I want to become you I need your life I will suck your life I want you here with me I will take you in my arms and suck your blood my lover my other my betrayer my victim See my hammer see my nails…I will crucify you, alongside me on the hanging tree I love you I love you let me penetrate you as you penetrated me my lover my other I have the hammer I have the nails I want to kill you now as you killed me become me give me your blood Tom Tom six inches of nail six inches of pleasure I will have my way with you we are the winners of the world Tom we are together now with these six inches of pain O come to me Tom let me* <u>*fuck*</u> *you…*

For hours…...

During this nightmare it seems I smashed the door open. I don't remember doing it. Nor being sick all over the kitchen. I must have sprung leaks everywhere, for there was vomit, piss, sperm, blood.

Julia came home next morning. Saturday. And took me to hospital where they stitched cuts on my arms. I cried a lot and begged forgiveness. At first she was so angry. Then when I told her I had a whole pill she understood, teeth gritted, forgave.

I swore I would never take acid again and I meant it.

We tidied up together when we got home. I was feeling terribly sick but I had to remove every trace of the night. Of her. Of Mona. She did this. I knew then she was dead. Only the dead can get such revenge.

Tidying took all day. Julia was grim, silent with revulsion at the mess. Me silent with guilt and sickness. Finally things looked almost normal. We even fixed my bedroom door. I went out and got us a couple of pizzas. We sat at opposite ends of the Georgian dining table eating the stuff. I avoided her eyes. Until I had to say something. 'Julia, do you want me to go?' I couldn't stop a tear escaping.

She leaned across the table and took both my hands. Eyes met. Both wept. 'Little wounded soldier,' she said, and came around the table and put her strong arms round me and led me to her bedroom and held me on her bed a long time until we made love.

Next morning I went down to the car and it sat flopped on its wheel rims like a pudding. Each tyre had a nail in it. Impaled by one of the nails was a note:

HELLO LOVER. I GOT YOU NOW!

Just that.

Alive? After all? Dead? How?

Terror.

Alive or dead Mona would never allow me to find happiness.

I sat on the sidewalk for maybe half an hour, staring at the car, wishing Mona would come swaying down the street in all her Laura Ashley purple with her black lips and her eyeliner, and just...kill me. Or die.

Julia shouted from the balcony. 'Hey! I thought you were going for the Sunday papers!'

'Look! Look at the car!'

'Who?! What?'

'Come down,'

A couple of minutes and she was staring at my legless steed. 'I don't believe this,' she said, reading the note, 'Your ex-girlfriends really take you seriously don't they?'

'Ex wife,' I corrected. And while we waited upstairs for the AA I told her the sad story of my marriage. 'Hell,' she said.

'Only some of it,' I said.

And she told me the story of her one and only boyfriend.

JULIA'S STORY

I grew up in La Jolla, San Diego, California. Pronounced 'La Hoia' meaning The Jewel, which was what the Spanish missionaries who founded the place thought of this perfect little stretch of perfect ocean with its perfect beach…until, I presume, a bunch of Americans arrived and shot them all. My dad was a dentist. Mom shopped. Her upbringing was as conventionally middle class as America could make it, at least on the surface as shiny and perfect as money can buy. Every piece of furniture, every piece of Art on the walls or in the garden, utterly perfect. Each blade of grass in the lawn sweeping down to the swimming pool snipped to a perfect length and finished marvellously by Juan the gardener. 'I swear he polished the grass,' she said. 'With wax.'

There was, of course, the Other Side of La Jolla. Pacific Beach, where the surfers and the hippies smoked joints and did acid. Where there were all night parties, the kind the kids at school boasted about going to, but very few had actually been to! A bit like the way the boys all pretended they'd laid a hundred chicks when the closest they'd been to a girl was the centrefold of Playboy.

It couldn't work of course because I knew there was something in me that could never be satisfied by a man. I had been attracted to girls all my life. But everyone seemed to think girls had crushes on each other in adolescence, sure, but they would pass. I mean – hell, you know what there is about girls…! Anyway Greg was really macho. This was High School, right? We started being real competitors – he Captain of the football team, me of basketball. We were the stars at school. It seemed written in the stars we would be together. Mr and Mrs American Dream. And the prom – oh God, and finally at Graduation, there we were both *summa cum laude*….

Ok so you want to know about the sex. The sex. Just like in the movies, groping in his car. He made me suck him. It was expected. It used to make me heave. Once I puked on his jeans. He was mad! I felt it was my fault, I felt so guilty I couldn't blow him properly, so when the day came when he wanted to do the whole thing I was grateful, because I thought somehow now I would be able to make it up to him….

Gee I hate talking about this.

Ok, this is when I have to tell you about the Birds. See, his dad had a hobby. Well, an obsession. I mean he was some guy with a Ford dealership so he had to have some kind of life outside his car showroom. Also, because his wife was so fat and lazy and foul-mouthed and Mexican, he hated socialising. I guess people looked down on him for marrying a Mexican, especially since the rumour was she was once a maid he got pregnant with Greg and he didn't like showing her around. Anyway, Greg never had any brothers and sisters so I reckon the poor guy only had sex the once. I mean, she had a moustache! No, a real proper one I swear. So she'd lie about eating and swearing. I only met her once. It went something like this:

'Helloooo my leetle one, who and what is the *chica?'* She lay on a lounger on the terrace of their strange, overblown house in which just everything was slightly bigger than it should have been. The dining table soared for feet away into the distance. The sofas and chairs, built for giants, were deep enough to need an expedition to search for lost guests. So the lounger on which the huge woman lounged, cupped her and cared for her and made her look almost human sized. 'You come and seet here, by me. '*Cabron*!' she shouted, 'breeng dreenks for my son and hees *puta*!'

Hey you need to know by now I was mad. She'd called me a bitch! She assumed I knew no Spanish and felt quite free to insult me! Juan the gardener taught me all the bad words, he was a really good friend in his way.

A maid bustled in, petite and frowning with hatred, with four huge glasses of iced water on a massive tray.

'Thank you *Cochina*,' she beamed at the maid who, I'll swear, as soon as she could get away with it, spat in the drink. Well, she'd just been called a dirty pig.

'Aww, such a sweeeet one! Where you find these chocho! You maricon, you so lucky!'

At which point I smashed the glass of iced water to smithereens on the terrace and headed down the perfect garden (with its HUGE lawn), hoping there was a back gate and I could leave that horrible nightmare behind me…it was that or punch her, hard.

Greg however, being the athlete he was, soon caught up with me and flying-tackled me to the ground. He was laughing.

'Hey babe, never let Maria get to you! She doesn't mean it, really! I should have warned you. She's just so bored, she loves to bug people to see how they react! That's all! Hey – laugh! '

I stared at him unbelieving.

'You're real privileged! She likes you! If she didn't she'd have called you a *callientapollas!* Told me I was a *tontopollas* and suggested I *besame el culo'*

'Are you serious?'

'Sure!'

So then I did start laughing, so did he, and there we were rolling around on that gorgeous soft yielding loving perfect grass and I guess we just started kissing and somehow tongues got into the game…for the first time, and I thought, Oh shit this is it. And the phrase that kept coming back to me I had heard the day before in the Perfume Shop – 'Try it! You don't have to buy it!'

'Come with me,' he said and led me to the back of the garden…. did you forget about the birds? The daddy hobby?

Well, right at the bottom of the garden there was this huge cage, full of the most glorious, the most perfect, the biggest, the most expensive tropical birds you will ever see. Greens! Reds! Whites! Yellows! Cockatoos and Cockatiels, Parrots and Parakeets, Birds of Paradise, Scarlet Macaws, Toucans, Kookaburras, Touracos….all squawking, eating, preening, shitting, flapping, even flying the few feet allowed…

And right behind the cage there was this huge bench, big enough to shelter the Great Bed of Ware. Underneath. Ok, so I'm exaggerating. It was big, padded, had a canopy above it, and, above all, couldn't be seen from the house.

….was I the first girl who had been led sacrificially to this bower…?

…by Greg?........?

He lay me on the bench.

Sacrificially.

Began to unbutton me. Hands expertly behind me, slipping the bra off, then all over my breasts.

I didn't like my breasts.

Then he began all the slobbering… ok I didn't mind the nipple play, it was a turn on, I don't deny it. 'Come on baby…' 'Mmmmmm….' 'God you're beautiful….'

And those hands then like creatures with their own minds, freed from all impediments, roamed on, around, down, inside….

'Wow baby….'

Ok so I was still turned on but nervous! Worried! Thinking about contraception…which made me think about his smelly dick…which made me think about being sick all over him….but I suppressed it! Because it was nearly. Quite. Nice….

'*You're so fucking gorgeous….*'

Hold on! How could he have said that when his face is smothered in breast?

That wasn't him.

'My *cucaracha….puta….besa mi culo….*' It wasn't his voice! Was she there? Was his mother watching?

I writhed, trying to get away. He held on. 'Don't worry don't worry…it's all right…'

'*Me encanta tu culo….*' '*Vete a la verga culero*' '*Give it to me bitch…*' 'It's all right! It's not *me*!'

'Get OFF me!'

'It's all right!'

I began to fight. No rape for me! I writhed. He held on more tightly. So I punched him on the nose. REALLY hard.

He let go. His nose streamed blood. Just like Pieter hitting you! There was blood everywhere. 'For fucksake!' – he was crying. 'It's not me! It's the birds! I thought you'd find it funny!'

'*Funny*?' pulling my clothes on.

'La concha tuya'... 'Yo cago en la leche de tu puta madre' ...More and more, I can't remember them all.... There were plenty! It was like a barrage. In all different bird voices. Even some Juan had never taught me!

Greg buried his battered face in his t-shirt. He was sobbing with pain, frustration, disappointment. 'I'm sorry, I'm so sorry. I've spoilt it all haven't I?'

'Yes.'

'She's taught it to them. She thinks it's funny. I think it's to stop my dad taking the maid out here...'

'I don't think it's funny. I think it's horrible, and dirty, and I never want to see you again.'

'Really?'

'Really!'

And I didn't. Look: that wasn't 'a traumatic incident that put me off men and made me a lesbian!' I hate that shit! What made me a lesbian is I find women sexy! They turn me on! There's nothing I hate more than 'you're a lesbian because of a childhood trauma....' Or *worse,* 'you're a lesbian because you've never had a real man...' Bullshit! I can fuck with a man. Easy. But women turn me on. Men don't.'

'So tell me about your first girl friend,' I said.

Ok. Like I said, I had crushes when I was young. Plenty. I had girlfriends, passionate, deep girlfriends but there was never sex. Well, real sex. Gee, I guess there was even kissing but there was a point with Caroline when we just stopped just short. She stopped it. And things weren't the same with us after.

It was when I went to Bryn Mawr things got serious. Yep, I got accepted by one of the best Girls' colleges in the world. And the BEST thing about it, it was miles from La Jolla! Philadelphia is such a great place. I just fell in love with it. And that wasn't all I fell in love with! One day I met a girl. Well, it wasn't quite that simple. I knew her a little. We were in the same sorority, Alpha Chi Ro. You English don't understand this fraternity shit we have there. Each named in Greek, for some reason. Anyway, it was real Ivy League place, you know?

Our sorority house was a grey stone building, must have been a hundred years old, all oak panelled and stuff. Very prim and proper. So many rules, so much shit in those days…I mean, you had to be a rebel! You had to fight the whole time or the walls would just fold in and crush you.

Anyway this girl came along in my second year with the new freshie intake.

They had to be initiated, you see. We call it Hazing. Maybe you don't know about these things, coming from where you do. Well, our initiation was standard for Bryn, which is pretty wild. So she had to clean toilets with a toothbrush, all kinds of shit I don't want to tell you about. For part of it of all the Seniors would line up either side of the dorm. The freshies would have to walk the gauntlet. I spotted her right away, amongst all those fresh-faced femmes. Her name was Marie, by the way. I have to tell you she was quite butch. I don't think I'd ever seen a proper butch chick before, maybe in pictures, but not for real. There she was dressed in denims, a red and blue check shirt, rolled up sleeves but really showing her tits. Grrrrreat. As she walked, each girl she passed had to cut off a piece of her clothing. They went for the shirt natch, the pants were too tight. She didn't like it! She kinda put up with it but I could tell she was mad. Ok? Anyway, I found it terribly erotic. Each bit of flesh revealed made me drool. I couldn't take my eyes off her. I knew there was no bra. I couldn't wait…I couldn't breathe…

Four came past me. I made token snips. Then she reached me. Her shirt hanging in tatters. Girls laughing. Eyes meeting. Wow. I knew. She knew. I went on my knees. Started cutting her pants from the ankle up. She was breathing hard. First with anger. Then, there was no other word for it, as my scissors approached came within a hairsbreadth of her wet snatch, with pure lust.

I was shaking! I had to stop when I got too near, I was sweating and shaking so much…

Shit! Then they had to sing while we threw tampons smeared with ketchup and condoms dipped in mayo at them, and a whole lot more stuff…through it all I just knew what was going through her mind. Exactly the same as went through mine, when, a year before I had to do the same shit. Namely, wow, this is ritual humiliation. I hate it! And at the same time: wow, this is pure sex. This is SUCH a turn on…..

That night I couldn't sleep because that Marie kept coming into my mind so I climbed into her bed – she had her own room! – and it was like she had been waiting for me. We just ate each-other up!

So that's what happened. We became lovers. I had never been so happy! It was like discovering sex for the first time. I also thought I had discovered true and everlasting love. Of course I was wrong and when Marie was thrown out of school (went back to her parents in Maine. Why?) when our stash of weed was carelessly left in full view of the darned sorority cops, we parted without deep regrets.

I realised I had only been using her, really. To discover myself. And once I was discovered, boy, did I ever let loose! Once I left college, got a job with Citibank in New York - talk about promiscuity. I had so much time to make up. I just crammed it in… I found the local girls' bar, the club, I had so many girls…I mean, you've realised, I'm pretty highly sexed. Otherwise NO WAY would we have had sex – oops, sorry Tom but it's true. A man is sometimes better than nothing. Occasionally. Well, *hardly* ever…

Oh I fell in love a couple of times. Fell out of love more often. I realised that the concept of faithfulness just wasn't for me. And it isn't!

I know you straights think girls, even gay girls, are supposed to be more interested in relationships than just sex for sex' sake. Not me! I just wanted more, more, all the time because I knew that however wonderful the person was, there was someone even more wonderful just a few minutes away.

By the time I realised that I was hooked, like on a drug, I was almost totally worn out. Well, it felt that way. I had to stop and look at myself in the mirror. I was at my parents' holiday house in Shelter Island at the time and believe me, a girl's got as much chance of finding a girl to love there as you have of finding a monkey in Piccadilly Square. So I had some time to think about myself and reassess. I just knew I had to get out of the Scene. I was sick of the bars, the clubs. Gosh, I knew most of the girls in most of them! I'd *had* most of them!

So I asked my Company if there was any chance of a transfer anywhere. And here I am!

'Here you are. What happened to him? Whatsname?'

'Greg? Gee, who knows. Went off to marry Miss Orange County or somebody. Who cares?'

'You broke his heart.'

'No I didn't. He broke his own heart. He would have raped me if I hadn't punched him.'

'You don't know that!'

'Sure I do. His dick took over his head! Those birds – they just reflected the way he was - he was a bird brain, that's all.' She grinned.

'All men aren't like that.'

'I know that! That's not why I'm a lesbian! I like, I fancy, I *love* women!'

'Me too...I want to ask you something,' I said, 'You say you were sick of bars and clubs and stuff. But when I met you, you were on the prowl, weren't you?'

'It's not that simple.'

'What do you mean? You were looking for something.'

'Yeh…can't a girl go out just for a good time? It's a mixed club…'

'Oh come on. What are you looking for?'

'I don't care if it sounds corny. What's everyone looking for? Yes, now I'm looking for love.'

'Oh,' I said, hurt by the present tense.

'Tom, have I hurt you?'

'No no, of course I understand.' Yes, but I had thought we had found – at least some – love together. I thought we had love in bed with us last night.

'Do you? Tom, I like you a lot. Sometimes I like you so much I'll even lend you my body for just a little while. But it can't work. Not like that.

'Yes. Yes. Sure.' Whew. I really thought she'd shared at least some of the absolute joy I'd felt. Did she orgasm? Yes, sure. Unless she was absolutely a brilliant actress.

'It's just part of me. Not a phase, or an aberration, or anything like that. It's fixed in concrete. If you and me got, say, permanent, I'd cheat! I'd have to.'

'I understand.'

'Lucky for you I'm not a man hater, like some of my sisters. I can meet men on their own ground. No man will ever get the better of me.'

'Hm. Well, I've learned one thing,' I said.

'What?'

'I know how to get you to bed!'

'Huh? How?'

'All I have to do is start crying!'

'Idiot!' she said, punching me painfully and playfully on my upper arm.

She never told me why she had stayed out the previous night. I didn't ask. I knew I wouldn't like the answer. And that wasn't the last time she stayed out all night. It became a regular feature of our weekends. On Friday or Saturday she would announce her intention of going out. My heart sank every time. I never became hardened to it.

At first I stayed in, hoping she would return. But as time went on I realised I was losing all my friends.

She said I herself. 'What's happened to all your friends? You used to have plenty of friends. Though you haven't introduced me to any of them,' This was true. I hadn't introduced her to anybody, possibly because I thought they would see her as my new girlfriend and I knew she wouldn't like that. Besides, she could seem brash and arrogant and I could imagine her frightening or infuriating some of them to death.

So I started to pick up on old acquaintances and friends again. Telephone numbers were dusted off. Arrangements were made to meet, always with a get-out clause in case Julia happened to be home that night.

I even got up the courage to invite myself to dinner with Nora and Grant in Bromley. I casually asked if Pieter would be there. 'Probably not', Nora said, to my relief. I knew that if he heard I was coming, he'd vanish.

I went to movies with Brian and Kathe. Steeped myself in music. Dragged myself to concerts and festivals. Knebworth, Earl's Court, Wembley. Rolling Stones! David Bowie! Pink Floyd in Hyde Park, Cambridge…this was the bright and perfect and fuzzy and druggy and flowery and hairy 1970/1, with the world reeling from Peace, Flower Power, all the stuff that puts our teeth on edge nowadays, so I won't burden you with too much of it. But you should have been there! The Who, for one!...what an evening…the Stones! When Mick stood in mid air, I swear, feet above the crowd, looking down, playing and singing like a wounded ecstatic angel…

The Bowie concert in Earl's Court stays in my mind. It was a Friday night, I think. I was there with Brian and Kathe, stoned out of mind and time on some incredible Nepalese. I had come from work, so was in a suit. We were in row 5. And during an instrumental (probably Low, I can't remember) Bowie crouched in front of a speaker and with a huge smile, his eyes absolutely met mine! The only person there in a suit, I must have stood out like a sore prick. And he gave me such a wide, such a true, such a warm smile, he's the only man I ever fell in love with…

Julia never accompanied me. She viewed my times with my friends as opportunities to escape to her world guilt-free. The more friends I had, the freer she felt.

I promised not to go on. The plot beckons.

Five

Withers Stronglode Withers and Truelove
Solicitors and Commissioners for Oaths
5a London Wall London EC4

17th July 1970

Dear Tom,

You will forgive my using your first name I trust. We have been working together so long, I am beginning to understand you quite well.

Who knows, perhaps if we knew each other under different circumstances, we could be friends? I too have my ideals, though I am sensible enough not to let them interfere with my work. This is a lesson you seem to be learning.

This new spirit of realism is giving all of us here a great deal of pleasure. As long as you always remember to keep the two sides of your life separate, you will be all right. As a well-known guru said to me the other day, 'A man who is IN this world learns how useful a tool Confusion can be.'

I suggest you study Yoga and get to know yourself a bit better.

Yours etc

James

J. T. Truelove BA LLB
James Truelove, Executor of the Estate of the Late Hazel Stone

He must be mad. Who the hell decided this weirdo should make decisions about *me*?

I enclosed his letter with a brief note of my own and sent it to Father. My note said 'This is the asshole who's making decisions about *my* sanity!'

A week later I received Father's reply:

> *Dear Tom,*
>
> *It's about time you learned respect for your elders and better. That is the point of his letter. You think you're so smart, don't you. Where is Mona anyway? Is she still with you?*

Well I shouldn't have expected him to understand.

Man on mountain pierced by the peak can say either 'Help! I am alone! I am lonely! Or simply admire the view.

This was my little estate of one when the tramp sat next to me on the tube, as I was on my way from the office to Park Lane, where I left the car everyday.

I had been summoned to Boles' office that morning. As I entered I knew he was having a mindstorm, because he paced up and down like a clockwork chicken, and I could hear the crackle of joints and the rustle of skin.

'Sit!' he ordered. And as I made my way towards the small group of chairs around the coffee table he said 'Not there boy!' and pointed to the tiny guest chair facing him across his desk.

Oh dear, I thought, trouble.

He wheeled in mid-pace. 'Well!' he snapped, 'you've been working here two months now, am I right?'

'Yes.'

'AND?' he howled into my face, inches away. Dry spittle spattered me like minuscule spads of sea-foam. I tried to stop myself wiping it away.

'Thank you very much,' I said, having decided that some in-depth grovelling was being called for.

He grabbed a handful of my hair. 'What the fuck are you thanking me for?' he asked more quietly, voice dribbling with menace.

'For giving me a job,' I said, wondering whether it would be tactful to writhe away.

He picked me up by the hank of hair. 'Yes, I gave you a job. And WHY did I give you a job?'

'I don't know,' I said, saying to myself, Don't hit him, whatever you do, don't hit him.

'Atkins said you wouldn't be another one. Parkinson said you wouldn't be another one. I believed them. I should have *known!'* He let go of my hair and I sank down into the chair. He went around to his side of the desk and sat facing me. 'I should know by now not to listen to other people. I know what I am doing. They are all out to cheat me. Do you realise that I could run this whole show on my own?'

'Yes.'

'I asked you if you are one of them and you denied it.'

'One of whom?'

'Don't play Clever Boy with me! Never try play clever with me. I'll spell it for you: S K I V E R!'

Oh no….! He knew about all my clever strategies to avoid work….! I'm doomed! 'But – '

'Tell me this, my boy: how much business have you done? How many actual SALES?'

'I – '

'I'll tell you how much. Eight.'

'?'

'Eight'

'?'

'Pounds.'

Gosh.

'And NONE of it with South Africa!' He paused for effect.

'For buttons. Buttons! To the Canary Islands...'

He made a strangled noise as if I'd placed a garrotte around his neck.

'Why do I bother?' It's great. It's a lot. I was so proud of those buttons. My first trade! 'I wasn't meant to be a businessman. I'm a kind man, a good-natured man. What I always wanted was to own a zoo. I love animals. Little furry things. The furrier the better. They don't argue. They never skive. So much better than humans. Did I tell you about my zoo?'

'No sir,' I said.

'Yes my boy. I have my own little zoo in Hampshire. I have lots of furry things. Hamsters, rats, agoras, all with fur. So when I go home I can go into my zoo and play with them. I feed them myself, care for them.

'Do you understand?' His eyes brimmed. Someone else on a mountain impaled by the peak. 'And every day I have to leave my little darlings and come here. And why do I do this?' he asked, dabbing away tears with a handkerchief I couldn't help noticing was speckled with blood, 'because you stupid cunts couldn't wipe your own arses if I wasn't here. Who would keep you if it wasn't for me? Eh? Eh?' He pocketed the handkerchief with an air of finality.

He was getting mad again. A ruby droplet of blood appeared on the corner of his nostril and hung there. I considered pointing it out.

'At least when *animals* stop being useful and die, I can eat them! Eh? Eh?'

'Sir – '

'And I thought you were different. I thought, this Bloch, he's a go-getter, non skiver. He could almost be my own very own son! ' He contemplated flaking fingers. The tiny drop of blood migrated thoughtfully to the end of his nose and poised, dramatically.

'Sir – ' I said, half standing and looking him straight in the eye, 'I *am* different sir,' I said, meaning it, 'I promise!' I realised that my eyes too were brimming with tears. I had been sucked into his mad little world, and there was nothing I wanted so much as to make him happy.

'Get out,' he said, swivelling round in his chair.

As I passed through the outer office Monica beckoned me over. 'Has he fired you?' she whispered.

'No,' I said.

'I thought he was going to,' she sighed. 'My gosh he's *wonderful…*'

Good God I thought. What's wrong with us. 'Yes isn't he.'

For the rest of the day I was in a mindboil over all this. Now the hand grenades had come home to roost, and they were roosting with pulled firing pins. I couldn't hold out any longer. I had to do the business, and some of it would have to be with South Africa, like it or not. The choice was simple – do what he wanted or at least *appear* to do what he wanted, or Boles would stop the application for my Work Permit, and back! I would have to go to the Fascist Republic of Apartheid, police state, hate hate and hate….and definitely no Laszlo's millions! When Mona and I had left SA, we had done so with a bitter hatred for those who ruled the country with greed lies and guns. We had decided to put the place behind us. The Revolution was coming, we were sure, and White Liberals would be in the way. I had finally realised that there was nothing I could do to change things or make them better.

So there I was faced with a dilemma as disagreeable as a soiled nappy stuck in the loo: expand trade with South Africa or have to go back there – and forget my millions….!

I had to do a lot of double-think. I had to do a lot of self-justification and self-deception. Me then sickens me now.

Aaargh. Maybe selling things to South Africa wasn't as morally wrong as *buying* things from them. It was taking their money after all, not giving them any. Depriving them of Foreign Exchange. Or was that just weasel thinking? And then on the other hand buying things would help to put food into poor black's mouths. But MUCH more caviar and lobster into fat white faces! And guns into the hands of the cops and army. And more cells and torture equipment into the prisons...

Filled with a mad jumble of thoughts and despair, it took me a while to notice the tramp sat next to me on the tube.

What do you do when a tramp sits next to you? Same as me, I suppose. Cringe away, subtly. Try to breathe as little as possible, to avoid the mixed odour of sweat booze cigarettes and solidified despair. Try to avoid touching them. Pretend to be deaf or foreign if addressed.

'Hello Tom,' he whispered.

'What?' I dropped my Evening Standard, open on the crossword page.

'Don't be frightened,' he giggled and offered me a bottle in a brown paper bag. 'It's all right,' he nodded reassuringly, 'It's KWV.'

'Oh,' I said, as if it was quite natural for a strange tramp to offer me a slug of South African brandy on a London tube. I accepted the bottle and drank. Nice. 'Who are you? How do you know me?'

'What a couple of stupid questions hey, Tom?'

'Is it?'

'I want you to come with me to Sloane Square. Keep by me. Is that clear? ' With a wide smile, he indicated a menacing bulge in his pocket. So I agreed. Mostly because I was curious. Not frightened.

When we arrived at Sloane Square I alighted with him and he led me to the Gents' toilets in the middle of the square itself. We went down the stairs. An attendant emerged from the office. The tramp whispered to him. He nodded, mounted the stairs and locked the sliding gate, returned. Suddenly, at an unheard signal, three closet doors opened and three burly men in three-piece suits emerged.

'So this is him!' one said.

'He looks like a blerry idiot to me,' said another, who wore a deerstalker and a bushy ginger moustache.

'No no,' said the third, a pudgy minuscule version of Alfred Hichcock, with far less hair. 'He's the one. I got his picture.'

Shit, I thought. South Africans.

'Well?' said the tramp.

'Who are you?' I asked, a little panicked, 'what do you want?'

'No no,' said the tramp. 'It's a question of what *you* want!' He grinned and offered me the bottle. 'Have a *sluk*,' he said. 'We thought you was a commie.'

'And it turns out we should have been proud of you all along,' the Baldy said.

'We has been watching you for quite some time,' said the Deerstalker, 'and we wants to help.'

'Are you guys Jurors?' I asked stupidly.

'I don't know what you are talking about,' he answered. 'I see you still don't trust us, is that it?'

'Who the hell *are* you?' I blathered, though I had a suspicion…

Baldy clapped his hands. 'Mostert!' he shouted, and a cubicle door opposite me opened and Pieter came out. 'You said you wouldn't call on me,' he complained, avoiding my eyes.

'Unless necessary. Unless necessary,' the Deerstalker man said. 'He doesn't trust us, see?'

'Pieter what are you doing here? What the hell is all this about?'

'Tom, I'm sorry.' He looked as if he'd just shot his mother by mistake. 'I didn't want you involved. This,' he sighed, pointing to the Attendant who was listlessly dragging a broom over the floor, 'is Brigadier Maartens.'

I stared at the man, and suddenly, with a shock, I recognised him. This was the man who was responsible for my escaping South Africa and the attentions of the security services. (The full story is in Umfaan's Heroes. To sum it up for those of meager pockets, Tom and Pieter tried to undermine the South African State along with Absalom, an ANC fighter. Their effort went wrong – Absalom died, Pieter and Tom were lauded as heroes of the state who had fought so bravely against the ANC – a misimpression neither chose to contradict.) His usually expressionless face managed to beam. He was still a large as ever, a genial giant with a chopped-up moustache and a pocket full, no doubt, of plots and poisons. About fifty, his body showing the surrender of the attempts of his stomach muscles to keep some sort of order.

'Well hello again,' the man grinned, extending a rubber-gloved hand. I shivered. Touched one of the fingers.

'You see Tom we need you. These gentlemen represent the finest minds we have in London – '

'I see,' I said. 'BOSS.'

'You got it boy,' the tramp said triumphantly. 'See? I told you he was a clever clogs!'

Baldy produced a chequered picnic cloth, laid it on the toilet floor while the others arranged cushions, bottles of wine, cold meats, baguettes.

'Sit,' said the Brigadier. 'Relax. Have some wine.'

'You want a smoke?' the tramp asked, rolling a joint.

'I'm dreaming,' I said.

'Well there's no reason not to enjoy your dream,' Baldy smirked.

We sat on the cushions and I picked gingerly at the food. Eating a meal in a public toilet was not slightly appealing. And as I ate, I gagged at the memory of the last time I saw the Brigadier.

In a military hospital outside Pretoria, pain, lies, end of the road, despair.

'What do you want from me?' I asked, bored with the silence and embarrassed by the slurps and gulps of my fellow picnickers.

'No no it's what *you* want my boy,' Maartens said, 'We only want to help!'

'Help? With what?'

'Don't act stupid, boy.' He said, 'You want to be a multimillionaire isn't it? We know everything. Mostert told us. And we want to help you get that money!'

Everything? 'Pieter you're a bastard,' I said. 'I thought I could trust you.'

'Don't be like that,' Deerstalker said, 'He's your best friend. He only wants the best for you.'

'Let's get down to business,' Maartens said, passing me the joints. 'Let's work out how we are going to help you.'

Now I was frightened. If I had a machine gun I would have turned them all into lead salad. Including Pieter. But I was also curious.

'Now it seems to me the first priority is to make sure you are successful in your job *ne*? '

I nodded dumbly. 'And?'

'Well, we're just the people to help. You're in the South Africa section at Grabkin, hey?'

I nodded.

'So all we have to do is push some business your way. And for us, nothing could be easier.'

I began to see where all this was heading.

'Karlsen, explain to our friend.'

'Very well,' said Baldy, 'Let's discuss, say, steel.'

'Steel.'

'If you were able to make a deal for say, ten million dollars, would that be nice?'

'Uh.Yes.'

'Your boss would like you hey?'

'Yes.'

'Like you say, yes. Now this is what you are going to have to do. Have a look at this.' He handed me a telephone number scrawled on a piece of toilet paper. 'This is a number in the Ivory Coast. You can phone them tomorrow. Ask for Monsieur Talon. You will say "Mother sent me". You got that?'

I nodded.

'Tell him, two hundred USD per MT. Then give him the name of your company, the address, the Bank details. Jalon will open a Letter of Credit. Then you phone this number.' He handed me another piece of toilet paper. 'This is the number of ISCOR, the South African steel company. Ask for Hennie De Vries. He's expecting you. Tell him, "Mother sent me". See? Tell him, ten mill

USD. Give your name, the Company name and address. And that's it. Understand?'

I understood all right. 'I thought the black nations didn't buy from South Africa.'

The others laughed. A horrible noise.

'Of course they *say* they don't *domkop*!' Maartens exploded. 'But they know they get a good deal, see! You're not *selling*. You're facilitating!'

'But – '

'Never mind but. We take care of all the details. It's all perfectly legal. The steel is shipped to the Azores. The marks are all put on there, see? "Product of the Azores", see?' He guffawed. 'And your Company gets ten million pounds! See how easy it is for you? You then send an ILC for seven millions to ISCOR, your Company makes three. Good hey?' He sat back smugly wiping chicken fat off his thick lips.

I let my anger rise at last. 'It's – it's – ' I stopped the words. Stood. 'Well, I'll be off. Thank you very much for your time.'

'Stay where you are,' the Brigadier hissed.

'No no, must be going, my – uh – wife will be worried. Maybe I'll give your proposition some thought. Maybe I won't!' and I made a dash for the exit.

But there was a steel gate between me and freedom. And a huge body rugby-tackled me and I fell down the stairs shouting Help!

I must have blacked out for a few seconds I suppose, because when I came to Deerstalker was sitting on my chest. Pieter crouched by the urinals in terror. The picnic had been spattered about the place by my flailing feet. The others stood around me.

'Listen to me boy,' Maartens said, his face inches from mine. 'If we ever let you get out of here, you will do as we say. Because if you don't, you will have to die. Do you understand?'

I nodded, thinking, I'll go to the police. The minute I get out of here.

'And I can assure you, Bloch,' Baldy added cheerfully, 'if you fuck up, if you go to the police or anybody, that lesbian you live with – and her little girlfriend – are going to get very badly cut up. And don't forget, you got a wife too, and family in South Africa. *Verstaan jy*?'
I nodded. I understood.

I staggered down the Kings Road. Ignoring all the stares, I set my jaw and walked. Hang on, people are staring. Why are people staring.

When Julia saw me she told me why. 'Tom! What happened?'

'What happened,' I echoed numbly.

'There's blood all over your shirt! What happened to your *clothes*?'

'I – I was mugged.' I said.

'You were *mugged*? Where?'

I buried head in hands and slumped on the couch. 'Let me clean you up,' she said, and led me to the bathroom.

Later she asked for details. By then I had invented a story. I told her I had left the car at Park Lane Garage, taken the tube 'on a whim'. Been attacked. ('*In rush hour*?' 'Yes.') But I had fought back. This explained the fact that I still had my cheque book.

She didn't believe me. Insisted I go to the police. I refused adamantly. 'What for? They didn't steal anything in the end.' (Except my integrity.) (Except my pride.)

She decided that I had reasons.

And later she had reasons for refusing me the consolation I craved.

The next day I made two international calls. 'Mother sent me.'

'Who's your girlfriend?' I asked Julia casually on the next Saturday morning at breakfast. (Alpen. Toasted wholegrain bread with miso. Korean Boricha coffee substitute. She'd have nothing else.)

She looked up, startled, from her muesli. 'How did you know?'

'Oh, just something someone said.' I answered. 'Tell me about it.'

'What's to tell?' she said and shovelled a spoonful of fibre-rich mush into her mouth.

'Like, where did you meet her? How long it's been going on, what she looks like, all that stuff. Not to mention why you haven't introduced us…'I smiled thinly.

'Tom, I just didn't think it would be a good idea to tell you yet. Why are you forcing me?'

'Why shouldn't you tell me? I've accepted it, after all. I know I can't give you what you need. So share with me.'

'I don't want to hurt you. I didn't want you to be jealous.'

'Jealous? Me?' I'll bet my voice was sick and hollow. 'Don't be silly. Tell me.'

Julia sighed. 'Ok, she's called Amber. She's twenty-six. Five foot nothing. Lives alone. Works in a library. And I think she's really sweet. Is that what you want to know?'

'What does she look like?'

'Blond. Slim. Like that.'

'Oh.' A tasteless mouthful stuck in my throat.

'You *are* jealous!'

'No I'm not. When did you meet her?'

'A long time ago. The first night I didn't come home. The night you – '

'I see.' The night I wrecked the place.

'That's why I didn't tell you,' she said, seeing me replaying the night behind my eyes.

'Uh huh.'

We continued eating in silence for a while. I tried to control my breathing.

'I knew I shouldn't have told you,' she said eventually.

'Don't be ridiculous,' I nearly snapped. 'Of course you should have told me. I'm just upset you didn't tell me sooner, that's all.'

'No. I shouldn't have told you. You're all upset.'

'I am not.'

'You are. I can tell. You're all pink and you haven't finished. Do you want an egg?'

'No I do not want an egg.'

'See? You're shouting.'

'I'm not shouting!'

'I'm going out,' she announced, standing up so quickly her chair overbalanced and made a soft 'whup' on the carpet.

'To see her?' I asked.

'None of your goddam business!' she yelled and grabbed her bag and made for the door.

Oh shit. I've done it now. What I dreaded. I have frightened her another two feet way from me. I must try to do better than this! Get a hold of myself. Apologise.

I went into my bedroom where I climbed into shorts, put on a t-shirt and raced out of the flat across Albert Bridge and into Battersea Park.

I panted furiously around the running track, the smell of burning rubber and sweat following me like exhaust fumes.

There was someone dogging my footsteps. As I sped up so did he. Aha, a challenger is it? Dammit, no way are you going to catch me! Faster, bugger, faster! Still on my bloody tail! Is this Roger Bannister or what? Faster faster fas – gotta stop! Can't stop! Gotta! Wheeze. Puff. Pant. Stop.

So you've stopped. Puff. Too. Pant.

Puff puff. Puff.

Pieter!

'You. You. Bastard. Puff.'

'You're. Puff. Not so bad. Puff. Yourself.'

'Whew. Puff. What the hell are you doing here?'

'I. Puff. Got to talk to you.'

'Ever (puff) heard of the telephone?'

'Aaah. (Fyoo!) Don't be silly. Your telephone's tapped.'

'Whew. Surprise, surprise, I should have known that. Anyway, I don't want to talk to you. Ever.'

'Why? What have I done?'

'What the fuck do you mean what have I done? All that stuff with BOSS. Got to sit down.' I plopped down next to the track. He sat next to me. We breathed ourselves back to normal. 'I mean, how could you have gotten me into *that*?'

'Hell I'm sorry Tom. I want you to understand. I'm trying to save you – '

'*Save* me?'

'Listen! Not just you! This is the greatest chance we've ever had to do some real damage to the racist regime – don't you see? I *had* to get you involved!'

A runner came puffing by. 'Peter, don't you think we should get off the running track?'

'Of course not! No-one can hear us here!'

'What do you mean about damage to the regime?'

'Listen,' he said, ignoring the nubile legs that went pop-popping by. 'This deal they want you to do –'

'I've done it. I made the calls. It makes me sick.'

'Fine, fine! Don't you see the power we have?'

'What do you mean?'

'Power to blow the whole dirty business wide open! What do you think would happen if we gave the press all the info about South Africa's trade routes to the black states?

'What would happen, Pieter, is they'd kill my girlfriend. Sorry, my *ex* girlfriend. And *her* girlfriend. And my wife. Or *ex*-wife, and my whole family. That's what would happen.'

'Not if we do it right. We could blow the whole thing! The whole connection!'

'Then they'll kill *us*.'

'Maybe. Maybe not. We'll be *fucking* careful.'

'Fucking hell…..' I said.

Six

I got home to find a letter waiting which did nothing for my peace of mind. Mother. The usual blah about not writing. I skipped. Then a cutting fell out with a photograph of Ian Smith, PM of Rhodesia, looking gaunt angry and arrogant. The caption said 'Brave Rhodesia defies the Brits'.

> *'…Things are very bleak here now. Last week Mrs Gilchrist, you know, Pattie's mother, the one we thought you'd marry just to spite us, was arrested while trying to help some of those poor people in one of the squatter camps they call "homelands". They said she was "disseminating Communist propaganda". Actually she was giving out leaflets about the food distribution points. There seems to be no end to the suffering the Nationalists are prepared to cause the black people.*
>
> *'Now that sanctions against Rhodesia are beginning to bite, most South African businesses are treating it as a golden opportunity to make money by supplying those racists there with all sorts of things they can't get from Europe. Your father is having a terrible fight with his Board of Directors; they're all for stepping up trade with Rhodesia and he isn't. He is looking into the possibilities of a job in the US.*
>
> *'Sorry to be so gloomy but you refugees have a very easy life.*
>
> *Your loving*
>
> *Mother.*
>
> *P.s. we were sorry to hear that you and Mona had parted, but your father says he did warn you. Did he? Anyway, I trust your new girlfriend is loving, kind and Jewish. (supposed to be a joke, dear, don't get upset. At the same time, do tell us if she is.*

I looked around the empty flat. There was no answer to that.

'So tell me darling, how are things going with your new girlfriend?', said Noel, with a burp. 'What's her name? Julia. Is she loving, kind and Jewish?'

We were sitting in his lounge. He had made dinner. Julia hadn't returned by eight in the evening so I had phoned Noel and invited myself over. I didn't want to be in when Julia got home. I wanted her to feel free. And I wanted to get stoned.

'I don't want to talk about it,' I said, sucking on a joint.

'Not wanting to talk about it means there's something wrong. What is it?'

'Oh hell, Noel, it's just so – ' I really didn't want to talk about it. Or did I. Originally, my decision to see Noel was tied up with a desire to forget the whole thing. Or was it.

'Tom, give!'

'All right, if you insist. She's one of your lot.'

'Do you know, I thought so! My intuition strikes gold. And you're in love with her, n'est-ce pas?'

'I suppose I am.' Glumness settled on my gut.

'You're on a hiding to nothing, darling. No, don't look so sad. Have you two made love at all?'

'Yes.'

'What was it like?'

'Well,' I sighed, 'I liked it a lot. She seemed to as well. But the only time she'd go to bed with me is if I'm really upset or freaked out. It's like a nurse doing her duty. Or someone stroking a puppy in pain. I don't know…' I trailed off.

'Darling, you're going to have to try to understand her. I understand. I've been to bed with women. Did you know that?'

'My gosh!' I said. 'The idea of someone as camp as Noel going to bed with a woman was ridiculous.

'Why not? I like women a lot, you know that. I'm not one of those queens who speak of women as "fishes". No. I have occasionally been so close to a woman when she wanted it and so did I.'

'Well then – '

'No, that shouldn't give you hope. What do I feel in bed? I'll take you on a guided tour of my mind. Firstly, her nude body leaves me cold. It's so other to what I find erotic. So I have to call on my imagination. And believe me, dear, it's hard work. The main problem being the erection, getting it and keeping it. So, once we're together entwined, I start to imagine I'm with the most gorgeous and manly man my little mind can conjure up. And so, with the aid of my brain and a lot of application of her mouth, we both manage to have a satisfactory time.'

'You're saying you do your duty, you put on an act and you don't really get anything out of it?'

'Well I do get something out of it. I make her happy and I ejaculate. It's nearly fun! Luckily for you and Julia she doesn't have to get an erection and if she doesn't orgasm, like all girls, she knows how to fake it. Sorry darling. She makes all the right noises so you'll never know.'

Suddenly I knew exactly what it as like for Julia making love with me. A task. A job. A kindness. 'That's awful!'

'Darling, you'll have to accept it. You can't change he. You will never "convert" her. I heard a good saying on "Thought for the Day" this morning. "Don't waste hay", the priest said, "on a dying horse"'

'Oh shit!' I said. I wished there was a bucket around for me to put my head in. How could I have been so selfish! So blind! So stupid! Julia had given me love. Why did I have to insist on sex as part of that package?

'Don't look so bloody miserable,' Noel said. 'It's all part of growing up, Tom.'

'Don't patronise me Noel.'

'Sorry darling. Try to understand her. Why do you think, in all the time I've known you, I never made a serious attempt to seduce you?'

'Yeh, I wondered about that'

'Because, darling, it would be unnatural for you with your erotic "set" to make love with a man. It's the same for her. Or for me, making love with a woman.'

'Ho hum.'

'Shall we go out? Find a fuck? That'll fix you!'

'That's what you said last time.'

When I got home next morning after a fruitless and boring night smoking, discoing, Julia wasn't there. OK, I thought, she's spent the weekend with her girlfriend. She's upset with me, wants to teach me a lesson.

But when she gets home I'm going to be different. A reformed character. I'm going to promise her that I will never try to get her to bed again. I will be her best friend. Her platonic lover. I'll ask to meet Amber. I will force Amber to like me. I will find a lover of my own. I promise you'll be happy, Julia. I promise.

I went to bed. I slept until six in the evening.

No Julia.

Sunday night. She has to come home tonight. She's working tomorrow. Her clothes are here.

I turned the telly on. I watched without interest, waiting for Julia to arrive so that I could introduce her to the new me. She would be apprehensive, on edge; maybe she would come in with the decision to turf me out. Fine, if that's what she wants.

The telly finished.

I went to bed.

I lay awake all night turning the light on and off, reading, trying to sleep again, trying to meditate. There was no way I could entice sleep in. When the alarm went off I was headachy and drained. I dashed to her bedroom, but she hadn't slipped in.

I dressed and wrote a note which I sellotaped to her dressing-room mirror.

Dear Julia

I have been worried sick about you. I want you to know that I have had a revelation. I love you too much to make you unhappy. So I will never beg, cajole, force or con you into making love ever again. This way we can stay friends, closer than lovers.

On the way back to work I stopped to pick up a Guardian. As usual I glanced through the headlines of the trash press on the newsagent's rack.

LESBIAN LOVERS IN GRUESOME SUICIDE PACT ran the headline in the Sun.

With an awful foreboding I bought the Sun too.

Sitting in the car I read the report:

> *An American banker and her lesbian lover were found dead yesterday in a flat in Chiswick. Julia Pemberton, 26, a leading Broker for Citibank, the posh US bank in the city, had died with her partner, Amber Morton in a bizarre suicide pact – "It appears," said Superintendent Brokenshaw of Scotland Yard, "they killed each other in a ritual suicide, by hammering six inch nails into each-others' chests" Nobody else is being sought in connection with the incident….*

Sick…sick….I stared….I pushed the car door open and retched…

M O N A A A A A A A A A A A A A A A A A A A A A A A A A A A A A A AAAAAAAAAAAAAAAAAAA!!!!!!!!

In a storm of misery, fury, helplessness, panic I went into the office and offered my resignation. It was not accepted.

'Don't come in here and give me nonsense my boy. Have you been drinking?'

'Yes sir. No sir. It's – personal reasons.'

'Rubbish. Just when you're about to pull off one of the biggest deals this Company has ever seen. Impossible!'

Instead he gave me a week's holiday. Unpaid of course.

'And be back here Monday! Get!!!'

The attendant at the Sloane Square gents dragged a listless mop over a perfectly clean floor. 'Close up!' I said.

'What?'

'Close up Brigadier! I have to talk to you.'

He grinned and clapped his hands. 'Right! All you *moffies* perverts and wankers,' he yelled sergeant-major like at the cubicles 'Everybody out! This is a fire drill!'

Chains clanked, cisterns flushed. Far too many men exited hastily from the cubicles puling trousers up over pink knees.

The Brigadier locked up, took me into the office. 'Sit down my boy. *Koffie*?'

'Ok.'

'So. You like my setup eh?'

'What?'

'Did you see how clean and tidy this place is! Hey? Only a Brigadier can do it this good!'

I stared at him. So glad he took pride in his work.

'So how's it going with you?' he asked, giving me a steaming mug of Camp Coffee.

'Everything,' I said, 'is going famously!'

'So why are we all in a flutter then?'

'I've got a couple of rather nasty personal problems.'

'Haven't we all?' he asked, sighing. 'My daughter wants to marry a Sikh. A brown one! My youngest son wants to be an actor. An actor! That's what comes of living in a permissive Commie society.'

I tried to look sympathetic.

'I believe you've started the process? Made those telephone calls?'

'Yes I have. That's not what I came to talk to you about. I want you to sort someone out for me.'

'Of course *pellie*. Anything for you. Who is this person?'

I was a little taken aback. 'Just like that?' I asked. 'You – you'd *kill* someone just because I ask you to?'

'Why not? You're one of us now. Only – ' he leaned forward confidentially – 'we don't say "kill" in this profession. We say "endorse out". It's our little joke you see.'

'Very funny.'

'Don't get stroppy. Now who do you want endorsed out?'

'My wife.'

'Ah,' he said, 'Now that's different.' He was shocked. 'We don't get involved in domestic quarrels. Hell, if every time my wife nagged me I got her killed, uh, endorsed out, she would have died a hundred deaths!'

'It's not that – '

'Marriage is a state made in heaven, you see. Now how can we interfere with Heaven?'

'You don't understand! She's crazy! Off her head! She's going around killing people!'

'Well, if God means her to around killing people maybe it's for the best. Have you told he Police?'

'They don't believe me.'

'Well I don't like it one bit. Coming between man and wife. We'll have to discuss it.'

'Promise?'

'Don't you worry. Go on home and try to make it up with her! Now *voetsek*. I've got work to do,' he said, taking up his mop.

In my lonely journey along King's Road, cursing the idle window-shoppers whose only problem was whether to buy the purple or the red, Mona's face hung before me like a discorporate hologram, desperate, deluded, frightened, lost. And I felt her grab for my heart again. But no! This time, Mona, you've gone too. Damn. Far.

I let myself in and clumped up the stairs to Julia's flat, muttering a prayer. God, if when I open the door Julia come toward me smiling her smile and asking whether I had a good day, I might start believing in You.

I offered the key to the door and it accepted. Emptiness. The breeze through the open window flapping the curtain. The ashtray with a half-smoked Marlboro. A hairbrush with strands of hair that were not mine. I went into the bathroom and stared at the cabinet full of cosmetics which were mostly gifts from months ago, unused and dusty. I took a handful of them and, shaking, stuffed them into the full waste bin. A Mary Quant eyeliner fell onto the tiled floor. I kicked it hard. It shattered against the bath, blackening the tiles.

And before I knew it I was on the floor crying bitterly for the death of one woman and the resurrection of another.

'You're Mr Block are you?' The voice was female, American, seething.

'Yes. Bloch.'

'This is Mrs Grice here.' She waited for my reaction. 'Julia's – '

'Mother. Yes.' I didn't know what to say. The telephone writhed in my hand. I forgot to breathe. Eventually – ' Mrs Grice I – ' I was going to say something weak and stupid like I'm so sorry, I'm deeply…

'Why didn't you DO something? Why didn't you SAVE her?' The attack was so sudden, cruel. I reeled back, looking for defence. 'But '

'It's your fault! It's your fault…'

'Give me that.' A man's voice. American, domineering, deep. 'Hello? This is Torrance Grice here.'

I could hear the woman weeping. 'Now I don't understand what happened here,' he continued. She screamed, off, 'I do! He could have saved her!'

'Hello,' I said.

'She's just too upset to think. I am too. She won't accept what's happened. Do you understand?'

'Yes,' I said. Taking her back 'I'm upset too. I loved her Mr Grice.'

'Whatever. Be that as it may. Now listen to me. We're here at the Hyde Park Hotel. We've done all the paperwork and such. We're taking her back with us see?'

'Yes,' I said, blurred with tears. 'What can I do to – '

'Ok, she wrote us about you. Said you were a friend, and a couple other things. Whatever. So I want you to do something for us, for her.'

'Yes.' It was a hard word to say.

'We want you to pack all her things and send them round to mr at the Hotel, understand? We want her things.'

'Yes,' I said, 'I'll bring them to you – '

'No need. Put everything in a cab, there can't be much.' Then, trying to lump some words together, 'Look. Don't blame yourself. It wasn't your fault.' It was, it was! The wife screamed, off. 'Shut up Martha. Well – so long.' Then the telephone clicked and I was alone again.

With her things. In her flat. Two wet hours, packing her case with her clothes, smelling her sweat and her perfume, cleaning her out of my life, sweeping her under the carpet.

I stared at her diary. I did not open it. I could not. I packed it into a cardboard box with her books. Phoned a cab, sent him off with her…

Shit I hate writing this. I know I'm supposed to tell you everything, but I don't want to. I will confess though that I wanted her parents to read the diary, her letters (there was a bundle of them in the carton. I wish now I had read them!) and know that I had loved her, would never have harmed her, would have protected her with my life, against anybody. Even Mona. But I can't say I had nothing to do with her death, can I? To an extent, it was my fault!

The flat was mine now, so I stayed. Her Company had paid the rent for a year and didn't seem bothered that she was no longer there. So I claimed the place, right of abode. Just in case one day her key was offered to the lock, and it accepted….

Seven

'Well, the deal's going through puff,' I said as Pieter and I made another circuit of the running track.

'I hope you're keeping photocopies of all the correspondence,' he said, 'puff.'

'Of course I am. But what's next? How are we going to build up the evidence puff so that we've got them where we want them?'

'You know what the trouble is puff?'

'What?'

'No-one's done anything puff – *illegal* yet!'

'No, that's true. Just helluva fucking extremely fucking puff *immoral.*' I realised that I didn't want the whole thing to blow up just yet. I wanted the job to last until I got thr whole Inheritance thing sorted out.

'That's not enough. Maybe we should let the deal go ahead.'

'Why?' I asked hopefully.

'I mean maybe you should do a few more deals. Build up a picture. Besides, I've got feeling there's more really *bad* stuff, puff, '

'I've been thinking much the same thing.' I stopped, hands on knees, to catch breath.

He stood panting next to me. 'I know. You're thinking about your millions aren't you?'

'Now look – ' (I'm not going to put all the pants in. I can't remember exactly when they were anyway)

'I've been thinking about that as well.'

'Eh?....Don't tell me you've changed your mind?'

'I feel pretty strange about it,' he said. 'I don't feel as if I want to – I don't know – interfere with your Karma – do you know what I mean?'

'It's not that simple. Anyway, Karma has been pretty shitty to me recently.'

'You mean Julia.'

'Let's run,' I said. A couple of silent circuits. Then I said, 'You know when Julia died – was killed – ' I swallowed 'I felt like I'd forfeited my right.'

'Why?'

'I can't help feeling it's my fault in some way.'

'You think Mona killed them don't you.'

'I'm sure!'

'I don't know,' he said, 'there's something – not quite – right.' I felt numb incredulity at his reluctance to believe me. And rising irritation. 'Anyway, you couldn't have prevented it.'

'Hell Pieter I should have! I should have stopped Julia going out that day. I should have sorted out Mona long ago, had her committed. I should have – jeez, if only I had….' Here I go again.

'You know what? We all cause deaths every day, do you realise that?'

'What are you talking about?'

'Think of all the little fling creatures that get sucked into the engine of your car. Mr and Mrs Bug flying along nonchalantly after having a jolly bug screw, all in a jolly post-coital happy-with the world view, chatting about the weather when suddenly *whap*! Squashed killed and roasted. Killed by a Ford. Never mind. The end.'

'Shut up you fucking hippie weirdo.'

'Not to mention the steak you had last night! Huh? Charming Mrs Moo never did any harm to anybody, taken all confused, mouth full of mush, into a huge room full of blood and guts and corpses and screaming where she's murdered by a stranger, someone she wouldn't have *dreamed* of harming in any way, having committed no crime ever in her life! Zappo. Eight minutes of pleasure for little Tommy here and a coupla others. See? Every day you and me commit millions of murders.'

'Bollocks Pieter. It's not the same thing.'

'Why not? Because most of our victims are not people? Every day people die because other people don't do this or that. Usually because some bastard somewhere wants a bit of land or some more power or money or revenge – '

'You're saying I'm one of those, that because I want that money people are dying around me? Is that it?'

'Oh jeez Tom, stop!'. I stopped. He put both arms around me and hugged my sweating body to his, right there in the middle of the running track, and the other runners didn't mind because they thought we were just two machos like them who needed to give some comfort to one-another.

I had to fight tears. I broke away after a few seconds. 'You are my brother, Tom, and I love you. I want you to have whatever makes you happy.'

'I know.'

We ran some more. It was pretty chilly that day. A dull Autumn was following a dull Summer, and a dull Winter was gathering itself for a half-hearted assault on this island, somewhere to the north of the running track at Battersea Park.

'So you want me to make a few more deals before we blow the whistle,' I said.

'If that's what you want. Yes, of course. The more we have the more stink we can make. Everything this country buys from South Africa just helps the fat white cats grow fatter. I don't have to tell you. We've got to blow the whole BOSS network wide open. We have it in our hands. We've got to stop companies like yours who don't give a damn about supporting an evil fascist racist regime because they only care about profit. We've got to hurt the people who deserve to be hurt. At least we can make a little scratch in history.'

'Right on,' I said.

Winter settled in like a geriatric aunt come to stay. Trees held on to shreds of browned-off leaves. The streets were littered with cold. My life fell into a routine which was so different to the way I used to live that I began to believe I was someone else.

The only reminders that I was the Tom I had once been were the letters from James Truelove Esq., Executor of the Estate of the Late.

Extracts:

October:

> *'...pleased to see you are settling in so well. But never forget that there is a Spiritual Dimension to all our struggles. Do not fail to keep a cool head on your young shoulders...'*

November:

> *'I want you to know we are swelling with pride at your continuing excellence. It is obvious to us that you are in possession of an excellent brain for business. I do hope you will find a little more time for recreation, though, young man. Too much work and no play will make Tommy a very drear young man. What?'*

December:

> *'Do not become obsessed with your work to the exclusion of all else, my boy. This is merely a Word from the Wise. As the Guru says, "between each breath there must be a pause." I do recommend meditation. Failing that, some sex.'*

Each letter was shoved savagely into the drawer where it joined the others in the Drawer of Shame.

Meanwhile I worked hard at selling steel to the Lebanon, Zaire, the Cameroons. Steel made in South Africa. The Escom labels were removed. 'Made in Swaziland' substituted. Specification documents were in Afrikaans.

I kept copies of all telexes, invoices, made recordings of telephone calls. Pieter and I were building up a sizeable file. Though what Grabkin was doing was not strictly illegal in British law (things changed later on) the member countries of the OAU (Organisation of African Unity) – many of them our clients - had their own views of that! We knew that publicising the dirty deals would cause storms, upset, that the various Anti-Apartheid organisations would love it… and any company dirtying its hands with this triangulated travesty would be made a pariah.

One day all my work was rewarded.

I sat in Boles' office drinking a cup of tea. He smiled atwinkle at me from across the rosewood coffee table. There was so much smile on his face that all his wrinkles joined. 'We're very proud of you my boy,' he said. 'You've shown them all. I knew you would. That's why I hired you.'

'Well, thank you sir.'

'I think you have learned the first law of business.'

'What's that, sir?' I asked.

'Don't ask what is that. You know what is that.' Danger crackled for a minute over his face. Then the wrinkles spread themselves into smile mode again. 'That what comes first, boy, is Business. And second. And third. And last! Right? That *winning* is the only what is that. That is what! I'm increasing your salary.'

'Gosh.'

'Gosh? Not "gosh". Thank me!'

'Thank you.'

'I may even get you a new car.'

'Gosh. I mean, thank you.'

'Yes. And now you are legal, I may even put you on our private medical scheme.'

'Legal?'

'Work permit came through. The Home Office is our friend!'

'Gee. Thank you.'

'Yes.' He leaned back in his fat chair, took a fat cigar from a fat box, snipped it, set fire and sucked. Then, suddenly, 'Rhodesia.'

'Huh?'

'"Huh" is not what I want to hear!'

'I mean – very interesting. Um. Smith seems to be holding his own rather well. From what I hear they get everything they need from South Africa. Uh – '

'Yes yes, *nearly* right. There are still some things they can't get, because South Africa doesn't produce them, or has difficulty importing them.'

'Aha!'

'A good word. Aha. I like aha. And everything that goes to Rhodesia has to go through South Africa, so the South Africans are critical to their survival. Are you following me?'

I tried another 'aha'.

'Hmm. Yes. Aha indeed. And with your wonderful South African connections, do you get my drift?

'Yes sir,' I said.

'I need Grabkin to be right there, as the main supplier. Of everything. Do you get me? *Everything*. There's much money to be made. Profit, boy, profit!' His eyes glinted through the cigar smoke. 'Profit!!!' he almost screamed. Then, almost without a pause, 'Go! Get me profit! *Raus*!'

As soon as I shut his office door behind me the strained smile left and went off somewhere on its own.

'What's the matter?' Monica asked. 'He's just given you a raise!'

'I know.'

'He's ordered you a car!'

'I know.'

'Your work permit is through!'

'I know.'

'He's asked me to get a quote for putting you on BUPA'

'I know!'

'So?'

I couldn't explain to her how much the idea of being involved in actual sanctions-busting dismayed me. Even though I knew that this was exactly what Pieter and I had been waiting for. But sanctions busting was not just immoral, it was illegal too.

As I stared blankly at Monica's concerned and smiling face I realised that the Pieter Project, up to now, had been a game I was playing to ease my conscience. But now I was being asked to go another step into the muck. This is a Police matter. Prison calling. Wrath of the Law.

'I can't explain,' I said.

'Tom,' she looked gently into my eyes, 'it would help to talk about your problems.' Oh dear, I thought, she's *so* cliché driven….

'I know,' I said.

'You listened to me when I told you my troubles. You're the only person I've ever discussed the Boyfriend Problem with.'

'Oh good.'

'I'll tell you what,' she said, 'Meet me after work. The Runt' – her name for the boyfriend – 'is working late. Let's go and have coffee somewhere. Then you can tell me all about it.'

So after work we had coffee in a little Italian place near Leicester Square and I told her an assortment of lies about what was bothering me. Imagine if I'd told her the truth!

She listened with a small soft frown on her downy face.

'Cluck cluck,' she said, 'you have been having a hard time, haven't you?'

'I suppose so,' I said as her little hand with the too-big engagement ring reached across the table and took mine.

I flinched at the unexpected touch but then I thought, hello, this could be rather useful. Monica knows all sorts of things. She knows all the Boles dirt, for example. And probably everything about everyone in the firm.

She's not unattractive either, for a woman of her age. And maybe I need a bit of mothering right now. I've looked through the Lonely Hearts columns (never contacted anybody. They all seemed rather sad and shallow). I've shared some things with friends, and discovered how little they could really understand. I need to feel protected, by somebody who knew actually nothing about me. I want warmth and intimate dinners. And sex. Truelove was right about that!

I squeezed her hand back.

We walked out into the buzz stink and bustle of the rush hour. People zoomed past with Evening Newses or Evening Standards clutched between briefcases and raincoats. Cold this evening, but warmer than the last few days. Drizzle hanging in the dirty air.

'Tom,' she said, voice biting through the bustle, 'can I say something?'

'Of course you can,' I said, giving her Smile of Encouragement number 3.

'I've – oh dear, I can't believe I'm going to say it – uh fancied you rotten ever since I saw you that first day.'

Hah. The mouse hath roared! But I couldn't say what she wanted me to.

'Is that so awful?' She waited meekly for my response as we waited for the traffic light to change.

'Of course not!' I said, laughing. 'I've always thought of you as –' and I slipped an arm around her tiny waist. What was I getting myself into? Her too? Another six inch nail? Ah, but my poor neglected loins. All work and no play. Truelove, you shit. Your fault.

'What are you thinking?' she asked.

'Just – how dangerous it would be if you were to fall in love with me, I guess.'

'Far too early to be thinking about that!' she said. We sat on a bench. 'I don't want love,' she said and pulled me towards her with surprising strength. 'Just sex.'

Monica loved sex. Well, this shouldn't have been a surprise. She had told me that her main complaint against the Runt was his unavailability – and the more often I saw her, the more I sympathised with him. Her appetite was awesome. Every opportunity she had she'd make a grab for whatever part of me was within grabbing distance. We did it in the stock cupboard, we did it in the male toilet, we even did it in Boles' office one glorious afternoon when he was 'at a meeting'. She had no limits – once we did it four times in a day. Ok - me young and fit and spunky, I admit, but there were times frankly when I would have preferred to have been able to go a few days unmolested!

What was missing was the full bed scene. I didn't want to screw her in the flat. Three reasons. Julia. Mona. And, of course, the Runt! This mysterious elusive man in her life.

The subject of Mona started to blur. Either BOSS had found her or she was lying low, waiting. Maybe she had fallen into the Thames. Or overdosed. Or been murdered for the contents of her carrier bag.

I certainly hoped so.

THE XXTH CONGRESS OF THE DEPARTMENT FOR THE DEVELOPMENT OF THE BLACK RACES

The meeting was called to order by the Brigadier. 'All right everybody,' he said, 'settle down. Everybody got some champers, *ja*? All got enough to eat?

We nodded in an exaggerated display of happiness and satisfaction.

The interior of the Sloane Square Gents was decorated in orange, red and white bunting – the colours of the South African flag. The urinals were screened off by display boards carrying a photographic exhibition featuring pictures of happy smiling black faces in nice little box houses with flowers staggering bravely over yellow brick walls. A banner screamed

THE DEPARTMENT FOR THE DEVELOPMENT OF THE BLACK RACES – 20 YEARS OF PROGRESS

Proteas and other native South African flowers sagged in vases about the place.

In the middle of all this patriotic paraphernalia was a great stinkwood table laid with fourteen places. The cutlery was Cape silver, made by Daniel Hendrik Schmidt in 1794.

Fourteen men sat around the table on camp chairs and drank champagne from sparkling crystal glasses. The Brigadier sat at the head of the table, beaming like a bucolic godfather. Steaming plates of boerewors and pap, T-bone steaks and mash waited for the massed teeth of the men of BOSS. And Pieter. And me.

'Before we enjoy the marvellous fruits of our beautiful homeland – which, I must tell you, were flown out this morning especially for us by South African Airways – ' he paused so that we could clap appreciatively, 'I would like to say a few words.' Pieter kicked me under the table. 'This is a very special occasion, occasioned, as you may say, by our good friend Thomas Bloch.' I rose, bowed, sat. They clapped.

'This Bloch, this Thomas – I used to call him "doubting Thomas", didn't I, boy? – has served us very well. This is the very same Bloch who was once suspected to be a Commie. But I took him under my wing, and he has come through with flying colours.' They clapped again.

'This man, this Thomas – has been responsible for revenue to the South African treasury amounting to more than thirteen million dollars US. No mean sum, hey?' He beamed.

I turned up the volume on the pocket tape recorder in my jacket and hoped it was getting all this.

'And now I want you all to charge your glasses and drink a toast to the one pinko Jewboy who has seen the light. I give you, Thomas Bloch!'

They all rose and drank to me. Pieter's eyes met mine in a glancing blow of co-conspiracy. Did he, too, sense my twinge of guilt and betrayal?

We ticked into the pile of cooling, congealing food and drank in the air of camaraderie and bubbly and the reek of cigarettes, cigars and toilet disinfectant. Then we polished off vast heaped plates of koeksusters and sat back, full to bursting.

'Did you like that Bloch?' the Brigadier asked smugly. 'You see, like I said, we know how to reward our friends.'

'You certainly do,' I said.

'Ye well I hope this will be only the first of our celebrations Tom. We can only go from strength to strength from now on. Well, we'd better do the other toasts, hey?'

We all stood and the ritual toasts were gone through. To the Republic!' To Paul Kruger!' 'To the Voortrekkers!' 'To Hendrik Verwoerd the saint who discovered Apartheid!' 'To the Prime Minister Vorster!' Cheers. 'And now…to business!' Cheers. 'That wasn't a toast! *Fokken dom*… Siddown!!' Embarrassed laughter as we sat.

He turned to me. 'Now let's talk. Let's talk about our allies. Let's talk about Rhodesia.'

'Huh?'

'What are your thoughts about Rhodesia? Have you thought about how we can help our allies to the north to resist black domination and terrorists?'

'Coincidentally,' I said, 'I have.'

'Good!' he beamed.

'So, if you've been thinking, what do you think the Rhodesians need most?'

'Oil?' I asked.

'Good answer, intelligent answer. But silly. We got that problem well in hand my boy!' The men gave mild conspiratorial titter. 'No no my boy, there's something far more useful than mere oil. Now what can that be?' Suddenly he turned to the others in the room. 'Now my little man and me need a little bit of privacy. *Verstaan*?'

Blank faces.

'*Jislaik! Ek bedoel, voetsek*!' (If you must know, that means, 'Jeez! I mean, fuck off!')

Hurriedly and with some knocking over of glasses, they all vanished through a hastily unlocked entrance. Including Pieter.

While he relocked the entrance I reached nervously into my pocket and turned the tape-recorder on again.

'Uh – arms?' I asked with a sick, sinking feeling.

'You are getting a little warm.' He let out a guffaw of appreciation of his own wit. 'No no. What they need at the moment is rather more – *nuclear* than that!'

'You mean – '

'Use your wits!' The smile was gone. 'I'm talking about *survival* now, boy! The survival of the whole white race in Africa!'

'Survival?' I said.

'Now listen. We got all the basic materials for atomic power in South Africa, right? And already Rhodesia – this is not known, except by a handful of people – is building a reactor.' He sat back to study my reaction. So did I.

'Yes my boy! But it's even bigger than that. So you got to listen to me really carefully, Tom. What I'm telling you I wouldn't trust to my old mother. And she's a real old fashioned *boerevrou*. Eats blacks for breakfast'

More reaction studying. More sitting back, twiddling fingers. Lighting of a cigarette.

'Our backs are against the wall. If we let it happen, Rhodesia will fall to the Commies and we'll be next. Can you imagine what it would be like to have another bloody black state on our borders? A home for the ANC and the PAC and the bloody Russians right next door?'

'Terrible,' I said.

'Yes. That's the exact right word. Terrible.' He paused, sat back in his chair and sipped at his brandy. 'So we have devised a plan. It's called "Operation Deus Ex Machina." And that's where you come in.'

'Oh,' I said.

'Well? Do I have to spell it out? Are you as clever as I think? Huh?'

'Spell it out please Brigadier.'

'Very well then I will. The objective of Operation Deus Ex Machina is to give Rhodesia, and of course us as well, the only weapon that can save civilisation in Africa.' He paused, looked at me, waiting for me to say the words.

'The atomic bomb,' I said, hoping that the fear and despair I felt was somehow hidden behind my strained smile.

'Exactly. Well, aren't you honoured to be involved? Thrilled by this opportunity? Come on boy, show some enthusiasm!'

'Yes of course. Thrilled. Excited. Honoured. The lot!'

'Now listen carefully. We have in SA all the raw materials. We've got uranium, plutonium, whatever hey need. We also got good scientists and technicians. Our plant at Phalaborwa is as advanced as any in the world. But what we need is the computer backup, the control mechanisms, the ways of dealing with the Hard Water and whatnot, I don't understand he science part. The only people that have all this knowledge and equipment are he Superpowers. And of course they would never consider it officially. Especially the Brits. So that's where you come in.

'So here's your list!' He handed me sheaves of printouts, lists of equipment. 'You will have to use your head hey? Never get too much stuff from only one supplier. We don't want people to begin to add two and two. Spread your orders over a few months as well. Israel will supply lot of it, but the rest will have to come from the US and Europe. We will inform you of a number of different destinations you will dispatch to for transhipment. You will liaise with me at every stage. I'll want a preliminary report in ten days. Our friends in the north are in real trouble. Do you understand the importance of this mission for civilisation?'

'Yes,' I said hollowly. 'What an honour.'

He stood. 'Well, better get on with the washing up. Give me a hand.' He chortled as we collected the plates, glasses, cutlery. '*Ag*, where are the staff when you need them? Bloody proof we're more civilised than the Brits – at least we got servants!'

'One thing,' I said, as we piled dishes into a washbasin, 'have you – uh – our discussion last time about my wife – '

He clucked and shook his head. 'I told you what my attitude to that is,' he said, 'Yoyur domestic quarrels are your own affair. Marriage is qa holy state Ordered by God. You must go to this woman and make up your differences.'

'But I *explained* – '

'Think about what I said. My wife nags me all the time, says she can't understand why a full Brigadier in the SA Armed Forces has to be a toilet attendant. Sometimes my boy,' he put a wet hand comfortingly on my shoulder, 'I would dearly like her endorsed out but I stop myself. You should do the same'

'Easy for you to say!' I said, 'But just how can you expect me to really focus on my work when I'm worrying about her all the time? I mean, I want to give my job my fullest possible effort.'

'You'd better do that. The whole future of Africa could be on your shoulders.'

'I know.'

'I'll think about it.'

'Thank you.'

'Now hand me the Vim.'

There was one small pleasure Julia had left behind her, a legacy of joy, her two litre six cylinder Triumph GT6.

Dear monster of growl, no-one claimed it after she died. I had forgotten to mention it to her parents. I felt she would have wanted me to have it. So I did. Mine! Poor man's E-type they called it, because of its pocket-sized resemblance to the classic Jag. Sleek. Powerful. Hot. Gorgeous. Valencia blue.

On weekends I would leave the puce coloured Company Ford outside the flat, climb into the GT6 and let myself go.

Inside that hot fusty messy cockpit Julia was with me, at my side, her laugh, her perfume. Her litter – fag ends, unread letters, tissues, a lipstick - lolled about the carpets. I left it there. I never even emptied the ashtray.

I would point the bumptious little nose north or south or east or west and go like hell. Roar up the motorway, ignoring silly things like pig patrols or petrol or pricks in Capris. A tickle of the foot and dust behind!

And I would chat with Julia in my head. Clear my mind, share funnies or seriouses or ideas or annoyances.

This was what I did when I got home from that dreadful meeting. Roared off down the M4, my dead girl and me.

'You're in up over the very top of your little head now,' she said.

'I know that.' I swung us past a huge pantechnicon laden with boots. 'What am I going to do about it?'

'Oh I expect you'll take the Aquarian line.'

'Which is - ?'

'Oh, letting things happen, seeing how they turn out. Never making anything remotely resembling an actual *decision.*'

'I can make decisions! You know that!'

'Balls,' she said. 'You really are totally wet sometimes. Mind that truck!'

I swerved. 'I'm sure about one thing,' I said. 'There's no way I am going to help those racists in Rhodesia and the fascists in South Africa get the bomb!'

'Why do you say South Africa? I thought you said the stuff was for Rhodesia.'

'No way. They want the bomb for themselves. The Rhodesia story is just a little fiction, specially invented for me. They know Rhodesia will fall. They want the bomb so they can hold the whole continent to ransom. They think I'm an idiot.'

'Well you are sometimes.'

'Don't get tetchy. Why are you tetchy tonight?'

'You annoy me sometimes. I'm sorry.'

'That's all right,' I said, lapsing into a sulky silence.

'It's no bed of roses, you know. Being dead.'

'I really wish you were here…' I said, eye watering. 'If only…'

'Shut up your "if onlies"', she said and I swear I felt a ghostly hand touch lightly on mine.

Eight

One icy bright freezing snowless Tuesday morning in December I stepped out of the flat and there was a taxi between me and my company car. In my way. So naturally I went up to the window and said 'You fucking selfish bastard why don't you let your passengers off at that perfectly good parking space over there? I have to get to work! Fine for you, you're already *at* work!...'

'You don't have to swear at the man Tom, he's just doing his job.'

Shit. Voice from the past – 'Father!'

'Darling!'

'Mother!'

'*Hoesit Boetie*?'

'Plowsky!'

'Hello Tom,'

'Michelle!'

Then they all tumbled out of the taxi, a mess of family an baggage, and they were all over me. Especially Mother, who hugged and wept and there was a general babble of 'Why didn't you tell me you were coming?' and 'You look so *thin*!' and '*Fifteen pounds*! It's a fortune!' and 'Mommy I'm tired' and 'So this is London eh?'

'What are you all *doing* here?' I said finally as the taxi muttered off ('bloody mean Australians!') and the baggage lay about on the Cheyne Row sidewalk like victims on a battlefield.

'Well, we hoped it would be a nice surprise!' Mother said, a little hurt. 'Aren't you happy to see us?'

'Of course! It is! It is!' I said. To be fairly honest, it was. I had always suspected that I secretly quite liked my family.

'Come on darling, show us your flat. Here, grab the bags,' Mother said and we staggered upstairs, sharing the mass of suitcases between us.

'I was going to work,' I grinned as they flopped on the sofa and armchairs.

'We got here just in time then,' Father said.

'What can I offer you? How long are you here for? Where are you staying?' The questions bubbled out.

'I want a coffee. I'm going to stay awake,' brother Plowsky said.

'We're only here for the day,' Father said. 'We fly to Zurich tonight.'

'Switzerland?' I said, going into the kitchen. 'What are you all going there for?'

'This is such a lovely flat,' Mother said, coming after me. 'Can I help with anything?'

'No no. Coffee for everybody? I'd better phone work…'

'Things are hotting up at home,' Father's voice from the lounge. 'We have to get our money out. If Rhodesia goes, we're all for it'

'I see,' I said, filling the kettle. 'So why did you all come?'

'Allowances. We each have an Allowance of money to take out.'

'I see.' I grinned at Mother. 'Is this what they call "the Chicken Run", eh?'

'There's also another reason we're here,' Mother said quietly so the others couldn't hear. 'We want you to come back Tom.'

'Where's your bathroom?' Michelle's voice. 'I want to splash my face.'

'So do I!'

'So do I!'

'So do I!'

'Down that small flight of stairs,' I shouted, 'First door on the left.' Then, more quietly, 'I won't be doing that Mother.'

'Just listen to what your Father has to say.' She said. 'Now tell me darling,' she was rooting through my cupboard for unchipped mugs. And also to inventory my food. 'Tell me about Mona.'

I groaned.

''We know she's no longer with you,' she said. 'And that you have someone new. So tell me dear,' she stroked my shoulder gently, 'what happened?'

'Oh she's just. I mean, we. It didn't work out. She went off. That's all I want to say.'

'Poor darling. It hurts, doesn't it?' She rescued sugar bowl and tray from behind the sink.

'Yes,' I said, surprised at how she had wrung a pang out of me. I changed the subject. 'So how is everybody back – back there?'

Mother was not to be deflected. 'Funny thing,' she went on, 'her parents don't seem worried. They had a letter from her he other day. Her father tells me she was going on about how much she still loves you.'

'*Was* she?' This was confusing information. 'Where is she? Did they say? What is she doing?'

'They didn't say. They're not worried. I suppose she'll find her feet. She's awfully self-confident, isn't she?'

'Not really,' I said glumly. I wanted to tell Mother that Mona was no longer the girl she had known. I wanted to tell her everything, but I couldn't bear her reactions. Or the flood of bridge-table bromides I would be submerged in.

'Well, take the tray dear,' she said and I carried the steaming cups into the lounge.

'What were you two whispering about?' Father asked.

'He was telling me about Mona,' Mother said. 'She's gone, dear. I explained to you what happened. Anyway, the subject's closed.'

'Why?' he asked. 'Why is it closed?'

'He doesn't want to talk about it.'

'Finished!' Michelle emerged from the bathroom, pink and glowing. 'I feel much better now. Didn't sleep a *minute* on the plane!'

'My turn!' Plowsky said, pushing Father out of the way in his rush for the bathroom. 'Need a shit! Now!'

'Rude boy,' Mother muttered. 'Darling,' she turned to Michelle who was dabbing at wet hair, 'why don't you go and have a lie-down?'

'I don't want a lie-down,' she said. 'I'm just waking up now.'

'Go on Michelle. We need to talk to Tom.' Father said, attempting authority.

'Oh all *right*!' Michelle whinged. 'I suppose that's the bedroom? Do you only have *one*?' she pointed to a door.

'Yes,' I said, thinking, no change. Still a cat. Still no tits.

She went in, slammed the door and no doubt attached her ear to the keyhole.

'Ok, what?' I sat on an armchair facing them. The coffee between us on the sofa table.

They seemed to have aged quite a lot in the twelve months I had been away from home. Father was lined and ragged, dressed in his old tweed jacket and slacks. Mother had lost or smeared makeup and looked vulnerable. I tried to suppress the warmth for them that wanted to rise.

Hell! I suppose they were just exhausted after sixteen hours on a night flight.

'Hang on. Before you talk I have to phone.' I said and dialled work. 'Migraine,' I gasped to Monica.

'You poor darling. Well go to bed. I'll tell God. I'll see he doesn't 'phone you.'

'Thank you,' I moaned, replaced the receiver.

'Was that work? You don't have a migraine really do you dear? I don't understand why you have to lie. You could just say your family are here from abroad...'

Groan...Which, I was thinking, was beginning to feel just like a migraine, without the headache. 'So what do you want to talk about?' I asked.

'I've said it once. Tom, we need you to come back with us. Come back home.' Father said.

'What, now?' I asked with a grin.

'Don't be sarcastic. Just listen to me for the first time in your life. I have been right about quite a lot of things in my life, haven't I? You have to admit. You remember I said that woman wasn't right for you?'

I didn't remember. 'I don't remember,' I said.

'Well, I did. You probably weren't listening. No, what I want to say is – '

'Now I know why you look so thin! It's that ridiculous beard thing you used to wear. It's gone! Do you see that? His beard is gone!'

'I'm *talking*, Anne.'

'Sorry dear. Go on. He looks so much better. Sorry.'

'Listen here my boy. I mean, we're really very proud of you, now you have a flat and a job and so on – '

'We thought we'd find you in a squat, to tell you the truth dear,' Mother interrupted.

'Let me talk, Anne. The fact is my boy, I will have to retire some time in the next few years. So I came to tell you, I want you to come back so I can train you to take my place.'

'What?'

'Yes dear, he means it. You've proved that you can be a businessman – '

'Well I believe you are doing well at Grabkin. Like I said, I'm proud of you.'

'*We're* proud of you.'

'Thank you.'

'So what do you say?'

I shook my head. It was both an expression of amazement and a negative.

'Why are you shaking your head? Is it the new girlfriend or what?'

'There's no girlfriend. Any more.' I said, though I felt Julia at that moment looking over my shoulder and laughing at me. If only they knew! I shook my head again.

'So what's the matter with you? What's stopping you?'

'You know...' I said, 'I always thought you thought I was an idiot. A dreamer. Never be good at anything. You told me that often enough.'

'All right. I was wrong. I can see how well you're doing. You even *look* like a businessman, for once. Nice suit!'

'Ok dad, let's get to it: is this about the Inheritance?'

'Yes, there is that.'

'There is that.'

Pause.

'*Think*, boy. No-one could ever imagine you not to be – "sane and responsible"' (he actually did the two finger thing in the air at this, 'if you're in training to be the MD of one of the biggest companies in South Africa! There where there is so much support for you.'

'And so many fewer temptations,' Mother said confusingly. 'Tell him the rest Danny,'

He gave her an angry glance. Then, after reflecting awhile, added 'Perhaps you're right dear. Tom, we have to make *sure* you inherit, understand? The Revolution is just around the corner. I give it one year, maybe two at the most. Once you get that money, it's all payable in the UK! There it will be, a nest egg for us all to live on happily when the country blows up. Let's face it, the amounts we are getting out of the country are a pittance. Especially when you look at the costs of setting up house in a new country. And once you're in SA, we can pull a few strings, you know, with the lawyers and such. We know the lawyers there. Old man Goldberg plays golf with me! And this fellow over here, what's his name, Truelove. There's no chance with him making the decision! So what do you say?'

A depression wafted in through the window and settled on me. I didn't want to answer. Or even talk.

'Tell us what you think darling, or do you want some time - ?' Mother said.

I just sat there shaking my head.

'Come on boy, what are you thinking? Share it with us. Say it.'

'You really want to know?' I raised my head from my hands. 'Iwas thinking, nothing's changed. You *still* think I'm useless, you still think I can't handle this business on my own. So you want to take over. Once you didn't care if I got the money or not! Now that your little fascist state looks wobbly, you want to make sure I inherit. For you!'

I didn't mean it to come out like that. I certainly didn't mean the 'for you' to be quite so – so – nasty.

There was a silence while they stared unbelievingly at each other. Father's face arranged itself into 'I told you so'. Mother's fell into 'No darling please don't...'

'You think *we* want *your* money?' Father spat out at last. 'You think we want to rob our own son?'

'No Father that's not what I meant – '

'It's what you *said*! I can't believe it! Like we want to cheat you!' He was going a perfect purple. 'We came here to make you the best offer you've had in your life!'

'- only because we love you – ' Mother slipped in.

' – and to help *you*!'

'I told you he'd say no!' Michelle came out of the bedroom, triumphant.

'So did I!' Plowsky emerged from the bathroom. 'Hey haven't you got any shaving cream?'

'Never mind shaving cream!' Father said, standing dramatically. Then, as in a Victorian melodrama, 'We're leaving!'

'But – '

'But – '

'But – '

'But – '

I escorted them to the King's Road to find a cab and we were an ambulatory shouting seething protesting and (as far as Mother was concerned) weeping melodrama. W must have entertained hundreds of people in Cheyne Row, Upper Cheyne Row and Oakley Street.

The babble died down somewhat as we stood and waited. Each was all bawled out. A cab was hailed. Father ushered them all in. Grabbed me by the arm as they waited to go. 'Listen oy, one more time. Think hard. Let me know if you change your mind.' He turned as if to get in, then stopped, pulled me very close. 'I'm sorry you sold out,' he said, 'I could have used you. Have you lost *all* your principles?'

'What do you mean?'

'I can't explain. Not now. Just come to your senses, that's all I ask.

And my family was gone and this time I really felt as if I'd lost them forever.

Nine

I spent Christmas with Grant, Nora, Brian and the rest in Bromley style. Grant and Nora couldn't hide their smug delight and the reconciliation between me and Pieter and lavished nut loaf on the lot of us.

And then quite suddenly it was January. One more month to go. The last month in which to wind up. Or down. In which to become. Or cease to become. Like a condemned man. The old Tom, marching to the gallows. The new Tom, stinking of compromise, writhing with guilt, brimming with power.

I went about in a daze. Everything I saw, everything I did, I kept thinking, This Could be the Last Time. Stones! Played itself again and again in my mind. May beee the lassst time, I don't know....OH NO...

Withers Stronglode Withers and Truelove
Solicitors and Commissioners for Oaths
5a London Wall London EC4

January 1st, 1970

Dear boy

This is the penultimate letter from your friend James Truelove and I would like to herewith formally express what a pleasure it has been working with you.

This is the appropriate time to sum up my personal feelings, as well as those of some of my associates whom it has pleased us to call the Jurors in the matter of your late Grandmother's will.

As far as your Personality Assessment goes, we have concluded that your intelligence and creativity remain intact despite. The fact you have not made any major effort to discover the identities of your Jurors has been somewhat puzzling to say the least; I had thought that your acuity would lead you straight to their lairs and by now you would have disposed of at least three.

Your commercial acumen will no doubt count heavily in your favour. I would add that this statement is not in itself to be taken as my endorsement of your capacity to inherit. This will depend on the evidence and opinions of all the Jurors who have given so generously of their time.

I am pleased you have found some pleasure in your own company and do hope that in your solitary moments you have found the time for meditation as I suggested. Spiritually, we are all of us able to change.

Wishing you luck and good judgement! Do not fuck it up.

Yours truly

James

James Truelove BA LLB
UK Executor for the Estate of the late Hazel Stone

January rolled out like a Disney movie – very pretty, very brief and terribly corny. The weather was still, cold, clear. Occasional snow fluttered prettily about the windows, showing off some fancy acrobatics. By the next day it had vanished with no trace, as if someone had switched off the projector.

Work was easy. I was left alone to get on with the shopping on the shopping list. That list! All my precious evidence. All Pieter and I had to do now was to collect and collate the tape recordings, the photocopied documents for the triangulated steel deals and above all the Deus Ex Machina project. All the dirt. The Grabkin filth. The BOSS elephant shit. It was all coming together. All so easy. It felt as if everything was just falling into place…

During the Sunday run we discussed our plans. 'The main thing puff,' Pieter said, 'is to get the stuff to the newspapers and the police – '

'What, both? Why?'

'If we only hand the stuff to the police,' he puffed, 'the main bit – the stuff that's immoral as well as illegal – will never be known. What's more,' he went on. 'it's got to be done in such a way that neither of us is connected with the disclosures. We'll be dead if they find out it was us, that's for sure!'

'Ha! Fat chance! Of COURSE they'll know it was us! I don't care, myself. We just have to stop them getting hold of the Bomb. That's all that really matters!'

'Hey, I care,' he said. 'I don't want to end up falling out of a window or being knocked over by a hit-and run driver!'

'You should have thought of that when we started this thing! I can't believe you're *now* thinking about yourself...'

We ran in silence for a bit while I bit my tongue.

'Sorry Pieter I didn't mean it that way. They'll be in jail, anyway! Those BOSS idiots. They can't get us from there.'

'Don't be so sure... shit! It's cold!' he remarked, speeding up.

I kept pace.

'There'll be others,' he continued. 'If this ring is broken, they'll just send another lot over. They'll just start up again....and you know what? If they still trust me...I'll just do it all again!'

'Do you really think they won't realise you shopped them?'

'Bugger it...' he said, 'I suppose I'll have to be arrested along with those bastards.'

'You can turn Queen's Evidence. We are going to have to go public – '

'Either way I lose,' he said sadly.

'You should have thought of this when we started the whole thing.' I snapped, impatient. 'Shit Pieter, you knew what the odds were!'

'Yes I knew. But now everything's coming to a head I – '

'You don't fancy martyrdom.'

'Right.'

'And what about me?' I asked. 'They'll be after my blood too.'

'Hah!' he said. 'You'll have your money to protect you!'

'Maybe. To protect *us*.'

'*Ons moet 'n plan maak'* he said. We must make a plan.

We ran on in silence.

There was something wrong at home. I knew as soon as I opened the door. There was a strange sort of displacement of the air, as if it had moved in some way since I left. As if it had passed through someone else's lungs...then I knew.

Someone had been through the place. Someone had opened all the drawers and closed them again. Moved everything about. Just a bit. And the strangest thing about it all was it looked – well – a bit *cleaner.* And tidier.

Hmm. If Truelove had sent his spies into my life, why had they cleaned all the glasses? Emptied out all the kitchen cupboards and cleaned them, before refilling them in perfect order? Was it BOSS maybe? The Brigadier loved cleaning things! The cooker shone. The bathroom and kitchen floors glowed. Even the windows were entirely faultlessly blemishlessly see-through, for the first time since before I moved in.

Who? Why? I rushed to the small piano stool that I used to store evidence. The papers appeared untouched, though the stool's mahogany shone with beeswax.

I had to talk to Pieter. But there was no way I could get hold of him without being monitored in some way. I would have to wait a week, until our next run.

On Monday I went to work as usual. Worried silly all day. Was I going crazy? No, this wasn't my imagination! The place had been securely locked as usual. Yet somebody...somebody...

When I got back that evening the Good Fairy had been again. Ashtrays had been emptied and washed. The bath was free of scum. Everything was neat and tidy and in its place.

Tuesday the same. I had deliberately left a pile of washed clothes on the bed. When I returned they had bee folded and put away.

Surely this had something to do with Truelove. It seemed the sort of thing that creep would get up to just to remind me I am being watched. Maybe he's just obsessed with me. Trying to make me happy? Must change the locks, must change the locks! How do I change locks?

If it was BOSS, they would have taken the papers. And I'd be dead, not cleaned. The piano stool would not have fooled them.

Only one way to find out.

On Wednesday I left for work at the usual time. Halfway through the day I threw a migraine and went home.

I parked around the corner. I let myself in and closed the front door very quietly. Tiptoed up the stairs to the door of the flat. As I turned the key I heard a panicky scuffle inside. Banging the door open, I heard a clatter, and ran up the stairs which led from the lobby to the lounge. No one. Then, suddenly, footsteps behind me from the bedroom! I dashed to the bedroom too late to catch whoever it was flying down the stairs. Looking out of the window I was just in time to see a flutter of skirt vanish around the corner.

So the phantom cleaner is a woman! But how the hell did she get in? And – well, how did she get out? And!

At least she seemed in no way dangerous. And at least she wasn't the Brigadier! Well, apparently not. Though was my flat now full of bugging devices? If that was her purpose, why clean the place?

I went back into the lounge, confused and frustrated. The television was on. A box of chocolates lay open on the sofa table.

Evidently the Phantom Char liked to relax between cleans.

I felt frightened for the first time in ages. I had always known that Pieter and I were playing a dangerous game, but I had never felt so vulnerable before.

Somebody was getting into my locked flat regularly. There were murderous racist spies who didn't trust me. There was a lunatic hippie lawyer wanting to know my every move. And somewhere out there Mona was lurking, madness and murder in her eyes…

Every night after locking myself into the flat I'd hook a chair under each doorknob, like in the movies. Every curtain was closed, every window secured. I searched the place assiduously several times for bugs, never found any. What does a bug look like? I presume the clue is in the name. Electric beetles. I felt under siege. Waiting. Listening. Jumpy as a kangaroo on speed.

Sunday dragged itself at last into my life. I met Pieter at the running track but no running was possible because the world had turned white, the sky was full of gentle snow, vast flakes motionless in the still air. The running track was bleached out of sight. We sat on the bench outside the changing room, sheltered by a few inches of roof. I was shivering in my tracksuit and Pieter was shivering in his.

'What are we going to do?' I asked.

'I've been thinking a lot,' Pieter said. 'This is how I see it: if we follow our original plan, both of us will have to give evidence. We'll be right in the eye of the hurricane. If we follow plan B and *you* do the gaff-blowing, then I'll go to prison with the rest and *you'll* be the one BOSS will be after. For the rest of your life. Yet I favour plan B.'

'Why?'

'Because it leaves me where I am now. Fifth Column.'

I stared at the motionless snowflakes, hypnotised. 'Alternatively,' I suggested sadly, 'we could do nothing.'

'And let those bastards hold the world to ransom? You're crazy.'

'You're right Pieter. But there's something else. Someone's been in my flat.'

'*What?*'

'I don't think it was them. Whoever it is cleans and tidies the flat. Watches television. Eats chocolates. And the actual evidence hasn't been touched.'

'Maybe they didn't find it?'

'I thought of that. I put a hair on the clasp which shuts the piano stool where I've hidden the papers. The hair was gone next day, so the stool was opened. But everything was still there. I just don't understand.'

'I don't like it,' Pieter said glumly. Then, after a while, 'Well? What do you think we should do?'

'I dunno.' The snowflakes began to make pictures. A great white horseman an a massive white steed dressed in ancient armour, fierce. 'I dunno if I'm meant to be a hero.' The horse reared, hooves striking at me. 'Am I?'

'You remember our discussion about how many millions of things we kill just because we don't think about it?'

'Um.'

'Stop dreaming! Here's our chance to maybe save thousands of lives. Just by speaking up. Just by actually *doing* something!'

'Do you realise that whatever we do, we're betraying somebody? I'm talking about Morality now. Big M.'

'How so?'

'Well, if we blow the gaff I'm betraying my Company. You're betraying yur bosses. Sorry about the pun. And we put loads of people out of work. Friends. Noel. Monica.'

'If we *don't* do it, we're betraying ourselves. And millions of people struggling under Apartheid. How can you weigh – '

'It's just not that simple - !'

'You can't get cold feet now. I mean, if I'm prepared to go to prison – '

'I could get killed!'

'I know. I know. Look. You are going to have to decide. It's all up to you. If you decide to do nothing, I'll go it alone. It'll be hard without your evidence. But we've got to get those bastards! Why should evil survive and thrive? Didn't you read all those books when you were young, all those novels in which the Hero always wins? Good triumphs over evil?'

'Life isn't like that.'

'Don't give me bullshit clichés. Why shouldn't it be? Why should those cynical swine who believe that the way to profit and power is through screwing people, *why* should they win? When we've actually got the goods on them? When we could bring them low? – ' He was getting very angry.

'I have to think,' I said and walked out into the snow, right through the White Knight.

I suppose I was hesitating because I didn't know what was going to become of me in a few weeks' time. Because of the Inheritance. Because of the morality of the whole thing. Because I was shitscared of the consequences of making *any* decisions.

I kicked my way through the powdery snow, looking back now and then at the white-smudgy lonely figure of my friend on the bench. And battling the buzzing whirrs of the 'whatifs' which crowded the air around me like a million snowflakes.

What if I didn't inherit and I blow the whole Deus Ex Machina? No job, for sure! Bole would make sure no-one would ever employ me again. The fate of the whistle-blower.

What if Boles disowned me? Claimed to have known nothing about the triangulations I'd apparently set up with BOSS' help?

Most of what I had done, though had actually been legal. Except of course for the sanctions busting for Rhodesia. And then, what about the Nuclear stuff? There could be prison for that.

And I'd be on the BOSS death list. For sure.

Yes....

Wait a minute. Starting to get an idea.

What if I actually pull the Inheritance? If we were to hold back until that was finalised? I'll be rich as. Rich enough o pay for a load of plastic surgery. For passports from any damn country I chose. Lots of houses...Bermuda, the Seychelles, Transylvania...

Well, there'd certainly be enough for both of us.

Strange that. In the beginning, when I first heard about the Inheritance I'd thought, nah. Could never happen to me! Who would ever think me 'sane', 'responsible'? They would only have to ask the people who know me. Father for instance.

Then I thought, whatthefuck, I'll show them. I can be whtever I want to be. It was as if fate conspired with me. Things fell into some sort of place.

And then, what happened was, with all that shit with Mona, then with Julia, I kind of. Forgot. Kind of. All about it. It became one of those things that *could have* happened. Like breaking the bank at Monte Carlo.

But surely, just on the surface at least, had I not been exemplary? Working! Solid citizen! Not even doing much drugs.

Could it just – happen? Not if I blow the gaff on Boles and BOSS, that's for sure! The Establishment protects it own. It would rather see me crushed to bloody porridge than give me a massive fortune which would invite me right in to their dirty club.

There was a white soup of snow now between Pieter and me. I was halfway across the track and all I could see of the other side was the looming shape of the changing rooms, and I knew that in that gloom somewhere was a tiny pinprick of light, a lonely and vulnerable man, shivering and staring into the whiteness knowing that somewhere his Fate mused and muttered to itself.

The White Knight is back now, rearing between us, and I don't know if it is me or if I am the dragon it's here to slay.

Yes I always wanted to be a hero, always secretly hoping the ship would sink so that I could rescue everybody. Or the building burn so I could be the one who carries the President to safety through the flames…

Pieter are you still out there?

Bugger it! I peered through the Knight, and there they were, the muzzy changing rooms…The changing rooms!

Yes, it's about changing. I have to change, yes! Change! I ran then, slipping often in the new snow, heading for Pieter. Oh yes Pieter, how could I have hesitated, how could I have considered escaping my duty! Why did we wait so long – *whoops!* – ha ha!

The building takes shape, I can see the shape of it, the pillars even.

I see the small dark form huddled on the bench waiting for me.

'Pieter! Pieter! I'm going to do it! We've got to do it. I don't care how! Pieter damn it. Pieter. Pieter wake up. Pieter? Pieter….NO! No no no no NOOOOOOOO….!'

I screamed and screamed I don't know how many times – anger, rage, madness. And hugged the cold bony body to me.

There was a hole in his head, the size of a walnut. His life had fallen out of it.

I never knew he was so bony.

It's All Right, Piccanin

One night Pieter and I sat on the hillside above Trichardsdal watching the stars come out – boys then, virgins still I think, we hadn't even killed anybody – we had spoken of Umfaan, whose name means 'boy' in his language, and Pieter told me one of the Old Man's stories.

Listen, he said, and I'll tell you the story just the way the Old Man told it to me.

'One time', said Umfaan, drawing deeply on the long pipe which was filled with a foul mixture of mouldy tobacco and best dagga from Rhodesia. 'I was a member of a gang of *tsotsis* who were the terror of the township of Alexandria by Johannesburg.

'Well at the time I had never killed anybody before because I was the piccanin of the gang, I was only eight years old. I was used as a spy, to find out everything that was happening like who had just got paid so we could rob him or what the other gangs were doing so we could stay out of their way or fight them if they were weaker, or where the police was patrolling so we would know when it would be safe to raid the tobacco shop.

'We were called the Redskins, our gang, and our greatest rivals were the Mofolos. They were a band of ruffians like you've never seen! *Au!* Those fellows were tough. They were all so big they looked like Springbok rugby players and we were all much smaller, but there were more of us and we reckoned we were better, because we were faster, see?

'And these were the gangs that were fighting for the control of that section of the township where the Garage was and the poorest of the poor people lived.

'Alright, so this one night we were preparing ourselves for one helluva big robbery, the biggest one we ever attempted. There was a rich man who lived a little way away who was called Albert Phoma, who owned the Store you see. Now he had all his money from preying on the people and his house was said to be full up with antiques and all valuable things. So we believed this Ft Cat deserved to be robbed and I was sent out to scout.

'We planned it really well. There was barbed wire and glass on top of the wall, so they put blankets on it. There was three dogs, they had to die. Poisoned chicken.

'Then they sends me over the wall and I let myself in the bathroom window which only little piccaninny could get in. So that way I entered the house.

'I was so scared I can tell you! I was shaking like an old alkie deprived of his *skokiaan*. But the house was very quiet. I could hear this tok tok, a huge clock like I never saw before. My heart was making the same noise.

'So I tiptoes towards the lounge, and there what do I see? I see two men in the light of the street lamp shining through the window. The one was very big and fat and he was lying on the floor like a dead elephant.

'And standing over him with a big knife like a butcher is Jim Mofolo himself, leader of the Mofolo gang! And this I swear: he also is shaking like *another* old alkie deprived of his *skokiaan* as he stood there and stared at what he had done. This boy was only about eighteen but as I saw him standing there though he was full of muscles like Charles Atlas he looked very small to me.

'Then he looked up and saw me. First he got a fright, then when he saw just a little boy he gave a sort of brave sideways grin. "What are you doing here piccaninny?" he whispered.

'Well I could see what *he* had been doing. "The same as you", I answered bravely.

'"You have better fok off," he said, "This is Mofolo business."

'Well, I was annoyed! "This is not your territory", I said, "*You* fok off!"

'He laughed. "My men are outside. I am going to let them in now. If you're still here when I come back we will give you the same what we gave him!" gesturing contemptuously at the huge corpse at his feet.

'I was going to say, so are mine! But then I thought, they can't be. When they saw the Mofolos about the place they probably ran. How did this guy get in?

'And then he turned away and as he did so I saw clasped in the dead man's hand a poker that he had probably picked up when he came into the lounge to see who was robbing him. So with a *flash*! I grabbed that poker and jumped up on the couch to give me enough height and I *hit!* him with that poker, and it went *crunch!* on Big Jim's head and he went down on the carpet, next to his victim.

'Well, I stood there on the couch and stared in shock at these two men lying together like husband and wife. Mofolo was still breathing and I remember thinking, "Don't die, Big Jim, please don't die," and you know, I started to cry.

'Then I got down from the couch and kneeled next to him and held his bleeding head in my hands. His breathing got harder and I knew he was going.

'And you know what, just then his eyes focussed on me, and he looked me straight in the eyes, and you know what he said? Like this, "It's all right piccanin, it's no big deal…"

'Then he died and I heard his soul flutter out of the window like a bird.'

I swear I saw those same words hanging in the snow-filled air as Pieter fluttered out of my life like a bird.

'It's all right piccannin…'

Ten

I missed Pieter's funeral. It wasn't my fault. Nora had telephoned me tearfully to tell me about his death, 'mugged in the Park'. I didn't tell her that I knew better. I told nobody except you. I had just left him, well, it. Pieter had left me, actually. I left it. The body. Because hell, I didn't want to have to talk to the police, not with what had happened with Mona and Julia and all that…as if deaths follow me everywhere, this is not something tat happens to everybody. Besides no way did I want BOSS to know Pieter and me had secret meetings. He had left his body. He had been expelled from it. He didn't care what happened to his body once he had left. He always said that.

I set out from work for the funeral on a chilly Thursday at 2pm. I drove like a maniac. I did actually want to get there. Not for Pieter, for Nora. And the others. The funeral was at 3.00 in the South London Cemetery. The traffic was snarled up all the way down Park Lane. Bomb scare or something. There was no way around.

When eventually I got south of the river traffic was at a standstill again. So I sat in my car and screamed, drew in deep breaths of carbon monoxide and hash, muttered, turned the radio on and off. I was only going because of Nora…she wouldn't understand if I was late. All the Bromley people would be there. Nora had apparently sent a telegram to Pieter's parents, but I doubted they would fly from South Africa.

And as I sat in my car the only emotion I could feel was Hate. The only desire I had was Revenge. It addled my brain with the exhaust fumes. Mona, I was convinced, was the cause. She had killed my friend, I had no doubt of it. She killed him! Before I could *tell* him, before I could explain that whatever happened I would support him, be with him. He never knew about my revelation… My mind went red. That hole - ! …..the traffic moved on an inch. It could only have been Mona. She who would never let me alone, never let me get anything that would make me happy! And Nora called it a 'mugging'. Trying to protect me, bless her.

By 2.30 I was still on Chelsea Bridge. To my right Battersea Park lay like a rape victim under its cosy burden of snow. Mixed in somewhere in all that snow was blood and my tracks and the tracks of my brother and the tracks of his murderer. Frozen in. A mute, frozen tragedy.

'*Ag* it's nothing *Broer*, just no big deal' Huh? Pieter's voice. Certainly! Pieter's voice!

'Pieter! What?'

His voice I swear had been as clear and bright as if he was sitting right next to me. Was it him? Or Mr Wishful Thinking? But the voice didn't come again. I shouted his name. But he had just been passing by and had popped into my car to give me a little bit of comfort.

'Pieter,' I promised, 'whatever happens, before this Project goes much further I'm gonna make sure the bitch gets it!' and I banged the dashboard in angry confirmation, in case he was still hanging about.

2.45. No chance of getting there on time. Nora and Grant won't understand.

Damn, I thought, to hell with it.

And I decided I have to take my life by the neck *now*. I'm never going to be manipulated again. I have to take control!

And for the first time in years, as I breathed in deeply, suddenly I felt strong. I felt sure. I felt *right*. There were much more important things than the Millions. Things that had to be done, whatever the consequences!

Ripping through the gears I made a perilous U-turn and headed back towards Chelsea.

'Pieter's dead,' I told the Brigadier who, leaning on his mop, looked up startled and lost his smile.

'I know,' he said. 'Tragic hey? What a mystery!'

'Yes,' I said bitterly. 'Tragic. Now I have an ultimatum to put to you.'

'What the hell do you mean ultimatum?'

'Like this: either you – what was your silly phrase? – "endorse out" my wife, or I stop work on Deus Ex Machina.'

Then before he could answer or yell for his louts to beat me up, I left.

5

One

Withers Stronglode Withers and Truelove
Solicitors and Commissioners for Oaths
5a London Wall London EC4

February 1st 1970

Dear Tom

This is my final letter to you. Although you and I have never met, I now know you far better than any of my other clients. As you can imagine, I have a very large file indeed of documents relating to the last nine months of your life, as well as the considerable data relating to your previous history.

I tell you this in order to reassure you that the decision which will be made when you reach your majority will be based on sound evidence from impeccable sources and will therefore be as fair and true as any verdict reached in the Old Bailey its very self.

The nub of the question at issue which will be discussed and debated in your presence will be, 'Is Thomas Bloch now of 9 Cheyne Row Chelsea SW3 a sane, fit and responsible person to be awarded a sum of money exceeding fifty million pounds sterling? Should the decision be in the affirmative, you will be immediately put in possession of the financial instruments and documentation relating to your inheritance, including the deeds to various properties which appertain to the said estate.

I wish to add a small personal note here. It is of course possible that the decision will go against you. Should this happen, I beg you to consider what you have gained in the past months. You now have a respectable job with an international company. You own a beautiful car and live in a flat in one of the smartest parts of London. You are no longer dependent on mind-changing drugs. You may well feel this has been worth the other sacrifices you have been obliged to make.

The world is your oyster young man, all because your saintly Grandmother was concerned about what would happen to you after her death.

She evidently loved you very much, just as Count Laszlo Mindchyck, whose millions were bequeathed to her, loved your dear Grandmother. The message of this short informal sermon my boy is this: Love is the most important thing in the world and it gets you where you are today. As Guru Jenkins says, 'Death is merely Love's way of renewing itself. And vice versa.' I hope that whatever happens, you will continue to consider me an ally. Please always remember our services are extensive, relatively inexpensive and guaranteed by the Law Society to be of the utmost probity.

Please note: the date of the Hearing is Sunday the Fifteenth of February. Kindly present yourself at your place of work, as your Employer has very kindly allowed us the use of his premises, at 20.00 hours precisely.

Yours,

James

James Truelove BA LLB
UK Executor for the Estate of the late Hazel Stone

'So what is all this Jenkins rubbish Truelove? I ask you to write a simple letter and you put all this crap in. Why?' Laszlo paced up and down Truelove's office, waving the letter furiously.

'You never complained when I mentioned the Swami in my other letters –' Truelove whined. 'Besides, the boy needs to understand there is another side to these things, the spiritual side – '

'*Spiritual*!? Huh!'

'Yes. He needs a refuge in case there's a negative result – '

The old man came to a halt like the Road Runner at the cliff edge. Carefully, he uncrumpled the letter and re-read it, one foot immobilising the bean-bag opposite Truelove's desk as if to stop it escaping. Then he forced a thin smile. 'I'm sorry young man. You're right of course. I am nervous for him too! After all, I have my furry spiritual side of course.'

The Truelove eyebrows rose involuntarily. Never before had he experienced his employer admitting to any depth of sensitivity to the spiritual. 'Do you want to sit down?' he asked, jumping up from his chair and offering it to the old man, who sat gratefully.

'Yes yes sometimes I get a little tired,' Laszlo sighed. 'Now you sit too, eh?'

Automatically Truelove looked about for a chair even though he knew there wasn't one. So he sat on a beanbag on the floor. Crossed his legs. Uncrossed them. Sat on his haunches. Could not decide whether his client would regard a lotus position as appropriate to the circumstances.

The Count watched his discomfort with a slow triumphant smile.

'So tell me,' he said, 'How do you think young Tom is standing up to all this at present?'

'Well sir his friend died you know.' Truelove said, pushing his legs out in front of him.

'I know that. So? Lots of my friends died. In the war, in the peace, even in the bathroom. I know much more dead people than live people. So what. He was mugged, wasn't he?'

'Well, the Police seem to think so,' Truelove said sceptically. 'But I'm looking into it.'

'Do that. There are some very strange things going on here. I don't like strange things unless I'm doing them. Find out why and fix it.'

Truelove shifted his weight again. His back was aching. He yearned for the Calm the Ravaged Mind position. But as it included placing the left foot behind the neck he thought better of it. 'By the fifteenth all will be known,' he said, 'I promise you.'

'Well you had better make sure all the arrangements are perfect. Is that clear? You'd better send this.' He threw the letter, twisted like a pretzel, at the lawyer.

'One thing I have to ask you sir,' Truelove said, retrieving the creased sheet of paper.

'Yes ….?' The grinning Count looked exactly like an ancient Zen Master eliciting the Ultimate Cliché from a naïve acolyte, in preparation for giving him a sharp slap in reply.

'What happens if the decision is positive? I mean, how can he inherit your wealth if you are still alive?'

'Good question. It took you long enough to ask!'

Truelove stared up at Laszlo for a long time, waiting for the answer.

And the count stared straight back, face wreathed with smiles, deep in Samadhi.

I scrunched the letter up and threw it into the bin. Then I took it out again and re-read it. O.k., Truelove, I'll be there! I took out my pocket diary and on the page on which I had already written myself a Happy Birthday greeting I wrote 'Oh yeah?' and added, '8pm, the Office.'

Then I went out to work.

For the next two weeks I kept to myself. Did all my regular security checks. Whenever I saw a suspicious looking woman on the street I went to other way or down a side street or stopped suddenly to let her past. Jumped whenever the telephone rang.

Whatever I did, the Phantom Cleaner couldn't be deterred or stopped. I even changed the locks. In she went every day, tidied and cleaned. Then left, leaving only a few chocolate wrappers in the bin. I gave up trying to catch her. Maybe she was after all benevolent. Maybe my only friend. And I needed friends.

All the others seemed to have dropped away. Even Noel avoided me. And Monica was always busy whenever I came near. I didn't mind, I wanted to be left alone. I was the White Knight. I was on a Quest. That was all that mattered.

Nora did phone to ask me to dinner and to quiz me about missing Pieter's funeral. ('But dear you were like *brothers*!) I tried to make her understand that it would be better for everyone if they just let me be. But she went on and on…'We're your family dear. We care about you' until I said cruelly, 'Nora for God's sake forget it! Forget you ever knew me. I am just too much danger for everyone who knows me! For *your* sake!' And then I slammed the phone down on her.

So that makes two families I've lost in two weeks. But it was only protecting them! I seemed to bring misery and death to everyone who knew me. In a way, I was proud of myself: I had the Project, and that came first. The White Knight has no time for gravy and mash.

Any day now, I thought, BOSS will contact me. A tramp will sit next to me on the tube and say, 'by the way, the little matter of the Endorsing Out has been attended to.' And I'll say 'Good.' And stare into his face and grin to myself as I mentally inventories the lusts I have of BOSS agents, the details as to when and how they meet, the tape recordings and all the other evidence of their filthy doings…

And then when I go into work, I'll be called into Boles' office so thathe can ask me how I am doing on the Rhodesia Project and as I say 'Fine, everything's coming together very satisfactorily,' and smile my winning smile at that Captain of Evil, I'll count off in my mind all the photocopies I have of the orders for nuclear equipment I sent out on behalf of Grabkin to major munitions manufacturers all over the globe. The shipping notes and Bills of Lading showing the routes to Rhodesia via Phalaborwa in South Africa. The telexes from ARMSCOR acknowledging receipt. The tape recordings of telephone conversations with the mad jackals who feed off the international trade in death.

Oh yes, I thought, for once in Real Life the baddies are going to *get* theirs!

Two

Friday the 13th of February 1970. Nothing happened. No saviours died. So nothing new then. There was a thin pile of post on the doormat, picked up as I rushed out of the door to work. One hand clutched my briefcase. The other clutched two big packets. One was addressed to New Scotland Yard, the other to the Editor, the Observer. They contained duplicate sets of photocopied documents, transcripts of recorded conversations, telexes, everything.

Fate now on board and running. Battle lines drawn. The timing perfect. By Tuesday, the parcels would be opened, the fan and the shit would begin to meet each other and…by then I would either be rich enough to vanish anywhere I wanted in the world, or I would be penniless, jobless, probably homeless and free as a wingless bird!

I stopped off at the Trafalgar Square Post Office, where they were ceremoniously consigned to Fate and her minions.

Once at wok I sat at my desk and read my cards. Amongst them were two valentine's cards. One was obviously from Monica.

Here's a VALENTINE
From one who PINES
For someone QUICK
I MISS YOUR DICK!

The other had a picture of two hearts on the cover. The message read:

There is no escape from me. I love you, darling. I love you so much I want to be with you always and I know you still feel the same. We are twinned by fate always to be together. Soon, my love, soon.

In case I had any doubts about the identity of the sender, it was signed, '*Your wife*'.

So, confirmed. She was still alive. Yesterday at least! The madness of her valentine made me feel more guilty than angry. Inside me there was still a nest of sorrow and loss. I brushed it away, thinking, 'yes! You love me! So who are you going to kill next to prove it?'

I couldn't concentrate at work. I kept stopping and going to the coffee machine, ot the toilet. Finding any excuse to do nothing.

I popped into Noel's office. 'Noel,' I said, 'can I see you?'

'I'm a bit busy...' he was half way through dialling a number.

'Don't do that! I need to talk to you!

'That's what you're doing love,' he said, replacing the telephone. 'What's the matter?'

'I don't know. Yes I do. It's tomorrow.'

'Uh huh. Your Red Letter Day.'

'How did you know that?' I asked, pulling a chair up to the desk and seating myself.

'You told me last week.'

'Oh yes. I'm so jumpy! Last week I felt as if I didn't care about anything. Now everything is coming to a head and – I dunno...' I ached to tell him everything. But No Way. Did I implicate him? Probably not. His territories and his business was mostly within the law. I sighed. “My best friend is dead. The girl I loved is dead. My wife is mad. I'm surrounded by bad people....I don't know if I *want* to be twenty-one!'

'Goodness darling you *are* in a bad way. Why don't you go home. You're doing yourself no good here. Throw a sickie.'

'What will I do at home? I'll get bored crazy!'

'Here,' he said, handing me a lump of dope,' Go home and smoke yourself stupid. Time will go faster than you think.'

I walked through the midday West End streets to the Park Lane Garage. When I got to the car, a tramp was idling against the bonnet. I nearly ran away. Then reminded myself: the papers were in the post; there was no way they would yet know how I had betrayed them.

'Hello Thomas', he said cheerfully. 'What took you so long?'

'What do you want?'

He held out a paperbagged bottle of KWV Brandy. 'Have a *sluk*' he said. 'It'll make you feel better, hey?'

'Don't mind if I do,' I said and drank deeply until the burning in throat and stomach spread to the head.

'Just came to tell you not to worry,' he said.

'Not to worry? What about?'

'You know. The little matter of the Endorsing Out. We've had the go-ahead from Pretoria. Though if I say so myself, I don't like it one little bit.'

'Oh,' I said.

'So you can just forget all your little worries and concentrate solely on the Project on Monday, hey?'

'Of course.' (you bastard) 'Thank you.' (By Monday you'll be on your way to prison you slime) 'Goodbye.' (Goodbye!)

All the way home all that played in my head was Mona and the horror of what I had set in train. Against the horror at what she had done. Against my hatred of capital punishment. Against the only way to stop her being to Stop. Her. Could I stop stopping her? Probably not. They had the 'go ahead from Pretoria.' Once they had the Go Ahead, they went ahead.

I reached home at two thirty, vast acres of afternoon still to be got through. At least I had my lump of time-killer clutched in my pocket!

I opened the door. Heard the TV jabbering. Funny. I leapt up the stairs to the lounge and –

She was asleep on the couch, wearing a smart cotton dress and an apron. She looked slim, healthy. Not haunted and thin as in our first months in London. I didn't recognise her at first. There was a bloom to her cheeks that made her quite beautiful – or handsome, rather. Strong. Lovely.

As I stared emotions fought a pitched battle in my skull.

Her eyes flickered open. 'Tom! Oh, Tom!' she extended her arms joyfully to me.

I stared. I stared. Mouth open.

'I knew you would come to me!,' she said. 'When you got my valentine you knew I'd be waiting. I was right! You came!'

I tried breathing myself into a semblance of control. What does one do when confronted by a murdering madwoman? Humour her? But what if she attacks? Is she armed? I must get to the phone, call the cops. Hell, they've been useless up to now. Must keep distance. Appear unconcerned.

But I couldn't stop shaking. 'What are you doing here?' I managed.

'Don't ask me that,' she pleaded softly. 'I'm your wife. I've come back. And I'm going to be such a good wife, you'll see! Haven't you noticed how well I've cleaned our flat for three weeks now?'

There was no resemblance between this sweetly smiling and beautiful girl and the screaming virago I remembered. 'You've ruined my life,' I whispered, 'and you expect me to be happy to see you?'

She sat up. 'I know,' she said, and a tear escaped, 'and I'm so sorry Tom, I'm SO sorry. I want to make up for – for everything. I want to give you the new self, the new Mona – '

'You could never make up for everything you've done. You could never give back the lives you have taken.'

'But – but I haven't *taken* any lives! Not in this life anyway. What are you talking about? What do you mean?' She started crying and I had to force myself to keep away so that my arms wouldn't cuddle her of their own volition.

'You're a lying bitch! You killed Pieter – '

'Pieter's dead?' She peered through her wet fingers.

'You *know* he's dead! And Julia – I loved her and you killed her!'

'Who's Julia?'

'What game are you playing you crazy bitch? Are you denying you killed them? I didn't mind so much when you killed the Rat but they – ' I leapt across the room before I could stop myself and grabbed her by the hair.

'I didn't! I didn't!' she cried as my hand went back for a blow which would have been superpowered by all the anger and horror and bitterness that was in me – easily enough to kill her – but the blow stopped ungiven –

'And if you didn't, who the fuck did?'

'I don't know I don't know I don't know! Oh Tom if I knew you were going through all that I would have com back, I would have escaped somehow, and come back! How could you think I would kill Pieter? I loved him too! And this Julia? I never even *knew* her....' She subsided into a torrent of weeping and I let go of her hair. 'I didn't even kill Nick,' she blubbered.

'Mona, you're *mad*. Don't you realise! You don't even *know* you killed all those people!'

'But I didn't! I couldn't have! I've been in Gloucestershire for six months. I wasn't even sure where you were. What you were doing. What was happening to you. I sent you letters, but I couldn't give my address in case – '

'*Gloucestershire?*'

'Yes, there's a therapeutic community there called the Refuge, based on RD Laing's work. I've been having intensive therapy.'

'Huh?'

'Don't look at me like that. You remember Nick, the one you called the Rat? Well, when you left that night he started talking about Death and all that stuff again and as usual I pretended to go along with him – '

'*Pretended*?'

'I wasn't as mad as you thought I was. I had to humour him because I knew if I didn't, he would kill himself. And that was exactly what he did! After you telephoned, remember, I went to our room and sulked for a while. Then I decided to go to his room to see what he was doing. And he was dead! Lying there all blood and everything, I didn't know what to do! I first tried to pull that great nail out of his chest and then something just clicked in my head. Just snapped. And then these men came into the room – '

'Who?'

'I didn't know who they were. I *was* crazy then, I can tell you. They just grabbed me. I put up quite a fight. But they grabbed me anyway and next thing I knew I was in a car, all tied up, I think they sedated me because I passed out, and when I awoke – Gloucestershire!'

'Who the hell were they?'

'I still don't know. Whoever they were, they had taken me to the right place. It was fantastic, Tom, the therapy I mean. I was taken through my whole life in those six months. There was the whole alternative therapy shebang. Even a guided acid trip. It was like being put through a grinder and then being put back together again. They used everything, Rebirthing, Biodynamics, Gestalt…they made me a new woman!'

'And the voices?'

'I'll always have the voices. I just know exactly how to deal with them now. They can't frighten me anymore, those crazy disappointed broken dead things. I won't say I'm *cured*, but I'm a functioning person fully in control. And I've got a great therapist in London too. He gave me the courage to come back to you. Says it's part of my process. He says in time I will heal completely. You know what kept me going all the time Tom, what made me want to get better? You. You're the one I've welded my life to.

'That's why, when I got back to London I decided I had to do something for you. He told me where to live and I don't know how he did it, he gave me a set of keys for your flat. Anyway, you're such a chauvinist, you think cleaning is for women so I had to show you that being filthy is no proof you're a man! All that grime in the kitchen! Honestly!

'Anyway, so I sent you the valentine so you'd know and I fell asleep and when I woke up it was as if my dream had come true and there you were standing there like a knight in ar5mour or the handsome prince come to kiss me back to life and – and – '

She was weeping again. I stood, strode to and fro, fists clenched, shaking, holding myself in, because half of me believed her and the other half kept saying, 'Watch out, beware, she's schizo, she can say anything and make it sound so real…'

'Don't *do* that! You 've *got* to believe me! *Believe* me!'

'Wait!' I said, and dashed to my desk, opened my Things Pending drawer. I riffled through a pile of letters and found the letters from her I had stashed there, maybe hoping to show them to the police some time. Some in envelopes with her writing. There it was, clear as daylight, on each envelope. The postmark. *Collingsf'd Gloucs.*

The truth, after all.

I just sat on the floor and wept. Within seconds she was next to me, and her so-well known and so-longed for arms were around me.

After a night of talking and making hungry love, the next day, my birthday, was a day of shopping and doing domestic things in a daze of delight. An incredible lunch at Wheeler's with oysters and salmon and birthday cake. Celebrating everything! Suddenly it was as if happiness had scoured out every bad memory, every stress, every 'whatif' in the world. Suddenly I didn't actually care about the Inheritance, or about the meeting scheduled for the evening. I only wanted to be with my new Mona, this incredibly beautiful, knowing, clever person with the gorgeous body....all that gaudy claustrophobic dirty stuff seemed quite irrelevant.

I told her everything. I even told her about BOSS and the Deus Ex Machina and my plans for destroying their London cell, Boles and his dirty business and just about everything except…except…except of course for my request to the Brigadier. She laughed at most of it. And we decided to do what I had planned to do with Pieter. That is, vanish. Win or lose, straight after the Hearing we'd be off, rich or poor, heading South with every penny and everything saleable if there were no millions; and with a fat cheque book if there were.

With cheque book – Brazil!

With no cheque book – Bournemouth!

We didn't care. We would change passports, faces, everything. We would elude BOSS and make a new life. 'All I want is to be with you,' she said, 'Whithersoever thou goest and all that.' And as she kissed me goodbye I was contented. 'I'll be waiting,' she said. 'Don't worry about me. I've got chockies and the telly. And when you get back we'll have the best celebration ever!'

I had told her only one lie. I said the hearing was at 6, not 8. My idea was to get to the Brigadier before the meeting, (in my mind I was calling it a Hearing) cancel out the Endorsing Out. I felt quite confident about this. They were always there in the evenings. That was when they had their meetings.

Besides, I wanted to be alone for a bit to think and commune with my ghosts. My voices.

Three

But when I got to Chelsea the Gents was locked. A sign, 'Closed for Maintenance' on the gate. Frustration! Where was that number, the 'use only for emergencies' number he'd given me once? Ages ago?

I ran back to the car, parked on Sloane Avenue and rooted through it like an addict desperately seeking the only drug in town and eventually, there it was screwed up on the floor, footprint across its face, but readable.

A phone box!

A phone box.

A coin! No coin! Big shit!

Back to the car.

Flying roaches and papers and mess and there on the floor and in the glove compartment, a few pennies.

Back to the phone box. Lift receiver. Pennies in. Dial the number. Wait, wait and wait. Wait. Hurrrry upppppppp. 'Hello?' a posh little girl's voice. 'This is Gemma Louise. How can I help you?'

'Hello. This is Tom. I need to speak to the – to Brigadier – I mean Mr Maartens.'

'I am terribly sorry Mr Tom, my daddy is not in at the moment' Exaggeratedly cultured, carefully enunciated with just the merest squeezing of vowels showing her South African origin.

'Oh,' I said. 'When will he be back?'

'I'm afraid he is to be out the entire evening Mr Tom. Can I take a message?'

'It's really very urgent!'

'Oh dear I am so sorry. Are you from the council? Do we have blocked lavatories again?'

'No, I work with him. It's about work.'

'Oh I see. Which work exactly?'

'It's a matter of life and death! Is your mommy home?'

'I do not have a mommy at present. Can I help you? Is it about BOSS?'

Totally taken aback. '*What*?'

'Because if it is you have to give me the password.'

'*Password???*'

'Yes. Do you have it?'

'No I don't!'

bleebleeblee – another penny ching

'In that case I cannot help you.'

'Wait! Wait! Don't hang up!'

'Yes?'

'Can you give me a clue?'

'A clue?'

'Yes!'

'Oh all right then as you say it's life or death. It's in Afrikaans.'

'Yes, fine, and…..???'

'Don't you know?' She's enjoying this.

'No! Can I have another clue?'

'Oh all right, if you must. Think of an Afrikaans word starting with S'

'I don't believe this!'

'You only get three goes. So what is it?'

'Uh… *suiker*? '

'No!!!' Delighted. 'Have another go!'

bleebleebleeeeep ching. One penny left.

'Listen to me PLEEEEASE! It's life or death! If I don't speak to him he'll – uh. He'll- damn!'

'No need to *swear,* sir!'

'I'm so sorry. Please, please. If I don't speak to him he'll – he'll – endorse out! He'll endorse out! Mona! You have to tell him NOT to!'

'Only if you give me the password!'

Nooooooo…. 'Is it *seker*?' 'Sous?' Sarie?'

'Yes…. But which one? One chance left!'

'Please! Please! Just tell him, don't endorse Mona out!!!'

'One chance. One chance!'

'One more clue. Just one more!'

'All right, because I like you sir. It's a song.'

'A song! A song!' Almost ecstatic,' Sarie!' (sings) '*O Sarie Marais is so ver van my hart….*'

'Hurray! Hurray!'

Beebleeblee no more pennies

'Give him the message! Give him the message!'

'I will!'

'Promise?'

'Promise!'

Bleeeeeeeeeeeeeeeeeeeeeee……….

Happy, relieved, excited, and it's only 5.45! Need air, need fresh air, need speed. Up! The King's Road. Up! Warwick Road. Left! On the A4. Straight! Up the M4. Vroom. And as the Triumph growled along the motorway, the words of Truelove's last letter kept echoing in my head. '….what you have gained in the past months…respectable job… international company…beautiful car….'

'Blah! I said to the car. 'Everything I've gained has been at the expense of something or *someone* I've lost!'

'Yes! Almost everyone I know is either *dead* or *bought* or both…' said a sad ghostly voice in my ear.

But the White Knight is immortal, I said, laughing.

The day had been bright and crisp. The heavy snows of January had vanished from the city like a stage set at the end of a spectacular performance. But in the countryside the signs of the winter were still about. Sodden snow lying heavily on fields and in dirty patches next to the motorway, like the fleeces of huge drowned sheep. But the sky was clear with early stars.

Despite the cold air outside I was so warm. From within. Whatever happened now, I had Mona back. Together we could face anything. If somehow I were to win all that money, she would know what to do with it. Do *good* with it, once we'd changed identities and vanished. Grand plans!

'That's how they all start out, the do-gooders, ' the ghostly voice resumed. 'Then they get bought!'

'Not us,' I replied, 'Not Mona. She's good and true and incorruptible. Not Mona.'

And if I didn't win? Well, we were all packed and ready. I had a few pounds put by. And we'd still be able to vanish. We'd give them all a run for their money!

I pressed the accelerator hard down and that six-cylinder growl went straight to my stomach.

'I wonder if there'll be any food at the hearing?'

'Don't be silly,' said the ghost. 'They specified 8pm because they know you always eat at 7. Think of the money they're saving.'

'Excuse me,' I said very reasonably, 'but I don't think I know you.'

'You don't,' the voice answered. 'My name was Armand Bennett. I was assigned to your case – '

'What? By whom?'

'Oh, you'll find out soon enough. I'm the fellow who bugged your sex life and nailed your tyres too!' He chortled. 'I enjoyed that. All in the name of Duty, of course. For *your* good, really! Anyway, I was knocked off by the competition the day I handed in my resignation... Ah well,' the ghost sighed, 'it seems I'm doomed to go on observing you even after my body has ceased to be of use...'

'Bit of a waste surely?' I said, 'since you can't report back. Anyway, this maybe our last meeting, so let's have some dinner together!'

And having bolted a horrible snack at the Chieveley service station (yes there was a sausage roll involved) and chewed an antacid I had found in a bottle in the glove compartment, we headed back to London. Never had I been so happy. Never felt so strong. I lit a massive joint and my heart lifted and my mind sang.

'Well, you seem to have everything you want,' said the voice in my ear. 'Everything's in your own hands now, or will be after this evening...'

'That's right,' I said smugly, 'and that's how it's going to be from now on'

'Well I suppose my job is finished, now the circus is about to begin...'

'Eh? What do you mean?'

'Bring on the clowns! Tarantara!'

'So where are you going?'

'I'm just – ' said a faint voice, mimicking Captain Oates, 'going outside. I may be a while.'

I parked carelessly on a double yellow line in Half Moon Street and walked jauntily down Piccadilly, carving my way between the thronging tourists shivering in their layers of coats, wraps, scarves. But I was warm from the inside! I was indomitable.

I strode down Jermyn Street. Fancy being able to order my shirts from Turnbull & Asser, have my shoes hand-made! Mona too. A Dior dress or two, set of by chains of gold and sparkles of jewels, why not.

What am I *thinking*! We were going to do *good* with the money. That's what we'd agreed! IF we get it...

Suddenly there it was – headquarters. The Neo-Georgian stinking monster in red brick stucco and sandstone. Grabkin Incorporated. With nothing more than a modest brass plaque to trumpet its magnificence.

Hawkins, man-mountain of a commissionaire, greeted me cheerily. 'Evening sir,' he said, 'nice night for it.'

'Hello Hawkeye,' I answered. 'Where am I to go?'

'Top floor, sir, there's a little gathering, cocktails an' that. But first I am to take you to the changing room.'

'Changing room?'

'Yes sir, that's right.' He ushered me into a cubbyhole of a room, behind the main reception desk.

The room smelled of old sweat and tobacco. On a row of pegs there were all sorts of costumes. Military uniforms, clown suits, crinolines. 'What the – '

'Didn't they tell you sir? S'pose not. Couldn't organise a pissup in a brewery. No, it's fancy-dress you see, sir. Boss thought it'd make everything a bit less formal, like.'

'Fancy dress?' I grinned, a mischievous delight prickling at my scalp. 'The bugger!' Truelove was even crazier than I thought. 'All right,' I said, 'I'll play!'

'Well you just help yourself to whatever you want,' the Commissionaire said. 'I'd better get back out front. Though I think most of the guests have arrived.' He said this last with just a hint of disapproval at my having arrived fifteen minutes late. Hold-up on the motorway. Not my fault.

About to close the door behind him, he poked his bull snout in and said 'By the way sir,'

'Yes?'

'A word to the wise. It's Haw*kins*, yes? Not Hawkeye. Just so you know.' And was gone.

Leaving me running my hands over the sumptuous silks, lace, velvet, wool…very clever! Fancy dress eh. Fantasy fulfilment. So who exactly am I? And who do I want to be?

There was only one obvious choice and five minutes later I emerged wearing a suit of armour, which, though it was cardboard and tin, clunked awesomely as I walked. 'Ready!' I announced to the lobby.

'Righto.' Hawkins looked up from his copy of the Sun and led me to the lift. 'Jolly good, Sir Lunch a lot is it! Haw haw.' Ching! The door slid open. Voom! The lift raised us heavenward. Ding! We were at Boardroom level. Fuff! Voom! The door slid open.

Hawkins knocked respectfully on the veneered rosewood door. It was opened by Julia. I dropped the helmet I had been clutching under my arm.

'Julia!!!' I wanted to say, Gee Julia you look remarkably good for a dead person. Especially dressed as Scarlett O'Hara. But all I could say was 'Julia!!!'

'Hello Tom.'

'But – what – you – '

'I'm so sorry Tom, I – everything will be explained later. I promise. Come in, take a seat.' She dismissed Hawkins with a 'Thank you Hawkins' at showed me to a chair at the foot of the table. I sat, feeling definitely woozy. 'You seem to have dropped your head,' she said, sweeping up my helmet and placing it on the gleaming oak boardroom table in front of me.

'But – but you have to tell me – why – what happened – ' I blurted and then the door opposite me opened and in came a thin angular man in a flowing yellow robe with a garland of plastic flowers around his neck, beneath which protruded a large silver ankh. Young, maybe early thirties, blond hair thinning. I stared uncomprehendingly.

I wasn't just woozy, I began to realise. This was so unreal! I felt very very stoned...

'Thomas Bloch,' he said, eying me like an old friend newly rediscovered. 'We meet at last.'

We shook hands.

'This is my boss, James Truelove,' Julia said.

'Uh – nice to meet you,' I burbled. This! This thin, nervous-looking man was Truelove? He seemed alien, also very familiar...

'Happy birthday young man,' he said. 'We must get you a drink. Beer, I suppose?' He grinned archly and I remembered. I remembered the bastard who poured beer over me the night I met Julia.

'Don't taunt him James,' Julia said. 'He'll have enough to contend with tonight.'

Thank you Julia, I thought, still trying to work out how a dead person could be standing there, protecting me.

'If you say so dear. Well, we'd better prepare you hadn't we? How are you feeling? Confused?'

A good question. How was I feeling. I interrogated myself. Yes, confused summed it up rather well. But above confused, beside it and next to it, a kind of elation – in some ways, crystal clear. A very familiar elation. A bit more than high.

I nodded.

'Never mind, we'll soon have everything sorted out. Now the procedure is as follows.' His voice became business-like. 'The first stage is we go into Mr Boles' office, so that you can formally meet the Jurors. We have arranged a little cocktail party, so that everyone will feel relaxed and you won't feel as if you're on trial. Is that all right with you?'

I shook my head as if to clear it of cobwebs. It didn't clear. Quite unaccountably, the wall seemed to have turned into viscous liquid and was noticeably flowing. What the – 'Yes, fine.'

'Good good.' He rubbed his hands. 'Then at ten o'clock precisely we'll all come back here and the Reports will be read. After that, in the spirit of true democracy, there will be a vote and a decision will be taken. Is that clear?'

I nodded. There was no reason it shouldn't be. Except it was all getting tangled up with this feeling…this familiar feeling…this invasion of my head by….

'Ready?' He stood an arms length away and scrutinised my costume. 'So you chose armour, eh? I *said* you'd choose the armour! You feel as if you're under attack do you? Well, gird up your loins, boy. It'll soon be over now.'

As I stood to follow him, I suddenly realised how absurd and ridiculous all this…me…and then it clicked! This detachment. This high. Flowing walls. Only one thing can do this.

Acid.

LSD.

How? Had someone spiked me? WHO - ?

I knew who. The glove compartment. The bottle of white pills labelled Phillips Milk of Magnesia, which I'd used after the horrible meal at the motorway services. The acid! The acid in the antacids! The same I had taken that horrible night weeks ago….of course Julia had stashed it in the car! To keep it out of my grasppppppp…..!

Oh no. Not this. Not now.

'Look,' I managed to say, 'I don't think I can…Look, I need to go home. I need to go home now. It's not –'

'Come now boy, don't be scared! It will all soon be over! Be brave. Get up now, take up your sword and your mace! Let's see what you're made of!'

Julia put a hand on my armoured shoulder and shook it. 'This is all about *you*, Tom,' she said. 'You can't go home. Let's get it over with.'

Muzzy, I stood. 'Over with' I said. Right, got to! Got to get through this! It's a movie. It's only a movie. I'm strong enough. White knight! (Who am I kidding? Me.) I took up my helmet. And thus absurdly burdened, in a bizarre suit of fake armour I followed Julia and Truelove to my fate.

Four

Boles' office was a swirl of low lights, clinking cocktails, sugary music dribbling out of concealed speakers. The room was full of tobacco smoke and people in masks and frills and flounces. 'Tommy baby!' Monica emerged from the mass in a cat costume in black and white, grabbed my arm. She tripped over her tail. 'Oops!' she giggled. She was very drunk.

'Surprise surprise' I said in what I imagined may be a sardonic tone.

'I've been missing you soooo much. Gimme kiss.'

'Later later' I said, pushing her away. I was unaccountably angry with her. Probably because she was drunk, but mostly because she was *there*. Also because she was getting between me and my view of the room. Who else? Who else?

The room was too dim, though, for me to be able to see very much. Besides, much of it was flowing about. A trace of nausea mounted, but I managed to breathe deeply, dissolved some of it. Cocktail voices filtered through the gloom. '*Then* I told him I was a virgin – ' 'She said then I said, I've *never* eaten chrysanthemums!' 'You'd never believe how much I paid for a blow job –' 'Darling, what a perfectly *horrible* costume. I love it!' Gradually my eyes began to focus. I took deep breaths. Centre. Grounding. Be Here Now.

But.

'Thomas! Come here boy. Welcome!' A man hunched in a doctor's white coat, stethoscope hanging from wrinkled neck. It was Boles. You too, eh? I should have realised when I was told where the Hearing was to take place. 'Good heavens, what are you supposed to be?' he asked. 'A Crusader, eh? Very appropriate. Well well. How are you my boy?'

'Fine' I said with an insincere grin.

'That's my boy!' He slapped me on the back and withdrew with an 'ouch'. The blow swung me around into a Marie Antoinette.

'Hello darling.'

'Noel!' I started to giggle. Then I stopped. 'You shit!'

'Don't swear darling. Do you like my outfit?'

'Very appropriate. "Let them eat cake" eh?'

He grinned under a mess of powder, his red bowed lips and beauty spot making him look more like a cheap whore. Yes, looking beyond and inside, that's what he was. Anger visited.

'Don't be so serious darling. This is the most important night of your life so far so you may as well enjoy it. We're all your friends here you know!'

And so, exactly, it seemed. The next person to greet me was Nora, dressed as a peasant in smock and bonnet. With Grant as a Regency beau.

'The whole orchestra...' I said and my heart sank, remembering how unceremoniously I had dumped the Bromley set. I seemed to have managed to offend everybody.

But Grant grabbed my hand and pumped it. 'We're so *pleased* for you, Tom, aren't we Nora?'

Confused. 'Why?' I asked.

'I hope you'll give some consideration to a little plan I have in mind. It's to do with buying an aircraft and – ' Grant conspired with my ear.

'Come on Grant, you can tell him all that later,' Nora said, trying to drag him off. 'Come *away,* dear...'

But Grant clung on. Leaning back to my ear, whispering, 'Listen Tom, just between ourselves I can promise you my vote if you'll just give me your word you'll listen to my idea!'

He was a cartoon. A bunny. I leaned away in pretended Elmer Fudd shock. 'Bwibewy? Are you twying to *bwibe* me?'

He stepped back, offended. 'Don't take it like that, I just – ' This time Nora exerted all her considerable muscle in pulling him away. 'We'll see you later,' she hissed.

Oh shit, that's TWO votes lost.

Tweedledum and Tweedledee pretending to be Dick and Moira waved at me from across the room. Brian and Kathe dressed as pirates were standing next to them.

You too you too you tooooooo! I knew I should be annoyed. Or maybe offended. Perhaps affronted. But seeing these caricatures these exaggerated facsimiles of those who had been my friends, everything just became totally absurd. It was as if everybody I knew in England had been in on this plot, spying on me!

A stab of panic, laced with paranoia. Didn't any of my friends actually *like* me?

Oh if only Pieter would pop out of the crowd. If others could get away with playing dead, why couldn't he?

I breathed myself back to a giggle and snatched at a glass of champagne from a passing tray. May as well add some alcohol to the mix! I no longer wanted to recognise the faces in the crowd. Better not to know who else I should not have trusted.

I put on the helmet and lowered the visor. This felt like a good place to be, although access to the champagne glass became a ridiculous endeavour. Experimentally, I tried throwing my head back and splashing the stuff in the vague direction of my mouth. Messy, but refreshing!

'Tom?' I jumped. The voice sounded right inside the helmet, next to my ear.

'Who? Where?'

'You don't know me. I'm dead.'

'Pieter?'

'My name is Ian. I'm your step-great uncle. Or your great step-uncle. No idea which is right. Your granny Hazel's brother, perhaps she told you about me. I died in Europe in 1936. I do recommend being dead, you know. Look, I've brought a friend!'

'Please no more,' I groaned. I just hoped Mona still had the address of that place in Gloucs…

'Hello Tom,' a woman's voice.

'Whosat?'

'Don't you know my voice? Your Granny Hazel.'

'I'm going mad,' I said.

'We just came to see how you're getting along. It's going to be such fun!'

I whipped off the helmet. How could I call Mona mad when I heard voices and voices!

'Stop talking to yourself.' It was Maria. The Night of the Flaming Curtain intruded into memory like a slug into lettuce.

'Well, *you're* no surprise!' I muttered.

'It wasn't nice what you did to me. I've waited all this time to tell you. You nearly lost me my job!'

'Well what about me? I was nearly in love with you!'

'Were you really?' A smile. 'Say, when this is over, how about coming to my place?'

I laughed. 'I'm a happily married man now my darling'

'And....?' On tiptoe, she brushed my nose with a kiss. 'Tell you what darling boy. If you want my vote you'd better come to my house and fuck me like you've never fucked before...' She was dressed as a Victorian whore, a Jack the Ripper victim. There was stage blood all over her neck. I backed away in a wave of disgust.

'Heyyyy lover boy, it's only tomato sauce! Taste!' She dipped a finger into the red and held it out to be licked.

'Aaaargh no!' The last time I saw blood it was very real. I bolted to the door and banged it open. Hawkins stood there like a man mountain. Pushed me back into the room with an unceremonious sharp shove.

No-one seemed to have noticed my re-entry except Truelove who grabbed me by an arm. 'Well my little friend, getting on swimmingly are we? Having fun?' He was drunk and getting drunker.

'All right,' I said. 'I want a piss. Where's a piss?' Looking for an escape.

He ignored the question. 'Any surprises here for you?'

'Full of surprises. You're all full of surprises,' I said.

'Good good. So glad you're enjoying your little party! But will it be your last? Who knows!' He chortled. 'Oh well, I'll be over by tomorrow won't it.'

'Is that supposed to make me feel good?' I asked sweetly.

He squeezed my arm as if to steady himself. It hurt. And looked me in the eyes. 'Wait and see,' he said.

Then the door banged open and all the lights went on full. Julia stood in the doorway ringing a brass handbell. 'Ten o clock' she intoned. 'Time, gentlemen and ladies. Court's in session. Everybody into the Boardroom please!'

So this was it. Involuntarily I put the helmet on and immediately 'can we come with you?' Hazel's voice inquired.

'You can't fool me,' I said inside my head. 'You're not real.'

'Don't be such a killjoy,' Ian's voice snapped. 'We'll be good, promise!'

'What are you doing here anyway?' I asked petulantly.

'You don't think Ian and I are prepared to go through the whole damn boring trauma of being reborn yet again without knowing how this is going to turn out, do you?' Hazel's voice answered.

Someone grabbed the helmet from behind and pulled it off bruisingly. Ow my ears. It was Truelove. 'You won't be needing that boy. It'll all be over tomorrow. Come on now.' He propelled me into the Boardroom ahead of him. 'Sit!' He pushed me down into a Hepplewhite chair at the foot end of the oval table. And the others took their places.

Julia sat next to Truelove. Noel next to me. Nora opposite him. Then Brian, Kathe, Dick, Moira, Grant, Boles, Monica, Maria. The whole panoply of my friends in London were there.

Only two faces were missing. Pieter and Mona. Thank God those two faces were missing.

'Is everybody comfortable? Truelove's voice floated from the head of the table. 'Well, let's get started.' He cleared his throat, rustled his notes. 'Ahem! Well, it's a great pleasure to welcome you here tonight. This as you know is the culmination of nine months of hard work for us all and the end of a romantic story that began before the last war. You all know the story, don't you? How - uh - ' he was losing his place, began fumbling with the notes ' - uh - Count Laszlo's Mindchyck met a pretty young girl called Hazel - uh - something - and - ' he abandoned the notes, 'and began a love story sadder than Romeo and Julia, sadder than Helen of Tree and whatsname, oh bugger. Sadder than Adam and Eve, Tom and Jerry, milk and sugar.'

'Doesn't Laszlo look awful?' Hazel's voice again. 'So shrunk and old. When I knew him he was six foot something.'

'Pay attention Thomas,' Truelove's voice sounded like that of a spinster schoolmarm. 'This is for your benefit you know. Where was I? Oh yes, sadder than. I've done that. Anyway - and never saw her again. Alas, by the time we found Hazel in South Africa she was too old to take the strain and sadly she passed away.'

A sadly groan went up around the table.

'Yes yes! And then we discovered she had made this preposterous will.'

'How rude!' Hazel's ghost sputtered.

'And - ' he paused, looking directly at me, 'we find ourselves having to decide whether to give all this lovely money to that idiot over there!'

'That's not fair!' Julia piped. 'You're supposed to be the Chairman. You're supposed to be impartial!'

'It *is* fair. I am a juror as well, see? They're only eleven now, if there were twelve as there's *supposed* to be…'

'No James!' Something was frightening her. 'Don't! Not now!'

'Arright aright, but it's his own fault…'

'Shut up, James, for God's sake!'

'S'allright, I won't say. But you'd think she'd have learned – ' he was incapacitated by a fit of giggles 'not to….not to take sweeties from strangers! Haw!'

Julia cringed away. The others looked blank. Here there was mystery. This did not feel right.

'Let's just get the Reports out of the way,' Julia commanded.

'All right, all right. God you're such a *nag*. Oh hell I shouldn't have had that last drinkie. It's supposed to be your job to stop me – '

'Get on with it man!' Boles' temper snapped.

Truelove reeled as if slapped. 'All right,' he said, 'all right,' pulling himself together and straightening the plastic garland around his neck. 'Subject, Thomas Bloch….uh…' interrogating his notes myopically 'Thomas, you need to remember all these good people have your interests at heart. Which means that whatever is decided will be in your best interests. Am I right?'

Everybody nodded. Even I nodded.

'Of course if the vote is – whatsname – split, I will have an extra vote. One as Chairman, one as proxy for the absent Juror. Now if you would all read your reports aloud, in a nice clear voice so we can all hear, children, let's go clockwise around the table.'

Maria was first. She stood. Then she sat. Then she started. 'I met the accused, sorry, the Tom, at a night club as instructed. I was delegated to eggzamine sexual proclivities awareness and orientation and to that purpose you made me let the awful detective man set up a camera and sound equipment in my flat.

'Well, he rumbled me. The Tom that is.' She looked up from her Report which, I could see, was grubby and beer-stained. 'And everything went phut. And the Fire Brigade had to come and – Tom, are you coming back with me after or not?'

Monica reared out of her seat perfectly cat-like, and flipped a cup of coffee across the table soaking Maria in streaks of brown to join the streaks of tomato ketchup on her whore's costume. 'Bitch!' Maria screamed.

'Whore' Monica shouted.

'Catfight!' snarked Brian with delight.

Maria leapt onto the table, talons out and ready for battle. Monica leaned forward and whipped her legs from under her and there was a screeowl as stiletto heels gouged a deep scratch in the polished oak, a screaming crunch of bodies as Maria fell onto her fellow jurors.

'Hells bells women please! Please! Get back to your seats!' Truelove shouted.

Eventually the tangle was untangled, although not without minor injuries to several of those present. I don't know which. I just cowered out of the way. I think Dick may have had a tooth broken. His fault for getting between them. Maria returned to her seat and wiping her face with a paper napkin, carried on. 'Sniff. Well, the orientation analysis was completed in the end by that bitch there.'

'Hm,' Truelove said, 'Now,' referring to his notes, 'You have to give a verdict. Do you consider Thomas Bloch here present to be a fit, *sane* and proper person to handle the great responsibility of this considerable inheritance as per the conditions of the will made plain to you?'

Arms akimbo, she stared at me for a while. I looked back miserably. 'No,' she said. 'Not. I vote not.'

'Well thank you for your evidence. Brief as it was. Next!'

First Kathe and then Brian stood up. One after the other they unfurled my time at Bromley. Not just the drugs and stuff, but the times I had missed my turn at washing-up; how chaotic my bedroom was ('shoulda seen *theirs*! I muttered); my rows with Pieter. Then each gave a vote. The pirates decreed that I walk the plank.

This was not going well.

I seethed in my suit. What was this, revenge? For what? All that nonsense about My Best Interests. Maybe it was because they regarded me as a traitor? To the hippie cause? A sellout? I should have *explained...*

I clamped the helmet down on my head as Nora and Grant got up together to make their joint report. A clucking hen in a peasant smock, puk puk puk and a low petulant groan melding together and becoming mush in my brain. My mind wandered. Then they shook their heads and I knew it was another negative. I should have brought Mona, she'd stand by me!

'Listen to their stupid prattle,' Hazel's voice. 'Blah blah blah. I know what I'd say if I were here!'

Now Noel speaks. I push the earpieces aside. Surely he won't let me down? '...I have known Tom for three years now and I think you're all being perfectly beastly....' Then a long spiel recounting our friendship and all its harrows and hollows. '...and in that time I have seen much evidence of his innate compassion, inner sweetness, vulnerability, lack of self-confidence...and while he was extremely successful in his work, this may have been more luck than judgement. I really think he's not a natural at Business....' Oh shit. That'll teach me to be nice to people who are nice to me….I stare at the plaster-decorated Edwardian ceiling. I can hear a waltz. Was this a ballroom? 'I am so sorry to be negative, but much as I like him I cannot advise leaving any large sum of money at his mercy.'

You bastard.

Tweedledum and Tweedledee were next. They spoke in near tandem, completing each-others' sentences as usual. 'One time we…' 'I remember the day when he…' Much repetition of the other Bromley reports. All true! All awful! In their eyes anyway.

Another no and no.

Monica next. She stands up swaying, lurches toward me and tries to kiss me through the helmet. I pull away. She grabs the helmet, drags it off (ow nose), throws it across the room. 'I want you to listen to *me* now, Tom! *Listen* to me!'

'Fuck off Monica!'

'Sit down you stupid girl!' Boles snaps.

'Are you going t give us a Report or not?' Truelove asks wearily, testily.

'Ge' way. I been on this case same as you. No skiving for the Monica! Ono! Day and night trying to get him to bed. And yes, in the end we did it. A coupla times. Ooooooh. I can tell you he's all there in *that* department! Unlike you, you eunuch!'

'No need for that! Just give your vote, woman!'

'Don't be absurd. She's far too drunk'

'Mr – uh – Boles, I'd be very grateful if you wouldn't interrupt. We have to follow the proper legal procedure. There's nothing in *here*,' slapping the pile of paper in front of him on the table, 'that says the jurors have to be sober.'

Could it be that Monica is going to give me my first and only yes? Drunk as she is, she's got more sense than the rest of them.

Boles looks furious. 'Nonsense young man – '

'Don't nonsense young man me!' Truelove is too tired and too drunk to care. 'If his wretched wife had been here *she* would have told you – '

Huh? What? There's something going on here. Something I have to focus on. Concentrate.

'Truelove, if you don't get *on* with it – ' Boles' threat is delivered in a grinding half-whisper like sandstone over my flesh.

'Can we carry on? It's my turn,' Julia said desperately.

Hang on a minute. There's something not right here. What did he mean about Mona?

'No it isn't. It's Mr Boles' turn. And that woman hasn't given her vote yet!'

'Not guilty! Not guilty!' Monica shrieked.

'Do we take that as a no?'

Everybody started to talk at once.' Quiet!' Julia shouted, and rang her handbell. 'Let's get on! We're nearly finished.'

Slowly, the room came to order. But my mind didn't. Mona's face flashed in front of me. Her eyes were staring. She was trying to scream.

'All right let's get on with it as the lady says. Julia, proceed.'

'I only wanted to say I'm sorry Tom.'

I longed for my helmet. To hide in. To think.

'I'm sorry I had to pretend to be dead.'

I focussed. This was disturbing. 'But you – '

'Yes. But you were just too much for me. Even when you were trying to be considerate. Those eyes! Hanging around me like a sick puppy all the time. Hell I'm sorry.'

'But what about the newspaper - ?' That article and all its horror came back like a pendulum hitting me in the face.

'It's amazing what some newspapers will print if you phone in a story with plenty sex and gore.'

'But I spoke with your mother and father – '

'Actors. I needed my things, see. I didn't mind your keeping the car. It's a better fit with you than me.'

'Oh,' I said, feeling sick.

'I wanted to move in with Cassie,' she said. 'I couldn't take the drama there would have been if we'd tried to discuss it.'

'Huh,' I said, remembering that gruesome weekend; my resolution to accept her as she was. I wished I could tell her, but words refused to come together.

'Are you going to give us a Report,' Truelove's query tinged with sarcasm, ' or is this to be an apology session?'

'Damn your Report,' said Julia.

'Julia!' Truelove was aghast at the defection.

'Just get on with it!' Brian shouted. Others joined in. 'Stick to the rules!' 'I'd call that a yes!'

As they babbled I decided, well, have to grab hold, have to ask, ask now…I stood up, took a deep breath, and they all went silent. 'What – ' I said, and all eyes turned to me, 'What has happened to Mona?'

Truelove's eyes swung away. Julia stared at her lap. Maria dabbed at a coffee stain. 'Nothing,' Truelove muttered glumly. Then, looking up, 'We've done absolutely nothing.'

Julia spoke quietly. 'It wasn't us, Tom. It was Them.'

I began to shake. Eventually I managed 'Who? What? WHAT HAS HAPPENED TO MONA?'

'We didn't do anything Tom, I swear!' Julia got up, came around the table, tried to put an arm around me. I shook it off. 'I went to get her earlier, to give her a lift over here. She was – she was – she was already dead, Tom.'

'No….'

'Dead. Lying in front of the TV. Next to a half-empty box of chocolates.'

'Noooooo………'

'Poisoned of course,' Truelove's voice was jagged and cruel. 'It's *your* fault!' He gave his anger full rein. 'If you hadn't got yourselves involved with those disgusting – '

'Who? WHO? WHO?' But I knew who. They had only been carrying out orders. Originating from me.

'Do you deny you have been working for the South African Secret Service?' Truelove orated as if in court. 'I was going to tell you this,' he addressed himself to Boles, 'when it came to my turn. But I'm telling you all now!' The others gawped in disbelief. 'He has been working for BOSS, their Bureau of State Security, for at least nine months now, maybe longer. Well now he's paid the traitor's price.'

I ran for the door. Hawkins blocked the exit.

'See how they've paid you for your *services*?' Truelove spat. 'Or did you *ask* them to do it?' I felt as if arrows were splatting into my back. 'And it's not the first time you've paid in blood! Remember Pieter?'

'Pieter?' I turned from the door.

'Yes your dear friend the double agent. You must have found out he was working with MI5, eh? How did you find out? Was it you who betrayed him?'

'WHAT?'

'Did you want him dead? Well you had your wish. They got him in the park. Your BOSS buddies. Oh yes, dear Nora, that was no mugging. Did you do it yourself, Tom? Did you pull the trigger?'

The room was too silent for me to scream. Too closed to escape. 'No!!! NO!!! I loved Pieter! He and I – we – together we – '

Boles stood and his chair fell backwards, making a woof! on the soft carpet. Our eyes met. I silenced myself.

'SIT! Both of you! I've had enough! Sit!' His voice boomed. He had taken control of the Hearing as he had taken control of so many Board Meetings in this room…Truelove and I sat, dumb.

Everybody turned expectantly to the old man as he put his hands to his neck, removed his stethoscope and dropped it to the floor. Then with his fingers at the back of his neck, he started to peel the face off his head. The mask unrolled – soft, painted rubber. Popped off the top of his head, dropped onto the table.

We stared uncomprehendingly at the face of the unknown man who stood before us. He was old, very old. Much older than Boles had seemed.

'Yes boy, Count Laszlo Mindchyk! I thought you had guessed that long ago. Apparently I was wrong. Well, how do you do?' he said blandly and came around the table to shake my hand.

'How do you do,' I said expressionlessly.

'Yes you see before you the very man who loved your dear dead grandmother.' His voice had changed considerably since he removal of the mask. It was deep, rich, continental, like ground coffee. Cultured. A man who kissed ladies' hands. 'And I have a great deal of apologising to do for putting you through all this…'

'Mona…' hoarsely.

'You've had a shock boy, but you're with me now! With me all things are possible.'

'So what - ?' I wanted to know, could he make everything better, could he wave a magic wand, and what the hell was he doing disguising a person I didn't know as another person I didn't know…?

He misunderstood the what. 'You see my boy; I wanted an heir – someone to take over from me when I am gone. I have quite an empire boy! Record companies, timber, diamonds, stocks and shares in all the major corporations, property – heavens, even I don't know everything I own. So all of you, sit comfortably, I'll tell you my story.'

No escape. Hawkins at the door. A boardroom of pale people I thought I knew.

'Once upon a time I met the most beautiful girl in the world and she ran away from me. You know that part of the story Tom, she must have told you. And after she ran away there came a nasty little man with a silly moustache. He wanted my country. You all know that part too.

'I watched the tanks come rolling down the road and then one night my chauffeur and I mined that road. There was quite some fuss about that. They shot all the men in the village. Then they came for me and my family. I never found out what happened to my lovely little girls, or their grandmother – perhaps it's better I don't know.' He sighed and we sighed with him.

'Well I escaped from the prison camp. It wasn't easy. I had many adventures…anyway, I ended up in London. In the course of the war I worked in propaganda at Bush House, broadcasting to my Homeland. And during this period I made many friends amongst other exiles from my country including many musicians, as well as a handful of people who managed to escape with some of their money.

'After the war it was natural for me to put these parts together and form a little classical record company. It was successful. Then in the fifties I realised there was so much more money to be made from rock and roll and I bought a small nearly bankrupt label called Drama Records. Nowadays everyone knows the name and it did so well I was able to invest in a number of other ventures. Someone must have been smiling on me. I made my millions.

'But all this time a spectre haunted me. And you could say it became an obsession. It was the spectre, Tom, of your grandmother's lovely face. Everything I did I did for her. When I commissioned music, it was would she like it. When I bought apartments it was could she live here. When I bought a gold mine it was because of how much I know she loved gold. I so much wanted her to approve of what I had achieved but most of all I wanted to become successful so I could find her and marry her.

'When finally I felt secure and rich and ready I hired detectives to search for her. Eventually they brought me the good news that she was still living, and in Johannesburg. But alas,' he gave a great sigh, 'she was married. I had waited so long, too long. And so what could I do? Did she remember me? I wondered. Did she regret leaving me? I thought I would never find out. But then one day her husband died.

'You can imagine how I felt. Sad for her, happy for me. But what to do? So my solicitor here, Truelove, and I concocted this terrible, this stupid plan. Which I now realise! Which was to send somebody to tell her I had died and she would inherit my fortune, so that I could know from her reaction if she still felt for me after all this time. And if there was still love there I would come and I don't know what, jump out at her from behind a tree or something and shout "surprise surprise" and we would live happily ever after.

'But it wasn't to be. You know what happened.' He turned to the others, tears in his eyes. 'When she heard, when she heard this terrible news the shock was so great it killed her!' His hands went to his eyes. Monica handed him a handkerchief and he dabbed. 'Stupid idea! But nobody's fault but my own! I take all the blame.'

The audience, too, dabbed at their eyes.

'So what was I to do? The reckless will she made, you know all about that. So I decided to find you, Tom, and because she loved you, make you my son and heir.'

I stared at the wreck of his face and tried not to feel anything.

'Incredibly, we find you in London! So we set up this Company and make it look like it's here forever. And when we look for you, what do we find? A hippie, living with a madwoman.' He shook his head sadly. 'So to give you a chance to redeem yourself we kidnap the woman, send her to a sanatorium, a very special one where she can get cured. And when they cured her, I took her into my confidence and made her the twelfth Juror. For she loved you and I knew she would look after you. Then I sent her back to you. And now she's dead. How sad, how sad. I lost two wives altogether. Two daughters. People die.'

A sob came out of me unbidden and the Jurors turned, broadcasting sympathy.

'You know what my greatest mistake was?' He pointed at Truelove. 'Hiring this idiot. I listened to his advices. Pah! Truelove, I should have done this long ago. You're fired! Get out!'

The lawyer stood up, face frozen. Then muttering furiously to himself, he assembled the pile of papers before him. Then on second thoughts he swept them to the floor and exited, elbowing past an amused Hawkins and slamming the door.

Laszlo stared around the table, eyes boring into those of each Juror in turn. 'What a bunch, eh? What a bunch! These are the people this Truelove thinks were fit to judge you. Hah! Hippies, faggots, arty farty people I wouldn't spend a *fart* on! What were you mixing with such people for? You're not one of them!'

'Dunno,' I said.

'Good answer! I have to tell you how proud I am of you. In my disguise of Boles I tested you every which way I could. And the way you handled every test! Sewed up that steel contract! And using the whatchamacallit – BOSS – the way you did to make profit for us! This idiot lawyer should have worked that out. And this new project you're working on! Very hush hush eh? My goodness, you *tower* over this bunch of nogoodniks like a Samson!'

'Do I?'

'Be bold boy! Don't be modest! What has this bunch of jerks ever done for the Balance of Trade, eh? Name one export they have contributed to. Eh?'

I looked at my friends. Their eyes avoided mine as if guilty.

'Useless, every one of them! Tom, when you go from this room you are never to see any of them again. I will find plenty new friends for you. Bankers, industrialists, politicians. These will al be blown away. Blown away!' A manic edge crept into his voice. 'They are the half men. It is dog eat dog in this world. If you don't have sharp teeth, you go under! This world is only predator and prey! So welcome to our world!' His mantle of sanity was showing cracks.

'Here!' He reached under the table and pulled out a large battered cardboard suitcase which he plonked on the table with an effort. "This case is what I brought with me from Poland! Everything I had was in this case. Now I give it to you! Your first instalment, what Truelove was to give to you if these morons had seen your true quality. Just paper, boy. Stocks, bonds, directorships, title deeds, all in your name. A few bundles of real money just so you can feel what it's like to be truly rich. It's all yours!'

'I – '

'This is only the first instalment. The second is called POWER. When you come into the office on Monday I'll show you what it is like to be the partner of and the successor to Count Laszlo Mindchyck! CONGRATULATIONS!' He pumped my hand and then kissed me on both cheeks. 'Now off you go. Piss off. I want to argue about fees with these idiots. They don't get a penny from me!'

I turned to say goodbye to everybody. 'Shall I help you with your case sir?' Hawkins appeared, snatched the case off the table and pushed me out of the door. It slammed to behind us.

'But I wanted to say goodbye – '

'No need for that sir. Now where is your car?'

Out into the cold night. The fresh air! As we sweep up Piccadilly, I unbuckle the armour and leave it in a cardboard trail behind us. Hawkins scrabbling after me.

By Hatchards, a tramp. Can I trouble you – '

'Give me the case!' I snatched it from Hawkins, wrenched it open and gave the startled tramp a handful of money.

'Come on Hawkeye!' Half Moon Street. The car waiting for me. Hawkins helps me heave the case onto the passenger seat.

'Well goodbye sir! See you Monday.'

Fat chance! 'Goodbye Hawkeye!' Get in, start up and as the big man disappears muttering down the street roll a fat jay.

Growl through freezing sparsely trafficked streets across town heading for the M4 empty now

Haha you wait till Monday you *wait*! You murderers you thieves you fascist predators, you wait!

The car gives a gleeful shudder of pleasure as

60 climbs to 70

Yahooooo! Open the case!

75

Handful of paper out the window whipped away by the freezing wind

80

Car swerves as another handful snatched away by the greedy fingers of he wind

85

Handsful of litter lungsful of laughter for the countryside

90

Paper for cows to eat

100

Paper birds for the wind to play with

105

My fingers can't keep up with the hungry wind

With me in the car laughing with me a car full of my dead friends, Mona, Pieter, Hazel, Ian. 'Faster! Faster!' 'Where next Tommy baby?' 'Hurray! Hurray!'

Vrooooooooooooooooooom...

Finis

?

23387452R00166

Printed in Great Britain
by Amazon